Pr...
Tw...

"Excellent . . . [An] endearing take on the enemies-to-lovers trope . . . Readers are sure to be enchanted by this couple and their deeply felt struggle to open their hearts." —*Publishers Weekly* (starred review)

"If fixer-upper fantasies are your thing, don't miss *Twice Shy* by Sarah Hogle. . . . Maybell's voice and point of view make the story funny, engaging, and enchanting." —NPR.org

"Hogle did a marvelous job of turning what could be a heavy and predictable tale into a lighthearted story full of surprises, redemption, and love." —*USA Today*

"The perfect springtime romance." —PopSugar

"Hogle's story takes a gentle, knowing look at anxiety, its debilitating effects, and the importance of stepping outside our comfort zones in this slow-burn romance with plenty of charm and witty banter." —*Country Living*

"This book is the softest, sweetest book releasing this year." —*Frolic*

Praise for
You Deserve Each Other

"Deliciously wicked [and] truly hysterical. Naomi especially is laugh-out-loud funny." —NPR

"[A] hilarious debut romance . . . [that] rewards readers with laugh-out-loud moments and a satisfyingly sweet and redeeming ending." —*Booklist*

＊

Just Like
Magic

ALSO BY SARAH HOGLE

* * *

You Deserve Each Other

Twice Shy

Just Like Magic

A NOVEL

SARAH HOGLE

G. P. PUTNAM'S SONS
New York

✳

PUTNAM
—EST. 1838—

G. P. Putnam's Sons
Publishers Since 1838
An imprint of Penguin Random House LLC
penguinrandomhouse.com

Library of Congress Cataloging-in-Publication Data

Names: Hogle, Sarah, author.
Title: Just like magic: a novel / Sarah Hogle.
Description: New York: G. P. Putnam's Sons, 2022.
Identifiers: LCCN 2022026816 (print) | LCCN 2022026817 (ebook) |
ISBN 9780593539859 (trade paperback) | ISBN 9780593539866 (ebook)
Subjects: LCGFT: Novels.
Classification: LCC PS3608.O48268 J87 2022 (print) |
LCC PS3608.O48268 (ebook) | DDC 813/.6—dc23
LC record available at https://lccn.loc.gov/2022026816
LC ebook record available at https://lccn.loc.gov/2022026817

Printed in the United States of America
2nd Printing

Book design by Katy Riegel

This is a work of fiction. Names, characters, places, and incidents either are
the product of the author's imagination or are used fictitiously, and any
resemblance to actual persons, living or dead, businesses, companies,
events, or locales is entirely coincidental.

To Samantha Tan and Gritty:
the greatest love pairing that never
should have been

*

Just Like
Magic

CHAPTER ONE

....

Countdown to Christmas: 11 Days

LUMPY SNOWFLAKES TUMBLE from above, "Blue Christmas" dancing out of the speakers of Mary Had a Little Boutique. The historical brick buildings glisten like icicles in the pearly dusk that shadows Old Homestead Road, all of their names hand-lettered across display windows. This tiny Colorado valley town has a population south of two thousand, composed of six blocks neatly divided between three roads, the middle one the commercial strip. Despite having lived here for about eight months, I've never ventured into town before, since I might be recognized (wearing off-the-rack Rue 21!). Or worse: I might not be recognized at all.

Everything here has a cutesy name, usually Old West or mountain inspired, as if anyone could forget we're in the Rocky Mountains when we're literally shaded by them—Spruce It Up Hair Saloon, Frontier Hardware, Silver Mine Dining, Rocky Road Ice Cream Parlor. The boutique glowing in front of me is rustic-wedding-in-a-barn trendy. Like if the Lumineers were a store.

Surely I'll find gifts for my prickly, difficult-to-please relatives in here.

I *have* to.

The store is small and brightly lit, so it's impossible to avoid the attention of its manager, leaning eagerly across the counter when I push open the door, its bells chiming. Her eyes squint, then widen. "You look familiar. Are you—?"

"No," I'm quick to respond, turning to run an idle finger over a cloth napkin. My stomach churns at the forty-dollar price tag. "I'm nobody."

She snaps her fingers. "Bettie Hughes! Oh my goodness! You must be here visiting your grandparents. I'm always seeing Lawrence's car whizzing around. It's such a treat, every time, always waves hello, stops for a chat if he has a minute. Couldn't be nicer." Her voice goes a bit wobbly. "Your grandmother isn't as . . . well, she's busy. Probably gets tired of being stopped all the time for autographs." She tries to sound cheerful about whatever memory she's reliving, in which my grandmother crushed the warm, friendly image this woman had held of her like a sorceress grinding the bones of her admirers.

I smile tightly. "Sorry to disappoint. I get that comparison a lot, but I'm not Bettie."

She's confused for a moment, and then she winks exaggeratedly. "Ahh, gotcha. Don't worry, I won't say anything. Not a peep."

We're in on a secret together as she watches me browse. I can't concentrate, painfully aware of her attention. This is what's popular now: high-quality, artisanal presents from small but expensive holes-in-the-wall. I can see my younger sister Kaia now, gifting me a secret, never-before-released album from one of my favorite bands that she procured in a water-tower-turned-musical-speakeasy somewhere in New York; Athena, my other sister, topping her by gifting me a bathtub fashioned from a rare type of volcanic rock that self-heats, which she got from a store in Denmark that disappeared the day after she made her purchase. My relatives and I don't give each other anything with a recognizable label: the more obscure and personalized, the more exclusive. I'm tired of giving the family's worst gifts. I'm tired of everyone pretending my offerings weigh the same as theirs.

"Do you need help? Hunting for a present for someone special? Look at this," the manager says, emerging over my shoulder with a clay pitcher. "I think your grandfather might like this."

I jump. "Ah!" I twist a *You don't even know my grandfather* into submission, because maybe that's not true. Maybe Mary from Mary Had a Little Boutique knows Lawrence Watson better than I do. After all, he's lived in Teller City half his life. "I'm not who you think I am."

"Right, right." She glances at the window, at all the cars parked along the slushy street. Business is booming at the evil shop next door. "They're gonna run me out of business," she laments. Then she cranes up at the sky, as if photographers might be dangling from helicopters. "We got this in today." She shows me a crocheted sweater with a price tag of one hundred forty-five dollars. "*Beautiful*. Isn't it beautiful? Handmade, too. Lady by the name of Daisy makes these, told me she only crochets one a month, they're so much effort."

"Mm."

I'm going through the motions, picking up ceramic pots, feigning interest in cakes of handmade soap. Twenty-seven dollars. I need twenty-seven-dollar handcrafted soap that costs five bucks. I suppose it's nice that everything here is sourced from local entrepreneurs, but there's nothing in this store I can afford. A tiny knife for cutting cheese would prevent me from filling my car with gas for a week.

The manager grins with dollar signs for eyes. "Do you like coffee? We sell the most amazing ground coffee you've ever tried. Here, I can give you a sample."

I'm given free samples of coffee, cologne, a bag of muffin mix, and tinted moisturizer. Eventually, I contrive an excuse to leave ("very busy, got a 'thing'") and she's visibly disappointed but expresses hopes that I'll return tomorrow.

Back out on the sidewalk in "downtown" Teller City, I force a slow exhale between my teeth, tightening my purse against my body. Wind snaps and belts like the feedback in an old home camcorder video. Next door, the mutual nemesis of Mary Had a Little Boutique and myself stares down with big block letters and Edison lanterns.

Magnolia Hope Chest.

In their plot to take over society with shiplap and oversized wall clocks, *Fixer Upper* home renovation stars Chip and Joanna Gaines have conquered the western U.S. state by state with their cute little stores. Even towns as bite-sized as this one have fallen prey to Joanna's love of industrial farmhouse chic and white subway tile. This location is less than a year old. I can see their thinking: the rural, down-home image looks good on their website, and they know that their star power will draw shoppers from every town in the county. That a sleek bronze glass-front building such as this one, while scaled back in comparison to its Texan motherland, is permitted to sit comfortably between Shahad's Toy Shop and Mary Had a Little Boutique is an abomination.

My mind flickers to my sister Athena, who loves the Gaines style: rustic décor with an upper-middle-class price tag that makes her feel she's relatable and down to earth. I remember being in the upper *upper* class, trying to persuade Macy's to stock my perfume label while considering myself too good to shop at Macy's. Now I clip Dollar General coupons.

After my finances imploded, I dreaded my shopping runs for fear of being photographed perusing the clearance sections. Even though I couldn't afford high-end products anymore, I still had my pride. But with Christmas around the corner, I've been frantic to find gifts for my wealthy family, who are congregating up the mountain three days from now. A couple of weeks ago, I bit the bullet and entered the contact sport beloved by millions of American citizens known as Black Friday shopping.

There I was, skulking into Magnolia (with sunglasses and a wig) at six in the morning the day after Thanksgiving—a little bit hungover, brooding over spending the holiday alone—and I began filling my cart.

Prices were low. Adrenaline was high. I'd just nabbed an antique-style wall sconce at half off, which I knew Athena would love—the rush gave me such tunnel vision that, medically, I cannot be held liable for my actions. A woman and I brawled over a reclaimed-wood recipe box, the police were called, and we were both dragged from the store with lifetime bans.

I kept shouting "It's not me!" for some reason. I remember being devastated to lose the wall sconce, which I'd never be able to afford at regular price. I was also devastated by the teenage assistant manager, who called me *ma'am*, which resulted in a full breakdown. I can't be a ma'am, I'm only twenty-three! Or I was a few years ago, anyway. I'm pretty sure I'm twenty-six, but I spent so many years being twenty-one that I'd have to check my driver's license to be sure.

Chip and Joanna are my mortal enemies now, discriminating by expecting customers to pay with money rather than exposure, even though I would have basically done them a favor by letting them give me merchandise. I have 9.3 million followers on Instagram.

Frustrated that this shopping trip proved fruitless, I slam my car door, which I like to imagine is still my sleek, deep red Aston Martin Vantage rather than a 2003 Chevrolet Impala in bird-poop white.

I ignore the stoplight since nobody's here to see me run a red, thinking about how utterly rude it is that I peaked at twenty-four and didn't even appreciate it, because I thought the money would keep flowing forever. I leveraged my name to broker deals for a fragrance line, a clothing line, a jewelry line, one right after the other under bad advisement, a horde of yes-men bleeding me dry without my knowledge, because I trusted anyone who said they believed in my creative vision. With ten million dollars in the bank, I began spending like an idiot, assuming that every year I'd double those millions. I bought a top-of-the-line car. A Hawaiian villa. I invested in all my friends' loose-threaded start-ups, all high promises, no substance.

I was sitting in one of the most expensive restaurants on Melrose Avenue, celebrating my rise to the Top Thirty Entrepreneurs under Thirty, when I got the call that I was broke. The restaurant declined my credit card.

Halfway up a mountain at the north end of Old Homestead

Road, a big, shuddersome house gazes down at me like a beady-eyed crow, tracking my progress to the opposite side of town. Even though that house and its occupants don't know I've been hiding out in Teller City for the last several months, I feel it watching me all the time. It's why I do all my shopping in nearby Springhedge. Needing to keep a low profile means I can't risk trying to make any friends here, so I sit alone on the couch night after night, dreaming of the good old days.

I scurry like a beetle back into my rotting log, a small dwelling on the wooded outskirts of town with no cable, where the electricity and Wi-Fi are unwittingly being powered by one of the neighbors. (I run an extension cord from their outdoor outlet.) I stopped paying the water bill, so I've been waiting on that to dry up: my future holds either getting a job or showering at the YMCA in Springhedge and doing my toilet business unspeakably. I subsist on frozen pizza and peanut butter sandwiches. And Evian bottled water, of course. I'm not a pleb.

Once inside, I collapse onto the couch to feel sorry for myself. "Why couldn't you have lived somewhere else?" I moan to Eileen. "Or had a bigger television?" This one is twenty-four inches.

Eileen doesn't respond, as she is very busy being dead in Florida. She was only supposed to be in Florida for a three-week vacation last February, but the ninety-year-old lady snuffed it at Disney World during week two. I had needed money and a place to stay, and found her advertisement asking for someone to water her plants at a time when the situation was dire (I had been staying with a woman I'd just met, who said I could take her sofa if I acted as lookout whenever she was doing illegal tattooing). My three-week stay has grown into nearly a year. Every single day, I am terrified a cop is going to show up and arrest me for squatting, or a long-lost relative will come to claim Eileen's house and belongings. I can't believe no one's kicked me out yet.

It's a drafty little place, musty-smelling, like it knows Eileen is dead and has decided to die right along with her even though someone's still trying to live in it. The walls are dark wood paneling, the carpet gray shag that's crunchy in areas. Crayons and dead mice have melted under the radiators to form the world's most grotesque rainbow. There isn't a single decent wall to pose in front of for pictures. I had to nail a tie-dye tapestry up on the wall with the best lighting, which as far as my followers and family know, is the "bohemian room" in my private Hawaiian villa. Don't ask to visit me because I am simply too busy to accommodate guests—I am making a fortune as an influencer for a nonexistent company called verdIgRIS Tea, a multilevel marketing venture I made up. Allegedly, if you drink the tea it can make your eyes greener. I'll send details to you in the mail, which will then be lost by our inefficient postal system.

Even though verdIgRIS isn't real, other brands will surely see my sponsorships, so the goal is to make them think I'm in demand. If you build it (the lie), they will come (with enough cash to get me out of Teller City before my grandmother discovers I'm here and heckles me for being a failure).

I swallow, staring at the ceiling. Three days.

Only three days left until I have to see everyone and put on a convincing show that I'm Doing Great, Actually. No, I certainly did not make a huge deal out of how rich I was, then blow my money on big, elaborate parties for fair-weather friends I haven't heard a peep from since my brands went kaput. The media didn't overexpose me to the point where everyone hates me. My face wasn't all over tabloids, first for my success, and then for my lavish parties, and finally as a target of ridicule. Constant accusations of cheating on partners or being cheated on. Plastic surgery. Debt. (They got that one right, at least.) I didn't lose job opportunities, left with nothing except for credit too bad to get a loan.

It's what my parents have been warning me about since I was four years old and crying that I wanted to be a Disney star. My frugal, responsible, ordinary parents, who shunned the limelight my grandmother casts, who've been scrupulously saving for their retirement since they were in their twenties. I certainly couldn't approach them for help, not when my dad tried so hard to keep his kids from chasing fame but we all did, anyway, because bad people in nice suits offer fame-adjacent children the world the second they turn eighteen, exploiting their connections, sweet-talking them right into ruin, and then moving promptly along. Dad hoped we'd choose normal lives, too. He was worried we'd end up spoiled or broken. Joke's on him: I'm both!

I get up and pour the remaining quarter of a bottle from the fridge into a glass. California zinfandel has never let me down.

Three days. The ticking clock is a roar.

"This sucks," I tell my wine. "And so do you, but at least you're trying."

I have nothing to give to anyone.

All of my possessions have already been featured in social media posts. Athena will know if I'm giving out my own stuff as Christmas presents, she will *absolutely* say something, and then what? At any rate, I couldn't possibly part with the few belongings I own from my old life. Gold-infused essential oils recommended by my aromatherapist, a prosperity-boosting body scrub that only works if you're a Scorpio. Musk-scented CBD oil made especially for depressed blue tang fish. Most of these are GOOP products, obtained through my persistent extortion of Gwyneth Paltrow. She's in the wind now and hasn't sent me anything in months.

I pop open a fresh bottle. "It's not fair!" The closer Christmas gets, the sicker I feel.

I rev up social media to do the number one no-no: look up my own name.

What I find is bad.

Tweets with the highest engagement accompany the hashtag #BettieHughesIsCanceled, followed closely by #LucasDodgedA Bullet.

This was the fallout after I tried to tell people that my ex-boyfriend, Lucas Dormer, was emotionally abusive, via an interview with *Andromeda Magazine*. Lucas's fans swiftly crushed me. We've been broken up for years now, but they still won't let their hatred go, dogging me all over the internet, posting GIFs of people throwing Raisin Creme Pies at each other's faces (I'll explain that reference later).

I pour another drink, digging into TikTok. The only time I'm mentioned by the merciless teens of today's society is in mean hashtags on videos they post of themselves dancing to Lucas Dormer's songs. One of them green-screened my years-old mug shot into the background.

I'm making a bad day much worse. I need to put my phone away, but I can't. I have to know what people—people who think I'm too rich and busy to look it up—are saying about me.

Some of the girls I used to be friendly with before their modeling or acting careers took off have posted cryptic tweets like *It's so sad to see what's happened to her*, and I don't know who they're referencing, but just the fact that it *might* be me pumps my body full of furious adrenaline. How dare they!

I'm drying up my second bottle. Every boyfriend I've ever had has, at one point, used a #BettieHughesIsOverParty comment to link to their melodramatic "What's It Like to Date a Watson-Hughes" exposés on Medium.com from two, three, four years ago.

I "like" a few of them, just so they'll know I see what kind of shitfuckery they're up to. A reporter at the *New York Times*, Kelly Frederick, who used to dig around in my finances and tell everyone my companies were drowning, declared she was praying for me. She tagged @BettieHughes, the wrong handle, as mine is @Real-BettieHughes. Her thirty most recent tweets are gushing over Lucas Dormer's guest appearance on some teen drama, tagging him in every one. I know she's hoping he'll show interest, maybe gratitude. I know he'll probably flirt with her a little from afar but never date her, because he's a celebrity whose public persona doesn't match up with reality behind the scenes, and she's a reporter.

The worst part?

Almost all of these tweets are from last year. Hardly anyone's been talking about me since, except to make jabs. A theory that I'm in rehab is floating around. Some people think I'm dead.

Even my unpopularity isn't popular anymore.

I can't let this be my legacy. I had no idea how pathetic my public image has gotten. I'm going to have to deplete my vault of Photoshopped pictures. Each one takes hours to perfect, which is fine because I don't have anything else to do. I have no real skills, so I can't find lasting employment anywhere. The few places that would take me, I can't work at without being recognized. I can see the trending topic now: *Is Bettie Hughes working at Speedway?*

I unleash the whole collection: myself Photoshopped in front of private jets. Hotel rooms with Versace shopping bags on the bed, lobster dinners in restaurants that require a reservation made months in advance. I'm not an amateur; I know I have to alter enough details in these pictures that no one can trace back to the originals. There's a forty-year-old Swiss woman with two followers who has the best life I've ever seen, and she's usually my go-to. I change the shape of clouds in her backgrounds, tint the coloring of her clothes. Apply filters liberally. Now her life is mine.

My brain waves blur as I open a new bottle of wine, footsteps unsteady. I pass thirty reflections of myself in Eileen's hallway endcap of mirrors and record a TikTok soliloquy about how I could've been a movie star if I wanted. If I had the time, which I don't. I'm a busy business lady, lots of green-eye tea to peddle. Would anybody else like to sponsor me? Except I'm highly exclusive, you probably can't afford me. But you should definitely put in an offer. And you know what? Nobody invited me to any Halloween parties, which is bullshit, but I don't care, I don't want anything to do with all those two-faced . . . with all those people and their however many faces. I don't even care! What happened to all the friends I used to have and why did they leave when I stopped paying for group vacations?

In my fizzy state, my attention turns inexplicably toward that hack Kelly Frederick, spamming her socials with pictures of my Nickelodeon Kids' Choice Awards surfboard, which I won for being a Red Carpet Fashion Icon in 2010 (it was the Before Times, when the populace still liked my fashion). "Suck on that," I mutter. "They don't give you surfboards at the . . . the goddamn New Year's Times, do they."

Then I drift back to Twitter, perhaps unwisely. *Magnolia stores are unethical. Don't shop there!!*

This garners a comment from my sister Athena (who has double the followers I have): *I love those stores!* In under two minutes, a dozen people reply to say that by promoting Magnolia, Athena just convinced them to shop there. The official @magnolia Twitter account "likes" all of these tweets, even mine, which feels passive-aggressive.

I envision myself on Christmas Day in Grandma and Grandpa's living room, handing them the free samples from Mary Had a Little Boutique because that's all I've got. You can forget presents for my nieces and nephews; those gremlins are money pits. They'll each get a hug.

Nothing is cheering me up. Not the wine, not the spare Christmas decorations I found in Eileen's closet. I can't even plug in the artificial tree, a kitschy, miniature pink thing, because I don't know what happens when alcohol and electricity mix. I could be electrocuted. Or the tree could end up drunk. Nobody knows.

For my birthday last year, my grandmother sent a Kinollghy record player to my PO box in L.A. It's styled to resemble yesteryear but with Bluetooth compatibility, and it looks damn spanking good on Eileen's coffee table. I only have two Christmassy records (packaged together—a gift from my sister-in-law), one of which I tip out of a big square envelope-looking thing and onto the big black round thing that makes music happen. Presumably. This is my first time using the record player. I've been holding out to spite my grandmother, who would probably be able to sense it in the air if I did something she wanted me to. Like a bloodhound.

The volume isn't quite high enough, so I try to notch it up by zipping the needle around. Some wine splashes onto the red disc, but that's fine. "Mariah Carey is thirsty today," I remark.

The record squeals and skips to the second track, "All I Want for Christmas Is You."

Mariah Carey isn't thirsty, Mariah Carey is possessed by demons. The song spitting out of my record player with a weird succession of *thwip-thwip-thwip*s sounds like an attack, the beats arising not from Mimi's unparalleled vocal range but rather from a dark temple at the earth's core, storming and sinister, some creature chanting in a haunted language with the exception of one clear refrain: "Ooooooooh, Chriiiiiiistmaaaas!" The lights brighten and then dim, buzzing in discordant sync with the *thwip-thwip-thwip*, the high, mangled "Ooooooooh Chriiiiistmaaaas, Ooooooooh Chriiiiistmaaaas."

The hairs on the back of my neck stand on end; I am instantly and unfortunately sober.

I try to pry the record off the player, but the needle grates a hot spray of sparks that burns my hand and I shriek, springing back. Everything electric is going haywire: the overhead light, a Himalayan salt lamp, the miniature twenty-four-inch television, my Ocean Galaxy Light Projector. They're all drunk, pulsating wildly, bright and then dim, bright and then dim—my head spins along, stomach roiling. I'm about to paint the walls with pizza rolls. It's an earthquake! It's Revelation! Quick, Bettie, be religious!

"Dear sir, baby God," I cry, reaching for more wine. "Small, holy bundle." You know, on second thought, perhaps the wine can wait. "Forgive me. I won't do again whatever it was that you're mad about, you've got my word. I swear on Bettie Watson's life." Not Bettie Hughes, mind you. Bettie Watson. My grandmother's lived long enough, whereas I've got so much ahead of me.

I yank the record player's cord out of the wall right as Mariah's distorted soprano reaches a fever pitch, all six bulbs in the ceiling fan popping in an explosion of glass, a table lamp behind me catching fire.

"Agghhhh, shit! What the hell! What the ever-loving hell!" I seize my weighted throw blanket and almost use it to tamp out the flames, but it's a remnant from The Time I Had Money and, more importantly, it's been discontinued. I know for a fact that Carrie Underwood has publicly bemoaned not having one. I simply cannot destroy a thing so exclusive that Carrie Underwood will never have it.

I use an afghan Eileen crocheted instead, thankfully succeeding in beating the fire into submission. The electricity stabilizes, that piercing buzzing noise ebbing away. Smoke lingers in the room, and my mind flashes with ideas for utilizing this near-death experience to come back into public favor. I'll post a picture of the exploded bulbs in the Clarendon filter, an afghan singed with black craters. *Lost my only memento of my great-grandmother*, I'll caption it, *but I'm thankful to still be here. I'M SO SORRY*, Kelly Frederick will type-sob in a front-page headline. Then the byline: *The world almost lost Bettie that day. And I . . . can't help but feel responsible, after I exposed her money problems to her investors and ruined her life.* I'll forgive her, but only after Oprah gently advises me on national television to take the high road.

"Whew." I blow out a shaky exhale, then revolve to find a man in my living room, standing not five feet away from me.

He waves. "Oh, hey!"

I scream and fall down, frantically scuttling backward like a crab, broken glass biting into the pad of my hand. A swift glance at the door shows me it's still shut. The man is speaking, although whatever he's saying can't be heard over my never-ending scream. He's a blur of colors, mostly red and green with a squiggle of brown on top, wearing what I think is (but cannot possibly be) a sweater featuring a *T. rex* eating a candy cane.

"I'll never drink again," I vow. "Please, Mariah, release me from your curse. I'll be good."

"As I'm sure you've already guessed, I am the Holiday Spirit," the man tells me mildly. "Due to an obscure typo in the Festivities Legislation, the Holiday Spirit can be conjured by playing the current Billboard Hot 100 number one hit, if it is a holiday hit, and if it is played backwards, on vinyl." He gestures to the scarlet record on display, sticky with wine. "Well done, Miss Carey. I'm as shocked as you are that it's taken until now for that typo to be pressed into action."

The last of my air abandons me in a wheeze.

"But you can call me Hall, as in Holiday." He beams, head slanting.

"Oh, right," I reply faintly, and then pass out.

*

CHAPTER TWO

....

CALIFORNIA ZINFANDEL HAS let me down. It has pushed me all the way down a broken elevator shaft, in fact. It's well past dark when I roll off the couch onto the shag carpet, skull thumping with a migraine, and release a pitiful wail. The house smells like dessert for some reason, and there's a stretchy beige bandage on my right hand that I don't remember putting there. This is what happens when you day-drink.

"What have I done to deserve this," I murmur forlornly. My phone lies inches away on the carpet. I must pull through for the sake of my fans, which I'm going to have again someday.

Zero outreach from Dad, Felix, or Athena, as per usual. Felix and Athena never check in because they're snobs, and Dad never checks in because he's a quiet, private soul who doesn't contact anyone unless it's an emergency. One single text from Kaia, which she meant to send to a friend. Six from Mom in the few hours since I last glanced at my phone, asking how I'm doing, if I've booked my flight, when I'll be getting in, if she needs to pick me

up from the airport. Directions in case I rent a car. She wants to
know if it's still raining on my end and I have to look up the current weather in Haiku, Hawaii, before I respond. My house,
which the bank took away, has been bought and sold twice over.
It's been relisted on Zillow, which I stare at nightly through my
tears. The fact that my mother keeps an eye on what the weather
is like where all of her children live makes me feel so much worse
about lying and being the only Hughes child who didn't show up
at Thanksgiving.

Thanksgiving just reminds me of Christmas, which reminds
me that I'm a failure with no presents to give everybody, a spon-
sorless woman in her midtwenties who steals Wi-Fi. And now I
wish I were unconscious again.

"What am I gonna do," I mutter into the carpet. From this
angle, I can see everything going on under the couch but pretend
I do not see it. An exterminator isn't in the budget. I'm barely
scraping by with my OnlyFans earnings, since ninety percent of
my subscribers bailed after I said I wouldn't post nudes.

I scroll through my many, many notifications. The unofficial
BettieHughesUpdates account, which has mostly evaporated—its
organizers moving on to shiny new starlets—has retweeted low-
hanging gossip about my "clearly shopped photos," even though
they have no proof of that. I've endured too much. Like the fire
from earlier. It's frankly miraculous that I survived, since I drank
so much wine that going anywhere near that fire should have
turned me into a Molotov cocktail.

I decide to deactivate my Twitter. It's the equivalent of a tan-
trum, and I've done it before, but it makes me feel better.

Then I mosey over to Instagram, where I post stories en-
couraging my followers to enter a sixty-day "A Healthier New

Me" pledge with VerdIgRIS Tea. *Sign up today with my promo code HUGHMONGOUSSALE.* I find one of my best selfies, change my dark brown eyes to green, and post that, too.

I receive immediate replies: some asking for more information on the tea, some calling me out for MLM scheming, some asking for nudes. Even when the interaction isn't positive, at least people are responding. People remember me. Right at this very moment, while they type their comments, they're thinking about me.

"There." I toss my phone aside. "Now I can spend the rest of the night hating my life."

"Anything I can do to help?"

I jump off the couch, entire body vibrating with a bloodcurdling shriek. A man wearing a sweater with blinking red and green lights sewn into it is standing in Eileen's living room. "Get out!" I yell. "Get out of my house! How'd you sneak through my alarm system?" I really could not explain why this is one of the first things I shout. I don't even have an alarm system.

He flinches. Holds up a tentative finger. "But you . . ."

"What are you, a stalker? One of my fans?" Maybe I'm still drunk, and right now I'm yelling at some guy on my television screen.

But he looks real. He could be a detective, or a real estate agent. No! Anything but a real estate agent! I start throwing things. My G. Label x Tabitha Simmons Heli Sandals. My Alexis Steelwood Charcuterie Board. Even my Stinson Studios Natural Oak Serving Bowl, 14". The charcuterie board cracks him over the knee, and he jerks to gape at it, then me. When the serving bowl goes flying, he's prepared for it, and with a twist of his hand, the bowl rebounds seconds before making contact with his chest. It lands on the floor at my feet, cracking into three pieces.

I shriek again. "My bowl!"

"I'm sorry—I—"

I hurl the pieces at him and he does that thing again, waving his hand to halt their travel in midair without physically touching them. I stare at his hand, beginning to reexamine this situation from a different angle than "but what about my bowl."

"Please don't do that," he entreats politely.

"Was that . . ." I sputter. "Are you . . ."

"Telekinetic, yes," he replies as I say, "Jesus."

He pauses, eyebrows lifting. "Ah, no, I am not Jesus. I am Hall!" He smiles broadly, which forces me to take proper notice of his brilliant smile, deep smile lines bracketing his mouth. Then I notice other details, like his mop of chestnut brown hair, olive skin with a dash of freckles, and long lashes framing green eyes. *Arrestingly* green, like my fake posts for verdIgRIS Tea results. They're the clearest jade I've ever seen. I'd peg him as in his midtwenties, with boyish good looks and good humor that I find suspicious.

"Do you not remember me?" His face falls, hand landing squarely over his heart. All of the blinking red and green lights on his sweater start flickering. "Oh, *no*! But that makes me so sad! I remember absolutely, wonderfully everything about how we met. I put it all down here! For posterity!" He plucks a large red book from somewhere behind him and flips to the first page. It features a Polaroid of the two of us, me sprawled on the couch unconscious, eyeliner and mascara smudged. He's giving the camera a thumbs-up and a happy, lopsided grin, eyes crinkling at the corners. It's a tight race, but I think the most alarming aspect here is that I can see both of his hands in the picture.

Which raises the question: "Who the hell took this picture?"

"I did," he replies, flipping to the second page. This one's got a

Polaroid of the two of us with a broken bowl on the floor at our feet. In the picture, he's holding the red book, showing it to me. A caption in gold ink shimmers beneath:

*"Who the **** took this picture?"*
"I did."

The asterisks intended to preserve sensitive eyes from the word *hell* are, upon closer inspection, miniature poinsettias. "Ahhh," he sighs, gaze welling with fond emotion as he strokes the book's spine. "Memories."

I grab the book. It's labeled THE TIME I WAS INVITED TO THE PHYSICAL PLANE BY BETTIE MONICA HUGHES AND TRIED SUNNY D FOR THE FIRST TIME EVER AND IT WAS SO AWESOME. The title's a combination of alphabet stickers and cut-out magazine headlines. "My middle name is Gardenia," I say, dumbstruck.

The word *Monica* disappears, *Gardenia* fading in. "That was a placeholder, since I didn't know. I really love the name Monica. It's technically the most beautiful human name, tracing back to the fourth century."

I stare at him.

"But Gardenia is fine." He snatches the scrapbook back. It vanishes. "I've been waiting forever for you to wake up again. Why are there so many dead plants in here? I bandaged your cut and put together a nice gingerbread loaf, if you're hungry."

That explains the smell and the stretchy beige material wrapped around my right hand. I don't know what to make of that. It strikes me as both kind and violating.

"Right," I croak.

"I think the reason why you slept so long is because you've

been consuming drinks that make you tired," he continues radiantly. "Not to worry. I've dumped them out."

"You *what*?"

"Gingerbread loaf?" he offers, snapping his fingers. A plate appears between us, floating, a slice of brown cake staring up at me. I say *staring* because it's got candy eyes, a red M&M for a nose, and pretzels sticking out the top to form antlers.

"What are you?" I demand, shoving the reindeer in my mouth even though I absolutely know better than to take food from strangers. Why stop making bad decisions now? "Where'd you come from? Where'd you get these pretzels?"

"I am the Holiday Spirit, but you can call me Hall. As in—"

I'm starting to remember his spiel. Or shreds of it, anyway. "Holiday."

"Yes!" His megawatt grin is a solar flare, painful to look at. He rocks back onto his heels. "Due to an obscure typo in the Festivities Legislation, the Holiday Spirit . . ." I'm walking into the kitchen now, checking on the stash of sherry bottles in the cabinet. They're gone. Hall follows, craning his head around the side of the cabinet door. ". . . can be conjured by playing the current Billboard Hot 100 number one hit, *if* it is a holiday hit, and *if* it is played backwards, on vinyl."

I replace the batteries in Eileen's carbon monoxide detector and test it. Seems to be working.

"The Holiday Spirit is an individualized experience. 'Holiday spirit' means something different to every person, so the makeup of a conjured Holiday Spirit would vary from person to person. I'm only a small part of a vast and intricate substance. Think of it like . . . a mist that covers the world. I'm a tiny piece that broke off to come to you when you summoned. Every drop of vapor in that mist is unique, with unique traditions, beliefs, behaviors. But *I'm* the one who most closely resembles your own personal idea of holiday spirit—ness, which is why *I* heard you, and why I'm here." He beams proudly. "I have a frenemy who holiday-spirits primarily in Canterbury, Australia, and he protests all snow- and Northern-Hemisphere-centered holiday songs."

If there's no gas leak, then what is the explanation for why I am seeing and hearing what I am seeing and hearing?

"Somehow," I mutter, "I just know that Kelly Frederick is behind this."

Hall slides narrowly past me to grab a mug—I blink and from one second to the next, the mug has filled itself with steaming hot chocolate. As he waves his hand, summoning marshmallows out of the ether, the air around us stirs, tinged faintly with peppermint.

Hall nudges the mug between my hands until I wrap my fingers around it. Coaxes me to sit down in a chair, which I don't remember ever tying a cushion to but there it is, festooned with snowmen. There's a snowman hand towel draped over the oven handle, too. I scour the remainder of the kitchen, discovering new bits and bobs: A crystal bowl filled with big, round, jewel-toned ornaments. Three different wreaths, each one bigger than the last. A bread box shaped like a sleigh. Hall nods at the marshmallows bobbing in my hot chocolate. "That'll make you feel better, I promise."

"I can't believe you dumped out my alcohol." I take a sip, because what else am I supposed to do? He's right, though—after a swallow, my head seems to be clearing, that terrible migraine a distant memory. I take two more sips, confusion dissolving like stepping into a sunny, picturesque meadow. By the time I've drained the mug, this all makes perfect sense! I've always known

Mariah Carey was powerful, so her ability to summon the personification of festive cheer honestly tracks.

"I can't believe the day's already gone," I sigh, checking the digital clock over my stove. "Now I've only got two left."

"Two left until what?"

"Until I have to go to a thing I really do not want to go to." I let my head fall into my hands. "I wish I had more time."

"If that's an explicit wish, you have to say the magic words."

I arch a brow. "What do you mean? You could literally give me more time?"

"If you say the magic words, yes."

"Which are?"

Hall grows cagey, magicking himself a mug of cocoa and lifting it to his lips coyly. "Can't tell you."

"Well," I deadpan. "How useful."

I think the insinuation of not being useful wounds him. "It's a lyric," he blurts, then gulps his cocoa. Spits it out. "That's not hot chocolate!" He looks down into his cup, giving it a slosh. "Oh, it's hot *chalk*. My bad." To me, he adds apologetically, "I'm new at this. Sometimes I get excited and things end up . . . half-magicked."

I'm still stuck on this magic-words-and-wishing thing. "A lyric to what?"

He leans an inch forward, eyes trained on me with laser focus, trying to tell me without telling me. "Oh!" I exclaim. "The song that conjured you? 'All I Want for Christmas Is You?'"

He nods, gaze glittering. *"Yes."*

I reach for my phone, but it's not in my pocket. "Where's my . . . ?"

"Other room," he supplies. "I'll get it." Then instantly, it appears on the kitchen table.

I Google the lyrics, reciting them out loud. When I complete the seventh line, he smacks the table so hard that I jolt.

I look up. "So I can just say that I want more time, and . . . ?"

"Correct." He leans ever forward, a touch of mania in those otherworldly eyes. They're the color of peeled grapes. "Do it."

Most of my ideas are bad. I ignore this. "I want more time. *Make my wish come true.*"

Hall grasps my hand, there's a flashbang of light, and we're barreling through a black hole, audibly ripping through the fabric of the universe. We're falling backward, my skin sucked tight against my bones, every single one of them on the verge of crushing into powder, into molecules. Gravity pulls at my hair, my fingernails, stripping my socks off. The speed at which we're traveling forces my mouth wide open, all moisture on my tongue and lips evaporating. My teeth rattle and the pressure against my eye sockets is unbearable, but all I can do is take it, I can't do anything, not even shout—

We both slam, hard, into a cold floor. As I drag my eyelids open, my vision crosses but I make out twin blurs of Eileen's withered fiddle leaf fig.

Hall groans nearby, rubbing his head. I think he smacked it on the microwave. "Ohhhh, that was bad. I did not enjoy that at all."

My response is a woozy "Errf." My mouth's the Sahara, lips cracked. That fierce wind is still in my head, howling between my ears. I clap my hands over them, tears pricking my eyes. "Make it stop."

Singing abruptly fills the room at a clamor that could wake the dead. It's BTS, and they're coming from every speaker. They're coming from the microwave. From a battery-operated Billy Bass fish on the wall that is wearing a Santa hat, which I did not put there. My desiccated throat manages a pathetic, barely audible "Eghh."

"Sorry," Hall rasps. "I accidentally made it pop instead of stop."

The noise dies at once, but Billy Bass's tail is still flapping. Now he's singing "A Holly Jolly Christmas" in Michael Bublé's voice.

The all-consuming, disorienting pain from moments before is replaced by a full-body ache accompanied by weird visions bursting in my mind's eye. An enormous pecan pie. Mountains of curled silver ribbons all over the living room floor, my own hand pointing, and Hall hanging his head like a shamed dog. "Oh my God," I groan. "What kind of fairy godmother are you?" I throw up; it's mostly cocoa, and it burns my nose. "What is happening?"

Hall retches, too, although I don't know if his retching is because of how he feels or if it was triggered by the sound of me retching.

I anchor my hands flat on the floor, eyes closed, trying to keep my breathing even as an endless stream of visions batters me upside the head. I see shaving cream all over my bathroom, and Hall crouching on the floor, putting the finishing touches on a *Home Alone* diorama. It includes tiny bricks for dropping onto Marv's face and a working staple gun the size of my pinky nail.

"I'm having psychic visions," I whisper. "You gave me superpowers."

I'm like Dr. Strangelove or whatever he's called, with the cape. My first thought is *How do I abuse these powers for personal gain?*

"I'm so thirsty," I mutter. "I need something to drink."

A cup appears, levitating level with my mouth. Hall's magic is on the fritz, evidently, the cup wobbling, shifting color from orange to yellow. I peer inside, croaking, "Is this tap water?"

He blinks. "Uhh. I don't know."

"I only . . ." I slump onto my side upon the unforgiving floor, eyes clenched tight, dying of thirst. ". . . drink . . . Evian."

He tips the cup against my lips, confirming my worst fears about the source of this water. It's inhumane, the atrocities I have endured today. Or . . . ?

"Is it yesterday, then? Did it work?"

"I think so. What you're seeing in your head are memories of things you *should* have done and said and experienced if time had proceeded as usual. And alternate possibilities of those memories, too. I just envisioned myself eating four possible breakfasts at Denny's, which is handy information, because now I know I want the fried potato tower." He coughs. "It's off-menu. You have to ask for it."

"You knew about these side effects?" I try to swat at him, but my arm flops uselessly.

"I knew that it might feel bad, in theory. But I was hoping to be an exception, in practice." He tries for a smile. "Sorry. I really wanted to flex those time travel powers. Never done it before."

"Never doing it again," I retort darkly. "Not with me, anyway."

"I would never do it with anybody else. I'm committed to you."

My eyes narrow. "What do you mean?"

"You're the one who conjured me. I'm yours. And I am here to fill you with the holiday spirit."

I raise my eyebrows, smirking.

Hall flushes. "Not like *that*!" He's so distressed that he starts knitting a tinsel scarf, which he completes with remarkable quickness, and drapes around the shoulders of a life-size Father Christmas I didn't know was behind me, and which I'll be seeing in my nightmares tonight. "Obviously, you brought me here because you need holiday spirit, right?"

I think of Eileen's sad pink Christmas tree and begin to argue that my spirit level is satisfactory when he adds, "My holiday magic is yours for the using until you're adequately filled with spirit of your own, remember."

I close my mouth. Turn his words over in my mind.

"Your holiday magic . . . is mine for the using? Mine? As in, I wish for something and you just make it happen?"

My mind wipes blank, like a giant white void. Then it begins to fill up—with Alexander McQueen jumpsuits and five-thousand-dollar shoes, and canapés, and an upgraded phone. I envision the Watsons' Christmas tree hidden behind boxes and boxes of presents I can't afford.

"I'm so pumped," he's chattering. "Been dreaming about getting an opportunity to try out some really neat stuff for *ages*! And by ages, I mean literally since the Neolithic period, when I was commonly referred to as the Spirit of Winter Solstice; then later on, Yule. Some have even called me a winter god. Before I was Hall, short for Holiday, I was Hall, short for Holly King." He puffs out his chest at this. "A long time ago, holiday spirits were allowed to come and go physically from our plane of existence to yours, but it ended up being too chaotic and that's why the legislation was introduced. Spirits would come to earth and start feeling differently about their role—they'd start to reconsider who they were, then become confused about what they wanted or who they were. *Or*, they'd go overboard in their magic-spreading, and that's how you ended up with flying reindeer, which at one point was the shenanigans of some overexcited spirit. I've personally never mingled physically with humans before, but ever since I learned about the legislation's typo, I've been hoping and waiting for someone to activate it. I think I could make great strides here, providing joy."

"Is that your purpose or something?"

"Exactly. Before I came here, I was just floating around as an incorporeal mass of pure joy, shining down on the world and making the humans I passed over feel joyful, too. But now I can really get *in there*, you know?"

"How long are you going to be down here 'providing joy'?"

"For as long as you need it."

"And how will you know when I no longer need it?"

He shrugs. "Not sure yet. I think I'll know when I know. Your holiday spirit is a miserably low one point five out of ten on the Holiday Scale."

"Listen, you. I'm a ten at everything."

"If your number stays low," he continues, "then I could end up hanging around here forever."

A forever filled with Valentino handlebags. No one will be able to accuse me of Photoshopping my lifestyle ever again. "You're right, I'm super miserable. Let's get started on the holiday magic right away."

I need to cast about a billion and one wishes, then find a way to get rid of him. I cannot be responsible for this man-shaped mass of sugar who was probably created in a Brach's candy laboratory. I'll use him for my own ends, and then we can see about forever.

Hall has transformed the left half of my fridge into a snow cone machine and is fixing himself a snow cone with toppings that absolutely do not go with it: fudge sauce, a banana, and sprinkles. He's in a whirl of peppermint fog, shimmering faintly as it curls off his skin. "Being incorporeal has its benefits, but I do so enjoy inhabiting a body. A human male body. Who knew I would have such an amazing human male body? I did. This is what I've always imagined I would look like."

I run an assessing gaze up and down him.

It feels wrong to find him attractive, so I'm trying not to. It's like eyeing a Keebler elf with seductive intentions. He's so *nice* and so *pure*, a glowing unicorn untainted by all that is crass and vulgar about the world. I'm practically a demon in comparison, which you'd think would prompt me to take it easy on him. But instead, it's really bringing out the demon. I find myself wanting to say inappropriate things just to see what his expression will do. All of my worst impulses are running amok.

Maybe I can see how my spirit might be a one point five.

"I've got it, Bettie, and I am *flaunting* it. The organ function. The blood, I have so much of it. It's exhilarating to be so full of blood. I could eat ten fried potato towers in a row if I wanted to, but I won't, because I listened to a radio report on amino acids while you were unconscious today and I've got so many amino acids to catch up on. We're going to have a ball together, you and I. Imagine! We can design snowball cannons, we can put twinkly lights up on people's houses and surprise them. We can go caroling in all fifty U.S. capitals. Montgomery! Juneau! Phoenix! Little Rock! Sacramento! Denver! Hartford!"

He runs through all the state capitals, and when he's finished, he gets started on every tourist attraction along Route 66.

CHAPTER THREE

························

Countdown to Christmas: 10 Days

T HIS ONE. MAKE my wish come true."

Hall skims the real estate listing. "A sale for this house is pending. I'd rather not take it away from the new owner."

Hearing that someone is buying a house that used to be mine stings, but I won't show it. Hall is a mirror for emotions and if I start to cry, so will he. "Fine. If I can't have *that* house, we'll just create a new one. An even better one. Can you do that?"

"I don't see why not."

"I want five bedrooms, at least two of them masters, and six bathrooms. At least five thousand square feet. I want a guest house, an infinity pool, a spa, and marble everything. Marble floors, marble countertops, a marble terrace. Make that two marble terraces. One of those massive water feature rock walls in the living room, with backlights. Open-floor-plan kitchen and living area, and I want it so big that it echoes. It *has* to be oceanfront."

He nods, furrowing his brow in concentration. "Is that everything?"

"Are you kidding? We're just getting started."

I go into lengthy detail on the size of the bathtubs, the color of kitchen cabinets, the landscaping. A pantry stocked with gourmet chocolate truffles. A walk-in closet bigger than Eileen's house. Valentino Rockstud Spike shoulder bags in pink, blue, yellow, black, white, and *poudre*. I used to have one of those bags in blue, and it was my very favorite possession until I had to pawn it to get myself out of trouble with a loan shark. (The loan was for an actual shark, too. I used to have a seven-hundred-gallon aquarium in my bedroom.)

"And in the driveway, a red Aston Martin DBS Superleggera," I conclude with a giddy clap, beyond ready to kiss this place goodbye. "Make my wish come true."

Hall's been taking feverish notes. "Okay. I think I got it all." He sucks in a deep breath, shutting his eyes. A moment later, he opens them but doesn't speak. Or look at me.

"So?" I prompt. "Did you do it?"

He still won't look at me, those limpid green eyes fixating on the threadbare sofa. A hand lifts to scratch his head. "Hmmm."

"Hmmm, what?"

"I mean, I *did*. I did do what you wanted. Sort of."

"Can I see?" I wait for him to cross his arms and tip his head like we're in *I Dream of Jeannie*.

He pauses. "You might have to live without the sauna."

"We can revisit that." I am not living without the sauna.

To my surprise, we don't teleport. Instead, he directs me to my car. "Are we driving to the airport?" I ask.

"We could walk, actually." He nods, shutting the passenger door. Its hinges scream.

"Where are we going?"

He doesn't reply. Hall is looking pretty nervous, and I find out why once we're standing on the sidewalk along Old Homestead Road, facing a block of four buildings. At the center, between Teller City Trading Company (*Gift Shoppe & Old West Portrait Studio*) and the Blue Moose Café, there's an empty plot fenced behind spiked wrought iron, with a carpet of soggy autumn leaves and a well-preserved vintage milk truck.

Next to the milk truck sits a dollhouse.

"Hall."

Hall searches the sky with deep interest, pretending not to hear.

"Hall, what am I looking at?"

"Don't worry, I'll fix it. It just needs some . . . tweaking." He glances around to see if anyone's out and about. It's a gray, drizzly day, which seems to have chased the town indoors.

"Why on earth would you put a dollhouse here? Hall, I want to go to Hawaii now."

"Shh, I'm concentrating. I'm very new at this sort of transfiguration thing, you know." He presses his fingers to his temples, knees bent. It's a funny sight, but I'm pulled away from it by the spectacle of the dollhouse, which is growing in size while the milk truck shrinks down to a toy.

The house rises like something from a pop-up book, a narrow Georgian rowhouse with cinnamon-colored stucco in four levels, all fudged together with gobs of white paint that drip down unevenly like icing. The roof is trimmed in red and green scalloping. Warm yellow light pours through tall casement windows, illuminating the frosting ledges to show off how they sparkle, and all the way at the top, faint gray smoke puffs from two (out of four) chimneys in the shape of hearts. The whole thing inflates as far as the two flanking buildings will allow, bursting until the squeeze is so tight that there's a loud, painful scraping of bricks that makes me wish my eardrums would pop. Only once half the shingles have peeled from the Blue Moose Café and all of Teller City Trading Company's shutters have fallen off does his creation give an audible sigh and fall to rest.

It's a gingerbread house. An inedible, goddamn gingerbread house.

My throat is dry. "What."

I check the street to see if passersby caught any of this spectacle (no one is around, thankfully), then turn to him. He's wearing a *Holiday Realty* badge on a lanyard around his neck, clipboard in hand. "Let's have a look!" he says brightly.

My scowl burns holes in the ozone. "This is not a Hawaiian villa. This is the opposite of a Hawaiian villa."

"I think my magic wants you to live here instead."

"Your magic, or *you*? I don't want to live here! I thought you were supposed to grant my wishes."

"I did! But I made it better. You'll thank me, I promise."

"I will *not*."

I don't appreciate the euphoric glitter in his great, big, I'm-loving-everything-about-this eyes as he forcibly leads me on a tour. A gate materializes in the fencing, which goes *cling!* as he pushes through, arm looped in mine to prevent me from running away. "It's a new build, got state-of-the-art plumbing and a Never Runs Out water heater. Catslide roof in the back." He gestures, grinning dazzlingly. I'm distracted by the cute swoop of his hair, how the ends curl. "Multi-pane sash windows with timber pilasters. What a nice touch! The architect considered a thatched roof but deemed it too ostentatious."

I emit a murderous grunt.

Christmas string lights, large 1960s bulbs, zigzagging across the front of the house blink intermittently. "I only put up four visible-to-humans strands," he says, "because I didn't want to overwhelm you. I did add a few extra strands that only I can see."

"Extra?"

"Yes. Thirty yards of lights invisible to mortal eyes."

I poke at one of the enormous Dots candies bordering the pathway up to the front door, which is painted red, with a gold mail slot (made redundant by the milk truck toy, which he's perched on the fence post and fashioned into a mailbox) and a green wreath with the letter *H* on it. I don't ask if the *H* is for *Hughes* or *Hall* because if he gives me the wrong answer I might kick him.

"Two of the chimneys are fully functioning, but the other two are rooftop-aesthetic only. Wait till you see the interior design."

He opens the door, jostling me ahead of him. "All right, I'm *going*," I mutter tersely.

My remaining crumb of patience instantly evaporates upon seeing what's inside. He's built four stories that are so cramped you can hardly appreciate the height. The first level is the kitchen and bathroom: you edge through the door and are squashed straight into the sink. More of the space would probably be useful were it not for the decorations jam-packed every-which-where— it's Santa's Workshop from floor to ceiling. Up the stairs is a sitting room, with a sixteen-inch television I can barely see. Stacked on top of that is the bedroom, outfitted in the wild, inexplicable guess that I might like the color yellow. Gingham yellow bedspread. Sunflower wallpaper. Marigold-hued carpeting.

Hall watches my expression closely. "You don't like it?"

"It's a lot of yellow. Can I have something blue?"

Hall brandishes an arm, melting down the wallpaper. He spreads the sunflowers back out, this time making them cerulean. The carpet peels itself up to expose a parquet floor and then vanishes. The gingham bedspread flips over to its reverse side, which is plain white quilting.

"Wow," is all I can manage. If I had powers like his, I would go around changing the colors of everybody's vehicles to cause bedlam.

The house smells predictably of sugar, cedar, and old-fashioned ornaments, which the attic contains two trunks of. They're locked, with no keys in sight ("For the mystery," Hall tells me). Hall has decided the attic should be creaky, dim, and swirling with dust despite being only a few minutes old. He shows me a strange human-shaped stain on the peeling '70s wallpaper. "Somebody could have died in here."

I give him a strangled look. "Did they?"

"Of course not!" He turns to survey his handwork. "But they could have."

I leave him in his terrible haunted attic to go downstairs, *all the way* downstairs, into the kitchen. I open a window and start tossing stuff out to make more room—nobody needs this many jingle bells—then check all the cabinets for wine, which is a futile effort. I don't miss that Hall's tacked an extra bedroom off the back of the house for himself, and it's bigger than mine. Most of the space is absorbed by the magnificent bed, the frame of which is shaped like a solid gold sleigh. Every Just For Men product on the market adorns his shelves, including mustache and beard dye, even though he doesn't have a mustache or beard.

"So." Hall appears behind me while my belongings from Eileen's house appear all around us. His magic mangled my Ocean Galaxy Light Projector and Himalayan salt lamp, combining them into one bizarre light fixture. "Do you love the house or what?"

"It's not quite what I designed," I reply darkly.

He nods in agreement. "I know. It's much better."

"Better than Eileen's, I suppose. I've been running through under-eye patches like nobody's business, draining all my youth away worrying that a long-lost relative would claim the place." I sigh. "Could I at least have the Aston Martin?"

His eyes grow large and eager. "What if I told you that you could have something ten times more luxurious than an Aston Martin?"

"A Rolls-Royce Sweptail?" I know a lot about luxury cars. Every night, I climb into bed and add two or three of them to my Aspirations Pinterest board.

"Cover your eyes."

"I really do not like the sound of that."

Hall slips his hands over my eyes, and I suppress a shiver. This will probably sound sad, but I haven't been touched by another person in a very long time, and the (sort of) human contact is both jarring and more comforting than I would've expected.

He bumps me into every conceivable sharp corner on our way outside. "Aaaaaand, you can open them!"

I do.

Parked out front, passenger-side wheel propped up on the curb, is a bulbous, old-fashioned red pickup truck with a Christmas tree poking out of the bed. The license plate reads *MMWCT* for reasons unknown to me.

"No!"

"The glovebox dispenses Linzer raspberry jam cookies," he reports exultantly. "Find *that* in an Aston Martin."

"I would rather find myself in an Aston Martin!" I feel my nose scrunching. "This isn't what I wished for."

The new neighborhood attraction has attracted gogglers. A few of the neighbors, and Town-Hall-walk-around-ers from across the street, have assembled to argue over how long both the house and truck have been here. Nothing gets missed in a town as small as this one—which is my largest gripe with it, aside from my relatives up the mountain and the fact that I'll have to show my face there soon.

If it weren't for Grandma and Grandpa's nearby residence and the fear of being spotted by them or someone who can tell them they spotted *me*, Teller City is an okay town. I appreciate the grocery deliveries on Wednesdays, which have pretty much kept me alive. Once a week, I look forward to the box of sauce, dry pasta, canned vegetables, batteries, and toilet paper on my doorstep. It's delivered by a kid named Rudy who also delivers the newspapers, and I tip him in a new cryptocurrency that I made up.

"I don't remember seeing any construction," one elderly lady is saying.

"Oh, it was built months ago!" one of her friends exclaims. "Don't you remember?"

The other one shakes her head.

"It's been around for ages," another one adds. "I pass that house every morning when I'm walking my dogs."

Then they notice me.

I feel myself shrink back, but it's too late. One face lights up, followed by another, like a strand of Christmas bulbs. "Oh! You're Bettie and Lawrence's granddaughter, aren't you?"

My mouth falls open to say no, but Hall declares proudly, "Yes, she is!"

The gogglers are magnets for more gogglers. My name is tossed around in the air like a volleyball. They chirp questions at me, but it's like my mouth is stuffed with cotton, heart pounding. It's only a matter of time before my current living situation is discovered and all of my lies revealed. It would have been one thing for my family to find out I gambled away my millions two years ago, when I went into a tailspin. But now, it'll look so much worse. They'll know that everything I've said to them about my amazing, spectacular life has been a lie—and I haven't been easy on the boasting. Last month, I told Athena I was having an affair with the king of Aldovia.

My nervous stare pans all the way down Old Homestead Road, to the gothic revival house on the mountain that you can see from anywhere in town, high enough on its perch to look down upon the rest of society. It's painted like a woody nightshade flower: poisonous red berry for the siding, amethyst petal for the trim. A sharp, jutting turret is the yellow stamen, from which spins a gruesome weathervane of a honey badger eating a scorpion. On every steeply pitched gable roosts a gargoyle, serpent-faced lions whose purpose, I assume, is to horrify grandchildren sleeping in the rooms below.

In a town dominated by cozy lodges and Bavarian style, that house stands out like a night terror. As intended.

I swallow.

Beside me, Hall is chattering away obliviously, using my first and last name several times per sentence, really hammering it home that I am, in fact, living in the town where my namesake resides. *Like the village witch*, I think, glancing at Bettie Watson's fortress of doom, and then at my new house, which is its polar opposite. Children will be shoving their wish lists for Santa through my mail slot by the end of the day.

So much for keeping a low profile.

※

"The *how* is every bit as baffling as the *why*—experts are at a loss as to how a fully grown water buffalo has ended up on the fourth floor of a Chelsea apartment building. I'm Francesca Grace with NBC News, here with you live on West Twenty-First Street in New York City, at eleven minutes to midnight. We're standing just outside a building where, believe it or not, a *water buffalo* has been found in the apartment belonging to *New York Times* reporter and pop culture critic Kelly Frederick." The reporter can barely suppress her glee. "Kelly Frederick is perhaps best known for her work as an editor at *The Hot Goss* and her snarky, claws-out critical style. Frederick has built a considerable fan base that delights in watching her no-holds-barred takedowns of celebrities."

The news station slaps two pictures next to Francesca on the screen: one, a stock image of a water buffalo; and the other, Kelly Frederick's headshot, smirking insufferably.

Hall turns from where he's sitting on the sofa and pins me with a disapproving look, as though I have done something unsavory, when actually what I have done is serve up vigilante justice. Nobody would frown disapprovingly like this at Batman. "I hope you're happy with yourself right now."

"Thanks, I definitely am." I wish I could pop a bottle of champagne, but hot chocolate will have to suffice. "Haven't had this much fun in a while."

He touches his temples. "My head hurts. I think you're breaking me. I thought we'd be spending more time engaged in marshmallow-oriented activities."

"Good idea. Let's cover Salt Lake City in exploded marshmallow goo."

"They're going to tranquilize the animal," Francesca says, and Hall gives me a pointed look. "Authorities are . . ."

I tune her out after the word *authorities*, as I do not respect authorities.

"There's a hole in my wall!"

I zip back to attention. Kelly's livid face appears on the screen, and it's better than a trip to the spa. Her anger cleanses my pores and irrigates the trenches in my universally underestimated brain. She's got a massive hole in her wall, and the buffalo defecated all over her couch. I'm overwhelmed with good tidings and joy— Hall's succeeding with flying colors, filling me all the way up with holiday cheer.

"All right, now put the water buffalo back wherever you found it," I tell him.

Hall waits expectantly.

"Oh, right. *Make my wish come true*." Hall grabs the remote and changes the channel now that my joyride is over. "What else can you do? Can you communicate with the dead?" I visualize a tea party with Cary Grant (I think he ought to have been my true love, but alas, the age gap was too vast and we're ships in the night), Leonardo da Vinci (he's there to paint my portrait), and a velociraptor.

"No."

"Establish world peace?"

"Afraid not."

"Start a war?"

"No. And I can't do mind control, emotional manipulation, or create a real-life Jurassic Park, either. Those are all out-of-bounds operations, as included in Section: Primarily to Avoid Narrative Scrutiny, Clause: *But Why Doesn't He Just*." He draws a breath, looking grave. "The most dire of consequences would await me for even attempting the Number One Most Forbidden Thing, which is to bring back the McRib when it isn't in season. Such is the corporate might of the Golden Arches."

Interesting. "Why can you say yes to some wishes but not to others?"

"For the most part, magic is left to my discretion, and I can grant your wishes if those wishes seem to bring you joy." His gaze flicks to the television. "But I may reject a wish if it would be damaging to history, the spacetime continuum, that sort of thing. Or if it would cause real harm, physical or otherwise, to others. Some wishes I might not personally reject, but holiday magic would, for unknown reasons. Which isn't something I knew before I arrived here, but that information's just been conveniently dropped into my head now that I'm in need of it." He stops on the local weather channel, leaning forward.

The weatherman's bedecked in a reindeer tie and a headband with antlers. "Look at this man, wearing his little tie and his little antlers on television," Hall says, utterly charmed. As he watches, the same tie and antlers appear on his person.

From over on the coffee table, my phone lights up, and I browse through a crop of texts from Mom that I haven't known how to respond to.

How are you doing

We love you very much

Your dad loves you too

**Don't forget, Grandma
and Grandpa's house,
December 18 at 5:00!!!!**

Ahhh, the holidays with Bettie Watson, who isn't impressed with any of her grandchildren but especially not with me, the stain on her legacy. She's an EGOT hoarder who worked for everything she's got, and here I am just waltzing around with her famous name, not living up to my potential. Which is quite a trip, because I'm supposedly a millionaire. What more does she want from me? I do love seeing Grandpa, though, who adores me to pieces, and who I avoid at all costs because I want him to keep on adoring me. I wish we could only go every other year, break up the pressure with trips to see Granny and Grandad Hughes in Cornwall, but my paternal grandparents feel our brood is too large and too loud for their small cottage.

I can elude most family functions, like the billion gender reveal parties thrown by my two older siblings, and pregnancy reveal parties, and soon enough it'll be ovulation day parties—but nobody tells Grandma they're not showing up for Christmas and lives to tell the tale. She will not be deprived of her yearly opportunity to lament, for a week straight, what a disappointment we are, and we must soldier through if we are to inherit anything. Like ten million dollars, or her collection of blood vials harvested from headliners of the '98 Warped Tour.

If she's disappointed in me *now*, when she thinks I'm flush with Instagram sponsor cash and relaxing in my beach bungalow, I shudder to think what she'd say if she knew the truth.

I'm especially dreading seeing my dad. He and I got into a fight over FaceTime when I said I wasn't visiting him and Mom in Los Angeles for Thanksgiving. Truthfully, I couldn't afford the plane ticket, and my car wouldn't survive the drive from Colorado. But I couldn't tell him that, because money talk is a dangerous thread to pull, and I'm too busy trying to look like I'm just as prosperous as my siblings. So I had to lie about having other plans.

"Your mom will be devastated," he'd said.

And then he'd corrected himself. "Your *mum* will be devastated."

(Too many years of living in America has sanded down the edges of his British accent. All of his British friends have been poking fun at him. *"Listen, Patrick. Listen to how he says the word* blueberry.*"*)

My parents were firm about giving us a normal upbringing—public school, making Kaia and me share a bedroom. We all had chores, we all had to get jobs when we were teenagers to buy our own cars, et cetera. Dad's a photographer who earns a modest living, and he and Mom have been together since he took her picture for a magazine spread when she was twenty and he was twenty-four. She had been an actor in her teens but didn't love the job. So she tried ballet, but it was too hard on her joints. She didn't discover her true passion, which is cooking, until she was fifty and finished raising all her kids. Now she writes cookbooks and hosts a holiday baking show on Netflix, which tapes in the summer. She does some voice-over work for a weird two a.m. show on Adult Swim, too.

While I was growing up, they wouldn't take any money from Grandma and Grandpa Watson. It was drilled into us kids ever since we were embryos that we'd be expected to forge our own paths as well. My brother and sisters have risen to the challenge, each famous for their achievements. I'm famous for being famous, for being related to famous people. And for my failures.

My older sister Athena is a commercial model who's worked her way up from Proactiv to Burberry. She doles out lukewarm fashion takes for E! during red carpet season, taking care to mention L'Oréal and bareMinerals because both companies contractually own her soul. She's got a sheet of shoulder-length white-blond hair, skin like a vampire, and wears pastels in solid colors, never patterns. She graces covers of parenting magazines with her latest (and therefore most favorite) child in her lap, the baby dressed like a Puritan. Athena has cultivated this soft-spoken, I-only-use-organic-oat-diapers-for-my-babies environmentally responsible persona that is patently false, with a loud, stupid husband who makes sure, everywhere he goes, that everyone knows he's married to Athena Hughes. I called her Ivanka Lite at her rehearsal dinner, and she had my car towed.

My younger sister Kaia's loved to sing all her life, but Dad wouldn't let her pursue any career avenue that might lead to fame while she was still a minor. She went on a road trip with a friend when she turned eighteen to hit up every open mic night on the

West Coast, and within a month she had a record deal. Of all of the Hughes siblings, she's the one with genuine talent. She's got a raspy, bluesy sound—she's been in four bands so far, an indie darling—but I've heard a couple tracks from her upcoming album and it's scary, how huge she's going to get. She'll be mainstream by this time next year.

Felix, my parents' only son as well as firstborn, has assistant-directed two films that both tanked at the box office, and he thinks he's Tarantino. After each divorce (right now he's on wife number four), he does something tragic to his hair, stirs media buzz by getting violently kicked out of a bar, and steals another man's wife. He pursues married women almost exclusively, as per-suading a woman to love him is one thing, but persuading a woman away from someone *else* is an even headier achievement. A year after each divorce, he tones up, gets a new tattoo, and lands interviews with teasers like HE'S BACK, AND HE'S READY FOR YOU TO TAKE HIM SERIOUSLY or THE PRODIGAL GRANDSON, REFORMED. *"I'm feeling better than ever. This is the happiest I've ever been—I'm done messing around. I've grown up, found a new project I'm passionate about, and you're going to see a Felix Hughes like you've never seen before."*

There's a saying about the dysfunctional black sheep of the family, the one who makes the others look better by comparison but, overall, makes the family look worse: *Every family's got one.* My family has two: Felix and me. He and I are pits of lawsuits and rumors, some of which we started ourselves. We're layers of aban-doned passion projects, struggling to find meaning in our lives, stumbling over and over on a world stage. The difference between us is that nothing ever keeps him down. Felix's success is his in-ability to quit trying.

Then it dawns on me: for the first time, I have an edge over my brother and sisters. I don't have their cherubic offspring or a Grammy in my future, but I've got unfettered access to any limited-edition, coveted, out-of-stock thing I can possibly dream of, and what's the use of having that if I'm not rubbing my loved ones' noses in it? If I can transport Niall Horan to a random Taco Bell in Chicago (I did that an hour ago and it was marvelous) and decorate a gossip columnist's apartment with a water buffalo, what else can I do?

Thanks to Hall, I've got the ability to make it look like I'm happier and more successful than any of them. They'll roast alive with jealousy, and I'll be the least dysfunctional one of us all!

Hall is still watching the weatherman raptly, imitating his hand motions as if practicing how to warn Colorado of snowstorm trajectories. I smile evilly at the back of his head.

He and I are going to make some magic together.

※

CHAPTER FOUR

························

*Countdown to Christmas:
8 Days*

THE AIR SMELLS like pulverized Thin Mints and triumph. We're at zero hour.

"This seems like a lot," Hall remarks as he helps pile Hefty bags full of presents into the red pickup, which was supposed to be mine, but Hall keeps changing the lock on it because he's worried I'll *drive it without the care it deserves.*

"It better be. I'm making up for a whole bunch of holidays in which all my presents were shit. Do you know what I gave everybody last year?"

He shakes his head.

"Books from Little Free Libraries. I had a job waiting tables and was saving up, because holidays are expensive in my family. Grandparents, parents, two sisters, a brother, a sister-in-law, a brother-in-law, and their monsoon of collective offspring."

"That's a lot of people to shop for."

"But then a customer recognized me and wouldn't stop taking

pictures, not even being sneaky about it, so I finally snapped at him. The manager took his side, of course, because the customer is always right. My boss ordered me to apologize. I chose to quit. That's what always happens. It isn't easy to get hired in the first place because of my arrest record, so when some restaurant or store takes me on, thinking maybe I'll bring attention to their business, people come in and act like total dillweeds to me, to look funny in front of their friends." I stomp back into the gingerbread town house and emerge with one of my suitcases on wheels. This is going to be a tight fit. "I'm supposed to stand there and take it while they laugh and ask why I'm working there." My face reddens just remembering. "Humiliating."

"Couldn't you work somewhere else, then? Find a job where you don't have to interact with the public?"

"I have no skills, Hall. I'm not good at anything. My only talent is being beautiful and talking my way out of parking tickets."

Hall frowns, a crease between his eyebrows. I bet he's never frowned this much before, in his entire existence, even when he was merely a collection of floating particles watching Stonehenge be erected.

Together, we manage to get the door to shut. I sag against it, breathing heavily. "Do you think we got enough?"

He reaches up over his head, hand-cranking a long receipt out of thin air. Reading glasses appear on his nose as he fires off my wishes. "So far, here's what you've already bought for your family: A sable. A '54 convertible in light blue. A duplex. Checks, specifically from Jeff Bezos. Amal Clooney's engagement ring. A yacht."

"The sable is fake. The convertible is the size of a shoe. The duplex is in Madagascar, which, whole lot of good it's doing for me over there. The checks from Jeff Bezos don't have his signature, which means I'll have to forge them, and the yacht is stuck in the mountains."

"You have the ring, though."

"Which is on the yacht that's stuck in the mountains."

His lips purse. "You seem upset about that."

I wave him off. It's yet another hiccup in my fun plan to enrich myself with the holiday spirit by requesting all of the presents in the song "Santa Baby." The worst hiccup was when Hall didn't get my wish quite right and ended up conjuring a baby Santa. It had the measurements of a newborn with the face of an elderly man, rosy-cheeked, bespectacled, with a full white beard, wailing *HO HO HO.*

"At least I have Jennifer Lopez's green Versace dress."

"You should have let me get you a replica."

"I need the warm, fond memories that go with the original. Athena will be able to smell them when she opens it up on Christmas morning, and it will hands-down beat anything she's ever gotten for me." Besides, I deserve this win. I work so hard.

"I work so hard," I say. "I need to treat myself. If I had a therapist, that's exactly what they would advise." I am between therapists at the moment, as I have a terrible penchant for developing the hots for anyone who uses soothing, validating language or tells me I should work on myself, and I keep trying to seduce them.

"Every time you ask me to grant wishes I'm morally opposed to, I get ill. Just because you *can* do something doesn't mean you *should.*" His face is tinged green. "The travesty we unleashed upon Magnolia Market in Waco, Texas." I smile, recollecting the wonderful two hours we spent cursing distressed farmhouse mirrors so that the wearer could only see Jamie Lee Curtis eating Activia.

"You can't tell me that wasn't fun."

His gaze flicks up to mine, stern. "The chicken nuggets thing."

I have to snicker. Tabloids, paparazzi, and anyone who's ever sued me has had their taste receptors tinkered with, so now sweet foods taste sour, and salty foods taste exactly like if you microwaved Stouffer's chicken nuggets for half the recommended time, so they're partly soggy, partly frozen. Are they eating chips? Fries? Pretzels? Not anymore! It's all flavorless chicken nuggets now!

"*Then*, there's the laundry list of requests I had to reject because they cost too much magic, or would change the fabric of history, or would punch a hole in time, et cetera." Hall conjures a second receipt from nowhere, unfurling a naughty list so long that it rolls across the street, right up the steps of Town Hall.

It's not as bad as he's making it sound. All I wanted was to put myself somewhere in the background of *The Wizard of Oz*, holding a cell phone, to confuse people in the present day. It would spawn so many delicious conspiracy theories.

Figuring out what Hall is and isn't able to do has been a fun system of trial and error. The rules of magic are ironclad in some areas, but overall, they bend toward randomness. Magic wouldn't allow me to illegally stream *Lost*, for example, but it let me conjure up the box set of DVDs. It said no to an inflatable pool filled with chocolate pudding for some reason, but yes to fireworks that yelled "Boom" with the voices of The Black Eyed Peas whenever they exploded. Sometimes it has high-strung principles and says no to requests, but after rephrasing them creatively, I get my yes. I'm the loophole whisperer. Hall is the unwilling admirer of this, since I can tell it amuses him whenever magic swerves me forty times and then I finally win. This has led to him *wanting* to grant most of my wishes, because his amusement amuses me in turn, and *my* amusement gives him that nice, bubbly feeling of doing his job well. Very symbiotic.

"Just one last thing before we go," I insist. "I would like a dead mackerel, please."

He conjures a dead mackerel. It has plastic googly eyes and is glued to a plaque, but close enough.

"I want you to put this in Ally Whitcross's pillowcase."

"The woman from the *Beverly Hillbillies* revival?"

"She's got it coming. We were best friends until she started leaking all my personal stuff to the press." Before he can interrupt, I add, "Make my wish come true."

I think it was a success, because he gags a little. "Reverse Apple Jacks taste so bad."

"Here." I hand him my thermos of orange juice (it's mostly absinthe). He takes a deep swig before spraying it out of his nose.

Hall is using a child-size box of Yoo-hoo as a neti pot when my mother texts to ask how far away from my grandparents' house I am. I bet she thinks I missed my flight and I'll be the last to show up, as always. To be frank, I have had it up to here with everybody treating me like I'm a flake with no sense of responsibility.

My sense of responsibility throws me a gloomy, end-of-the-world look over his shoulder. He's standing at an easel, painting a portrait of Lacey Chabert (who, he's told me on three separate occasions, has starred in more made-for-TV Christmas movies than any other *All My Children* alum). Not being punctual is one of the many (many, many) things about me that gives him a queasy stomach. It's not that I'm stalling. (It's only a little bit that I'm stalling.) It's mostly that after getting a taste of revenge, I don't know how to stop. I've got a long list of people who need their comeuppance. Ally Whitcross, Niall Horan, and Kelly Frederick were only the beginning. My ex-boyfriend, Lucas Dormer, has hell on his horizon.

"It's four forty-five," he reports forlornly. "We're going to be late, and your family will hate me, and I won't be able to live with myself, and I'll melt into a puddle—"

I hold up my hands. "We're going! We're going. We can do more dead-fish stuff later."

He spins around, emerging from a Hall tornado in a sweater that has a fireplace on it with fiber-optic lights, which somehow smells like gooey chocolate chip cookies. "This is so exciting! I've watched all of your grandmother's films."

"Really? Wow. Even I haven't seen all of them."

"She's the best actor who ever lived."

"Please don't tell her that."

"Does she like green bean casserole? Does she have a subscription to Discovery Plus? I should know as much about your family as possible, since I'm supposed to be your boyfriend." It's the only rationale for bringing Hall along that makes sense. He trips over the word *boyfriend* as he says it, unable to meet my eyes.

"It doesn't have to be weird, Hall. Don't make it weird."

"I'm not making it weird. I'm just . . . thinking." I step in front of him, but he doggedly won't look at me. What is eye contact? Hall doesn't know her.

"You're overthinking."

"I've seen every single romance film in existence, so I know how boyfriends and girlfriends interact." His cheeks are scribbles of pink, color seeping up his neck. "So, I was wondering, do you need me to kiss you in front of them?"

"God, no! You don't have to do anything like that. We're too repressed to show affection in front of other people."

Oh dear, I've broken his heart. It happens so easily with Hall.

"You don't show affection in front of your family?" he repeats softly. "Bettie, that's the saddest thing I've ever heard." He drapes a hand over his chest, and the fiber-optic fireplace on his sweater begins to smoke between his fingers.

"I show affection to Grandpa Lawrence. Really nice guy, just the loveliest person on earth. Used to be a set designer. Now he works on a miniature version of Teller City in his basement and collects wooden mallard ducks."

"And your grandmother?" He motions for me to join him in the truck. "Just think of the place, and we'll be there."

"My grandmother," I tell him, "destroyed my future by giving me her genes. She's had a long, successful career, a long, successful marriage. There are documentaries about her. Foundations in her name. A scholarship program. The future will remember Bettie Watson. Me, on the other hand? It's a compare-and-contrast Venn diagram that I'll never look good in. When you're unfavorably compared to someone who's the best at everything, when you fall short of expectations, you fall very, very far."

✳

Hall's teleportation has a few bugs. We arrive up on the mountain without the red pickup or any of the presents inside it. Our shoes were also left behind, and my hair's in a ponytail now for some reason.

Teleporting, thankfully, isn't as violent as time traveling. One second, we're right outside the town house, the next we're regaining our balance in a copse of trees. The property is situated on the edge of a steep hill, and if the copse weren't there acting as a guardrail we could easily roll off and die. Or I would die, at least. Notable side effects of teleportation are: (1) Your sinuses temporarily fill with ice-cold eggnog that drains down the back of your throat within seconds of landing. (2) The song "Video Killed the Radio Star" becomes stuck in your head.

"It's breathtaking," Hall declares in quiet rapture, staring at a Coca-Cola bottling plant that's been abandoned since the 1980s. "Precisely where I would imagine the great Bettie Watson to reside."

I grab his shoulders and wheel him around in the opposite direction, toward Grandma and Grandpa's small gothic castle. It's like 1313 Mockingbird Lane up here, thanks to Grandma's deep flair for the dramatic and free license to design whatever kind of house she wanted, in her and Grandpa's negotiations to retire here, in his hometown. "*That* is where the great Bettie Watson resides."

He lets out a startled "Egad."

"Don't worry, it's more normal on the inside. Grandpa makes her keep the worst stuff on the outside of the house so that he won't have to look at it."

I yank him behind a tree as a young woman zooms up the jagged driveway on a motorcycle and unclips her helmet, finger-combing her brown-blond pixie cut. She must have ridden here from her vacation home in Aspen, which she's turned into a recording studio. She's wearing a long navy tunic over a black lace skirt, over striped leggings and old-timey boots with a zillion decorative buttons up the sides. It's a bohemian-Victorian style that she calls *botorian*. "That's my sister Kaia," I hiss. The L.A. Dodgers ball cap she removes from her backpack to pull over her head shouldn't go with that outfit, but it does. One more detail to be envious of.

I narrow my eyes at curtains ruffling in an upper window. Judgment Time has begun. My heart leapfrogs around like it's looking for an exit, but I remind myself that this time I have backup.

"The thing that really sticks in my grandmother's craw is that I'm the spitting image of her, and she doesn't approve of what I'm doing with that image. Also, I'm named after her. As far as she's concerned, I've blighted the name, too."

Hall nods in agreement. "You do look like you could've been twins."

My brother and sisters (beneath Athena's peroxide) have medium brownish hair and blue eyes, like our dad. I inherited Grandma Bettie Watson's jet-black hair, her thick, expressive eyebrows, and eyes so dark you can't distinguish iris from pupil. As a child, all I *ever* heard was that I looked exactly like my glamorous Hollywood grandmother. No matter what I do, I can't weaken the resemblance. Whether I'm au naturel or wearing heavy eyeliner and glittering smoky eyes, denim halter tops or a little black dress, she's already perfected it, and I look like I'm trying to copy one of her countless phases. I refuse to wear the retro swing dresses I used to be famous for anymore, which ticks her off because she's adamant that those suit me the best. My wardrobe of late consists mainly of black tights, black sweatshirts three sizes too large, and a black rain slicker. I've been dressing like a burglar so that no one will notice me picking flowers and pumpkins from the neighbor's yard, to garnish my Instagram selfies.

You would be so much prettier if you did something with your hair is Grandma's favorite parting remark (I haven't changed my hair up in ages; it hangs limply to my shoulders and doesn't hold a curl. It bores her), especially while sobbing: *You could have been the face of*

Chanel. Chanel made the offer when I was an excited, Who Cares What's In The Contract, I Want To Do It fourteen-year-old, but Dad said no. He didn't like that I accompanied my grandmother on red carpets, or that my picture was so public when I was a child purely because I looked so uncannily like Bettie Watson.

All of the big fights my parents had when I was growing up were about parenting differences. Mom's a deeply compassionate, people-pleasing softie who couldn't tell any of us no when we wanted something (we were always wanting lots and lots of things), and Dad was the wary, serious sandbar against the wave of all his children's requests. I can never ask them for financial help because she'll want to say yes; he won't, and I'm not driving a wedge. Their relationship is so much better now as empty-nesters.

"Grandma was born in 1946 and grew up on television, which I'm sure you know," I tell Hall, diving into my messed-up-family history lesson. "When I came along and turned out to be her clone, she and Mom thought it'd be adorable to style me after Grandma's child self, dressing me in fifties clothes. Took me along to red carpets in her most famous vintage outfits, with my Care Bears purse. Everybody'd be screeching how adorable I looked. There was Real Bettie and then there was Little Bettie! How delightful."

Hall's watching me closely. "It sounds like you didn't enjoy that."

"I did at first. But the people who shout the loudest about how much they love you are finicky. The moment you step out of the box they put you in, they just want to watch you burn. Real Bettie got to try out styles from the sixties, seventies, and beyond as she aged, but I was trapped in the fifties. All my friends were wearing crop tops and bandage dresses, getting their hair dip-dyed neon colors, and I was sitting there like Lucille Ball in my polka dots. Which *evvvv*erybody loved. Those goddamn polka dots are my villain origin story."

Hall chews on his lip, stifling the tiniest of smiles.

"Fast-forward, I was arrested three days after I turned twenty-one and after that, the media wasn't so nice." I scrub my hands over my face. "And I hadn't even done anything wrong! It was just loitering on private property, which I still think was a setup."

While I was building my sandcastle empire, the media took turns lauding my success with one hand and writing scathingly about me with the other, depending on the current temperature of public opinion. In my periods of unpopularity, fewer and fewer legitimate industries wanted to do business with me. People I'd thought were friends turned on me, only wanting me when I was popular, when they could use my name and image to boost the power of their own. When my companies folded, I became a joke. I've been pretending that I bounced back from it, fooling just about everyone. But I can't fool myself. I know I'm a joke.

"Little Bettie" reminded someone very clever on the internet of "Little Debbie," which has morphed into a meme, strangers spamming me with dented boxes of Nutty Bars and pictures of Swiss Rolls smashed on grocery store floors. There was a TikTok Challenge a while back that involved microwaving Little Debbie Raisin Creme Pies until they exploded, and I was tagged in thousands of them.

"I wanted to be a celebrity without appreciating what all that entailed," I admit. "My every move has been judged: relationships, sexuality, reproductive health. There are only so many times a person can insist they're not pregnant, that they've just gained a bit of weight, before they blow up on an interviewer.

Which becomes an unflattering sound bite, a hashtag, another nasty story about Bettie Hughes being an ungrateful brat."

I reach the end of my rant and realize I'm shouting. There are tears in my eyes.

"You're not an ungrateful brat," Hall tells me gently, pulling me into a hug.

I sniffle into his shoulder. "I am what I am. Don't pity me."

He strokes my hair, and I burrow into the feeling, the attention. "Why not?"

"I don't want your pity." I back away, wiping my nose on my sleeve. "I want your revenge. On everyone. I want you to help me get back at them." The statement is supposed to sound scary, but the sniffling ruins it.

Hall's mouth twists. "I'm not made for revenge."

"I know. You're so nice to everybody, so upbeat all the time. It's unhealthy. What's up with that?" I try to lighten the mood, already embarrassed that he saw me cry over my undeniably privileged childhood. I'd meant to tell him about Bettie Watson and instead I told him everything about Bettie Hughes. *You do love to make it all about you*, I hear former friends sigh. I shake my head.

"I'm holiday cheer, Bettie. Merry and bright." Piercing green eyes fasten on mine as he wipes away one of my tears and offers a rueful smile. "Nobody says *holiday sass* or *holiday grouchiness*. There's especially no such thing as *holiday revenge*."

"How wrong you are! You need to brush up on your Grinch trivia."

He withdraws, expression clouding. His eyebrows slant down, lips pressing into a tight, white line. "The Grinch is everything I fight against. I can't bring myself to finish any version of that film because he is such a personal affront to me."

"Oh, wow. I really touched a nerve there."

His face is scarlet. "The Grinch is to me what polka dots are to you."

"I've never met anyone who hates the Grinch."

"I don't! I can't possibly hate anything. But he's terrible, Bettie. All the Whos wanted was to eat their roast beast and sing. They just wanted to celebrate. That's all they wanted! I don't understand why the cable network Freeform includes this insult to the holiday spirit in their Twenty-Five Days of Christmas lineup."

"You're absolutely right. He has no business being there."

Hall either doesn't notice my small grin, or he's too relieved that I agree with him to care. He offers me his elbow again, still huffy. "No more talk of such revolting matters. Are you ready to go spend a week with your family? Remember, I'm right here with you. I won't let them make you feel small."

I loop my arm through his, touched by Hall's firm solidarity. I've been envisioning our roles for this trip as Leader and Follower: I make the wishes and he grants them. But I can see now that this is a team project. Whatever happens, I'm not on my own. "Thank you."

"Oh, right." He snaps his fingers when we emerge from the trees so that six suitcases appear in the middle of the driveway. A horn honks, Athena's sleek black car swerving angrily around them.

She leans out the driver's-side window. "Do you mind?"

"No!" I yell back. I can't wait to wow her within an inch of her life when she sees how excellent my life has become. She'll feel so desperately inadequate.

Speaking of inadequacy. "Now, when we get inside here," I

murmur, yanking down Hall's collar so that I know he's paying attention, "no fawning over my grandma, capisce?"

Hall's brow furrows in torment. "But—"

"None," I growl.

"What constitutes fawning?"

"No knitting her face onto your sweaters. She'd enjoy it too much. And don't tell her you've seen all her movies, or she'll be *insufferable*. Don't you dare tell her she looks the same age as her daughter, either. People do that all the time, and she loathes them for it. Even though she sometimes corners them into saying so." I wave my hand. "She's a wicked old witch. My point is—"

Offended on my grandmother's behalf, he divests me of my suitcases and marches resolutely forward. I hope nobody is watching through the windows to see that a couple of the roller suitcases are rolling along of their own volition. "Don't worry, Bettie, this'll be great. You're going to spend a lovely week with your family. You're going to learn the true meaning of Christmas, which is different for every person, by the way. *And* you're going to replenish your holiday spirit. That's the reason I'm here."

"The reason you're here is to make me look spectacular. But don't do anything magical in front of other people without my go-ahead. They'll either have a heart attack and die or they'll dissect your brain and sell it to scientists."

Hall shudders. Which might also have something to do with the tombstones that Grandma has chosen as lawn ornaments. They're foam props from movies and soap operas in which her characters were killed off, a souvenir tradition that began as "Ha ha, look at my gravestones, how delightfully macabre" but has since grown into commentary about what sort of roles are offered to women, especially aging ones. *Time* magazine did a two-page spread on Grandma (she was pictured holding a scythe) and all the fictional women buried in her yard.

We should have prepared more rigorously for this. Now that our charade is about to begin, I'm breaking out in a sweat. "Remember to be the perfect boyfriend. You have to make me look good, okay? Don't go talking about your exes."

"That's an easy one, as I don't have any exes. I've never been a boyfriend before. To build a Perfect Boyfriend Profile, I can reference the Fifty Best Romances of All Time as listed on *just a movie lovin chick dot com.*" He begins ticking them off on his fingers. *"Moonstruck. Love and Basketball. Moulin Rouge! The Photograph. Monsoon Wedding. The Princess Bride. Hope Floats. Slumdog Millionaire. To All the Boys I've Loved Before."* Extra fingers begin sprouting from his hand. *"Like Water for Chocolate. The Shape of Water."*

"Maybe not that one. I don't want you acting like a fish in there."

"If Beale Street Could Talk," he goes on. *"His Girl Friday."*

I soften involuntarily. "That's my favorite."

"Yeah?" He looks at me intently. Leans in an inch, and rumbles in a deep voice that would give Cary Grant a run for his money, *"What did I treat you like, a water buffalo?"*

A slow smile creeps across my face. "You've seen it."

"I've seen them all. I love movies very, very much."

"Me, too."

He smiles back, and inexplicable goose bumps begin to rise on the back of my neck. But the moment snaps when I hear the screen door to the Watson house creak open.

"One last thing." I stare deeply into his eyes, words firm. "No. Autographs. Don't ask for autographs from anyone. If somebody offers an autograph, it's a trap. Don't touch any memorabilia. Show zero interest in anything rare or expensive. If Grandma offers to let you touch her Golden Globe, it's a trap. It's become a game to spot a user. Everyone in there is going to be watching you like an eagle."

Hall looks unnerved. "Erm. Okay."

We reach the porch, where my parents are lingering in the doorway, watching us curiously. Mom's looking prettier than ever, corn silk hair in a French braid, teardrop pearls in her ears wide-set blue eyes giving her the appearance of one who's viewing her surroundings for the very first time and is quite taken by it all. Dad's hair has gone fully silver but is still impressively thick, hair-line young, the color rather dashing against his tan and his arctic-blue eyes. He's wearing something between a smirk and a smile, a pained expression he defaults to whenever he doesn't like what's happening. I didn't tell them I'd be bringing a guest. I get so nervous that I forget to help Hall with the bags, and Hall's so nervous that he forgets them, too, so they're scattered all over the walkway now.

"Honey! I'm so glad you made it. How was your flight?" Mom peers over my shoulder, scanning the driveway. "Your rental car okay? No speeding tickets? Where'd you park?"

I look behind me, too, as though a car might appear that I could claim. A car *has* in fact appeared: instead of the pickup, Hall's conjured a bright red limousine, its front right wheel close to hitting a coffin (Grandma took it from the set of her campy '70s movie *Tango with Nosferatu*).

Dad stares. "Don't tell me that's yours."

"Is *that* yours?" Mom adds, smiling meaningfully at Hall.

"Um, yes. That's . . . this guy's with me!" I manage a high laugh.

"How exciting! How long have you two been together? Bettie, you never mentioned you had a boyfriend." She tries to hide it, but I can tell she's hurt by this.

"He's . . . shy."

Hall sweeps my mother off her feet in a strong bear hug, and she gasps. "I am *so* happy to be meeting you." Then he does the same to my dad, whose eyes bulge. "This is wonderful! You're both so good-looking." Dad isn't the touchy-feely sort. A gentleman suppresses his emotions.

Shy? Dad mouths at me, one eyebrow raised as Hall pats his back.

"Bettie! Sweetheart!" Grandpa shoulders through and catches me in one of his famous hugs (Grandpa, like Hall, is of the belief that the harder you squeeze, the more love you convey), snapping several of my bones. "It's been so long! You need to visit more often. Here, don't spend this all in one place." He presses twenty dollars into my left hand. "Got your favorite ice cream in the freezer." He winks, then notices Hall. "Who's this?"

"This is Hall, Grandpa. He's my—"

An imperious figure presses a hand to Mom's shoulder and Dad's face, pushing each of them to the side. Grandpa backs away hastily. A gust of frigid air wafts, and if this were a cartoon, the woman who appears would have crows perched up and down her arms. She's in a floor-length black velvet cloak with fuzzy cuffs, a multilayered necklace swinging, thirty-seven glass spheres containing the ashes of thirty-seven fans. I'm five seven, so I'm not exactly short, but with her heels and a jet-black, complicated high pony that used to be Barbara Eden's signature style, the woman soars. (Grandma demanded the exclusive legal rights to that hairstyle in an MGM contract.) Her lipstick is steal-your-husband-red, eyebrows impeccably arched. She smacks her lips together, dividing a gleaming, catlike look between Hall and me. "Interesting. Ohh, that's *interesting*, isn't it?" She crooks a finger at Hall. "You. Come here."

Hall releases a thin cry, chokes out the words, "I've seen every movie you've ever been in, also your soap operas, will you please sign my everything," and passes out at her feet.

CHAPTER FIVE

....

T HERE'S SOMETHING STRANGE about this one," Grandma
tells us all, watching shrewdly as Dad and I help Hall into
the sitting room. Grandpa announces he's going to go find a raw
steak for Hall's eye, because in Grandpa's opinion there are no ills
a good old raw steak to the face can't cure. Poor Hall slumps onto
a sofa between my parents, shoulders tucked inward, eyes cast
down.

"No, there isn't," I reply quickly.

Grandma ignores me, crouching until he's forced to meet her
gaze. "You're a pretty young man, aren't you? What's your name?"

He cuts me a furtive glance, eyes widening when she snaps
her long-nailed fingers in front of his nose. "Ah-ah. Don't look
to her for an answer. Don't you know your own name?"

He clears his throat. "Hall?"

"Hall? Is that a question? What, do you go by your last name?"
She stands upright again, annoyed. "I hate it when people do that.
It's obnoxious."

"My last name is . . . Day." He slides me another anxious glance.

"Hall Day," she repeats dully.

He brightens, having a lightbulb moment. "My middle initial is E."

She stares at him so fiercely that it's astonishing he doesn't melt. "What's your favorite film of mine, Mr. Day?"

"Grandma, don't," I interrupt, but she holds out a hand, not sparing me a look.

"*Marigold . . . Says . . . So Long*," he croaks.

"Incorrect!" She rears back in outrage, grabbing the throw pillow he's clutching for dear life and tossing it at one of her great-grandchildren. Athena and Felix have thirteen-ish children between them, and they seem to be in competition to see who can bequeath the most unfortunate name: they started out okay, with Olivers and Daisys, but now we've got Domino, Ichabod, Octavian, Honeysuckle Lou, Minnesota Moon, and Peach Tree. I'm pretty sure that the kid who just took a pillow to the face is called Frangipane.

"Your favorite film might be *That Feeling in the Air*," Mom supplies helpfully.

"I love that one," Hall insists, but Grandma scowls, waving him off.

"Too late. Don't patronize me." Then she glides out of the room without another word, and Hall's face blanches, mouth dropping open. He turns to me.

"Does she hate me?"

"Of course not!" Mom exclaims, then rushes after her mother.

Dad turns toward us. Digests the sight of Hall and me together. "So. Tell me about yourself, Hall. How'd you two meet?"

My mind goes blank.

"Whole Foods," I reply as Hall says, "Baseball."

Dad stares. "What?"

I want a private word with my so-called boyfriend, so I place my hand on Hall's knee. My father instantly jumps up, making a hasty exit. "Be right back."

Hall is still staring at my hand when I retract it, then pinch him. "Baseball?" I hiss.

"It's an American pastime," he hisses back.

I wave him off. "Fine, that one's on me. We should've come up with a How We Met story before we got here. Also. A *limo*? Why'd you get a limo!?"

"It's the classiest of all the vehicles. You name a classier vehicle than a limousine, I dare you."

"You watch too many movies." I wonder when he stole my father's entire outfit, copying not only Dad's shirt but his slacks and watch, as well. He's very suggestible. "Don't wear my dad's clothes, it's creepy."

"That's how I'll make him like me. Also, movies are my favorite thing in the universe." He's getting worked up. "After bayberry candles and Thomas Kinkade landscapes. I gave us an impressive limo. I'm using fashion psychology to earn your dad's approval. I'm pulling out all the stops here, and it's like you don't even appreciate it."

"You fainted in the doorway," I remind him. "I warned you my grandmother was a witch and not to fawn over her, but what did you do?"

"Okay, so yes, I fell to pieces. That is true. But in my defense, she looked directly at me. Her magnetism wasn't diluted through a television screen. It was a holiday miracle."

"You need to bulk up your armor or she's going to eat you alive. Less *merry and bright*, more hard-ass. The best way to repel this fanged, mind-reading predator is to be aloof, acting as if you're not impressed or interested in anything you see here. Like you've got dark secrets and a heart of steel." He looks devastated at the thought. "P.S., stay away from my brother, Felix. He's a snake."

"Hey, there," says my brother.

"Hey, there!" I echo loudly before Felix can finish speaking, turning to plaster on a huge smile as he enters the room. I can hear Mom's contagious, bubbly laughter from the kitchen. It sounds like she's talking to herself, which means she's probably talking to Athena, who floats from room to room with large, haunted eyes like a tragically drowned Shakespearean character who communicates in backhanded whispering. "Felix! I've missed you tons."

"Aw, you liar." He tosses a duffel bag of his belongings into my lap, which I throw off me, and takes a huge bite out of a cookie that I'm willing to bet he was just told he couldn't eat before dinner. Mouth full, he says to Hall, "Who're you?"

Hall is stricken. "Me?"

"Nice to meet you, Me." Felix goes to shake his hand, but withdraws as soon as Hall sticks his out.

"Don't be an asshole," I snap.

"I'm not an asshole. You're an asshole." He considers. "Did you hear about my new movie?"

Don't ask for details, I think forcefully in Hall's direction, wondering when somebody's going to notice my excellent clothes. I'm here to show off, but no one's commented on my Ariel Gordon Dynasty Diamond Necklace ($10,950.00) made with 324 diamonds, which

I've paired with the black vest Keanu Reeves wore in *Bill and Ted's Excellent Adventure* (priceless).

Hall doesn't heed my unspoken plea, perking up. "What movie?" I notice that a Band-Aid has appeared on his arm, just like the one Felix has.

Felix comes alive. "*Thornfield*. It's a *Jane Eyre* retelling, but, like, edgy. Think Jordan Peele. I'm playing the lead role, Mr. Rochester, this sophisticated recluse who keeps bringing in new governesses. But come to find out, there's no child to teach. Then he traps their souls inside books. Whenever he wants to interact with one of them, he opens one of the books. But get this: it's *modern day*. Not historical. And the latest trapped governess, Jane, is rewriting her story from inside the book, altering the fabric of Rochester's reality." He looks pleased with himself. "We're pushing the limits of cinema. Some films are afraid to get too dark or weird, to really *go there*, but I say, what's life without risk?"

"What's Jane like?" I ask, unable to help myself. I know what word he's going to use as a descriptor.

"Oh, a strong female character for sure. She's feminine, but resilient. A real ingénue. And she dies at the end."

There it is. *Ingénue*. Felix is obsessed with that word.

Felix stares at me for a moment, waiting expectantly. His expression clouds. "*Congratulations, Felix*," my brother says in an imitation of my voice.

"Congratulations, Felix," I echo robotically.

"You could at least pretend to mean it." He stands up, shaking his head. "You know, I work really hard. At least I'm making something of myself."

My face burns. "I'm making something of myself, too! I'm a social media influencer. Where's my congratulations?"

As he stalks away, I catch snatches of Dad's baritone questioning, followed by Felix's "*nasty all the time*," and then a round of murmuring from others. Must be cozy to be my relatives, united in their annoyance at me.

When I glance at Hall again, he's got Band-Aids on his forehead and nose. "What are you doing?" I loud-whisper.

"Blending in!" he whispers back.

I throw up my hands. "Into what? A hospital?"

"This is what humans do! They wear Band-Aids. They get scraped up a lot and don't have self-healing powers. How don't you know that?"

I peel them off him. He winces.

The many iterations of my grandmother gaze photogenically down at us from a hundred angles. Movie stills, professional headshots with bedroom eyes and a smirk, playbill posters, interspersed between portraits of other silver-screen stars she admires. Her offspring have been relegated to hallways. Black-and-white family candids of my grandparents in the grass, playing with my mother, a young, white-haired Madeline. According to Grandma and Grandpa Watson's house, I haven't aged past ten. I'm in the den and the hallway between a guest bathroom and one of the guest bedrooms, dolled up in a poodle skirt next to my still-brunette sisters. There are no pictures of me after my departure from the polka dot stage, even though Kaia's gig posters are framed next to her headshots and Athena has multiple weddings blown up in eight-by-eleven frames. Felix evidently isn't that interesting to Grandma, as he's only up on the wall twice (both are graduation pics).

"You're angry," Hall ventures. It doesn't sound like an accusation, but I bristle anyway.

"No, I'm not."

"Why?"

I shrug. "I just don't care."

I care so little, in fact, that I meander toward the sound of those voices, closer and closer until I can hear what they're saying. I know what it's going to be.

She ruins everything. Such a disappointment.

Except, they're not talking about me at all.

"I told him to pick up the thin-sliced kind," Mom's saying. "Lunch meat. But he brings home an entire turkey! So now he can't be trusted to do the shopping by himself."

"He did it on purpose, to get out of shopping from now on," Kaia suggests, and they all laugh. She and Athena haven't walked in to say hello to me and Hall. Who, I might add, is the first man I've ever brought to Grandma's house. You'd think Dad would be grilling him on his job and his past, weighing whether Hall deserves me. But no! My fake boyfriend and I are loitering awkwardly like uninvited guests.

I can't decide what's worse, animosity or indifference.

"Hall," I say quietly but urgently, leading him into the laundry room/bathroom and closing the door. A load is tumbling in the washer, masking my words. It's such a normal, innocuous room, smelling of Downy white tea and peony fabric softener. The sunset is broken up by a kaleidoscopic privacy film covering the window, smattering the linoleum with rainbows. The toilet seat has a soft lavender cover over it to match the lavender rugs and washcloths. An old-fashioned washboard hangs on the wall. This room is for normal, innocuous grandparents, right up until you get to the Tony award wedged between a box of detergent and a goat's skull.

"I want a do-over."

His head lists to the side as he studies me. "Are you certain? Remember how we both threw up the last time."

"I want to make a better impression. Look at me, I've only been here a few minutes and I'm already being ignored. I want to come in blazing."

"Me, too. It's embarrassing that I passed out in front of Bettie Watson."

"You sort of passed out *onto* Bettie Watson."

"A do-over it is." He stares at me steadily, the right half of his face lit up in rainbow, a groove between his brows. "Say the words."

"Take us back half an hour. Make my wish come true."

Hall grabs my arm, and we spin, feet lifting off the floor. We're flung through stark, heavy nothingness, compressing my lungs. I can't get enough air, I can't—

We land on our feet, but barely, toppling against the washing machine. It isn't as bad this time around, maybe because we only traveled half an hour, and we went backward instead of forward. He catches me, both of us staggering. I knock over the Tony, breaking off the iconic medallion that sits within the trophy's pewter swivel. Hall repairs it, but he's still unsteady on his feet and his magic comes out wrong. The trophy grows to six times its normal size.

"What'd you do?"

"Shh, I'm fixing it!" he hisses. Since we're still in the laundry room/bathroom, it's almost as if we never left at all—except that the prismatic window film strikes the left side of Hall's face now, the position of the sun rewound. He frowns determinedly at the trophy and it shrinks back to normal. The comedy and tragedy masks engraved in the medallion have been replaced with Idris Elba and James Corden as they appeared in the 2019 film *Cats*.

"Wait," I interrupt before Hall can mess with it again.

He pauses.

"Keep it that way."

"What?" His voice is high, and I gesture wildly to drive it back down into a whisper. It's supposed to be half an hour ago, which means he and I should be hiding behind the cluster of lodgepole pines that Grandpa planted to prevent us kids from whizzing down the mountain to our deaths in our sleds. I quickly lock the door. "I can't leave it like this. This is Bettie Watson's Tony award!"

"That's what she gets for not having enough pictures of me around. We're going to fix that, too. I want you to switch out those dreamy glamour photos of Grandma with my mug shot. Also switch out Athena's husband in all of their wedding pictures for Gritty, the mascot for the Philadelphia Flyers."

Hall's mouth pops open, terror in his eyes, as I say, "Make my wish come true."

His jaws snaps together. "Let me fix the Tony."

"How about instead of that, we give me a makeover." I survey myself. "I'm not impressive enough, it seems." Which is outrageous, because I'm wearing the vest from *Bill and Ted's Excellent Adventure*. Not a replica! It's the real thing! "Give me something dazzling? Make my wish come true."

Poof, and I'm in a Christmas sweater. Tinsel fringes the collar, hem, and both sleeves.

"Not dazzling enough."

Poof. My pants have tinsel fringe, too.

"You're thinking small scale," I tell him, and then convey us through a series of wardrobe changes. I try on Christina Aguilera's outfit from the "Lady Marmalade" music video, just for funsies. (Hall blushes.) Marilyn Monroe's white dress billowing in a blast of air. Every single outfit from *Crazy Rich Asians*. Sissy Spacek's blood-drenched prom gown. Björk's swan dress. None of them are grand enough. I begin to despair. "I want something big and powerful. A *statement*. Something fit for a queen."

Hall snaps his fingers and I'm in a dress of rich gold and crimson brocade, with a magnificently jeweled collar that fans up toward my chin and then flares out. It weighs about a hundred pounds. I admire myself in the medicine cabinet mirror. "Damn, boy, is this medieval?"

"I took it directly from the closet of Mary the First."

"See? This is what I deserve, Hall. Actual royalty." I do a twirl, with no small amount of effort, knocking him out of the way. My skirt takes up the whole room.

"You need to spiff up, too," I advise. "Try on that confusing cowboy archaeologist getup from *Indiana Jones*."

He does, but it's not enough drama. "We need a jaw-dropper, or Grandma's going to lacerate you from top to bottom again as soon as you walk through the door. It's those marshmallow snowmen on your sweater—she looks at them and sees a bull's-eye."

"Actually." He bites his lip, a bit bashful. "There *is* something I'd like to try."

"Go for it! Big guns."

"But don't laugh." He swallows, shutting his eyes tightly, a fog of mint enveloping him. When it's dispersed, he's decked out in a sharp white suit, chestnut hair slicked back. The crisp onyx collar beneath his white waistcoat is scandalously unbuttoned, exposing a distracting quantity of chest, and—is that—?

It is. A gold necklace winks at me. It flashes little cartoon sparkles and I swear I hear it make a *ding!* sound. He looks . . . unsettlingly attractive. If he were simply a guy I'd spotted in a bar, I would definitely ruin his life.

"Is the chest hair too much?" he asks self-consciously, skimming one hand along his truly spectacular coiffure. "I gave myself a lot more of it, to better emulate John Travolta." He strikes a pose. "I'm *Saturday Night Fever.*"

"You look great." I clear my throat.

"Are you all right? Your face is pink."

"No, it's not." I clap, and we both turn to check the crack of light bleeding under the bathroom door. No shadows of feet. "Let's go."

We teleport to the limo, and then, as soon as I'm finished sputtering out eggnog, we make our grand entrance. The Watsons' front door creaks open, Mom and Dad poking their heads out to watch. It's a suitably chatty affair, with many ooohs and ahhhs. Or at least I assume that's the noises they're making; I can't be sure until we're sauntering down the walkway.

"Helloooo!" I exclaim. "Wow, what a drive. What was that, like, fourteen hours in the car? You're right, I look good for someone who's been traveling for so long."

"Who's that?" Dad jerks his chin toward Hall, who has acquired sunglasses. He's swaggering up behind me, profile swung toward the dying sun in a way that shows off his bone structure. He's doing that frowny-squinty thing that men do on red carpets, where they're trying to look Serious but actually look Constipated.

"That's my date," I purr.

"Your date?" Athena repeats incredulously, cutting between our parents to emerge on the porch. "You brought a *date* to Christmas?"

"Well, why wouldn't I?" I huff. Then I stare at Mom, whose face has colored, fingertips pressing against her mouth. "What?"

"It's just . . ." She drops her hands, and her eyes are filled with tears. It's because she's so happy to see me. And so proud. Then a hysterical laugh bobs out of her throat. "Honey, what are you *wearing*?"

"It's wearing *her*, more like," Felix observes from somewhere behind Dad. They're trickling out onto the porch, gawking at us. There is good gawking and bad gawking, which I should know.

"It's a Halloween costume," Dad guesses, which clinches this as bad gawking. It's bullshit, if you ask me. I'm wearing a queen's dress! An actual queen! And I've got twenty-first-century hair and makeup, which means I'm pulling off this look. Bloody Mary could never. "Where'd you two meet?"

"Baseball," I say, as Hall replies, "Whole Foods." We both groan. Dad's confused, but he isn't a big talker so he drops it.

"Did you take a limo all the way from LAX after you flew in from Hawaii?" Kaia asks casually.

"That'd cost a fortune in gas," Athena's husband murmurs.

"Money is no object," I begin, but Grandma's verdict catches my ear:

"Limousines are tacky."

Beside me, Hall deflates. I mean that literally. He goes all flat, and I can hear the air whizz out of him like a punctured bouncy castle. He keels over onto his back in the dead December grass, thoroughly two-dimensional. My family screams and screams and screams.

✳

"No matter what she says," I warn Hall as we descend in our hot-air balloon, "don't make yourself flat again. They didn't much care for that. And remember: we met when our pedal boats bumped into each other on Echo Park Lake. You were instantly smitten. I had other boyfriends on the back burner, but you won me over on our first date by hiring Gordon Ramsay to cook me a personal pan pizza."

We've spun back the clock again and, this time around, we're in matching tuxedoes that glitter like disco balls. We're also in top hats, which I've decided to bring back in style. A scarlet birdcage veil wafts from the brim of mine, studded with tiny crystals.

"Hello, relatives!" I boom through a megaphone as the hot air balloon makes contact with the front yard. Mom, Dad, Grandma, Grandpa, Kaia, Felix, Athena, their spouses, and however many nieces and nephews I have (after five, one stops keeping track) gather on the lawn to gape at me.

I spread my arms, smacking Hall in the face. Behold! I am both fashionably late *and* making a hell of an entrance, which means I've won.

"Sweetheart!" Grandpa cries. "Love it! What a show!"

"What are you doing to my lawn?" Grandma hollers. "You can't just park that thing here! What if it blows into the house?"

"What if it blows down the mountain?" Felix adds. He elbows Kaia. "Or right into town. Punctured on the tower of Town Hall like the giant peach from that movie."

In spite of her incredible voice, Kaia is the quietest of the Hughes siblings, which has the effect of making her seem more intelligent. Her approval therefore matters more than Athena's or Felix's. She appraises me narrowly from under the brim of her hat, clothes hanging from her waifish frame. Minimalist floral tattoos swim up and down her arms. Her low, smoky-voiced verdict: "I think it's cool."

I preen.

But then she tacks on: "Did you fly that here all the way from Los Angeles? Did you have to make a stop nearby for the special purpose of getting in a hot-air balloon?" and I wish she'd be quiet again and stop considering logistics. She does go silent, but only because she can't go more than a minute without vaping.

"Where'd you even get one of those?" Dad wants to know. "Who let you fly that by yourself? Don't you need an instructor?"

Mom, who started this process being delighted, clutches his arm. "Oh, Jim, this looks dangerous. Help her get out of there."

I lower my megaphone, confidence wavering. "No! Because . . . I'm licensed! Frankly, this isn't the reception I was hoping for. I'm in a goddamn hot-air balloon! Why aren't you people clapping?"

"Who's that?" Felix asks, pointing at Hall.

Hall points at himself, grinning.

"My boyfriend," I reply soulfully. We bounce a bit along the ground, not stable yet. Hall conjures some sandbags on the floor of the basket, weighing us down properly. The flame in the balloon dies out. If I weren't me, I would throw myself upon the earth in a withered ball of envy, and then perish. Of envy.

While Grandpa claps me on the back and slips me twenty dollars, Athena smirks and murmurs, "Another boyfriend?" I don't know how she's still standing right now, when she should be perishing of envy.

"My *long-term* boyfriend," I add, with emphasis. "We've been keeping it under wraps, like mature adults. He's loyal and devoted and we are *serious*."

"Of course you are," Athena replies sardonically.

She and her husband exchange smug, self-satisfied looks. A child whose name is either Terracotta or Ricotta rolls her eyes.

Target once paid her fifteen grand to do that in a commercial, so now she keeps doing it. I glare at her. She isn't better than me.

"I proposed to my second wife in a hot-air balloon," Felix adds with an expression of distaste, banishing hot-air balloons to the Realm of Old News.

"That does it," I snap. "Hall!"

"Yes?" He springs so close that we knock elbows, his head cocked in that intent, absorbed way he has, as though every word from my mouth is spun from gold. He's about two inches taller than me, but in my modest platform shoes, we're eye to eye. I should ask for more height, so that I may look down on everyone both figuratively and physically.

"Make Felix flat."

I tack on the magic words, he makes Felix flat, and my family shrieks with terror again. It is very worth it.

"Take three!" I call, stomping away from the scene. "Or four, I don't know which we're on. I am too busy to care about consistency issues!"

✳

"And here is my *fiancé*," I announce as I alight from the onion carriage from *Shrek*, which is pulled by unicorns, proffering my hand so that they all might weep over the glorious diamond (thirty-three carats) weighing down my ring finger. "My loyal, devoted fiancé, which is even better than a serious boyfriend."

"That ring looks like the one Richard Burton gave to Liz Taylor," Grandma observes, correctly.

"Fascinating," Mom is remarking, bending her face close to a unicorn's head. "You can't even see the strap that keeps the horn on."

"That's because it's a real unicorn," I tell her, at which she laughs.

My siblings stare at the carriage with bulging eyes. They have no words. It is awesome.

"This is good footage," I murmur out of the corner of my mouth to Hall. "We'll use this one."

✳

CHAPTER SIX

....

I T'S ALL EYES on me at dinner, and I am *living*.

"So as you can see, I am more independently wealthy than ever," I gloat. "I independently found Hall and got engaged to him, so now his vast fortune is all mine." I slap a generous scoop of sweet potatoes onto my plate next to an entire turkey leg. "On top of my own fortune, of course, as a beloved influencer."

"What kind of fortune are we talking about?" Grandma inquires, sharp black eyes pinning my new fiancé.

The word *fortune* is Kaia's reminder to whip out her tarot cards. She doles out readings at every gathering, mostly for Mom and Grandma. Her cards are illustrated with skeletons that have flowers in their eye sockets and they creep me out.

Hall's forehead is sparkly with sweat. Inordinately sparkly, in fact, and unlike everyone else who perspires, his perspiration has a sweet smell to it. I peer closer. Holy cow. This man sweats sugar.

"Investments," he supplies, swallowing thickly.

"Hall's a movie producer," I inform everyone. "He invests in movies. Just finished wrapping up the most incredible project—tell them all about it, honey."

Hall stammers out an "Uhh," before I slide back in.

"It's a *Jane Eyre* retelling! Very modern. And I have the starring role as Jane."

"You're in a movie?" Athena is troubled. "How much did you get paid? Who's the director?"

"You're acting now?" Mom interrupts, right as Grandma tsks and mutters, "Vanity projects."

"I'm not allowed to discuss details yet, but the director's name rhymes with Bess Panderson," I reply, reaching across the table to fill Athena's glass of punch all the way to the rim so that if she moves it a millimeter, punch will spill down her hand. "And no. It isn't a vanity project."

She and Felix emit identical noises. It's the sound you make when you miss your flight by twenty seconds, and now your dream vacation's canceled.

Pleased, I continue: "Jane takes a job as the nanny of a rich man's daughter, but she's hiding dark secrets about her past. The little girl is evil. And a ghost. Mr. Rochester is murdered by his previous nanny, who he's stuffed into the attic. Then the two nannies live together in the house by themselves, throwing lots of parties. Also, the location is a reimagining of the Bellagio and there's a whole makeover montage as the nannies get their groove back."

"What?" Felix slams his fork onto the table. "When does it release? What stage of production are you in? I haven't heard anything about this!"

"What's it called?" Mom wants to know.

"My Eyre Ladies."

Kaia, who is busy flipping cards, pauses with an Ace of

Pentacles in the air when she hears this, snort-laughing. Grandma taps a different card, The Fool, and they share a grin.

Felix shoves to his feet. I watch him consider flipping the table. "That is the stupidest movie title I've ever heard."

"Felix!" Mom cries. "Don't be rude." She leans across Dad to pat Hall's hand. Dad's watching me closely. "It sounds wonderful, dear. Felix, apologize right now."

"But *I'm* doing a Jane Eyre movie."

"I'm sure yours is nice, too," I tell him calmly, cracking the turkey wishbone in half.

His face is red as burning coals. "You're making this up. You heard about my movie, and now you're fucking with me."

"Why can't you just be supportive?" Mom rebukes with a long-suffering sigh. I have become electric. This phrase has historically been used almost exclusively to me re: my siblings. I fix my brother with a wounded look.

"I support *you*," I murmur in a small, quivering voice.

"Congratulations," Dad forces himself to say during an awkward lull that follows. I think he's been holding out hope that I'd do something normal with my life, or maybe follow in his footsteps as a photographer. The most excited I've ever seen him was when I was briefly fascinated with his camera when I was about sixteen. Then I broke it. "An actor. Suppose it's fitting." I assume he means that he shouldn't be surprised because acting is somewhat of a family affair, but then he adds, "You've always been a bit melodramatic." With a meaningful look from Mom, he hastily adds, "Which is a good thing, if you're an actor."

"The only acting she's doing is right now, pretending she's in a movie," Felix shoots back. Then he points accusingly at Hall. "Did she hire you? Who are you? Tell me where you went to college."

"My name is Hall," Hall whispers, to which Athena's husband, Sean (Felix always pronounces it *Seen*, just to annoy him), asks, "Is that any relation to Hall and Oates?"

I beam. "Sure, why not."

Felix is tapping furiously on his phone. "I don't see anything on here about a forthcoming *Jane Eyre* movie. Besides *mine*."

I kick him under the table. "Mom! Tell Felix to stop Googling us. It's invasive."

"None of that Googling nonsense!" Grandpa joins in, passing behind me. He slides a twenty-dollar bill under the lip of my dinner plate. "Here you go, angel," he says in a gruff whisper. "Buy yourself some of those pretzel bites with the peanut butter in them. Get me a bag, too."

"Thank you, Grandpa."

My siblings glare, except for Kaia, who is being tut-tutted by our mother (*"You need to stop vaping. What if it damages your voice?"*) and declares, "Five of Wands. Five of Swords. Seven of Wands. Two of Swords. Are we predictable or what?" She puffs on her vape pen and blows the smoke sideways, concentrating. "All foreshadows conflict."

"None of that is real," Dad tells her, to which she replies, "That is such a Virgo thing to say."

Dad's gaze falls on the money Grandpa gave me, and he tries not to sigh. I know he's thinking that I'm being spoiled. Lawrence Watson has always been calm, eternally unruffled (which maddens Dad when he's looking for an ally against Grandma's overbearing personality), deferring to his wife and going with her flow. Mom parented us like her father parented her, generous to a fault, which was a cause of friction between her and Dad because it meant he had to be the no to her yes. Now that we're all older, he's trying to alter that dynamic but is struggling to stop being that balancing force of opposition. According to legend, he was fun when they first met.

Sean pries Felix off Hall. "I want to know who he is!" my brother rages. "Tell me where she hired you from!" It shouldn't surprise me that he suspects I'm lying. He and I are too similar.

Hall yanks me into the hallway, then with a flash and a bang teleports us to a small round room in the turret at the top of the house. He conjures a boulder to block the door, breathing heavily. "What is *wrong* with your brother?"

"We're not very good at sharing," I reply primly.

"No kidding." His gaze catches on a framed rectangle of gray-blue construction paper resting on a shelf. I recognize the hand-writing, two lines in scented brown marker.

He reaches. "What's—?"

"Oh, don't—" I move for it, but he senses my embarrassment and strikes too quick.

"*If I'm lucky, I'll get to be as old as you someday,*" he reads. "*I'll really miss you then. Happy birthday, Grandpa! Love, Bettie.*" He grins at me, the smile lines bracketing his mouth deep and devilish. "So, which Bettie made this?"

"I used to make cards for my family when I was a kid." I flip it over and show him my logo—*Hughes & Co.*, as if I had assistants, with a shapeless miniature leaf for pizzazz.

"That's so cute. I love cards. Handmade is always the best way to go, you know."

"I wish I could still get away with handmade presents as an adult."

There are a ton of boxes up here. I spy some of Mom's old

yearbooks, a wad of receipts from the nineties, and contracts. Stacks upon stacks of contracts and screenplays. I pick up one with a coffee ring on the top page, right over the title: LEON OF NAPLES, *written by Felix Hughes.*

"Oh my lord, Felix's first screenplay." I eagerly flip the pages. "Nowadays he goes for serious, gritty stuff, but he used to love farce. He tried to get Grandma to help him bring this one in front of producers, and she told him the only way she'd attach her name to this project was if the real Napoleon Bonaparte came back to life and starred in it."

Hall appears over my shoulder. "Napoleon? What's it about?"

SOMEWHERE IN FRANCE, IN THE NAPOLEON TIMES: A storm whips. Rain and darkness are all over the place. A ship tosses in the ocean. Napoleon Bon Appetit is up in the crow's nest. Twenty-something, with hollow eyes that have seen hardship. His mother died six years before he was born, taken by the whales while leaning against a railing. She was feeding breadcrumbs to the seagulls; now he's traumatized and can't go near whales. Or railings.

He docks his ship and heads to the nearest shelter. We see Lisabella McGovern, a beautiful ingénue standing in a ballroom. People tend to do as she tells them, and she has honorary degrees

```
from a lot of colleges she's never
visited. Queen Victoria is there.
Lisabella's sister Sabrina is sewing her
twenty-eighth pillowcase whilst dancing
with the handsomest Sterlinghoover son
(there are a lot of them and most are
named Roger), laughing merrily and
popularly. There's a crack of thunder as
she sees Napoleon is there.
```

NAPOLEON

[is strapping, brawny]

LISABELLA

Neapolitan! You came back for me!

NAPOLEON

All this time that I have been away conquering all of the wars, so many of them in fact, thoughts of you have fed and watered me. So many nights have I recollected the scent of your perfume and felt the blood pool to my nethers, like a snake swallowing a large egg.

LISABELLA

[is powerless in the face of such potent virility, such compelling seduction]

BILL O'REILLY

[is a lizard]

NAPOLEON

I shall rip your gown off and impale myself in you like a stiff cracker into soft cheese. You are brie, and I, your lover, am a pretzel stick. And together we shall make beautiful hors d'oeuvres to each other.

LISABELLA

[their connection is so powerful that memories flash behind her eyes that aren't even hers. She sees him as a child, catching frogs in a stream. She sees him disappointing his father as a teenager, unable to secure that letter of recommendation. As an adult man, rubbing one out to a painting of American Gothic, which led to a long period of disconcerted self-reflection.]

[sighing lustfully] "Take me, Neo!"

"Out of all of Felix's passion projects," I say, laughing so hard that I snort, "this is truly the one that got away. I remember he refused to talk to Grandma for months after she insulted this screenplay. He wouldn't let me look at it." I flip through more pages. It appears Lisabella endures two pregnancies that each reach full gestation, both occurring within a span of twelve months. She discovers that she isn't the mother of the second child she gives birth to, which prompts an investigation into who Napoleon might have been fooling around with. He also has an evil twin brother who steals his identity.

"Speaking of movies." Hall slumps down the wall, head lolling from one shoulder to the other. I've never seen him so stressed. "How are you going to back up this ruse? This pretend movie you just invented?"

"Can't you simply . . . make a movie? Make your hand go swishety-swish and *bam!* It's on Netflix. *My Eyre Ladies*, starring Bettie Hughes and Kat Dennings. Produced by Hall . . . Andaise."

"I don't know if I can do that."

"Because hollandaise is a sauce?"

"Because cinema is sacred to me."

I sigh, preparing to make my case, but an open-handed slap on the door interrupts. My grandmother never knocks. She likes to hit doors as if they've just mistaken her for Jane Fonda (they've been in a bitter feud for three decades). "What are you doing in there?" Grandma demands, trying the door handle. Hall evaporates the boulder, I stuff *Leon of Naples* back into its box, and we step far away from the door as my daunting grandmother (a beautiful and intimidating woman, five feet ten inches, somewhere between the ages of seventy and one hundred and four, her hair now in victory rolls) sweeps in. She likes to tell her granddaughters that older fashions are classier, as if none of us have seen posters of her enormous '80s perm and spandex bodysuits.

"I *said*, what are you doing?" she repeats crisply, sizing up our blood pressures and temperatures with one sweep. "Are you searching for the necklace?"

"No?" Maybe now I am. "What necklace? How many carats does it have?"

"There is no necklace. Never you mind." She analyzes me. "I thought you were taller."

"I'm five seven."

"Because you don't drink enough water. Just look at that crepey skin around your eyes! We must take care of our face." Before I can come up with a reply, she's already twisting, heading back downstairs. "Follow me. No more lurking in my tower like weird little Rapunzels."

Hall and I don't dare argue. We trail a healthy distance from Grandma (the black lace train of her cloak is seven feet long), who leads us past a number of small bedrooms where my family members are busy unpacking their suitcases. Kaia gets the third floor to herself, thanks to the migraine-inducing incense she burns all hours of the day. "Barely have enough room for you all, and yet you continue reproducing," she grumbles. "What is this, the Four Seasons?"

"We can stay at a hotel, if you want," I offer, thinking this will be a great excuse to stay out of the house as much as possible, but Grandma holds up her bejeweled hand and snaps her fingers closed like a conductor quieting her orchestra.

"Where are your manners, child? Staying at a hotel is rude."

Hall sneaks a glance at me, absolutely petrified. Clearly, he thought she'd be more like her spunky, pigtailed character from the olden-days sitcom *Here Come the Warrens*. Her role as Maggie Warren catapulted her to stardom, and her catchphrase was "You dare me to?" But if you say that to Grandma in real life, she locks you in the pantry and makes you listen through the door as she donates your inheritance to Scott Disick's Patreon.

"Here you are," Grandma barks, slamming a door wide open. The room is cramped, dim, with an odor of disuse. It comes with a single twin bed and one flat pillow. For comparison, Grandma has a temperature-controlled trophy room with four well-lit velvet stages that could each roomily support a hearse. Which one of them does. It's filled with all the awards she got for her guest stint on *CSI: Minneapolis.*

"This is so small, though," I hear myself whine, two seconds before I think better of it.

"Take it up with your older sister! If she and that man keep copulating, there'll be kids coming out of the vents." She brandishes her arms.

"I don't have any kids," I say haughtily, mentally stepping over Athena's fallen body.

"That's because you haven't found a man who wants to have them with you," Grandma replies, as if my devoted fiancé Hall isn't right here. "Not much to brag about, mm?"

"Can I have my own room?" I beg right as she starts to leave. "We'll put Hall on the couch."

"No! The couch is too comfortable. Somebody's bound to get pregnant on it—no guests are allowed to sleep on the couch. And don't be a diva about sharing a bedroom, Bettie. It's not like you're saving yourselves for marriage."

I begin to insist that we are, but it's too late. She's already gone, door slammed behind her, scolding Minnesota Moon for using too many consonants.

Hall and I carefully meet each other's eyes.

"This is . . . cozy."

"I can make it a bit more comfortable," he assures me. The

twin bed leaps up, a wooden ladder shooting out of it. Another bed pops into being right below, one outfitted in a red bedspread, the other in green. I watch the furniture connect, pillows fluffing themselves and sliding into silk covers with our names stitched onto them.

"Bunk beds?"

"Bunk beds make the most out of a small space." He tucks-and-rolls onto the bottom bunk, a yellow legal pad appearing in his hands. All around us, the room begins to decorate itself. He's definitely a man who needs a certain atmosphere in order to be at peace. "So here's our itinerary of activities to complete in the days leading up to December twenty-fifth: Make ornaments out of Popsicle sticks. Make tissue paper wreaths. Play cold-weather sports. Go sledding. Build a snowman. Have a snowball fight. All indisputable classics."

"There's not enough snow on the ground for that right now," I remind him, jerking my chin toward the window. We had a warm afternoon, so most of it's melted.

"Oh, that can be fixed." With a flourish of his hand, snow begins to cascade from the sky, sticking to the panes. Hall tugs on his collar, and the reindeer tie he copied from the weatherman loops itself around his neck. "Expect a foot by morning."

"You can control the weather?" My eyes light up. "Make tornadoes?"

He cuts me a narrow look. "Why would you even think about tornadoes? Why does that occur to you? I wish *nice* things would occur to you."

"I don't."

Hall snaps back to his list. Somewhere in the background,

Perry Como begins to sing: *Ohhh, there's no place like hooome for the holidaaayyys.* The melody seems to be emanating from the window itself. "Build a fort. Feed some birds! Throw a party. Do a one-thousand-piece puzzle. More birds! Repair your relationships with your family."

I snap to attention. "What?"

"Make a time capsule. Watch every Christmas movie. Drink hot cocoa until we're sick. Drink hot cocoa in front of birds. Bake cookies."

"Some of these sound unnecessary. Like the family part, and baking cookies. Why do we need to bake cookies if we can simply conjure some?"

He reels back in offense. "Baking cookies is a tenet of the season."

"How about," I counter, ripping the top sheet from his legal pad and tearing it into ribbons, "tomorrow we conjure up that green dinosaur from *Toy Story*, life-sized, except Athena's the only one who can see and hear it. Then we watch her freak out."

Hall reassembles the torn pieces of his itinerary, smoothing them back into their prior arrangement. "Bettie."

"Deadpool. Let's put Deadpool in the dining room, trying to engage whoever passes by in a game of charades. Athena's the only one who can't see him."

He jams a hand into his hair, tugging slightly. "We can't do that."

What a spoilsport. "Because you're so set on doing Christmas stuff?"

"No, because Deadpool isn't public domain. And we're not doing Christmas stuff, we're doing holiday stuff." He telekinetically opens the closet door and shoves it full of the presents we left in the red pickup, then shuts it. "I'm the *Holiday* Spirit."

"Looking pretty Christmassy in here to me." I spread my

hands at the decorations slowly eating the guest room: He's got a real thing for red vintage pickup trucks with felled evergreen trees in the cab. Wall hangings, *fresh cut from the farm* embroidered pillowcases. Every time I blink, the collection grows.

"Sixty-five percent of my matter has been trapped inside a ceramic gingerbread house cookie jar in the Ye Olde Christmas Shoppe in Disney World since 1996," he tells me. "Therefore, I've been disproportionately exposed to this particular holiday, helpless to resist absorbing its traditions. But only the secular ones, as is my preference. Especially Valentine's Day—I simply *adore* Valentine's Day, because its atmosphere is so nice with all the love and love-declaring and lacy Cupid decorations. Always wished I could physically participate in it, holding one of those bouquets of mixed flowers from the grocery store, and be somebody's secret admirer. Or have a secret admirer of my own, I haven't decided which would be better."

I stare at him, a slow grin unfurling. "A secret admirer, huh?"

He blushes. "Yeah, but I mean. I've never." Turns away. "I've never had real feelings for anyone before, but I'd love to experience it."

"You've never had a crush? No warm, jittery, googly-eyed Hall with cancan dancers in his nervous system?"

"Nope. Never had the opportunity. I was too preoccupied with doing my job, and it would've been fruitless, anyway, since I couldn't interact with others."

"Well, if you do get the chance to develop a crush, good luck to you. They're a pain."

He considers this. "I hope I do, pain or not. And, I can't help but notice how pretty you are. So. If I do develop a crush, you might be the first to find out."

It takes a lot to surprise me. But I gasp. My cheeks actually heat up. A little sunbeam sprouts from my heart and glitters between my fingers as I point to myself. "You think I'm pretty?"

The oddest sensation slides through me, with tiny cold spots blooming all over. It's like I'm being haunted in the pressure points of my arms, my legs. Simultaneously, my conscience, which isn't as much like Jiminy Cricket as it is like Scar from *The Lion King*, sits forward and raises an intrigued eyebrow. Why does this piece of news make Hall ten times cuter? Hearing that he thinks I'm pretty has moved him up in the rankings of Wholesome Men I Would Like to Corrupt, kicking Keanu Reeves out of his long-held spot at the top.

He dips his head in a slow, solemn nod. "Objectively."

Objectively. It takes some of the wind out of my sails. (But only some. He keeps a breeze wafting at me at all times so that my hair can ruffle majestically.)

He straightens, and I wonder when he changed his clothes—now he's in pajamas—to such a shiny silver that I can make out the dark outline of my reflection in them. He's so close that the splash of freckles across the bridge of his nose, wandering up his cheekbones, stands out in sharp relief. Then I notice something else: a thin band of brown around his left pupil, but not the right. Heterochromia. I could've sworn it wasn't like that yesterday.

"I'm a force of merriment and cheer," he says at length. "A feeling. Specifically for the long, cold, dark parts of the year. My purpose is to be a light. People need extra hope in the winter."

"True."

"I'm more of a winter entity than a holiday entity, if you want to get into it, but I came to be known as the Holiday Spirit since so many holidays happen to be clumped together at this time of year. I don't mind. Most of these celebrations are about joy and togetherness, which are my favorites. I suppose I could've evolved into one of the less-Christmassy holiday spirits, like National Pancake Day or National Hug Your Cat Day, but winter-specific fun is my favorite."

"You have a lot of favorites," I point out with a wry smile.

"Let's turn in early," he says, feverish with determination. "Wake up to watch the sunrise and get to work on this list. Your soul needs to bake cookies so badly."

"I have never seen a sunrise in my entire life."

Hall claps a hand over his heart. "Are you serious?"

I shrug, gathering up my nightclothes and toiletries to lug into the bathroom. "Probably."

"Bettie, that's awful."

"Why is that awful? It's just the sun coming up. Does it every day."

He throws himself flat on his back on the mattress, groaning. Satin candy cane pillows materialize over his face, burying him.

When I return from the bathroom, he's adding more activities to his list, mumbling under his breath. I can't help but think that Hall is wasted here, with the Watson-Hughes clan. Our Christmas traditions consist of sniping at each other, exchanging gifts for the sole purpose of one-upmanship, and complaining. Complaining around the dinner table. Complaining around the fireplace. Complaining at the airport about all the complaining everybody did. Hall deserves one of those *nice* families, who smile sincerely at each other while flipping pancakes and sing carols without rolling their eyes. Every time I see pictures of families in matching Christmas pajamas, I laugh derisively while admittedly getting this small pang of something disturbingly close to envy. What would it be like to be part of a functional family? Sounds like a myth.

My genetic pool doesn't rise early to admire the dawn. If we rise early, it's because there's a limited number of Krispy Kreme donuts. Hall's going to be so disappointed tomorrow when he watches us all slip off to different rooms to stare at our respective screens until dinnertime, when we meet to argue, then go to bed angry. It's how the week up until Christmas is spent. Christmas Day is the angriest of them all. Someone always gets somebody else a gift that they find belittling or offensive; someone always threatens to go home early; the family bonds by ganging up on someone (me) and making them sorry they came along. Last year I swore I'd never return.

I climb the ladder, lie down, and close my eyes, listening to small footsteps clattering above. Muffled warnings from parents to get in bed *right now*. Laughter, televisions, bickering, doors closing. A hair dryer. The dishwasher. Kaia strumming her guitar. We're a house full of reluctant acquaintances who get together once a year to tear each other apart.

I allow myself to imagine a What If world. Maybe we would stay up late in the living room, tipping our heads onto one another's shoulders, fuzzy socked feet in other laps, reluctant to go to bed because we enjoy each other's company so much. We'd still be up right now, sharing stories. Making each other *happy*. I wouldn't find it embarrassing if anyone caught me peering out the window at sunrise for the pure interest of seeing it unfold. I wouldn't be teased for it.

I roll over. It's stupid to roam around in What If world—it makes the real one look so much worse when I come back.

"Hall," I whisper a while later. "Are you awake?"

"Yeah. What do you need?"

"Is Dracula in the public domain?"

He sighs. "Good night, Bettie."

✳

CHAPTER SEVEN

....

Countdown to Christmas:
7 Days

I STRAGGLE OUT OF bed at eleven in the morning, finding the room empty. Hall's carefully made his bed, an outfit draped across it that I presume is for me: a gold sweater dangling with dozens of jingle bells, black leggings with a snowflake pattern, and a loud pair of socks. I mean that literally—every time I take a step, the socks start singing the song about hot chocolate from *The Polar Express.* I peel them right back off.

I open the door, ducking before paper snowflakes swinging inward on strings can bump me in the forehead. They're strung all down the hallway, toward the staircase, where I can't put my hands on the banister because it's encased in half a forest's worth of evergreen boughs with fake snow clinging to the needles. When I went to sleep last night, there were a few decorations here and there—a few sparkly baubles, a tastefully decorated tree in the living room, a wreath on the front door.

Now, there's a Christmas tree in every single room. Garland borders the signed portraits of Hollywood legends Grandma looks up to—Anna May Wong, Humphrey Bogart, Audrey Hepburn, and dozens of others who've adorned the walls of this house for decades. There are giant, solid glass peppermint candies propped in corners. Model trains whizzing along the baseboard trim, passing through miniature winter villages. Bows and holly and candles and stockings. The couch that is bound to impregnate somebody has six different throws on it now, and so many decorative pillows that there isn't room to conceive. The house smells powerfully of peppermint. When I sit down on the toilet to do my business, I'm met with the wide-eyed stare of a realistic North Pole elf mannequin, standing in the bathtub.

The family is in chaos.

"Who did this? What is the meaning of this?" Grandma cries, pointing at the fireplace. It used to be gas, but now it's wood-burning, and the flames are cartoon-animated.

"Sorry, that was supposed to be live-action," Hall mutters in my ear, sliding past. I whirl to watch him, and next thing I know, the hearth blazes with ordinary fire.

"Morning, Bettie!" my grandfather exclaims, curling an arm around my shoulders. "What a nice surprise! No wonder you slept in late. You were awake all night setting up this fantastical display for us."

I try to shape my mouth into a smile. "Y—es. That's. What I was doing."

"Even the cups," Kaia's remarking from the kitchen, prompting me to wander along. Sure enough, every cup in the cabinet has been replaced with a hand-painted mug in the shape of a snowman, a nutcracker, or Santa Claus. My gaze falls on Hall, shifting his weight from one foot to the other along the wall and watching us all excitedly. When his eyes flit to mine, my pulse skips. I frown at myself and my strange pulse-skipping. I need to cut back on sugar.

He's wearing a camel turtleneck. "Oh, so you get to look normal, but I have to wear *this*?" I grumble when I sidle close enough.

Hall smiles down at me. It's such a genuine, warm smile, the skin around his eyes crinkling, that suddenly I can't remember why I was annoyed.

"You look *amazing*," he tells me, voice low.

He would think that, since he picked it.

"If I have to wear jingle bells," I insist, "then so do—"

His sweater is infested with them before I can finish my sentence.

"Why didn't you make me say the magic words?" My eyes narrow.

"You really only need them when I'm not in total agreement with your wishes. It doesn't cost me anything to just grant wishes, if I feel like it. But sometimes I make you say the magic words because Mariah Carey is a legend and every time you recite her lyrics, the world becomes a sparklier place."

I stare at him. He holds my gaze, still beaming.

"You are unreal," I say.

We're not the only ones stumbling around in an unfamiliar environment. The local news is all in a tizzy over the unexpected overnight snowfall. It's the strangest phenomenon: snow has been falling nonstop, but the accumulation never exceeds twelve inches.

"What we've got here is a cold front," Hall informs everyone, turning down the volume of the weatherman on TV. "A level two nor'easter producing heavy preliminary snowfall across parts of northeastern Colorado and southwest Wyoming. There is wind movement, hail, ice pellets, and evaporation in inches. We're talking full coverage of I-22. Climate impact, et cetera."

"Interested in meteorology, are we?" Grandma observes dryly, taking his measure.

"Yes, I've been teaching myself. I think the weather is fascinating." Her sarcasm misses its target, and I recognize the exact second that his genuine smile hits: Grandma doesn't know how to react. Her eyes grow three sizes. His straightforward geniality has taken a whisk to her brain.

"Bettie!" Hall sings, steering me into the kitchen toward a buffet of sugar cookies. There's got to be over a hundred cookies here. He picks up a frosted poinsettia and shoves it in my mouth. "You need to eat something to get your energy up before we start the gingerbread house competition. I'm not going to tell you how you should construct yours, but I strongly recommend the use of Jolly Ranchers as bricks. Total game changer."

"It's too early for me to be any good at construction, Hall."

"What are you talking about? How are you still tired? I've been awake since four."

I skirt a glance around the room. "Yeah, I can see that."

"Doesn't it look so much better? Your mom walked in on me making candles, and my hands were covered in red wax. She screamed. I can't believe it didn't wake you up. Then I made cinnamon rolls for everyone and invited your dad to use one of my earbuds so that we could listen to *Celtic Christmas Podcast* together." His eyes darken. "He declined. Your father is in dreadful need of holiday spirit. He's a four point one."

My focus slides past him, to my father glowering mutinously in the doorway. He's wearing a Santa hat on his head, and I'm pretty sure he didn't put it there.

"You should probably leave Dad alone. He's not the kind of guy who shares earbuds. Or listens to podcasts."

Hall's mouth thins, looking drawn. "Maybe I should sing to him?"

"Please don't."

My phone keeps buzzing with notifications, which I'm not going to check here in public because there are too many busybodies. "I need a minute. *Don't* sing to my dad." I'm trying to impress him and make him regret all of his offenses against me, such as not letting MTV film in our house for my super-sweet sixteenth birthday. Also, for allowing me to be named after his mother-in-law.

As I slip past Dad, he seizes my sleeve.

"Where did you meet your boyfriend?" he whispers. "How long have you two been together? Something is *off* about him."

Athena and her husband are watching, tittering like two nosy old crones. The glue in their relationship is pettily judging everyone else's relationships to feel superior. "Fiancé, not boyfriend," I correct him, then hurry away.

I fish my phone out of my pocket, closing the door to the screened-in back porch behind me. I haven't posted anything on Instagram in a few days, which is the longest social media break I've ever taken.

I'm being tagged in stories from my followers, all screenshotting Lucas Dormer's latest post.

My arms are going tingly, blood pooling to my forehead, my ears, where my heartbeat rushes loud and swift. I lean against a support beam, index finger digging at a perfectly fingertip-sized hole in the screen, and brace myself for impact, as the name *Lucas Dormer* generally provokes in me a frothing swell of rage.

I have him blocked, which is why I didn't see until now that he posted a picture of me for Flashback Friday. I swipe over to his profile and grimace at a picture of us kissing, looking lovey-dovey. The next picture in the slide is an engagement ring, and he's captioned it with a broken-heart emoji. *Sometimes I think about what could've been.*

I suck in a sharp breath, scrolling through the flood of sympathetic comments. You've got to be kidding me.

Everyone loves Lucas Dormer. A real boy-next-door type, despite his rebellious phase after he left the boy band The Right Now to go solo.

Lucas is the sort of person who seems like a dream come true at first.

He was so much more attentive, so much more in love, so much more committed than any guy I'd ever been involved with which elevated our relationship status in record speed. We were using words like *soul mate* and spending every single second of every single day together. If I had to leave him for a couple hours, he'd text me long, heartfelt messages. After two weeks, we were talking about having children together. Big romantic gestures were everyday occurrences: a wall of roses, pink diamonds, spur-of-the-moment vacations, surprise fireworks. You know that high you get when you say *I love you* for the first time to someone? It was like that, nonstop. Whenever I started to drift down from that high—after a while, it was exhausting being up there all the time—he would outdo himself. Bring us back up to that level again. It was, in a word, intense. To me, intense = good, because?? Right?? It had to be a positive thing.

Most of my friends were exuberant in their jealousy, their happiness for me; his friends told me he was "a keeper." I didn't introduce him to the rest of my family, but Kaia met him by chance when we were out getting dinner and didn't like him because she thought that maybe he was like this with every girlfriend. I didn't want to hear it. Something about him nagged at her, so she started nagging at me. Which I thought was ridiculous, because *I'm* the older sister, which means I know better than she does. I defended him until I was blue in the face, even though my gut feeling was that she was right. Lucas told me that in previous relationships, he'd thought he was in love, but in retrospect, he actually hadn't been. It was like . . . if he was in a relationship and it ended, he canceled out the whole experience and decided it had no value. Wasn't real. This way, his next relationship going forward would be pure, and the new girlfriend would be the special, lucky girl to finally win his heart after a long string of users and fakers.

About a month in, paparazzi snapped pictures of him going to a private appointment at Cartier, and Kaia called me, freaking out. She was terrified he was shopping around for engagement rings and that I'd end up in his freezer. She said a lot of really bad things about Lucas that she'd been holding back, because she didn't know how to put it and didn't want to alienate me. I insisted we had the perfect relationship, that he was an outstanding boyfriend, more generous and complimentary than anyone else in existence. She asked one thing of me, one small request.

"Tell him you're going away with me for my birthday weekend."

I did, even though I felt sick with dread about how that would play out. Lucas did not want me to go. He volleyed back and forth between a few different manipulations: *I'll miss you too much. Can I come, too? If I can't come, then that means Kaia doesn't like me. And if Kaia doesn't support our relationship, she'll try to get you to break up with me. Kaia is against us being together. Kaia is a bad sister. Come to think of it, here's a bullet list of X, Y, and Z reasons why you should cut her out of your life. For*

starters, I think she's using you for attention because you're more famous than
she is, like everybody but me always tries to use you. She knows I see through
her bullshit, which is why she's trying to cut me out of the picture. Don't let
her do it, Bettie. Don't let her manipulate you.

I assured him I wouldn't be around any other men for the
weekend. I assured him I wouldn't drink. I would keep my phone
on me at all times. I would text him every half hour—actually,
even better, I would stay on the phone with him the whole time.
Yeah, it sucked that we were apart, and I didn't really want to go.
I didn't want to leave him behind. I loved him so much! More
than anyone.

Anyone.

After all, he pointed out, Kaia was just my sister, not my soul
mate, and blood isn't everything. Kaia had her own life going on,
we didn't hang out often, so what did she care? He was my future.
He was giving up all his free time to be with me, so shouldn't I do
the same? Why was he putting in more effort than I was? If I loved
him as much as I claimed, then why would I want to be anywhere
else but at his side? Kaia was against us. Soon, she'd turn the
whole family against us.

Lucas and I held each other, crying, passionately swearing
we'd never let anyone come between us. It was a lot. He needed
constant reassurance that I wanted to grow old with him. I'd
spend hours trying to convince him, until my voice was hoarse.
Each session would end with us being "closer than ever" even
though my nerves were frayed, and I'd think, *okay he's finally all*
right, we're settled—but then he'd plummet right back to that low
point, and I'd have to drop everything to reassure him all over
again. I began to suspect he was faking it, just to siphon my energy. To watch me prove myself over and over. Emotions were

running so high, all the time, and I was drained. Exhausted. I never had two minutes to myself to reflect on anything, to view this relationship from a distance.

Kaia dropped by my house (at the time, I was living in L.A.) on the pretense that she wanted to play a new track for me, and then Athena tumbled out of the passenger seat, grabbed my wrist, and stuffed me in the back. It was an intervention. Kaia held my phone hostage while we drove to Santa Cruz. We explored parks along the way, but I couldn't enjoy any of the sights. Aside from calling them every horrible name I could think of, I refused to speak to them. I had thirty nervous breakdowns per hour over what Lucas was going to do, how he would react. I begged for my phone so that I could call him and let him know I was okay, that I missed him, that this wasn't my idea, that I was forced. But not in a sinister way. I didn't want him calling the police on my sisters.

Kaia instructed me to dictate all my messages onto a notepad. She'd text them to Lucas herself.

As I sat in my hotel bed, surrounded by crumpled papers, my pen ran out of ink before I could come up with the right words that would make Lucas forgive me for going on an impromptu trip with my sisters. It was such an awful few days that I can't remember most of it. A trauma fog.

Do you know that feeling when out of nowhere, your ears pop and your equilibrium is shot, and you hear a high, thin ringing? That sensation knocked me over like an undertow. I couldn't stop staring at all the ink I'd used, all the paper I'd scribbled on and then discarded. The crossed-out words, because if I didn't use just the right words, he'd spiral. Or stop loving me. I couldn't predict what he'd do. Suddenly, I was so scared by what was happening that I did a one-eighty from being desperate to run into his arms to never wanting to be in Southern California again. I wanted to go into hiding. I was worried he had a tracker in my phone, that he'd find me. I was worried that if I called him and broke it off, he'd talk me out of it. I didn't have enough faith in myself to successfully break up with him in person, knowing that if I had to look into his eyes, I'd cave.

So I took what I thought was my only option: I broke up with him publicly, before I lost my nerve. I did it in a tweet.

I was slammed for that. Tactless! Vicious! Heartless! Poor Lucas Dormer dumped by "love of his life" Bettie Hughes via Twitter! Is she secretly hooking up with former flame Isaiah Redding?

Lucas's fans, who hated me when we were dating and sent me a ceaseless flow of death threats, took things to the next level. I was too ugly for Lucas. I was a slut. He's going to find a woman who deserves him, who's pretty and talented enough to be with him, and I'll regret what I did for the rest of my stupid, meaningless life. Emails and comments bombarded me until I locked my accounts (coward!), but they emailed my family members, friends I hadn't spoken to in ages, my middle school teachers, my neighbors.

Lucas milked the breakup for all it was worth, crying to every media outlet. Turned the whole world against me. I've seen video clips of him wiping his eyes on a concert stage: "She'll be sorry. I even pity her myself. Someday she'll look back and see what she had and be sorry." Waves of girls in the audience whooped in agreement, booing my name. I remember one of them held up a big white posterboard, covered in glitter, that had a picture of a Little Debbie Swiss Roll on it and the words BLINK IF YOU WANT ME TO KILL HER.

In less than two months, he was professing his love for someone else, a soccer star named Dani. He rewrote our story, claiming that now that he was in a perfect relationship and found his true soul mate, he could see that he never actually loved me at all. Dani was his first love. She'd be his love until his dying day. They lasted longer than I expected, breaking up only a few short weeks ago.

A slow, quivering exhale leaves my body as my stare burns through the picture of us kissing. I wish I could reach inside it and yank that Bettie out. There are a few comments mixed in with all the Bettie-bashing, about how fucking weird it is to ruminate over the marriage he might have had with an ex-girlfriend he'd never even been engaged to. Not to mention, the engagement ring he posted is the first picture that pops up when you Google "giant engagement ring." Others have tagged Dani with #DodgedABullet.

Any time I've ever tried to defend myself against Lucas, his horde of fans come back swinging with a vengeance. I am the villain. Any claims to the contrary don't fit their narrative.

Now that I've deprogrammed myself, I am able to identify this picture as staged. He took pictures of everything we did, planning activities around photo ops. Constantly grabbing me, pulling me to him, even when I was busy. Hugging me while I was on the phone, hugging me while I was typing up emails, hugging me when I was trying to get dressed, trying to eat. Holding his phone out, snapping pictures. He did it especially when I was in a bad mood, annoyed with him, because it forced me to put on a smile. Forced me to let him hold me, kiss me, for the camera, when I needed space. Love bombing.

In the time that I've been burning a furious hole through his latest story with my eyes, Lucas has added another post to his feed. It's a picture of him on a stage, baring all of his teeth in a smile, arm wrapped tightly around a pretty dark-haired woman wearing what looks like a tiny ice skater's costume with more cutouts than Swiss cheese. He's in a sharp black suit. *Tune in tonight 8/7c for the season finale! Jenna and I have an amazing one in store for ya.* 😊 *@dancingabc @DorminatorsOfficialUpdates #DancingWithTheStars #DWTS #Lucas AndJenna #TeamLucas #LucasDormer #DormerFansUnite #Domina tionNation #WeLoveLucasDormer #MCM #WCW #YouWannaWatch This #Hot #Muscles #Singer #Sexy #SoloArtists #BachelorABC #TheNextBachelor #TellABCYouWantLucasDormerToBeTheNextBachelor*

She didn't deserve you, one of the top comments says. I've worried the hole in the window screen until it's big enough for a golf ball to get through.

I think Bettie's news is a publicity stunt, says another, curiously tagging Callista Orjean in the comment. The name jumps out at me because Callista, a D-list celebrity, is one of Felix's ex-wives.

"What news?" I mutter.

I don't have Callista blocked, only muted, as she's such a wild card that I need to keep contained tabs on her movements. I click over to her profile and frown. No new posts for a week. The last one was a picture of her dog. Then I open her latest stories and almost drop my phone.

It's a picture of me and Hall from only ten or fifteen minutes ago: covered in bells, sugar cookies everywhere.

Look who's engaged! she's typed over it. *Congrats, Hal and Betty.*

"It's *Hall*, and *Bettie* with an *ie*, you plastic bag of lake water," I say to my phone, rapidly playing catch-up in my mind. How in the hell?! I haven't spoken to Callista in years. Someone *here* had to have snapped that picture, and then sent it to Callista . . .

The gears grind to a halt.

✳

CHAPTER EIGHT

·································

MARILOU IS FELIX'S fourth wife, a Filipino competitive surfer and the mother of his youngest, a baby boy named Adrian. She loves the Marvel Cinematic Universe and seahorses, runs three miles along the beach every morning, and can speak three languages—all of which she's teaching to her stepchildren. I have never heard a single judgmental word fall out of her mouth in relation to Felix's myriad faults. She is, far and away, the most sensible woman my idiot brother's ever met in his life, is light-years out of his league, and therefore it comes as no shock that he's sabotaging their relationship.

I grab an orange from the kitchen fruit bowl and hurl it at him. Felix ducks. "Hey!" he yells, patting the top of his head. That orange never came near his head.

"The fuck are you doing, texting Callista?" I yell back. "You're a moron."

Felix colors. "I haven't been texting Callista!"

"I've got proof."

He beckons, agitated. "Show me."

"Maybe I'll just forward it to Marilou." Right now, Marilou's visiting her sister in New Hampshire and is going to fly in closer to Christmas to be miserable with the Watson-Hugheses. Hughes's. Hughes'.

"No!" everybody yells in tandem. "Not Callista!" That woman's name is a plague, a dark shadow on Hughes history. Grandma even hired a witch to keep her out of our lives for good so I know somebody with the name Moon Goddess in their screen name is about to receive a scathing review on Yelp.

He bounds over. "Don't show anything to my wife. She'll leave me. I'm already paying a fortune in alimony and child support." He eyes my phone beadily, as if he can snatch it and delete whatever evidence I'm harboring.

"Oh, *Felix*." Mom's head drops to one side in disappointment. "What are you doing? I thought you were finally over that."

"You two were a nightmare," Dad rejoins. "I can't go through it again. I can't."

From a corner, Kaia strums her guitar and sings lowly, "Chea-ea-eating, chea-ea-eating, Felix's wives are flee-ee-eeing."

"I have to keep the lines of communication open with Callista," Felix interjects. Loudly. Whenever he knows he's in the wrong, he cranks up his volume. "We have . . ." His eyes shoot up to the ceiling as he calculates. "Two kids together. I told Marilou from the beginning that she has to respect the relationships I have with my kids' mothers. Those are protected bonds, to ensure healthy co-parenting." For Felix, co-parenting means he gets to see the majority of his kids one weekend out of every month. He also gets them all for the whole week of Christmas and then for two weeks in summer to celebrate his birthday.

"You don't have any kids with Callista," Athena points out. Felix glares at her. He was clearly banking on his relationship and co-parenting history being so convoluted that we'd mix up who the mothers of his children are.

Felix and Callista are a match made in hell. They get back together every other year or so, after sabotaging each other's healthier relationships, only to break up all over again. They've divorced twice. The second judge begged them to stay apart. "After the last intervention, you swore you were finished. What are you doing talking to her about my engagement?" I snap. Hall, in the process of building Marshmallow Fluff snowmen with two of my nieces, freezes in place. Stares at the ginormous ring on my left hand, as though he'd forgotten our ruse. "Callista posted it all over the Internet! She has no business doing that! You had no business telling her!"

"Why shouldn't I tell her about your *joyful news*?" he replies defensively. "What are you hiding?" He points at Hall, face contorting. "I don't like that guy. I wanna know more about this supposed 'movie.'" Hall's mouth opens, but Felix plows on: "And you're not even an actress, Bettie."

Aren't I?

"I'm telling Marilou," I say prissily, twitching my eye at Hall and pointing my finger at the floor. He obediently hurries over to stand at my side for backup. "She deserves to know."

"Do it. Do it, and I swear to God I will gouge your eyes out."

"And so he swears to gouge her eyes out," Kaia hums softly, fingers dancing up and down the guitar strings. "But you don't need eyes, to see all his lies . . ." She bends over her iPad to scribble that line down.

"Stop it," Mom snaps, smacking him on the shoulder. "Don't

talk to your sister like that. And Kaia, stop narrating. It's unsettling."

I turn to my brother. "Felix, have you lost your mind? That woman tried to burn your house down."

"The police never proved it was her," he begins, and I have to tune him out, because no way am I listening to the Callista Burned My House Down, That Bitch, Or Maybe She Didn't, We Might Be Getting Back Together, Except No We're Not, I Saw Her Out With Somebody Else, I'm Suing Her For Burning My House Down story again.

"How long do you give it until Marilou finds out?" Kaia wonders. She's investigating Callista's Instagram page. "Marilou follows all your exes on here. Did you know that?"

Felix has gone bone-pale.

"You sent Callista a picture of your grandparents' house?" his brother-in-law crows. "How dumb are you? Nobody else here is on speaking terms with your ex-wife, so it'll be obvious who sent it."

My brother is starting to panic. "I didn't do anything wrong."

"I *told* you not to get involved with that woman," Grandma declares smugly.

I study Athena, to see if she has any opinion on this, but she's decorating the Christmas tree with bottles of bareMinerals foundation in preparation for a social media post. Nothing, not even the likely disintegration of her brother's marriage, comes before the hustle.

Felix begins to rant that everyone is against him. Mom is suggesting alibis, ways she can cover this up, because he's her baby and he'll never have to take responsibility for his screwups if she can help it, and Grandpa's fallen asleep in a chair because he's too nice to be conscious for this. Grandma's polishing an archery bow the size of a toddler, giving me a brand-new reason to be scared of her. On the couch, surrounded by three jumping children, one of whom has scribbled all over his arm with a marker, Dad clasps his hands between his knees and stares heavily at the floor.

"You know what this family could use?"

We all look up at Hall, whose voice slices through the din with supernaturally amplified volume. "Counseling?" guesses eight-year-old Peach Tree as Mom ventures hopefully, "Pie?"

He holds up a pair of ice skates against his chest, grin a mile wide. "Ice skating!" He does finger guns at mom, shutting one eye. "But I like where your head's at, Madeline. Let me throw a few pies in the oven first."

She beams.

※

My relatives are mystified by the mountain of ice skates Hall was able to "rush order" in the correct size for every family member.

Felix, suspicious, demands to know how Hall knew all of our shoe sizes, if he has a fetish. Hall directs the wind strategically so that it blows away my brother's naysaying before it can infect the others. Luckily, most of us have an entitlement complex so like, why *shouldn't* someone surprise us with ice skates that fit perfectly?

Even more mystifying than the skates is the ice rink that's materialized where the defunct car lot used to sit on Old Homestead Road, just across the street and two spaces down from my ginger-bread town house, which I hope none of them notice.

"Who built this?" Grandpa asks wonderingly. "You know how long this has been here, Bettie?"

"Nope," I say. An old joke, replying when I know he's talking to Grandma. She hates it.

No one besides us is here. "It's probably a bribe from the mayor, hoping for reelection," suggests Grandma, who watches Frangipane lunge for the ice without skates on. Her eyes gleam like twin knives as they rest on me, then flick to Hall, who's smiling dreamily at what can only be his handiwork. Victorian lampposts hem in the rink, strung with twinkle lights and garland, each pole twined in ivy. There's a red bench, and a birdhouse over by the fountain in the town square, which is supposed to be covered with a tarp for the season but now spurts crystalline water. Puffy pink clouds tumble low, the spire of the church tower lancing through them.

"I'm pretty sure this rink has always been here," says my nephew Ichabod.

Dad grimaces without meaning to. (He's where I get my resting bitch face from.) "It must've. Skating rinks don't simply appear out of thin air."

"Don't forget your scarves," Hall says, probably to knock their thoughts off track. He hands out scarves to each Watson or Hughes as they pass, their eyebrows lifted as they appraise this fancy gift.

"Darling, did you make these yourself?" Mom exclaims, looping hers about her neck. Her name is stitched above the black trim in gold. "Where'd you find the time?"

Felix refuses his scarf. He'd probably refuse to skate, as well, but he considers himself to be pretty good at it and can't miss the opportunity to show off. Weak sunlight glints off his silver blades, harsh brow lowered, hands extended behind his back like a ski jumper as he pushes left, right, left, scaring off anyone in his path.

Sean veers too close and staggers, clawing at air for a few moments before running Kaia over.

Mom is doing graceful triple axels like they're nothing. Dad sits down on the bench, grousing that he's too old to skate, which makes Octavian burst into tears: *"Is Grandpa going to die?"*

Something touches my hand and I jump back, but it's just Hall.

He raises his eyebrows at me, a small smile touching the corners of his lips. Then, once again, he bumps his gloved fingers against mine. "Let's go."

"Me?" I point at myself.

He points at me, too. "You."

"Oh, nah, no thanks, I'm too full of pie. I'll just watch." I try to shove my hands into my pockets, but the pockets seal shut. I snap my head up to level him with a glare, and he shakes his head amiably, tugging on my arm. "Hall, I'm serious. I know you're really into this traditional holiday stuff—"

His head dips in a nod. "It's the whole reason I'm here."

"You're here because I got drunk and didn't know how to play a record."

"Why don't you want to skate, Bettie? What are you afraid of?"

I try to scowl. I do. But Hall's standing so close, analyzing me without meanness, without a biting remark waiting. I don't have to wonder what's brewing in the back of his mind. Don't have to be careful. All he wants is for me to skate with my family and enjoy myself. (And then probably carve an ice sculpture later. He's obsessed with them.)

"I don't want to fall down in front of them. They'll tease me until I die."

"I won't let you fall."

"I'm not any good at skating."

"Aren't you?" he asks, a sly sparkle to his eyes. "You should try it, just to be sure."

His hand in mine, we tread to the perimeter of the ice and . . . I feel it. A pull of magic.

You can do anything, it whispers.

The magic has Hall's voice, his peppermint scent. It feels exactly like a warm, conspiratorial smile pressed to my cheek, a steady hand on my back, which shouldn't make me shiver like it does. Even as he glides backward, one sure foot behind the other, away from me, I feel his hands. They're everywhere I need them: gripping mine, leading me; on my back, hovering just behind my shoulders. One very near my hip, but not quite touching. An invisible thumb pushes a wayward lock of hair away from my face, tucking it behind my ear.

He watches my reaction as I test the magic, discovering how firmly it holds me. Grins when my eyes widen in disbelief, either of my arms outstretched, gliding along on one leg. He laughs at my astonishment when I try a spin, which I shouldn't be able to pull off, and the spinning doesn't stop until I tell it to. However I want to leap and twist and spin, I leap and twist and spin.

Kaia hoots, her dozens of bracelets clinking together as she claps. "Look at you, Betts!"

It's not me, it's the magic, but I still soak up her praise. I close my eyes and tilt my face toward the sun like a flower, the best at something for once. All I want to do is race as fast as I can, spraying sparks behind me like comets. Quicker, quicker, wind-stung skin, digits numb, hair flying. Athena intercepts me and grips my arm, using my momentum to fling me toward Grandpa, who chuckles throatily as he catches me and flings me back again. Athena playfully tugs on my hat—an infinitesimal tweak—as my momentum curbs. I stare after her as she skates away, silvery-blond hair swishing back and forth like a unicorn's tail.

"Incoming!" a nephew cries, whooshing by. They're all a little faster, a little better coordinated than they ought to be, which I think is the reason we stay out on the ice as long as we do. The only thing better than being good at something is being good at something while other people watch. Or maybe that's just my mindset.

Dad, who resolutely told us all no, he would *not* get on the ice, has given in. Twirling my mother, admiring her skills with a besotted softness to his eyes until too many of us notice and he glares it into submission. The pair of them are night and day: she's quite verbose about her affection for him, whereas he photographs his feelings when he can't give them voice, leaving snapshots of her smile, his wedding ring, the dining room doorway where he notched the height of their kids every year, in places where she'll discover them and smile, clutching the pictures to her heart.

Athena and Felix are racing side by side as the kids scream, egging them on. Felix plays dirty, jabbing her with an elbow. Athena plays dirtier, closing him in until he topples off the rink's edge.

"Ragh!" Felix growls, tugging a scarf from around his neck. He's got another around his waist like a belt. The second he gets rid of it, the wind brings it right back like a boomerang and the fabric attaches itself to him with static cling. I ought to magic up some banana peels as punishment for him leaking pictures of me, but I don't have the heart. My brother's clueless and he's about to start over yet again, another spiral followed by a New and Improved Incarnation of Felix. It won't stop him from remarrying again in two years, though, promising his undying devotion to someone who won't keep it.

The magic eventually says goodbye to my family. I watch it leave them one by one—the children complain that they're cold and hungry. Grandma has three voicemail messages. Grandpa's missing a game on TV. Dad's knees are bothering him. Athena and Mom are the last holdouts, the former giving up only after she jumps and comes back down wobbly. Casting left and right to see if anyone witnessed the bumble, she shrugs and exits on stiff legs.

Mom's on fire. She doesn't need magic. She does trick after trick, arms extended in smooth lines, skates a blur. Dad, I can't help but notice, is lingering at the top of the hill where the base of the driveway begins, watching. Whenever she falls, she pushes herself right back up and keeps skating. She waves whenever she gets close to me, but mostly keeps to herself, doing her own thing. I bet they're both remembering the days when she wanted to be a dancer.

The sun is setting, firecracker orange wrapping around tree-tops, then their middles, sinking along the ground as if swirling the drain. Twilight marbles the ice, flashing new colors every few seconds, until I wonder if the ice has always been dusty rose or deep heliotrope. The magic rink is a vivid flame for the span of one minute; then the sun slips lower, lower, over to the opposite side of the world to clock in for its other shift, and now the ice is a mirror for starlight. I turn to ask Hall if he's ready to go back up the mountain, but he says, "One last go-round?"

I'm going to miss being an expert ice skater. Wonder what else he could make me miraculously excel at? I should take the bar exam.

I lace my fingers in his. Even through the cotton of our gloves, he gives off a shocking warmth. It pumps straight to my heart, turning me into a light, glowing from within.

I'm a force of merriment and cheer, he'd said. *A feeling.* That's how it feels to be in proximity to Hall, too.

Hand in hand, we glide, breathing in the frost. Hall's ears and nose are tinged pink, hair ruffling. "What's it like?" I ask. "Being in a body after so long without one?"

"Like my magic is more compact, more concentrated. You'd think I'd find the body cumbersome, but I actually feel like a feather now. I'm all right here"—he gestures to himself—"instead of spread out, stretching around the world."

There's no nice way of putting this. I'll have to be blunt.

"Ice skating isn't going to make me a good person, if that's your goal."

"You're already a good person. I have X-ray vision, I can see it. We're only doing *this* to have fun." His hand squeezes mine gently, and I could be imagining it, but I think the rink is growing. Broadening by the minute, so that our one last go-round stretches on. I glance over my shoulder at the Watson house, a tiny speck now on its piney ridge, shining with Christmas lights. Snow falls softly all around, but not directly over us. I ask Hall why that is.

He reddens, snowflakes belatedly speckling his hair as if, until now, they'd simply forgotten to.

"It wasn't intentional. Sometimes the magic responds to my subconscious."

"Why would you subconsciously not want it to snow over the skating rink?"

I can't imagine why this would be a point of embarrassment. Before I can question him further, music begins to rise up, filtering out of the silvery, snow-limned trees. Louder, louder, vibrating through the blades under my feet. It's like living inside a microphone as the Ronettes gather around it. Our surroundings have been magicked into loudspeakers, so that the trees, the geese flapping high overhead, every individual snowflake is emitting the sound Hall wants it to. I slide him an inquisitive look, but he faces determinedly forward. Is he trying to distract me?

A slow grin crosses my face. I think he notices it with his peripheral vision, because he fidgets. Scratches his cheek and turns his face farther away.

I hear an ever-so-faint *clip-clop* of horse hooves on cobblestones, shimmering sleigh bells, the crackling of a fire. I smell cinnamon, pine forest, peppermint, chestnuts. At first I think that Hall's infused these details into the environment, painting a scene, but whenever he flings me out, away from his body so that I can then twirl back into his arms, I notice how the sensations recede, go quiet. He's not *making* those sounds or scents. He *is* them. Being close to him is like huddling up before a hearth on the longest night of the year, a thick quilt wrapped around me, utterly safe and contented. It's like closing my eyes, lambent light warming me all over, and drifting away in a golden tint of nostalgia, toy drummers, and childhood things.

"Maybe a little bit of holiday cheer isn't so bad," I admit. The sky is black, with purple wispy clouds drifting like little ships sailing to the moon. "But I'll warn you, I might be a lost cause."

Hall's reflection in the ice is glowing. Actually glowing—a soft, blurry halo clinging to his edges, visible only from specific angles.

"What makes you think that?" he asks.

I stare at his radiant profile. I don't register the temperature anymore, or if music is playing, or if the rink is still growing. Maybe that was only an illusion. Maybe we've been circling the same small area over and over. I'm too riveted to question why he's cleared the snowfall away from my face as he looks down at me with star-bright eyes.

"The sort of person you are . . . all sweet and warm and fuzzy, is fiction to me. I'll never be able to let my guard down enough to be like that. Even with my mom, who's the nicest, most under-standing human I've ever known, I'm scared to open up, because what if the worst she's seen so far isn't my worst, which will be her limit. I don't want her to discover her limit with me."

"I can tell you have difficulty being yourself in front of others."

"It's a habit I can't shake. People are always using me to get more famous, or they want to schmooze Grandma. I dated this one guy for a few months, thinking he was so wonderful, until he revealed that he'd written a screenplay and wanted me to show it to Grandma. I told him I would, and it was like a flipped switch— all he could talk about from that point onward was whether I'd shown her the screenplay, when I was planning to do it, if I'd please hurry up. This is why I don't date anymore, why it's hard to maintain friendships. These friendships start off fun and light, with them treating me to margaritas, which evolves into *I need twelve hundred dollars for my cat's medicine, I'll pay you back. Hey, bestie, please loan me five grand? I'm only asking you because I know you're such a good friend, and nobody else will help.* At some point, they all reveal their true selves. Then I feel like a fool for believing they liked me for *me*. It even affects my relationships with people I *know* I should be able to trust, like my parents."

"I'm only one person," he says softly, "but Bettie, I'm not using you for anything."

I scan his face, but I'm not searching for proof that he's lying; he's so right, so inarguably right, that it brooks no challenge.

I sigh. "Sorry to bring the mood down. I suppose I've just been burned a lot. It's made me jaded."

"I've been burned, too," he volunteers, which successfully captures my undivided attention.

"What? By who?"

He nods. "By catching a falling star."

A laugh ruptures from my chest. "You *what?*"

"Well, more like it fell directly through me. But it was the first time I felt heat! Second time, I got struck by lightning. For a questionable century there, I confess I developed an addiction to getting struck by lightning."

All I can do is howl, which breaks his face into that boyish, irresistibly charming grin, and very quickly I can't remember why I'd been feeling low. The lamps he nicked from Victorian London burn lively and fierce as the moon arcs out of the trees. It's unusually large this evening, a milky round pearl. I don't know if Hall is affecting the appearance of our environment, making it picture-perfect for maximum holiday cheer. Does it matter? The stirring of pleasant feelings inside me is real.

Before my eyes, Hall scatters trees all over the town square and grows them up to maturity, adorning them with tinsel and jewels, lights that flash *Happy Holidays*. Hall's magic has been working seamlessly of late, *when* he's using it to execute his own ideas. I'm growing suspicious of magic's "total inability" to supply me with a luxury car rather than the pickup.

"He gives his harness bells a shake," Hall murmurs. "To ask if there is some mistake. The only other sound's the sweep of easy wind and downy flake."

I stare at him. "Is that poetry? Did you come up with it?" I don't know anything about poetry, but I know that it's romantic and elegant and whenever I envision myself far in the future as an eighty-year-old, Old Me is surrounded by poems bequeathed from the many brilliant, softhearted lovers to whom I was a muse.

He smiles. "Robert Frost did. Wish I could take credit! You look so impressed with me right now."

I look at the trees, the lights. He's an artist in his own way. "I've always thought I'd end up with a poet, if I ever got swept off my feet."

"Hmm," he says to himself, head bowed. "Bettie Hughes, carried away by a poet. I can see that."

"Thank you for this." I gesture to the rink. "I needed some fun." This man, if he can be called that, is indeed filling me up with the joy he promised to.

Hall's gaze flares with a bright emotion, open and honest, as he takes in my gratitude. A ring of brown encircles his right pupil, to match his left. I don't think it was like that yesterday, but the longer I think about it, the foggier yesterday becomes.

We step off the ice and head back up the hill, easy wind and downy flakes swirling behind us in a glitter spill of lights.

✳

CHAPTER NINE

M Y MUSCLES ARE sore and aching when we clomp our way back up the hill and into the house, shucking off our skates into a big pile on the snow-soaked rug covering the back porch.

Mom, Kaia, and Grandpa are bustling in the kitchen, clattering plates out of the cabinets to set the dining room table for butternut squash soup, lemon garlic chicken, and risotto. When Grandpa turns to look at us over his shoulder as Hall and I enter the room, something like amazement flits across his lined features. "Smells good in here."

His stare lingers on Hall for a few seconds more, then breaks. Did he forget about Hall? I study my grandfather, fairly youthful still, bright-eyed and suntanned, in a Denver Broncos sweatshirt. Mismatched socks, because it amuses his wife for some reason. He's still got a thick crop of gray hair, but he's climbing up there in age. I hope his memory isn't playing tricks on him.

But he turns to me as if nothing's amiss and crushes me with a hug. "Grandpa," I wheeze. "My liver."

"You don't need it." He chuckles that familiar rusty laugh I love so much, and predictably, passes a ten-dollar bill into my palm. "Some pocket money for you. Buy yourself a Tamagotchi."

"Thanks!" Grandpa doesn't know it, but all the money he gives me during my visits has been a lifesaver. Last Christmas I walked out of here with five hundred bucks, and this past summer he Venmo'd me fifty for no reason, which helped with my phone bill and a few other necessities. I'd never ask him for financial help, and he isn't aware that I need it, so I'm grateful beyond words that he is such a generous grandfather.

"And something for your boyfriend. What does he like?"

Before I can respond, he cranes his neck. "Hall, do you ever take my Bettie to the shopping mall? Take her to the pretzel place at the food court. They've always got the pretzel place, any food court you go. Bettie loves pretzels."

Hall blinks. "Oh?"

"It's all right that you don't know. You'll learn." Grandpa slips Hall a folded bill, too. "What do you like to do for fun?"

"Mini golf," Hall responds at once, his gaze straying over Grandpa's shoulder at a calendar on the wall depicting cats playing mini golf.

"Bettie, he likes mini golf," Grandpa booms. "There you go. Have yourself a nice date with mini golf and pretzels." He hums his way over to the sink and starts washing lettuce. Hall and I exchange a curious look behind his back.

We dive into our meal, and if anybody notices the basket of bread appearing, or the spontaneous dish of sugar cookies, they don't wonder aloud where they came from. Hall can't stop smiling, pleased with himself, listening to Grandma wax lyrical about skating at Rockefeller Center years ago for a movie and how glorious it was when Jane Fonda slipped and fell. This turns into an estimation of whether it's likely she will outlive Jane Fonda, and assurances from me that I will never agree to play the daughter of Jane Fonda in a movie. Since I am allegedly an actress now.

"I wouldn't ever cast her, myself," Felix offers, sucking up.

Grandma snorts at him. "Darling, you couldn't afford her."

A sullen Felix stabs at his chicken.

The rest of dinner, which began harmlessly enough, snaps back into its usual routine. Athena holds her four-month-old baby on her lap and feeds him mashed potatoes while Mom watches with pursed lips ("You should really hold off on solids until the baby is six months, and start with rice cereal"). Sean hears one of his offspring, Avenue, calling for him but pretends not to hear, scrolling through his phone under the table. Then he gets pissy when Kaia checks on Avenue, because that "makes him look like a bad dad." He points out to everyone that Kaia is vaping at the dinner table, which usually earns her a lecture, but Mom's too busy being annoyed with Dad for massaging his temples.

"Why do you have to go out of your way to look annoyed with us?"

"I have a headache. Am I not allowed to have a headache?"

Felix remembers that he's in method mode for his Rochester role, responding to everybody in clipped, guttural growls that I laugh at. Athena purses her lips at me, a startling clone of our mother. "Can't you be nice?"

Felix, angry that I'm not paying him the respect he is owed as Serious Filmmaker, tells Hall that he should pull his film so that it doesn't get bashed by critics for copying Felix's. "Can't you be

supportive?" Mom groans. Athena's baby sneezes mashed potatoes onto Dad's plate. He shoves to his feet.

"You can't get mad at a baby, James." Grandma, who has
never liked babies and whose upbringing of my mother in a big,
lonely house as an only child scarred her in such a way that Mom
brought four children into the world and then told them they were
all beautiful, perfect cherubs, says to Dad, "That's your grandson!"

"I'm not mad at a baby! I'm getting Tylenol. Am I not allowed
to get Tylenol?" Under his breath, he adds, "And never come
back."

Mom notes Athena's wineglass. "Are you breastfeeding?"

Athena's husband looks up, his brain registering only the word
breast. Grandma pinches his arm. He yells. His baby cries. I'd cry
too if my name was Fang.

"Can you just not?" he asks his unfortunately named infant.

"Don't snap at my great-grandson," Grandma tells him.

"He's *my* son, I can talk to him however I like."

Grandpa rises from his chair, as well, taking his turn to be the
one who gets to dramatically exit dinner. It's a coveted role. Sean
smirks at him, but I wouldn't be so confident. Grandpa was a Ma-
rine, briefly.

"Does anybody want a cookie?" Hall asks frantically, thrusting
the dish at everyone in turn. The magic of ice skating has already
worn off, and now we're all poking each other. The only person
who accepts a cookie is the four-month-old.

I tug Hall after me into the living room, but the hope of peace
is obliterated when I see what's happening on the television (105
inches—impossible to miss): the *Dancing with the Stars* title card
sparkles across the screen. Cannons shoot off in my gut.

I should go over and switch it off, but I can't move.

Athena's model friend Candy Olship sambas onstage, hips swishing. Instead of a skirt, she's wearing a few red tassels, and she's *stunning*. Athena wanders into the room, followed by the rest of the family. "Oh, look, it's Candy! We have to watch this."

I'm all braced for Lucas, but still flinch when he dances out, smiling the same smile I fell in love with. I wonder how many other women are haunted by that smile, and as his dancing partner beams back at him, my body is clinched by a funny, cold feeling. I was once hospitalized for dehydration after a day of sledding on sand dunes with friends. When they stuck the needle into my arm and started pumping me with fluids, the needle slipped out of the vein and I felt this horrible coldness seeping into all the wrong parts. Panic hit the roof. I slammed the call button to bring a nurse back in, wondering what would happen if too much fluid leaked out where it didn't belong, if I would die. Making one-way eye contact with Lucas feels exactly like that, except everywhere: my temples, behind my ears, double-helixing around my spine. An invasive foreign substance.

"Hall, I'd like for you to send Dani Seeley a gift basket of Godiva chocolates," I mutter quietly so that only he can hear me. "And some nice wine and cheese."

"Done."

The audience claps for the four pairs of dancers. I don't ordinarily watch this show, so I don't know who any of the professional dancers are, but I recognize the celebrities. Other than Candy and Lucas, there's also the well-known daughter of a Republican senator, her claim to fame being the daughter of a Republican senator, and Craig Robinson. The camera pans up to the balcony where past competitors are clapping, past Kimberly J.

Brown and Freddie Prinze Jr., to Lacey Chabert, the sight of whom makes Hall spring into the air.

"I *love* her!" he cries. He grabs my father and hugs him. Then sets him down immediately when he notes the look on Dad's face. "Sorry, I just *love* Lacey Chabert. Don't you just *love* Lacey Chabert?"

Hall cannot believe Lacey Chabert isn't competing in the finale, since she's more talented than anyone in the world. I try not to feel jealous. He gets as close to the TV as he's physically able, threading his hands through his hair as if prepping himself to meet her in person. All throughout Craig's and Candy's dances, he's filling us in on Lacey's film history like a talking IMDb page. "Doesn't this show usually air on Mondays?" Kaia asks in her lazy, vaguely interested way, but she's promptly drowned out by Hall's play-by-play of *Christmas Waltz*.

"It's one of her best," he informs us. "*Christmas in Rome* might be my favorite, but"—he frames his mouth with a curved hand, as if imparting a tremendous secret—"don't tell *Winter in Vail*."

"I won't," Felix and Mom say in unison, one of them sarcastic and the other sincere. I glare at my brother.

He crosses his eyes at me.

Hall's good humor evaporates when it's Lucas's time to shine. Strobe lights spangle Lucas's face as his charismatic essence unrolls from center stage like a fog. Lucas's most popular single, "Send Tweet," which he dropped a month after our breakup, begins to play, and I am struck with a very, very bad feeling.

I wish I had a thicker skin. I try to be a steel wall, but a deft jab sends my confidence plummeting. Lucas's dancing partner emerging from the shadows in a red polka-dotted swing dress is a throat punch, and I feel my mouth curving into a gruesome smile. So *this* is why Lucas posted about me, dragging my name, our relationship, back into the public consciousness.

They dance together, looking so in love, until she pretends to stab him in the heart with a toy knife, and Lucas death-drops to roaring applause. As he rises back to his feet, face twisted with emotion, the song fluidly rolls into a passionate instrumental cover of "Evil Woman." It's intolerably cheesy. I can barely see him, my vision is so red and pulsing.

Lucas goading his fans into attacking me anew was for votes on a dance competition show. Using me to stay relevant, to increase his odds of winning. He was in a relationship with Dani for so much longer than he was in a relationship with me, their breakup fresher, but I suppose their split wasn't sensational enough for a whole dance number. How must Dani feel, watching this?

"Oh, this little twat," Dad snarls, watching him. He never met Lucas, but he knew we dated, since the media documented every minute of our relationship with almost frightening obsession. My parents came by my house once when the paparazzi were hanging around, snapping pictures of me whenever I opened the door. A six-figure payout would go to whoever got the first clear shot of me wearing an engagement ring, so there were strangers with cameras outside my house day and night. One of their vans backed into Dad's car when we left to drive to a restaurant, busting his taillight, and he climbed out of the car to holler at them. After our relationship ended, my parents were relieved. I told them Lucas "didn't treat me right," so they likely deduced that he cheated. If Dad really knew what Lucas was like, he'd be in jail right now.

"Let's turn it off," suggests Mom, but we're all riveted. Nobody moves, except for Kaia, who turns around on the couch and rests her chin atop it, checking up on me. Worry sparks in her eyes.

You okay? she mouths.

I nod.

She extends an arm, hand squeezing mine. She yanks me closer, then whispers, "I've got a hex on him."

When she turns around again, Hall leans in. "You want to go bake some cookies?"

"No. I want you to have Lucas roll around on the floor like he's on fire."

Hall glances from me to the television. Thinks better of asking me if I'm sure. And then Lucas is dropping to his knees, onto his back, rolling around on the floor, just like he's on fire.

Power surges through my veins, blazing hot overtaking that horrible, eerie cold until it's burned away, until it's gone. I am the Goddess of Revenge, masterful, unstoppable.

Athena snorts. "What is he *doing?*"

"Interpretive dancing," her husband mansplains. "Very popular nowadays, on these sorts of shows. I don't like it."

Around and around he rolls, for long enough that his dancing partner, Jenna, starts to get concerned. She bends forward, whispering to him. I hear whispering, too—that of my fifth-grade language arts teacher: *Your only limit is your imagination!*

"Jump up," I murmur, staring at my weasel of an ex-boyfriend without blinking. Lucas jumps up.

"Macarena."

Lucas breaks into the Macarena. To save face, Jenna also does the Macarena. "What in the ever-loving hell," one of the judges can be heard saying.

Evil woman, indeed. "Pick her up," I mutter out of the corner of my mouth. My befuddled little puppet picks Jenna up. "Hold her high."

The audience, confused by his weird rolling and Macarena, cheers when Lucas, eyes wide with alarm, grips Jenna by the waist and hefts her over his head. Finally, he's doing something impressive! Something that makes sense. Except he doesn't put her down. He runs back and forth from one edge of the stage to the other, carrying Jenna, whose hair bounces along, hanging in her face.

I time this stunt to continue for exactly a minute. Which, in rushing-back-and-forth-carrying-a-woman time, feels like roughly an hour. He's pink in the face from exertion, arms wobbling, legs bowing. His grin is pained, big white teeth clenched like Bender's from *Futurama*. Jenna is clearly bewildered. It isn't her fault that he's such a douchewarbler, so I let him put her down. I am a benevolent goddess, after all.

"Rubber snakes," I whisper. "Rubber snakes everywhere."

Rubber snakes rain from the ceiling. Lucas jumps, dodging them, anxious fingers splaying. He's terrified of snakes. Jenna's head tilts, scouring the ceiling to find out where they're coming from.

This music will never do. I instruct Hall to replace it with a non-Auto-Tuned recording of "I Blame Myself," a song Lucas never sings live because he simply doesn't have the range. His unfiltered voice explodes across the room, embarrassingly pitchy. I cannot describe in words how cathartic this is for me.

"The fuck?" Dad says hoarsely.

I double over, clutching my stomach, muscles cramped from holding in laughter. Kaia throws me an electric smile, eyes wide—

"It's the hex!" she cries.

"Are you watching this?" Grandpa calls to Grandma. "Get in here! Look at this asshole."

Grandma, who'd wandered off, returns. Her brows lift, eyes

cool and haughty as they slide to mine. "You must've done a number on him."

You have no idea.

Her lips twist into a small but approving smile. She holds up her wineglass in a silent toast, then turns and leaves the room.

This salute is the first positive reinforcement I've received from her in years. It bolsters me. "Make Lucas crab-walk," I tell Hall.

We all delight in the crab-walk. Felix is crying real tears by the time Lucas, who has gone six minutes over his allotted time, slips his socks onto his hands and makes them talk to each other.

The show tries to cut to commercial, but I force them right back on the air. Lucas karate-chops the host and two judges when they attempt to coax him offstage.

"Maybe we should stop," Hall advises hesitantly. "Don't want to go overboard."

I'm too deep now. "Overboard! What a great suggestion. Does this stage come with curtains? Give it curtains and close them. I want a nautical scene."

"Bettie—"

"Make my wish come true."

His mouth snaps shut, grim. But curtains dutifully sweep across the stage, closing around Lucas. Cameras pan to the judges, some of whom are standing with their hands in their hair, jaws slack. A million reaction GIFs have just been born. I can't hear what they're saying over Kaia's hooting laughter. Then the cameras snag on Lucas again, curtains parting to reveal him wearing a gold-trimmed bicorne hat and black greatcoat atop a wooden prop ship. Three people Hall culled from the audience are circling him in Baby Shark costumes. The show attempts to cut to commercial again, but no dice.

My eyes are burning from not being able to blink, enraptured. "I want him to mime the content of *Leon of Naples*," I say, "while delivering lines from *Blade Runner*."

Lucas draws a long plastic sword from his scabbard. Begins to fight the same railing that took Napoleon's mother's life. Then, in a bid to colonize the ocean, he jumps off the ship, right over a shark, and launches into his monologue.

....

CHAPTER TEN

Countdown to Christmas: 6 Days

#DorminationElimination LUCAS DORMER UNHINGED ON DANCING WITH THE STARS.

JENNA JOHNSON SPEAKS OUT: "I don't know what happened. I couldn't make him stop."

DEREK HOUGH BREAKS HIS SILENCE ON LUCAS DORMER'S OFF-THE-RAILS PERFORMANCE ON DWTS WITH A COMMENT ON CANDY OLSHIP'S TIKTOK: [Pictured: A chocolate chip cookie emoji, thought to be a nod of support for Bettie Hughes. Fans and detractors associate the scandal-plagued star with the chocolate chip cookie emoji (in lieu of a Little Debbie Raisin Creme Pie).]

"NONE OF YOU UNDERSTAND ART!" NYT Writer Kelly Frederick Claps Back.

TONIGHT AT 11: INTERVIEW WITH DISGRUNTLED DWTS FOURTH-PLACE CONTESTANT, WHICH REMARKABLY ISN'T LUCAS DORMER. "Do you KNOW who my father is?"

"This is excellent," I snicker, scrolling through trending remarks on every social media platform. "Rot in social backlash hell, you dumb son of a bitch."

Hall shows his dissatisfaction today by wearing a sweater with Heat Miser's face knitted on it (I am also wearing a knitted sweater, made by request, which says BETTERIE THAN REVENGE). Last night after we went to bed, he was going on about how much he was looking forward to wrapping presents (A different bow for each box! Little sprigs of evergreen to look like miniature Christmas trees! Bells! We can get scented glitter!), to which I replied that most of us don't wrap our gifts, we simply slip them into bags. Mom wraps, because she's cute, but the rest of us don't bother with fancy packaging. What counts is the fancy present inside.

"Hall, come look at this one. Lucas is a meme." I'm joyscrolling through pictures of cats with bicorne hats Photoshopped on. Lucas has a song called "Exile" and Historical Twitter is having a field day with the lyrics.

When Hall chooses to ignore me, carefully pressing down the corners of his origami Kermit (he's making the cast of *The Muppet Christmas Carol*), I lower my phone with a frown. "Oh, come on, don't be mad about the present-wrapping. There's nothing wrong with using bags."

"I'm not mad," he says airily. "Just disappointed."

"What if I build a peanut butter bird feeder thing with you?"

He scowls. "A pity bird feeder."

"I mean, yes. I don't make a recreational activity out of smearing peanut butter onto pine cones, personally." I can't take him like this, in his Heat Miser sweater and pile of paper Muppets, hair magnificently rumpled from shoving his hand through it in frustration, not even humming Christmas classics under his breath. The full, sulky mouth and tense jawline that I certainly do not think about in a salacious way. "Do you want me to wish for a million rolls of gift wrap? We'll wrap up the kids like mummies, it'll be hilarious."

Hall shrugs, not taking his eyes off his project.

I exhale a sigh. "How does a white elephant gift exchange sound?"

He tosses Fozzie over his shoulder and stands abruptly. "It only sounds like the most incredible thing *ever*."

"Okay, calm down," I say, but I'm smiling.

"But it's got to be a proper white elephant," he tells me, pacing now. "No conjuring. We've got to get the presents ourselves, properly. No magic."

"Wait, what?" Maybe this wasn't such a good idea. "Never mind. I'll go get the peanut butter."

"Too late." His eyes sparkle, and an ominous sensation slides through me. "Bettie, do you know what this means?"

"I'm truly afraid to ask."

Hall spins, magicking himself up some sunglasses and a neon-green fanny pack. "Holiday road trip!"

✳

Hall's insisting we do this the *proper* way, building *proper* memories of the warm/fuzzy/hijinks variety, by forgoing magic for the entire day. Including teleportation. Sounds ridiculous to me—if one is capable of teleporting, why would one ever not teleport? "Use it or lose it," I intone ominously as we shut the front door behind us. "Think about that, Hall."

He smiles sweetly. "No."

We pick our way over patches of ice to the red pickup. He doesn't know how to drive it, but boy does he love sitting in front of various windows in the house with his forehead pressed to the glass, staring at that big, old-fashioned red truck with a Christmas tree poking out of the bed. Grandpa, who loves cars (he drives a '56 Bel Air, blue as a tropical summer sky), can't get over the fact that there's no indication of the make and model anywhere.

"Kinda miss the onion carriage," I muse, sliding into the driver's seat. The carriage, along with the unicorns, evaporated on our first day here. My family believes I hired the horses and carriage for an elaborate stunt, all except for young Honeysuckle Lou, who climbed on one of the unicorns and flew on its back for six whole minutes. ("But Mom! I was *flying*!" "Sure you were, sweetheart.") "Jeez, Hall, the smell in here."

He sniffs. "What's wrong with it?"

"I feel like I'm snorting candy cane dust every time I breathe."

"New York Peppermint Patties," he corrects. "This engine runs on them."

"It's just *York* Peppermint Patties, not New York. And of course it does." I blast the heat, but even when our vinyl seats are nice and toasty, the air retains a sharp bite.

Hall carefully buckles himself into his seat, spreading a new scrapbook open across his lap. He will be documenting the day's journey, writing our names in calligraphy across paper with foil swirls. *Holiday ro-oa-oa-oa-oa-oad triiip!*

"I wouldn't really call this a road trip," I caution, wary of bursting his bubble. "We're just going to go park in town and walk around. Where to first? There isn't much local shopping, but we've got Jackson County Hunting and Fishing Depot, Teller City

Market, Shahad's Toy Shop, Gold Rush Bookshop, and Teller City Trading Company. Or if you're in the mood for outdoorsy equipment, there's Ski You Later and Keziah's Snowmobile Rental." I remember sledding on these hills when I was younger and involuntarily smile. Felix, Athena, Kaia, and I had fun together, once upon a time.

"Gold Rush Bookshop," he decides. "But can we take the long way? I want time for road trip games."

"There is no long way." I gesture to the steep path wending down the mountainside, straight between Cheers Chocolatiers and Silver Mine Dining on Cottonwood Lane, to Old Homestead Road and Gold Rush Bookshop, two doors down from the gingerbread town house. I never paid much attention to its neighbors before, but I appreciate that he built my new place between a store and a café. Once Christmas with the Watsons is over, I can enjoy freshly baked scones every morning. Maybe we can get a pulley delivery system going on between our windows.

"Right there." He points as a new sign fizzles into existence. The sign directs left, into the mountains, where, one could assume, the road barrels its way through them and all the way around. The name on the green sign, predictably, reads *Holiday Road*. He definitely loves naming stuff after himself.

I indulge him with a left turn, and he grins. "What are your top three cities?" he shoots at me. "Go!"

"I like Hanoi. Umm." I consider the question. "Barcelona. And probably Amsterdam."

"Mine are Waikato, New Zealand; Santiago, Chile; and Santa Monica, California."

"Santa Monica?" I repeat with a laugh. The road is well paved, smooth as a ribbon. Spruces and firs jump out of the way as the road continuously forms ahead of us, sky foggy and white-gray whispering through the gaps between them.

"It has the two best words in it. Santa and Monica."

"Why do you like the name Monica so much?"

"It sounds musical, don't you think? *Monica*." He repeats the word in different registers. "Some words have a sound that I just like, don't know why. Like *belvedere* and *elephantine* and *polo*." I shake my head, smiling. I think that what I like the best about Hall is that even though he's seeing more of the world and its ugliness now that he's at ground level with us, he's remained steadfastly *nice*, viewing humanity through an optimistic, rosy lens. Nothing I have said or done, nor my family's occasionally rude or unseemly behavior, has corrupted that. He is so wonderfully different compared to most of the men who've been part of my life—so many of them strutting and showy, possessive, with tempers and dark moods. He is un-abashedly joyful. He is sweet with no self-consciousness. And the true kicker: he says exactly what he feels.

"I am very ecstatic about spending the day with you, shopping for your wonderful family," he gushes, which is a statement I never dreamed I'd hear uttered un-ironically. "Okay, now we have to play I Spy. I spy something . . ." He stares directly at his target. "White."

"Is it the sky?"

"Yes! It's the sky! This game is excellent. Now it's your turn."

"I spy—"

"Hold on." He holds a Polaroid camera against the windshield and squints through it, snapping a picture of the sky for posterity. "You'd think my favorite color would be red or green, but it's actu-ally white. An opalescent sort of white, with dashes of other color."

"Like the sky," I say, bemused. "Or snow, more like."

Hall gently grasps my arm. "We know each other so well."

"I think you know me a little better than I know you, actually. How did you come to be the Holiday Spirit?"

"I simply am."

"Yeah, but where did you *come* from?"

"Nothing."

I cut him an exasperated look. "I'm getting to know you so much better already. Where do you draw your power from, then? There has to be some kind of source for it. That's how magic systems work."

"I draw my power from nothing and everything." He's writing down whatever we say, hand a blur across the page. Now he's peeling off stickers. *That's how magic systems work* is bordered by an iridescent Pegasus and a rabbit peering out of a top hat. "Now that's pizzazz," he murmurs to himself, smoothing the edges.

I give up. "Nothing and everything is such a non-answer."

"No, this is a non-answer. The chicken parm sandwich from Domino's. That's where I draw my power."

I laugh. "Chicken parm powers, it is." We rattle over a long suspension bridge that, according to an elaborate overhanging sign, is called the Disbelief. Tufts of snow flurry directly into our path, like an airplane's condensation trails in reverse. "Are you making it snow? You're such a breaker of your own rules. I thought we weren't using magic today."

"I'm not doing anything," he replies evasively, jabbing the radio button to drown me out with "Last Christmas" by Wham! I wonder who taught him to lie.

Probably Felix.

"This time of year is unbeatable," he prattles on. "A sublime car ride through the snow—"

"Thanks to *you*, Elsa."

"Listening to music. This is one of my favorite songs in the history of songs. The lyrics remind me of this really amazing book I read before I was corporeal. It was difficult to read physical books, since I didn't have hands, but I listened to it on audio. What do you think?" He slides his sunglasses over his nose, then up on top of his head. "On or off?"

I glance at his thermos of coffee. "How many shots of espresso do you have in there?"

"What, this?" He holds it up. "None. This is Nestlé Coffee mate creamer. Spiced rum cake." He drinks it till the last drop, then refills it by tapping its side. "I watched a commercial with two people drinking Nestlé Coffee mate spiced rum cake creamer together, looking quite sated, and I thought, 'I must have that.' Highly recommend!"

I'm howling. "You're supposed to add creamer to coffee, not drink it by itself!"

"You want some?" He proffers it. I push it carefully away. Rocks and lumps of ice crunch under the tires, nothing to see but snow-dusted trees, the drab sky, and, to the right, Teller City nestled in the basin like a toy town. Hall takes pictures of the view on his gold Polaroid.

I glance his way. His sweater's changing patterns every two seconds, but he doesn't seem to be aware of it. When we left the house, he was wearing one with cats sitting in gift boxes in outer space, shooting laser beams from their eyes. Before we were out of my grandparents' driveway, it was Santa's boots sticking out of a chimney. My attention bats around between his shirts and the road, observing the procession: *Get lit*, with a Christmas tree. *Merry Christmas, Ya Filthy Animal.* Johnny from *Schitt's Creek*, saying *Ah, see, the Christmas spirit is all around us.*

It's his ability to be so open, I think, that loosens the lid on my jar of pleasantries that I normally keep airtight. "I'm glad to be spending the day with you, too," I tell him, then clear my throat. It's ridiculous that exposing sincere feelings makes me blush. "I hope it'll be everything you want it to be."

"This is my first holiday as part of a family. The white elephant gift I contribute must be absolutely perfect—I've been waiting to do this for years and years and years."

I sober right up. I hadn't thought about that—how much he'd be looking forward to this. He's been supplying the world with holiday cheer but wasn't able to participate in it, watching the fruits of his labor from a distance. This is the *Holiday Spirit's* first real holiday celebration, and out of any family he could be spending it with, he's getting the Watson-Hughes clan. It's tragic. I genuinely feel sorry for him.

I inwardly pledge to make it up to Hall somehow. Give back a little bit of that joy he's trying so hard to imbue in me.

"What else do you want to do, now that you're corporeal?" I ask.

Hall has a GOALS planner devoted entirely to this. "Go on a roller coaster with a friend. Share a Bloomin' Onion at Outback Steakhouse. Take a picture pretending to hold up the Leaning Tower of Pisa. Go see the Red Sox play. Volunteer at an animal rescue. Solve a crime. Go to adult magic camp again."

"Again?"

"I went a few times, but that was before I had hands." He acquires a wistful, faraway look in his eyes as he flexes his hands. We both have a silent moment of appreciation for them—Hall for their functionality and me for their appealing gracefulness, slightly roughened up from all the new use. Furthermore, it strikes me that he has *kind* hands. Which is nonsensical, hands can't be *kind*, but that's exactly the right word for them anyway. "I need a purple velvet cloak first, so that I look the part. Modern performers gravitate more toward sequins and feathers and flash, but I prefer the classic look—waistcoat, white shirt with a stiff collar, slicked-back hair, and a jewel-toned cloak with a deep hood for extra mystery. I know a million tricks already. I've been practicing them with my invisible tendrils of self, waiting for an opportunity to be able to hold cards."

"Can't you conjure up a purple velvet cloak?"

"When it comes to street magic, I can't cheat. It's against the code." He returns to his list, which goes on forever. "I want to stand under the stars on a balcony. Play mini golf. Go dancing in Paris. Make a smoothie while blindfolded. See a movie in a theater."

A lot of these are surprising to me. These are . . . very *human* desires. I would have expected a list like (1) Make a snowman. (2) Make another snowman. (3) Turn self into a living snowman.

"I'll eat a Bloomin' Onion with you," I say, shifting in my seat. Snow begins to fall harder, thicker, as he turns toward me. "We can stand under the stars on a balcony."

"Really?" A luminous grin spreads across his handsome face.

"Sure, why not?" Even though the thought of it makes me jittery for some reason, makes my foot apply more pressure to the gas pedal. *Whoa there*, I tell myself, slowing down.

"We probably won't have time for real magic camp," he says quietly after a while, mostly to himself. What a picture he makes. Honestly. I am sitting next to a magic man with the most devastating cheekbones the world has ever known, soulful hazel eyes that I really don't think have always been hazel, lips that can only be described as "pillowy," and cute, floppy hair. He's cologne advertisement handsome. And he is visibly destroyed by the thought of missing out on learning fake magic, because he has seen all that humanity has to offer, and assigns the most importance to what he views as the very best parts of humanity. It's a perspective that can only arise from observing the world for thousands and thousands of years and evaluating for himself what matters most in life.

"Maybe we can find some magic trick tutorials to watch on YouTube?" I offer him a smile and catch myself imagining that this is my real life. How nice would it be to share a Bloomin' Onion with somebody . . . nice?

My focus cuts to the ring on my left hand, a veritable disco ball, and I slip sideways into wondering if anyone will ever love me enough to offer me a real one. Aside from the three men who have proposed, of course. Among my social set, people get engaged just to get engaged. It's a whimsical flight of fancy that dies before it can become real. We celebrate our engagements with parties, demanding congratulations from people we haven't spoken to in years, but when someone asks *When's the big day* we only have a vague *Oh, probably springtime . . . a year or two from now. Or three. We're really not in a rush.*

None of my engagements have been real engagements. My engagement to Hall is the least real of them all, and yet, he's the best person I've ever been with. He pores over his list of hopes and dreams, his features serene, and I have to remind myself I'm not *with* a man like that. When I visualize Hall's perfect match, she looks like a woman from a Hallmark Christmas movie: She loves baking cupcakes for her many friends, has loosely curled blond hair, and never stops smiling. She organizes toy drives for orphans and is incapable of being mean. Her name is probably Tess.

I have plenty of good attributes, of course—I'm always down for a fun time, I can tie a cherry stem with my tongue, and I have a knack for finding hidden gems when traveling. But I'll admit I'm probably a *tad* more self-involved than is decent and am fond of revenge schemes. I have never baked a cupcake for a loved one. I glance sideways at Hall and twist my lips. Men like him don't want women like me.

✳

"Can we stop at Arby's, please?" he asks when the road he invented leads, not all the way around town and back again to the Watsons' like I thought, but into a town I don't recognize. The mountains have sunk down into the earth, replaced by shorn cornfields and lower elevation that messes with my balance. "They have the meats."

"I hate turning left across three lanes of traffic." I squint at the road signs. "Where *are* we?"

"Shelbyville, Indiana. It sounded like a magical place. We'll go back to Teller City, but I wanted to prolong our road trip."

I sit with that for a moment, waiting a beat too long to move when the light turns green. "We've been in the car for less than an hour, but somehow we've driven . . ."

"One thousand, two hundred and forty-one miles," he finishes. "What a trip, even with shortcuts! Anyway, I'm starving. How about you?"

I indicate. "There's a KFC." It's an easy right turn.

Hall sinks back against his seat, eyes narrowed. "I know too much about their eleven herbs and spices." Then he pitches forward again, pointing at a bank. "Can we go in there?"

"What for?"

"I like lobbies. I see a chandelier. I like chandeliers."

I deny Hall this request, because I think it would look suspicious to walk into a bank for the purposes of lurking. As I wend my way through town, focusing on the GPS (which I am almost positive speaks with the voice of Lacey Chabert), Hall asks to go inside every store that he recognizes from commercials. Big Lots. Chico's. Kroger. Jo-Ann Fabrics and Crafts. "The HOLIDAY INN EXPRESS!!!" He takes a hundred pictures, going out of his mind. "Bettie! You have to stop!"

We waste half an hour at the Holiday Inn, taking selfies in front of anything that says Holiday Inn. At first, someone on the staff looked like they wanted to get rid of us ("Are you booking a stay?" "No, we're just looking, thanks.") But one of their colleagues recognizes me, and they argue in whispers about whether or not I'm Bettie Hughes. It's absurd to think that Bettie Hughes is at a Holiday Inn Express in Shelbyville, Indiana. One of them raises their phone to snap a discreet picture, which is my cue to leave.

I steal a small Holiday Inn notepad and pen from the desk on our way out, which Hall admonishes me for, but he can't bring himself to give it back. He gingerly tears off the top sheet and sticks it inside his scrapbook.

"Take a right at the next exit," Hall tells me. I slow, whisking under an overpass and, impossibly, right out of the Wendy's drive-thru in Teller City.

I almost slam on the brake. "How did you do that!" I yell, stuttering along, checking my mirror. "Holy shit."

"Over there." He points the way to Gold Rush Bookshop.

"I know that! I can see where we are." My nerves fray as I edge into an ice-slicked parking space on the street. "You're insane. You need to give me warning before you change states in the blink of an eye."

Hall's barely listening. "Isn't it lovely?"

Gold Rush's display window is done up in festive lights. Next door, the Blue Moose Café is done up similarly, bulbs wrapped around the moose antlers on its hanging sign. They're both hopelessly outshined by the town house, however, which Hall's evidently been adding to. Along with enough blinking decorations to rival the Las Vegas strip, he's put an inflatable Santa Claus on the roof, boots sticking out of the chimney, and Christmas trees all over the small front yard, which are bathed in an inordinate quantity of snow. "I remember when I asked for a beach mansion," I sigh wistfully.

"Your mouth said *Hawaiian villa* but your heart said *gingerbread fairy tale*," he replies sagely, jumping out of the car before I can poke him.

"On second thought, if we're taking shortcuts, I want you to raise the *Titanic* out of the ocean and put it in Grandma's backyard. It's going to be my white elephant. Imagine the look on everybody's faces."

"No can do, we're not using magic to get whatever we want today."

"And by *we*, you mean me, because you're certainly still using it for yourself," I return grumpily.

He deliberately looks away. "It's in my nature to use it constantly, so I can't help it. But it isn't in *yours*. Shame on you for trying to break the rules."

I splutter, and he walks faster to avoid being called out.

I follow him inside the store, edgy by habit even though it

doesn't matter if someone tells Grandma they spotted me here. And if I stay in town for good (which, until Hall gives in and makes my beach house a reality, looks likely), I'll be *permanently* here. At some point, my family will notice. They'll ask why I moved to this town, how long I've been here . . .

The bell dings as the door opens. Hall enjoys it so much that he backtracks and reenters simply to hear it ding again. A guy around my age is browsing, and he goes bug-eyed at the sight of me. My stomach pinches, knowing what's going to happen next, already feeling like a piece of public property. He'll ask me to autograph a receipt. He'll want a selfie. If I say no, he'll call me awful, unspeakable names—

"I love your sweater," he remarks, then moves on. I watch to see if he'll covertly slip out his phone, but he doesn't. I'm in shock.

"Uh, thanks," I reply, not loud enough to be heard.

"Mine's nice, too." Hall glances down at his own LET'S GET ELFED UP sweater, then covers himself in horror. "I didn't put that there!" He quickly changes it to a rated-G OH, DEER.

"What happened to a proper day of doing things properly?" I can't help but tease.

He sidesteps behind a rack of keychains and lets out an annoyed exhale.

The store is tiny but whimsical, with trellises of ivy against one wall, the others brick and outfitted with modern industrial-style shelves. The Milky Way is painted on the ceiling. I fill my basket with multiple sets of finger paints, because it's important to nurture the arts in my beloved nieces and nephews, whom I cherish, and not at all because their parents are going to hate dealing with finger paints. Hall asks a friendly woman who works here if they've got "anything to do with magic" and is soon laden with books. *Iron and Magic* by Ilona Andrews. *Vanessa Yu's Magical Paris Tea Shop. Freddie Mercury: A Kind of Magic.*

"This is going to help me get in touch with my inner magician," he declares, holding up a copy of *Again the Magic* by Lisa Kleypas. I give him a thumbs-up. Hall is on his journey now.

As we leave, he compliments the workers' festive holiday vests, leaving all of them in great moods. "Thank you and good night! Let your hearts be light!" They wave at him, and a smile tugs at my mouth that I can't for the life of me put away.

"Find anything for white elephant?" I ask when we're back in the truck.

He shakes his head.

"Me, neither. I want something suitably bizarre."

"I want something unforgettable." He pages through one of his new books. "Un. For. Gettable."

I turn to him in the cab, rubbing my hands together in front of the vents. "Now what?"

Hall eyes the landscape. Purses his lips. "Go down to the end of the street and make a turn on the corner next to Last Dollar Lanes Bowling."

"What's back there? Hall, you have to tell me."

"I physically cannot. I like surprises too much."

I make the turn; right as the bowling alley flashes by, *bam!*, we're at an intersection in another town. "Damn it, Hall!"

"Brake! Brake! You have a red!" He halts the car with his magic, and I turn to glare at him.

"Where are we?"

His soulful gaze is a dangerous counterattack, melting my scowl away. "Morris, Wisconsin. I found a brochure in the tower room of your grandparents' house for this weird little place called . . ."

He fishes the brochure out of his pocket and smooths its trifold illustrations. "The Junk Yard. It's supposed to feature all kinds of curiosities, and you said you wanted a bizarre white elephant gift, so I think it might be the place. They have *Beetlejuice* wallpaper. A teapot engraved with the entire text of *Alice in Wonderland*. Taxidermied raccoons."

"Sounds promising." I'd love for Athena's husband to have to deal with a dead raccoon. "Which direction do I go?"

"Straight. According to the map, there's this big round bend in the road, and it's off to the right."

There's no snow on the ground here, but it's been raining, mixed with sleet. Only when my eyes are straining to glimpse past the windshield wipers and the headlights have automatically switched on do I realize the sun is going down. I hate that it gets dark so early in winter.

I spot a large building with bright-burning windows and Hall exclaims, "There!" I slow down, but there's no mistaking the timber sign out front, held up by the paws of an enormous metal grizzly bear standing on its hind legs. *Fireside*. The place is clearly a restaurant now.

"Sorry, Hall. Looks like they went out of business."

"Wanna go in, anyway? I'm famished."

"The parking lot's full." As I mention it, a Jeep passing in the other lane turns in front of us, on their way to dinner. "We'll be waiting ages for a table."

"If we keep looking, maybe we'll find another curiosities shop nearby. Sometimes when businesses close, it's because they're moving to a bigger location, right?"

"Worth a try."

I drive around, passing through a town called Beaufort, but we don't wander across anything that resembles the place in Hall's brochure. We try a couple regular stores, with little success aside from discovering a music album called *How to Be a Human Being*, which piques Hall's interest. I see several thousand things I'd want for myself, and Hall sees several thousand things he'd want to give out "as stocking stuffers," but nothing good enough for his white elephant. He's putting tremendous pressure on himself. This is going to be the gift of the century. The millennium.

Our trip should be considered a bust: we've been driving all day with not much to show for it aside from the indie rock album, finger paints, and Hall's new books. I glance sidelong at Hall as he pages through one of them, which he's angling away from me because *It contains too much magic for mortal eyes*, and I'm hit with a pang of disappointment that the day is drawing to an end.

Hall fiddles with the radio, trying to retain Christmas music stations as we move out of range. "You were right, we should have gone into that restaurant back there," I lament, my stomach grumbling. "I'm starving."

"Can I pick where we go? I love trying new places."

Hall wants to go to White Castle, because it's "majestic, don't you think?" but changes his mind at the last second. "Let's try Rally's." So I drive to Rally's, but right as I'm about to make the turn, he cries, "Little Caesars! Please? Sorry. I won't change my mind again. I just love that Little Caesars commercial, the one where the two people lay their heads flat on the table to look at how thin the crust is. It's so thin."

But the Little Caesars sign reminds him, somehow, that Dunkin' Donuts exists.

"Hall!" I snap through clenched teeth, switching my turn signal off. The car behind me has watched this happen twice, and honks.

"I *know*, but it's Dunkin' *Donuts*, Bettie." He gazes pleadingly at me. "I swear on my life, all I want is a donut hole. Give me a pile of donut holes, and I'll die happy." He pauses. "It's dawning on me that I might be able to die now that I'm in a human body. A beautiful human male body." Another pause. "I believe I am having an existential crisis."

Dunkin' Donuts is closed. His crisis escalates.

Hall is so heartbroken that he can't bear to commit to any other fast-food establishment but is somehow of sound enough mind to reject my suggestions. Ultimately we drive by every restaurant, blood sugar plummeting, barreling toward the outskirts of town. Then the outskirts of the outskirts.

Over the next forty-five minutes, snow steadily picks up ("I promise I'm not doing it this time. I was lying about not doing it last time, but this time I'm not lying"), making it difficult to discern roadside signs for food exits. "Hall, if you don't conjure me a burger right this second, I'm opening your door and kicking you out. Right into the road. We're lost somewhere in Wisconsin—"

"We're never lost. I know exactly where we are."

"—and we should be finished eating by now, but *no*, because you're too indecisive."

"I'm too sad to do magic." He slumps in his seat.

But not too sad to read. We discover that Hall gets carsick when he reads while in motion, but he won't stop. He switches on the interior light, refusing to put it down. I try to sneak a peek. "What are you reading?"

Hall shifts away. Says curtly, "Bettie, if you *please*."

"Why can't I look? Because of my mortal eyes?"

"Because you need to pay attention to the road, you reckless driver."

He's not wrong.

"It's getting too heavy to see through. Can't you teleport us to a Denny's?"

He sighs. It's a long, tortured sound, pickpocketed from Grandma's bag of theatrics. I'm going to have to talk with him about mimicking her. "I'm too motion sick to do magic."

I'm going to throttle him. We're in a town called Bonnaroo or Barryboo, flares of streetlights streaking through the blizzard. I hunt for a good place to pull over, because I cannot sit in this car for one more second. Luckily, an exit presents itself, and as soon as the car's in park, I jump out to walk off some steam.

Hall kills the engine, leaning across his seat to peer through the driver's-side window. His jaw goes slack.

We're in a half-filled parking lot, heavens violet and low, orange limning the skyline. The wonder transforming his features has a funny effect on me. A thin crack travels up my heart—I hear a breaking sound, like shattered glass.

There are tears in his eyes, big and shining with lamplight. "I've been all over the world," he whispers, "but this is the most beautiful place I've ever seen."

We're at a Cracker Barrel.

CHAPTER ELEVEN

································

A LONG, SKINNY FRONT porch with about twenty rocking chairs creaking in the wind is tacked onto the front of the restaurant. We step into a cozy, warmly lit shop rather than a dining area, which veers off to the left, separate from the retail section. It reminds me of stores from the Old West days, wood floor a gleaming blond, every nook and cranny teeming with Beanie Babies, Stewart's Cream Soda, and jars of hard candy. Christmassy merchandise is in full bloom: expensive Rankin-Bass, Americana primitives utilizing a lot of burlap, pip berry wreaths, rustic wall hangings, quilts made by the Amish. Teller City shops carry a similar atmosphere, but this is . . . a *lot*. Hall and I can't decide where to focus first, necks snapping as we gape all around like we've landed on another planet. "It smells like butter," he breathes, closing his eyes. "And maple syrup. Mmmm."

"I'm gonna go ask for a table. You stay over here and try not to alarm anyone."

Hall isn't listening. He's poking at a cast-iron skillet filled with Moon Pies.

"Table for two?" I ask the hostess, leaning for a better peek into the dining area. There's a lot going on in there, too. A bicycle and wagon wheels hang from the rafters. Every inch of wall space is adorned with old plates, black-and-white portraits of pioneers, deer heads, vintage tin signs, and banjos. Oil lamps are the centerpiece of every table, along with little triangular wooden blocks with pegs in them. Children are pulling the pegs out and sticking them back in, so it must be a game of some sort.

The hostess greets me with a friendly smile and an apology that it'll be a short wait. My stomach is eating itself. I join Hall in nosing around the shop, sniffing craft soaps and candles, tempted to nibble the ones that smell like food. Hall can't resist touching every single ornament, dropping borderline-inappropriate noises of appreciation. Other customers grant us a wide berth.

He picks up a rainbow swirl lollipop in the shape of a heart and holds it up to the light, a treasure in the wild.

A guy in a trucker hat nearby throws Hall a look that is crossed between confusion and annoyance, and I narrow my eyes at him until he turns away. I'm seized by feral protectiveness of Hall's personality, his worldview, what makes him different. It is so goddamn refreshing to spend time with a man who is this in touch with his emotions, who is respectful, sensitive, wise yet playful. He's made of literal holiday magic, not a single drop of toxic masculinity to be found. He wasn't raised with societal expectations baked into his every molecule, and the result is fascinating. A twinkling example of what could be.

I lean against a rack of quilted purses, the corner of my mouth kicking up. "I bet your heart is actually shaped like that." I point. "Like the hearts in cartoons."

He wings a brow. "My heart is the same as yours."

"Yours is sweeter."

"That's not true."

He's in denial. I show him a Grinch toy, and he scowls. "Ha!" I laugh. "That face! Now you look just like him."

He smooths his features. "Do not."

Hall is so much fun to tease. "You really ought to finish the movie. He redeems himself in the end."

"I find that highly unlikely."

"He does! He gives back all the stuff he took, and—"

"Your table is ready," the hostess says, appearing behind us. Hall pins me with a severe look, a reproach for defending the Grinch. His lashes are so dark along the lash line that from a few feet away, it appears like he could be wearing a hint of eyeliner. The jade in his irises is a stark contrast. Why would the universe make him this attractive?

As we're led through the din of the restaurant, I feel a rise of apprehension that's usually triggered by crowds, but luckily, no one notices me. Right as I reach to pull out my chair, Hall touches my shoulder gently. Begins to remove my coat. I revolve to help him tug me loose from my sleeves, and he grins at my obvious surprise. Then he pulls out my chair for me, gesturing for me to sit; after I do, he pushes me back in. We both order hot chocolate.

"You didn't have to do that," I mumble after the hostess leaves us, swallowing a lump in my throat. "You don't have to do fiancé things when we're alone."

He slants me a look. "Having good manners isn't a fiancé thing. It's a Hall thing."

I study him, thinking that being kind should be a Bettie thing, too, at least where it concerns him.

Hall's hot chocolate is gone before I'm finished ordering the wild Maine blueberry pancakes.

"I would like six more hot chocolates with my French toast," he tells our waitress. "And the Sunrise Sampler."

"Gotcha." She writes it down on her pad.

"I know the mini confetti pancakes are on the kids' menu, but could I have those, too?"

"You got it. Will that be it for you, sir?"

"No, I want the fish fry, too. With steak fries and cole slaw." He scrapes hot chocolate residue from the inside of his mug with a spoon. "This is the best hot chocolate in the world, did you know?"

"The secret is to heat the milk, add the cocoa, and then heat it up again for another thirty seconds," she stage-whispers, smiling as she scribbles down our order.

He hands the menu over with some reluctance, sorry to see it go. Then he says to me in a low, urgent murmur, "It was so hard to narrow that down."

"I can tell."

"I really, really wanted to try the chicken tenders." He stares longingly after our waitress, who disappears into the kitchen. "Maybe I'll get some to go."

"You'd have to. There won't be enough room on the table for anything else."

I glance curiously around the room, partially to take in the decorations and partially to make sure no one's surreptitiously snapping pictures of me. "No one's going to recognize you," he tells me softly, as if reading my mind.

I jerk back to attention. Hall's got his elbows on the table, fingers laced, chin on top of them as his eyes burn into me. They really do look like they're burning, an oil lamp flickering in them. It must be a trick of the light, but I imagine that I can see some of that unnatural green recede a fraction, giving way to caramel brown. And there's an otherworldly glimmer in there, twin sparks you can only make out if you're studying him extremely closely, from a specific angle. If I move just right, his irises become reflective.

"Did you put a spell on them? So that they won't recognize me?"

He shakes his head almost imperceptibly, mouth curving the tiniest bit. It is the softest curve there ever was. Everything about Hall is like that, easy and comfortable and happy. He's a collection of traits that adults like to scoff at as they grumble and age, as if contentment and curiosity should lie buried with childhood— but now that I think about it, it's an act of courage to march to the beat of your own drum, to behave with compassion and generosity, with wonder. Why are adults so serious, so cynical, anyway? Hall is warm sweaters and hot cocoa, face turned resolutely to the bright side. Every day is an exciting new adventure for him. He likes what he likes and doesn't care who knows, doesn't care what others think. I admire it so much.

I'm realizing just *how* much, sitting here across from him, batting back a warm feeling.

"You look different," he says calmly.

"How so?"

His shoulders lift, then let go. A slow blink of those long, dark lashes. Maybe he's putting a spell on *me*.

"You've been smiling more," he responds at last. "The first day we knew each other, you didn't smile as much. And it's something else, too." Another shrug. "Happiness can make someone look like a completely different person."

This gives me serious pause. Am I happy? My gaze slides to my glass of water, but I can't make out my reflection in it.

I look up again, and Hall smiles as he watches.

"What?"

"Nothing. You're just interesting to observe. Like a movie, except your movie is about someone who has been stuck in the *beginning* part of the movie for a long, long time. You know what I mean? The first half, before they've learned to grow and change."

"I'm like a movie?" I feel the confused expression I'm making, which makes him laugh. "What do you mean about a first half?"

"Nothing bad, only *interesting*. I've been people-watching since the Neanderthal days. So far, you're my favorite person to watch."

This stuns me for a moment. "I exasperate you all the time." I don't know why I feel the need to point this out. "When I make wishes you don't like."

"You know how I love movies? I've seen pretty much all of them, so I can usually guess where the plot will go. But with you?" Elbow on the table, hand against the side of his face to support it, he tilts his head in the opposite direction and raises his eyebrows in a *who knows?* sort of gesture. Then he casts his eyes down, lashes fanning crescent shadows on his cheeks, and idly begins to play the pegs-in-the-triangle game.

I'm still wondering if I'm bewitched, or if everybody else is, when our food arrives. "You went to magic camp when you were still a *spirit*." I stir my drink, watching him closely. "I can't get over it."

"Three summers in a row, and it ruled. Here, I'll show you some of my tricks."

He shakes a deck of cards out of his sleeve, earning himself an eyebrow raise. But his hands move too rapidly to follow, his smiles distracting me expertly. He's a master at sleight of hand. I've never found magic tricks attractive before and am shaken to my core by how hot I'm finding this.

Hall is unaware, happily making a quarter disappear. Then he makes me guess which hand it's in. (I'm never right.) Demonstrates the dexterity of his fingers by rolling it in front of and behind them in a swift flash of silver. It is honestly mesmerizing.

He plucks it from behind my ear. "Is this yours?"

"Look again. I think I dropped fifty bucks back there."

He reaches behind my other ear, revealing a handful of peanut butter pretzel bites. My favorite.

I munch on them. "You know, I think I'll keep you around."

He winks, and then his eyes widen in alarm. He stares at me strangely. A frown develops, brow creasing. "Uh-oh."

"What?"

"Nothing."

"Tell me."

He looks down, messing with the triangular peg game again. "Nothing," he mutters. "It's nothing."

I pry, but he's got whatever's bothering him under lock and key, so I eventually give up.

Hall overestimated the amount of food he can physically put inside of his body, facial muscles taut as three-fourths of his meal is shoveled into to-go boxes. He balances them in his arms as we weave back to the storefront to pay for dinner.

"Allow me," Hall murmurs before I can sidle in front of the cash register, bumping me out of the way with his hip.

"Where are you getting money from?" He's been buying stuff all day. Hall is only able to conjure Canadian money for some reason, which we exchange at the bank for American currency every couple of days.

"Somewhere in my pocket." Tucking his chin into the top to-go box to hold his tower steady, he fumbles in his pockets. "Here, hold this."

He hands me a lit sparkler.

"Jesus!" I cry, springing back. But then I take it from him before he can accidentally set something on fire as he keeps digging in his pockets.

"And this one," he adds, handing me another sparkler.

"Hey, you can't have that in here!" the cashier exclaims.

"Oh, hello," Hall tells the cashier. "Thank you so much for this experience. It's a magical wonderland here. You must love working at a place like this." He fills my hands with treasures: a bottle of cologne (Pitbull Man, by Pitbull), a train whistle, a miniature rhyming dictionary, a flashlight, a Pez dispenser, a hermit crab. The cashier monitors us with growing incredulity.

The sparklers finally burn to nothing. I cast around, not knowing what to do with the charred sticks.

"Do you sell Cracker Barrel postcards?" Hall asks, at last retrieving a wad of green bills. "I want to remember this."

The cashier rips her attention from my burnt-up sparklers, blinking. "Uh, yeah! We do, actually."

I offer to pay for his postcards, since he covered the meal, but Hall holds up a staying hand. "Keep your money, Bettie. You've got to start saving."

I snort. "Why on earth would I need to do that?"

He accepts his change and his bag of postcards, twisting to regard me with a serious expression that freezes my mocking smile in place. "You won't have my . . ." He almost says *magic*, but there are people around so he says, "*help*, forever. I'm going away as soon as you're sufficiently holiday-cheered."

"What? Didn't you say you might be here forever?"

"I can see now that I was wrong."

I can't believe what I'm hearing. "Do you *want* to go away?"

"Doesn't matter what I want. I thought maybe this would be a permanent thing; it's never happened to me before, so I didn't know exactly what to expect. But I can feel it." His brow furrows, sliding me an unsettled glance. The corners of his mouth are turned down, and for once he isn't cheerful at all. He looks older somehow, more like an entity that's lived for thousands of years. "My days are numbered. It's like a countdown clock in here." He taps his skull. "When everything is quiet, I hear the ticks."

I stare, heart beating fast. It's lucky that I'm ambivalent about holiday cheer, or else I might have reason to be worried. Very quickly, I've grown reliant on his magic, snapping his fingers to get me anything I want (or a skewed version of it, anyway). But I'll never be sufficiently holiday-cheered, which means that he's wrong, and isn't going anywhere. I have the vicious, cold, impenetrable heart of a withered old hag. It's half of my appeal.

"But I'm a one point five."

"Actually, you're a seven. You were at six point eight when we walked into this restaurant, then it shot up over dinner. My magic trick with the coin really did something for you."

My jaw drops. "There's no way. I'm a pitiful one point five. Look at how joyless and awful I am!"

He takes my measure, lips pressing into a smile that makes his eyes go soft, almost sad. "Our time will run out even faster if you continue caring like that."

I scoff. I can't think of anyone who's less in danger of evolving into a happy-go-lucky gingerbread-loving schmuck than myself.

"I don't know what you're talking about. I don't care about anything."

"Mm-hmm."

"It's true. I'm all about number one."

"Sure, sure."

As we pass the empty hostess station on our way out the door, Hall's gaze snags on the array of menus, and, on impulse, he snatches one and stuffs it up his shirt.

"Hall!" I whisper-gasp.

His face is pleading. "I know. I don't know what came over me. Should I put it back?"

The hostess has returned—it's too late now. I clamp my hands on his shoulders and maneuver him out the door before he can steal anything else.

Night has fallen, but, *oh, thank goodness*, it isn't raining or sleeting anymore. The clouds are in retreat, the sky a black inkwell glimmering with stars. He strolls over to the truck, half-terrified, half-gleeful, those strange irises burning bright. "I couldn't help it, Bettie. I need this keepsake. And I need to know what else the menu has to offer. I wasn't able to finish reading before she made me give it back."

"We've all stolen something," I reassure him. "Sometimes it's a Cracker Barrel menu . . . sometimes it's Williams-Sonoma bathroom accessories . . ."

Hall becomes more hysterical. "Bathroom accessories? Is that what I'll be moving on to next?" He leans all of his body weight against the passenger door, and I notice how the cold metal instantly fogs up in reaction to his warmth. There's a mild but steady blaze around him at all times, and if I listen close, I can hear the pop and crackle of embers. The shimmer of sleigh bells. "I'm a criminal."

"You're only human," I joke.

Hall delicately places his to-go boxes in the truck, then fishes out his menu to admire. He looks so melodramatic about it, I almost expect him to break into song.

"Do you want me to put it back?"

"No." He spins, menu strapped protectively to his chest.

"Well, I gotta use the bathroom before we take off. Don't do any more crimes until I come back."

He's already gnawing on an unfinished slice of bacon, even though I know he's full to bursting, concentration wholly riveted on his spoils. "Yeah, yeah, gotcha."

I do have to use the bathroom, but the main reason I dash back inside is to buy a magic kit that I spied on the wall while Hall was checking out. DAVID COPPERFIELD'S VAULT OF SECRETS. OVER 50 TRICKS INSIDE! Adult men might not be the target demo, but this is probably as close as he'll ever get to magic camp if it's true that his time really is limited. Not that it will be, because I don't feel cheerful at all. But just in case.

Bouncing back outside, I'm cold right down to the marrow, and when I catch my reflection in the window of the truck, I'm taken aback. I *do* look different, as if I have an inner light, almost like Hall does. This must be The Hall Effect, then—a consequence of being in his merry orbit. Right up until I hand the package to Hall, I'd planned on saving it for Christmas. He should get to tear open a gift along with everybody else, and not merely for appearances in front of my family.

I can't help myself. I want him to have it now.

He holds it in both hands, sucking in a little breath. "Oh, *Bettie*," he says quietly, gaze so starry that I can't look directly at him for long. It's like peering into the depths of a billion answered wishes. "Is this for me?"

I nod.

He cups the side of my face, then retracts. "This is my very first gift. I've never gotten one before." He slips it into the car and wraps me up in a hug. "*Thank you*," he murmurs into my hair.

I can't move, blinking rapidly at a streetlight over his shoulder. My throat begins to close, the corners of my eyes burning. As though a carver takes a chisel to my heart, I feel another sliver of ice chipping away.

When he lets me go, I smell faintly of peppermint and my fingertips are warm to the touch. "You're welcome."

I don't think Hall cares as much about the gift as he does about the fact that he was given one. "Wait until I learn all these tricks," he says with one of his lopsided smiles. "You won't know what to do with yourself. You'll be all in swoons."

"Swoons?"

Hall chucks my chin with his thumb, then drags it over to the base of my throat where my pulse thumps. "Yeah. You know? All aflutter." He can't see, but burnished gold washes over the red and green plaid of his sweater, starting at the shoulders like epaulets, trickling all the way down.

I stare at him, every ounce of amusement escaping through my cracks, evaporating in the chilly air. My pulse is hammering, pressing right into his hand. I feel like Hall is becoming more and more human before my eyes. Changing. The pure wonder remains, but on top of that, other pieces of what it means to be human, of what it means to be a human *Hall*, are layering one over the other in startlingly rapid succession.

"If I could summon special effects in real life," I force myself to say, throat bobbing, "I'd disappear in a puff of smoke whenever I leave a room instead of using the door."

His eyes twinkle. "I could make that happen."

"That would be incredibly extra."

"The only way to be." He withdraws his hand to snap his fingers, knave of hearts card appearing between his thumb and forefinger. "I'd have flames shooting out of my hands. And then I'd go like this"—he punches the air—"and—*fireball*! Swoosh, right through the wall."

"You're absurd." It comes out sounding like *You're adorable*.

"You'd love it." He grins. "Don't lie."

"If we were actually in a movie," I remark, "we wouldn't have to drive back through all this snow, we'd just slide from now into tomorrow, appearing in the living room out of thin air to admire this sunrise you've been talking up so much. I would simply clap my hands and—"

CHAPTER TWELVE

Countdown to Christmas: 5 Days

HALL'S ARMS ARE around me, just as they were in the snowy parking lot seconds ago, but fiery reds and yellows now burn across the right half of his face, all the colors of daybreak tracing lips that are unsmiling for once, catching every red ribbon in his rich brown hair. The colors enunciate shadows where they flatter most, carving out sinfully attractive cheekbones jawline like a blade. I watch his pupils flare even though the abrupt change of light should make them constrict. His Adam's apple works down a swallow, faint red blotches appearing on his throat. "Here we are," he says, pitch low.

"How does that work? I feel so well rested. Not at all like I stayed up all night."

"You didn't. I moved us through time. Gave all your systems a touch-up so that you won't feel the drag." He pauses, and suddenly I am hyperaware of each light press of his fingertips resting on my waist. He doesn't seem in a hurry to let go; after a moment of consideration I summon the bravery to slowly wrap my hands around his tan, freckle-splashed forearms. He feels so substantial beneath me. Strong and sure.

With literal light shining on our proximity, all of our easy playfulness from before dissolves. I'm wondering what's going on, question marks shooting off left and right in my brain like fireworks, but why should an embrace have to mean anything? Hall might not view this closeness as an intimacy cue like a human would. Also, he hasn't verbally indicated that his status as someone who's never crushed on anyone has changed, and I don't want to be presumptuous. He likes physical touch, period. He likes being close to all sorts of people, not just me. It's better to not ask if there's anything going on at all, to simply enjoy what I can.

"That's thoughtful of you," I manage as his gaze flicks upward to my forehead. He tucks an errant strand of black hair back into its pin. It's the perfect excuse to break away, but his hands return to me immediately, dropping a fraction lower on my hips. His thumb brushes the narrow gap between my shirt and waistband, the skin-on-skin contact sending up a shiver. His thumb quickly corrects to a higher location, ever the gentleman.

Standing this close, I am trying to breathe normally, trying to ignore how my heart rate has kicked up, how his touch has left behind a deliciously burning trail, and it's ridiculous. I don't usually react this way even when I'm making out with a boyfriend half-naked in his bedroom. And Hall and I aren't even being physical! All he's doing is *barely* touching me, watching me like . . . perhaps my pupils are dilating, too, like he hardly registers the play of light on my own face because he's becoming illuminated to other parts of me instead.

His eyes are liquid, attention dipping to my mouth. My heart accelerates. But then he smiles brightly, and it dissipates the haze; my vision's blurred his edges into the sunlight like a red-hot aura.

"What do you think?" he wants to know.

Oh, right. The whole bringing-me-to-the-sunrise-and-watching-it thing. A necessary experience, in his opinion. I haven't been able to bring myself to look away from Hall.

"Very romantic." My stomach drops. I wish I could rewind time like Hall can. "Kidding! Just kidding."

The tiniest of furrows creases his brow.

I rip my gaze away. Teller City is aglow, its hues and the depths of its buildings transformed by the sun, each rooftop a canary diamond. Bursts of orange peek between mountains, low-drifting clouds haloed with it. Hall was absolutely right to lament that I've never watched this part of the day unfold. "I thought it would be indistinguishable from sunset, but it's really not," I marvel. "There's a difference, isn't there?"

The white roads are unmarred by tire tracks or exhaust, no cars in motion from what I can see. Hall leans so close that the curling ends of his hair brush my temple. Whispers low and conspiratorial, breath ghosting over my lips, "There is. New beginnings are special. We're the only ones awake, watching the sky come alive." He pulls back just enough to view my reaction, the heat of his gaze pinning me in place. "Very romantic . . ." His gaze skitters lower again, glancing off the hollow between my collarbones. "As you said."

I think he's teasing, but it's hard to be sure. My mouth quivers slightly, as it does sometimes when I'm flustered and I like someone but I don't know if they feel the same, so I desperately don't want to be found out. "I—"

"If I'm going to be murdered, I want witnesses," someone cuts in loudly, and I whirl in alarm, breaking Hall's hold. Felix and Sean have wandered into the living room. "You have to pick Marilou up from the airport for me. I can't be alone with her."

I slide a hand up the nape of my neck, cheeks heating. What in the world were we doing? I remind myself, before I can start to feel too special, that he hugs everyone. He's a zealous hugger.

However. I do not think his expression is quite so *intent* when it comes to everyone else—eyes growing dark, slower to blink. Jaw tightened. Breathing quickened, more uneven.

I check to see if he's blushing like I am, but his back is turned as he absently straightens ornaments on the tree. Maybe I'm imagining that spark of interest. Maybe I'm projecting.

Our little moment that I'm going to spend the rest of the day overthinking is rapidly smashed by relatives clomping downstairs. Grandma has no qualms taking advantage of Hall's generosity, so she requests pancakes. Hall then takes advantage of my preoccupation by roping me into helping him, and before I know it I'm in an apron, adding blueberries to batter.

We take turns ruining Felix's morning by hugging him and giving our final goodbyes. Kaia gives him a tarot reading and draws the Seven of Swords, which none of us know anything about, but Kaia looks pretty grim. Even though Felix says he doesn't believe in tarot, he makes her do another reading. She pulls a Two of Swords for him this time and says nothing, only shakes her head. Felix is too green to eat breakfast. When at last Sean's car zips up the steep driveway with Marilou in the passenger seat, he hides behind the Christmas tree. "Callista started it. She brought all of this on. I think she's trying to sabotage my relationship."

"It takes two to let that happen," Mom points out. It's as close as she can come to chastising him.

But when Marilou pokes her head into the living room, calling out, "Knock, knock! Merry Christmas!" it would seem all of Felix's worries were for nothing.

"You feeling all right?" Marilou asks him, stretching up on tiptoe to kiss her husband's cheek. It should be noted that baby Adrian, bundled in her arms, wears a scrunched expression, as if disappointed in his father.

"Uhhhhh." Felix's stare follows her warily about the room.

＊

He's still twitchy two hours later, unwilling to trust Marilou's light, easy chatter. He thinks she'll bring up his contact with Callista the second he gets comfortable. But if she *doesn't* really know, he certainly isn't going to tell her. Every time Marilou speaks, Dad glares at Felix.

"I'm not cheating," he persists when she excuses herself to go nurse Adrian. "Callista keeps contacting me from new phone numbers. Stop looking at me like that."

"How you could get any woman interested in you is a mystery to me," Grandma replies frankly, enjoying her glass of cabernet. It is almost one in the afternoon.

"Mom," my mother says chidingly. "Felix is a good boy. A real catch!"

Felix is petulant. "I'm not a boy, I'm a *man*."

Kaia pats him on the back. Today she's smudged her thick black eyeliner in streaks that extend all the way to her ears, wearing a fitted black suit complete with a white cravat around her throat. "There, there, champ. Your balls will drop one day."

"I've sired seven children! That I know of!"

They bicker until Marilou returns, Felix pinching Kaia's knee under the kitchen table to shut her up. She quickly lifts her knee, smashing his hand into the table. Tears spring to his eyes. He tells her she looks like a postapocalyptic butler.

Dad frowns at Athena, who's been a statue in the corner by the pantry door for half an hour. "What are you doing?"

"It's the fan," I reply, pointing. Mom has a fan going to help with her hot flashes, oscillating back and forth. Athena's figured out that she looks the most attractive from this particular position, the airstream tossing her hair. The chair she usually claims is empty, since if she were sitting in it her hair would blow all over her face. She won't put it in a ponytail to keep it out of the way. The last time her hair was in a ponytail, Octavian said that it made her head look small.

"I'm over here because the fan makes it drafty," she snaps. "But I want to be part of the family conversation, so. It's fine. I'll stand over here in the corner, out of the way." She rubs her hands down her arms.

Felix coughs. "Martyr."

"Oh, honey, I'm sorry." Mom vaults out of her chair. "I didn't know the fan was bothering you! Here, I'll shut it off."

"*Aaand*, that's where she gets it," Grandma murmurs.

Felix, who needs to have menopause spelled out for him, loudly says, "I think the temperature in here is fine. You feeling all right, Mom?"

Marilou scoots her chair closer to me. Leans in. "Hey, you."

I nudge her shoulder with mine. "Hey."

"Congratulations on your engagement! Your fiancé's in the family room doing magic tricks for the kids. They *love* him. Daisy told him she's 'thrilled' he's going to be her uncle." The blood drains from my face. Marilou doesn't notice. "You picked a good one, Bettie."

She's right. I picked such a good one, in fact, that I can't see myself settling for my old type ever again. I used to be partial to artistic bad boys: brooding, sleep-deprived, tall and lanky. I couldn't count on getting a text back and was never sure of our status. It was as if they all had magnets that drew me, but those men all look so small and powerless now. What are troubled bass players and up-and-coming actors with ulterior motives compared to the Holiday Spirit?

Hall has been seamlessly ingratiating himself, especially with Grandpa and my parents. If I were actually engaged to him, this would be validating beyond my wildest dreams. I can't begin to imagine what they'll think about the guy I *do* end up marrying, if that ever happens.

It's just now hitting me that Hall masquerading as my significant other isn't merely covering up any magic I might want to deploy while visiting my family for the holidays. He's unwittingly setting a standard, which all men who come after him are going to fall short of. This is the only truly good man I've ever introduced to the Watson-Hugheses, which is . . . sad. They're all going to hate whoever I decide to date after Hall. *Hey, remember that happy young man in the wholesome sweaters who did magic tricks for the kids? Why couldn't you have made it work with that one, Betts?* And they'll say it right in front of my future boyfriend, because tactful they are not.

I should have introduced Hall as my personal assistant. Damn my love affair with engagement rings and attention!

"So helpful and considerate, too," Marilou's now telling me. "He carried my suitcases to my room for me."

Felix glowers at the table, profile turned away from Dad, who he's accurately guessed is mentally berating him for not carrying his wife's suitcases to their room himself. Mom accidentally knocks him in the cheek with her elbow while fanning her face with one hand.

"So sorry, dear." She kisses his boo-boo, and Felix allows himself one swift glance at me. My smirk prompts him to kick me under the table. I am briefly transported back to childhood vacations, my siblings and I crammed into the back of a van together, pinching each other as hard as we could and suppressing all our yells so we wouldn't get into trouble.

To Marilou, I say, "Hall is . . . great." It's a weak reply.

"How did he propose? I love proposal stories." She spins her engagement ring around her finger, reminding us all that Felix proposed to her at a small award ceremony televised only on local programming, high off the adrenaline of the evening. He didn't even win. It was, as Grandma decreed, *abominably gauche*.

Felix's glower has taken on a life of its own.

"He proposed spontaneously, on an ordinary day. He didn't even have a ring ready." I don't know why I say this, but it sounds right.

Marilou nods. "Love it."

I sit up straight, a flicker of pride running through me. "There I was, listening to Mariah Carey on the record player"—she brightens, as she's the one who gave me Mariah's albums—"and he came into the room, and I said, *Hey, there*, and it just happened. It's like he dropped out of the sky one day, being everything I needed."

"Do you have a dress picked out? A date? I love wedding dresses. *Say Yes to the Dress* is my favorite show."

She and Felix got married in Vegas, at his urging. He'd already *done the big wedding* multiple times, so by the time wife number four came along he thought big weddings might be a curse, dooming them to fail. If they went as low-key as possible, purposefully making choices that ran opposite to his previous ones, they'd last forever. Marilou, who was getting married for the first time, wore jeans and a tank top. I look at my brother, who is trying to change the subject to his movie. No one listens. Three different conversations are currently taking place in the kitchen, so he can either participate in (1) wedding talk, which doesn't cast him in the most flattering light, or (2) a conversation about hunting quail, which he's actively avoiding because he once shot Grandpa in the ass while hunting together, and which he's hoping no one will bring up, or (3) a heated debate about Minecraft between Octavian and Frangipane.

He shifts toward Octavian and Frangipane. "What are we talking about? *Enter the Dragon*?"

"*Ender* dragon."

"Oh. That's cool. I like dragons."

"You don't know what we're talking about." Frangipane rolls his eyes. "This is out of your depth, Felix." (Felix is his father.)

Hall, finished with his magic show, strides into the room and tells Mom he likes her hair.

Her hair looks the same as always to me, but she glows with pleasure, fluffing it. "I was feeling a bit daring this morning and gave myself a trim. Barely half an inch! I didn't think anybody would notice."

Felix rolls his eyes.

"Looks great, I meant to tell you," Dad cuts in hastily.

Ever the doting fiancé, Hall tells me I'm looking lovely, too, and sweeps by to get cracking on an apple pie. My mother's in love with his apple pies. "I can't wait to have you in the family," she gushes to him, drawing his hand between hers. "I'll finally have someone to bake with. None of my children have ever shown any interest."

A squeak sticks in my throat. I can't open my mouth, staring awkwardly at nothing. It's as if Marilou's congratulations have made it all real, and until now, my family thought we were only playacting. They didn't pepper Hall and me with questions about our big day, or if I wanted A-line, mermaid, or ball gown.

"Magic tricks," Felix heckles from out of nowhere. "What is he, twelve?"

"You shut your mouth," I return with a violence no one expects, judging by the looks on all their faces.

"Don't knock it till you try it," Hall tells him, mellow as a field of spring flowers.

Felix laughs without humor. "I've got better things to do."

"Like what?" I lean forward, burning holes into his eyes with my focus. "Texting? Sending someone pictures of my personal life?"

"Easy," he growls.

"You managing to find somebody's nine of diamonds in a deck of cards would be the single most remarkable thing you've ever done."

"Bettie," Hall warns gently. The warm, deep grumble of his tone makes the tiny hairs on my arms stand on end, not unpleasantly so.

"If you don't like card tricks," Hall tells Felix, "I've got a cup game, too, where you find out which one's hiding the Ping-Pong ball. And then *this*, which is my favorite." He holds out his hands, showing us that they're empty. Then he claps, and the cheap black wand from his David Copperfield kit appears between them. "Watch." He taps the wand against a cupboard door where salad bowls are kept, then opens the door. Pulls out a pineapple "Ta-dah!"

When only two people clap, he settles a fist on his hip. "Did the rest of you see? It's a pineapple!" He holds it aloft like a trophy. "I made it appear in the cupboard with this magic wand! I didn't even use . . . other . . . methods."

Felix leans back in his chair, doing his best to convey boredom. "Don't quit your day job."

Hall's eyes tighten to snappish red hots, and he is very likely about to shoot back a retort about his day job literally being magic production when Mom cuts in. "Let's go sit somewhere else," she suggests. "The oven makes it so hot in here, plus all the body heat. The heat is making us grumpy." Dad gets up, turns the fan back on. She tosses him a reproving look, but I can tell she's secretly grateful. He runs his fingers through her hair briefly while passing behind her.

"The children took over the TV in the living room, thanks to the Xbox *you* had to bring," Grandma says dryly, with an accusing glance at Felix.

"You wanna entertain them?" My brother raises a challenging eyebrow. "I would love to see that." Playing with Grandma when we were kids consisted of us lighting her cigarettes (before she quit) and painting her toenails. We spent summers eating Lunchables on the patio with our feet in buckets filled with water, since we weren't allowed in the Jacuzzi, while she watched her "stories" (soaps) and ate the most expensive chocolate truffles she could get shipped from France, pretending not to realize she'd locked us out of the house.

Grandma raises a brow, too, probably inwardly writing Felix out of the will.

Hall unspools colorful silk ribbons from his pockets, piles them in front of Felix in some sort of passive-aggressive display of power, and commences prepping ingredients for his pie. "Anyone want to help me cut out some snowflakes? Madeline?" He holds up a sheet of pie dough. "We'll make a decorating bar."

"Oh, that sounds delightful!" Mom exclaims.

Felix, who is usually her Best Boy, has had enough. "Pie isn't even that good," he mutters. "It's not like it's *cake*."

I'm trying to concentrate on Hall, worried Felix will hurt his feelings, while Marilou laments not getting to wear tulle for her wedding. Athena brags loudly about the tulle she wore for *her* wedding, and Kaia mutters, "Yeah, you love that dress so much that you keep your first wedding pictures up on the wall still."

"You can put that prejudice against divorcées back in the 1800s, where it belongs," Felix snaps. "Just wait till *you're* on your third divorce. Courtney will burn your house down, too, and then you'll know how it feels."

"Can't divorce if you never get married," she shoots back. "Courtney and I broke up. I don't have time for a relationship. Haven't you noticed that I never date anyone for longer than a month?" She raises a brow, flicking him a derisive look. "Take notes, big brother."

Mom gasps. "But you said you loved Courtney. Didn't you get her name tattooed on you?"

Kaia twists to show us all a delicate black-and-gray flower blooming on her shoulder blade. "Not her name. It's just a daffodil."

"Her birth month flower, though, right?" Mom replies. "That sounds serious."

Kaia shrugs. "Doesn't have to be. Now it's just another flower for my garden."

I didn't realize Kaia was breaking up with her girlfriends intentionally to avoid long-term relationships. Maybe this is why she always appears to be so chill: she cuts off anything and anyone that could distract from her career. Kaia has the type of personality that comes with a fence; you don't want to push her for details about her personal life. I've been trying to imitate it with no success, since *my* life is frequently turned inside out and dissected. But when Kaia settles her attention on you with placid aquamarine eyes, not a negative vibe in the wide blue sky of her mind, you mind your business.

Grandma levels a finger at Kaia, dark eyes fastened intensely on her. "You remember what I said."

"What'd she tell you?" Dad glances between them, circumspect.

Kaia peers at him over her iPad. "When I was six, Grandma yanked me into a closet and told me to wait for my career to be established before *popping them out*." She uses air quotes.

"Oh, for God's sakes." Dad throws his head back in exasperation. "Bettie!"

I jump. "What?"

"Not you!"

"Not her, what?" Mom is halfway listening. "What did Bettie do?"

"I'll tell you what Bettie did," Felix says mutinously. "She sprang some guy on us out of the blue, telling us they're engaged even though none of us had heard of him before."

"Well, *now* you've heard of him," I retort.

"You all knew Marilou for months before I proposed," he prattles on, refusing to let this go. "Why don't you have any pictures of Hall on your Instagram? It isn't *you* at all, to not put a thousand pictures of your boyfriends online."

I'm beginning to sweat. "So what if I don't? My relationship is nobody's business."

"What are you suggesting?" Kaia asks our brother. "Are you trying to say that Bettie and Hall aren't a real couple?" I'm grateful for the expression she throws my way, like, *can you believe this nonsense?* But since it isn't actually nonsense, my stomach tightens.

"No," Felix replies defensively. "But I think the engagement was obviously rushed. It just seems like something she'd do to get a reaction out of us."

I stand up. "I didn't get engaged for attention."

I absolutely did, but you'd never know it from the impassioned flames being ignited in me right now. Felix is feeling bad about himself because he didn't give Marilou her dream wedding, so he's poking holes in my love life, and I don't want to hear it. I've rapidly grown protective of my sham relationship and our future sham marriage. "Leave me alone, Felix. You thought the sun and the moon were the same size until you were thirty years old."

"What does that have to do with anything?" He stands up, too. "You launched a perfume that made people's hair fall out! And you melted the face off Athena's Celine Dion Barbies when we were kids." An entirely irrelevant cheap shot.

Athena gasps, eyes narrowing viciously. "Those were limited edition."

"Bettie, be honest," Felix interrupts, loud enough to steamroll Athena as she mutters to everyone that I pretend my eyes are green on social media and nobody ever calls me out on it. Which is throwing stones, if you ask me. I saw her in a commercial last week pretending she dyes her hair at home with Nice 'N Easy when I know for a fact that her platinum tresses are the work of a dedicated stylist. "Did you convince him to get engaged right before you came here?"

Someone else responds *"Excuse me?"* before I get the chance. There's a loud *thwick*, and quite suddenly, Felix can no longer argue.

As his head is covered in tinsel.

Directly behind me, Hall's armed with a T-shirt cannon stuffed with tinsel, wielding it like a machine gun.

"Bettie did not have to *convince* me to propose to her," he tells my brother darkly, an uncharacteristic hardness in his gaze. He doesn't glance at me, keeping that dangerous glare leveled on Felix. "It is all very well if you want to pass remarks about me, about my clothing or hobbies, but I won't sit by while you imply that I wasn't *on my knees* in front of this woman, absolutely gone for her, hoping with every fiber of my being that she would say yes to being mine forever, and to letting me be hers."

The authoritarian tone shuts everybody up.

"It is an honor to be Bettie's fiancé," he informs the stunned room. "Just as it was an honor to be her boyfriend before that, and her friend before *that*. I count myself lucky every day that I get to be the man who makes her smile, that I'm the one she wants."

Everything about my mother softens as she regards him, as if she always liked him but now her esteem is irreversibly fixed.

"Have we reached an understanding?" Hall asks Felix, more steely than I've ever heard him.

Felix blanches. Grandma's chin has dropped, appraising Hall with a delighted gleam. This is the best excitement this kitchen has gotten since she successfully drove a wedge between Liam and Noel Gallagher of the band Oasis.

I think something strange is happening to my face—it's somehow hot, cold, and also losing feeling. All I can do is gape at Hall, in disbelief that he would go to bat for me with this sort of fervor, all to deny an accusation that's actually true.

Felix blinks a few times. "I'm sorry." He's clearly guilt-ridden when he turns to me. "I don't know why I doubted you. I guess I was—"

Thwick, and more tinsel explodes everywhere, piled high on Felix's head like a snowdrift.

"Sorry," Hall says hastily, lowering his weapon. "I was expecting you to argue."

Felix shakes the silver out of his hair with a scowl, which transforms into a reluctant smile when he notices how hard Marilou's laughing at him.

"He's certainly got my blessing," Dad remarks to Grandpa, who nods thoughtfully, watching us.

As Hall meets my eyes, the world seems to tilt sideways, and I find myself tipping right into him. He catches me in his arms, faint surprise etched on his face, eyes curious.

Grandma raises her glass in a toast. "To Bettie and Hall! Long may they reign!"

I don't know what prompts me to do it—maybe it's because I've suddenly found my face so close to his, or maybe it's because my relatives are raising their glasses to us one by one and it feels perfectly natural to do so—but I cup the back of Hall's neck and shock him with a kiss on his smiling mouth.

He responds with a jolt of electricity, smile disappearing, arms automatically tightening around me. Warmth shoots through my veins, prickling the tips of my fingers, bright pops of color speckling my vision. The press of his lips is gentle but firm until it isn't: his fingers thread through my hair, bunching it for a moment in his fist, and the kiss turns bruising.

Before I can register the charge, he releases me. He brushes a kiss to the back of my hand while holding my gaze, and somehow the action feels like dropping out of the sky, hundreds of feet from the earth.

Has anyone ever kissed my hand before? It strikes me now as the sweetest possible gesture.

Then he raises our joined hands over my head and twirls me in one fluid motion.

As I revolve, I notice how impossibly slowly Mom's glass is moving as she lifts it in celebration of us; how Athena's words, midspeech, are emerging low and stretched, taking an eternity to tumble out. A child's laughter echoes from another room, sound visibly vibrating the airwaves. And from above, tinsel that landed on the ceiling fan earlier is drifting in slow motion, taking all the time in the world as it glitters past us like camera flashes.

I wonder if the slowing of time is intentional, or if he's done it subconsciously.

After spinning me in a full circle, my lips still tingling from how unexpectedly—how *fiercely*—he reciprocated the kiss, the world catches up at rapid speed and no one is any the wiser.

"To Bettie and Hall," he says quietly at my ear, one side of his mouth hooking back into a grin. The grin is a secret wink, a *we fooled 'em, didn't we.* My heart drops, rattling in the pit of my stomach. Of course. It's all part of the act. He's gotten uncommonly good at playing the hero.

I try to match his grin, but, foolish as it is, I can't help myself from thinking: *I wish this could have been real.*

✳

Chapter Thirteen

....

F OR THE REST of the day, all I can think about is that kiss. Hall doesn't mention it or behave as though it meant anything, acting his usual self. Am I making a big deal out of nothing? The kiss was fairly chaste, after all. Or is he just playing this incredibly cool? That evening, I march downstairs with the goal of cornering him alone in the kitchen—if I hint around the subject in circles, perhaps I can guess his feelings without having to ask what they are outright. Maybe we'll kiss some more.

But before I can pounce on him, I hear that somebody's already beaten me to it.

"So, what would you say your favorite thing about my granddaughter is?"

I wince, backtracking behind the door.

"How do I choose when there are so many options? She smells just *enchanting*," Hall informs my grandfather earnestly. "I like the way her hair swoops at the ends. You know? And when she's telling you to do something you know is bad, she stares at you with this nearly unbearable force, like you couldn't look away even if the ground opened up beneath your feet, and I find myself feeling quite warm, like I've run all the way here from Florida."

I bite my knuckles to keep a weird bubble of laughter from escaping.

"Tell me more about how you two met."

There's a strange note in Grandpa's voice, which I wonder if Hall will detect; it sounds an awful lot like he knows something he shouldn't and is toying with my fiancé.

"How we met," Hall repeats. You do not have to know Hall at all to detect his sudden nerves. A stranger would spot it from across the street. I appreciate poor Hall's dilemma here: he's goodness and light, but lying is required in this situation. Lying to my nice, polite grandpa twice in one day. While my nice, polite grandpa stares him directly in the eyes. In the sanctity of a kitchen brimming with Christmas desserts.

"Yes, I'd love to hear the whole story," Grandpa replies, and I'm very glad to be on this side of the door.

"Um. Well. We met, which was lovely. And we were both instantly attracted to each other. Physically and emotionally."

"Don't spare any details, son."

"I . . . we kissed. Twelve times, on that first day." He hesitates, perhaps gauging Grandpa's reaction. "Fifteen? Twenty. We kissed twenty times." His phony reminiscing goes a bit dreamy when he adds, "It was *wonderful*."

"I see." Grandpa is clearly entertained. "What makes you think you're ready to get married?"

I strain to pick up every syllable. Whatever Hall's about to say feels so significant that my balance is affected—I shift my weight from one foot to the other, a hot prickle on the nape of my neck, similar to the eerie sensation of being watched from afar. His answer doesn't matter. None of this does. I should flounce right in, interrupting them.

I'm a statue.

"When it's right, it's right, you know?" Hall's stock response is for the best, and I have no business being let down by it. We're not really engaged. So he doesn't really like me that way, even though I've felt myself growing to feel . . . differently, about him. I can't help it. He's so sweet, I really had no choice in the matter. "She and I are different, but . . ." He considers the question more carefully. "She's a type of fun that I admire but that wouldn't be natural if I tried to emulate it. And I'm a type of fun that I think is good for her to be around, but that she isn't vulnerable enough to emulate herself. It's an unusual match, maybe, but the influence we've been on each other is . . . pleasing."

An inner light clicks on. *Oh.*

"Anyway." Hall clears his throat. "Hear anything lately about the Wall Street? Or the Broncos? Let's talk about mallard ducks."

"Let's talk about the sequins I found glued to the mallard ducks in my study," Grandpa readily agrees.

"I bedazzled them. You're welcome."

"Do you think you and Bettie'll want kids?"

My forehead thuds against the door, which is thankfully masked by Hall's loud cough. He regains his composure after a few seconds, sputtering out: "Mallards are omnivores. Their outer feathers are waterproof. They are the most common wild duck in the Northern Hemisphere. Egg incubation takes twenty-seven to twenty-eight days."

Grandpa laughs. "Okay, I hear you. I'll leave you alone now."

"Gastropods are a staple of their diet."

"Good night, Hall."

My grandfather walks out of the kitchen, closes the door, and without even glancing at me where I've flattened myself to the wall off to the side, says in a low, amused voice, "Night, Bettie."

I straighten myself out, grand and dignified. "Lawrence."

His eyes gleam. "What an interesting couple you two make."

"I agree. We're the trendiest item ever."

"Mm-hmm. And are you going to keep him around after the holidays are over?"

My eyes narrow. "I don't understand your meaning."

He chuckles once, makes a gesture that is somewhere between wave and salute, and strolls off toward his study.

"You forgot my tip!" I call. Grandpa's deep laugh booms from the staircase.

As soon as he's gone, I immediately burst into the kitchen, startling Hall, who drops a rolling pin to the floor.

"It's just me," I say breezily. "What are we up to in here?"

Hall lays a hand over his heart; the color slowly returning to his stricken face.

"Nothing whatsoever."

I consider teasing him about mallard trivia but am delightfully distracted by his new *BBQ MASTER* apron. Flour and pumpkin pie ingredients cover every surface of the kitchen. "Here." I dig into my pocket. "I've got something for you."

He perks up. "Another present?"

"Sort of. It's nothing big. Remember that old birthday card I made for Grandpa?"

He examines the folded paper in my hands with interest. "Yes."

"It made you laugh, so I, um. Drew one for you."

It's rather pathetic, actually. Since I couldn't stop thinking about

Hall today but didn't have much opportunity to chat with him (Grandma was hogging him. He's an eager audience for all her wild stories that the rest of us have already heard), I was wandering in the tower room, reading more of Felix's old *Leon of Napies* script, when I saw the card again. I remembered how it made Hall laugh.

It got me thinking that I would very much like to make him laugh some more. At Cracker Barrel, he said he likes that I surprise him. With this information in mind, I schemed up one-liners designed to do just that.

He takes a look, and it's just as I hoped:

He laughs from the heart, hand on his chest. "'Congratulations on your engagement,'" he reads. "'You're lucky to have me.'" He raises an eyebrow, eyes mischievous. "Is that so?" Then, he admires my logo on the back, which I've updated from my childhood days. The *Hughes & Co.* is now accompanied by a holly leaf.

"What do you think of the drawing?"

He turns it over. "Very . . . why nachos?"

"I was hungry."

Another laugh from him, and now I've become quite smug. I used to make these sorts of cards all the time but grew out of it. After picking up the old hobby again today, I had a *ball*. Since I didn't have anything else to do, I spent an hour happily losing myself drawing a dozen other cards that nobody would ever want.

Thinking of (Doing) You

Retirement Is the Time for New Adventures! Let's Open Up Our Marriage

Beware, the Veil Is Thin Tonight. Xoxo Slugs and Hisses

Your Aunt's Been Talking About You Behind Your
Back. I Don't Want to Get Involved, Just Wanted to
Let You Know

The part that amuses me most is imagining the expressions on
people's faces if I inflicted these jokes from me to myself onto
them, with no further explanation.

"And here's another present, from you to me," I tell him, handing him a different piece of paper.

He's all anticipation, but as he scans the first few lines, I watch
his excitement melt away.

"It's a list of names," he remarks uncertainly. "Who are these
people?"

"They're gossip writers. I want you to wish them ill. Not *physically* ill, but, you know . . ." I gesture to the second column, labeled
Ideas.

"'Melt their shoes with liquid nitrogen,'" Hall reads. "'Remove their door handles. Make their hands smell like creamed
corn no matter how often they wash them. When they pass a window, have them see a giant sloth staring back.'" His stare flickers
back up to mine, no longer amused. "Bettie, I thought you'd gotten revenge out of your system."

"What gave you that impression?"

Hall lowers the list, a muscle ticking in his jaw. "This is what
you've been working on for the past two hours? You said you were
planning a fun Christmas surprise."

"I did! Fun for me, surprise for everyone else. And that's not *all*
I was doing. I was also making your card. Remember how much
you like your fun card?" I flash a winsome grin.

Hall rakes a hand through his hair and turns away, deliberating for a moment. Then I hear a *click* of the kitchen doorknob as it locks, and he picks me up by the waist without warning. I emit an "Ahh!" that is a cross between gasp and squeak as he deposits me onto the counter next to rolled pie crust and a sack of flour.

"Bettie," he says, stepping directly between my knees. He plants his fists on the countertop on either side of me. Tilts his head in faint exasperation. "What. Are. You. Doing."

Truthfully, I don't remember what I was doing. All I can concentrate on is Hall's intense eye contact. "Uhh."

"The water buffalo you had me put in that woman's apartment," he goes on when I remain too thunderstruck to speak. "Did it make you feel better?"

I swallow, then force out a "Yes."

When he merely keeps staring at me, I cross my arms over my chest. "It did! A little."

"In the moment, it made you feel better. But then later on? How did you feel the next day?"

I bite my lip. "I don't feel sorry for Kelly Frederick."

To my disappointment, he slips away, returning to his baking. He pats down flour, flattens his crust with a pin, going through each step manually rather than snapping his fingers to get the job done. The only light in the kitchen is the yellow bulb in the range hood over the stove, which splashes against his profile and flares it over the wall in shadow.

"How did it make you feel," he replies at length, "when you wrote down all these names?"

I watch him guardedly. He doesn't glance in my direction. "Satisfied."

"Mm. And how did you feel when you were making that?" Hall gestures to the doodled nachos.

I shrug. "Happy?"

As soon as the word trips out, I realize his trick.

"If you do things that make you *and* others happy, I promise you will find that happiness much more rewarding than revenge. You found yourself in a position of considerable power when you conjured me; what you do with it can change who you are for the better, or . . ." He drifts off lightly. "Not. Don't allow yourself to get wrapped up in bitterness."

"Listen, Hall, I appreciate that you're good and pure and Holiday Magic. But some of us are human with scores to settle. Why should I let those awful people get away with publishing awful stuff about me?"

He presses his cookie cutter into the dough, carving out maple leaves. "Maybe I'm not human, but I'm also not who I *was* anymore. Not all the way. I'm ancient, but everything feels new. My old life is so distant that I think I'll soon forget what it was like. I don't know who I'm becoming. But I *do* know that my choices decide that. Conscious, deliberate choices. I am magic from the inside out, but have you ever seen me eager to use my magic as a weapon against anyone? I see the strange looks some people give me. The smirks. I hear the laughing whispers. Not everybody likes me—"

"They're stupid, then," I cut in quickly, indignant. "Give me their names."

He slants me a meaningful look. "It's all right that not everyone likes me. I like *myself.*"

I twist the hem of my shirt around my finger, shame beginning to filter in along with the stubborn anger that surges whenever I reflect on all the ways I've been maligned.

I don't like that Bettie Hughes, I think, recalling the snide remark of a woman I once passed on Rodeo Drive. *She's not very nice. Kaia and Athena are probably fake, but at least they're nice.*

Plenty of people have said pleasant comments to me over the course of my life. I don't remember many of them. My brain keeps only the worst experiences intact, transferring them all to long-term memory storage while compliments and praise rot away.

I'm rattling and angry and I know it makes people like me less. Knowing this makes me angrier. "I'll never be good enough, smart enough, beautiful enough," I burst out. "I'll never be as successful as the legend I've been compared to all my life. If I was born blond and they'd named me Crystal, I'd be so well-adjusted right now, probably a preschool teacher or something. I'm not a decorated actress or a brilliant singer."

He faces me sharply, eyes alight with something shrewd and hunting as he scans every detail of my features. "And what *is* it, exactly, that you want?"

Staring at each other, he sees me, and I see him, too. How he likes the intimacy of feeling he's in a position to ask me questions and receive honest answers, ones I'd avoid if they were posed by someone else. He likes being the inside man sorting through my thoughts with me, being the person I open up to.

"To feel better about myself. I want to feel fulfilled," I reply bluntly. "I want my aha! moment, to see the path that's right for me and be able to recognize it clearly for what it is. Like my mom. She found her path with cooking, and now I can practically see the inner peace shining from her orifices. I want that. But my only skill is coming up with spiteful wishes. I'm drawn to men who make bad boyfriends, ideas that make bad business ventures. My impulses get me into trouble, and I say the wrong thing too often. I'll never get it right."

Hall abandons his work, pressing gentle hands to either side of my face. The rest of the kitchen lights flicker on, the room soon glowing merrily. "That isn't true."

"You're going to tell me to cheer up," I sigh.

"You have a right to feel what you feel," he says. "But Bettie, you've been burning so long, and I know you're tired. You can't change anyone's opinion of you by getting revenge on them, even though it might feel good for a few moments. You're hurting yourself trying to be a version of perfect that you've made up in your head. The only one who expects you to be that version is *you*. You can let it go, if you want." He drums his fingers on the counter. "Also? Some food for thought? Your mom was nearly twice your age when she discovered that her passion was cooking. Soul-searching takes however long it takes, and really, I don't think it ever ends. There's no deadline for figuring yourself out."

I watch him wearily. He's right.

"Damn," I croak.

He folds me into a hug, and I go very still before ultimately melting into him. "I know you've probably heard this advice before, but you don't have to forgive the people who are bad to you. However, if they're not ever going to give you the apology you require in order to move on, then you have to let it go for your own sake. The best revenge is making peace with a past you can't change and figuring out how to make the future a happier place for yourself to live in. That's how you come out on top."

"I should be happier now," I remark, sniffling into his shoulder. "I have Elizabeth Taylor's ring. It's thirty-three carats."

Hall laughs softly. "Ah, Bettie," he says in a tender tone, slipping his fingers in my hair. "That might not be enough."

His breath is a relaxant, every aspect of him promising safety, care, a sure and gentle touch. I want to lean into all that and breathe it. I want to feel like this all the time. I don't want to be this scared and bitter person keeping all my grudges alive like a muscle that never stops clenching. Hall has a point. Ultimately, I'm the only one who suffers from the effects.

"I didn't want to hear any of that," I tell him. "But thank you for saying it." After a pause, I venture, "What if I make a wish that's only a *tiny* part revenge, but also for the greater good?"

He quirks a brow.

"I want to steal a ton of Elon Musk's money and distribute it to world hunger organizations."

He blinks in astonishment, then taps my nose, dusting it with flour. That half smile is back, which warms my heart. *You're back on track*, it says. "All right, Robin Hood, you've got yourself a compromise. Let's do just a *little* bit of crime before bed."

"Really?"

"Stealing from the one percent isn't stealing, according to the legislation."

Relieved that he's no longer staring at me as if I've fallen short of his hopes, I hop down and press a brief kiss to Hall's cheek. It lasts only for the space of a heartbeat. When I withdraw, I'm arrested by the bands of brown ringing his pupils. There are striations now where there weren't before, adding depth, a dimension of colors. He holds his palm to the spot where I kissed him.

The doorknob rattles. "Is this locked?" Mom calls from the other side. "Who's in there?"

Hall's eyes widen, the lock clicks, and Mom enters, sniffing the air suspiciously.

"I knew I smelled pie!" She frowns at Hall. "You've been baking without me."

"I've never seen these pies before in my life," he insists, taking me by the shoulders and positioning me in front of him like a human shield. "They're Bettie's, I swear."

She laughs, he tosses her an apron, and as I seat myself on a counter bar stool to watch them have their fun, Hall turns and throws me a quick wink. I love my mom to pieces, but I wasn't ready to share Hall just yet.

Which gives me serious pause.

What is *happening*? I brought him here to help me impress my family. Now I just want to impress him.

＊

It's late, but I can't sleep. I watch the silhouettes of snowflakes tumbling down, dark spots against the frosted-silver glass and the moon through the window. My mind won't quiet, functioning on high alert as if there's an occasion I've forgotten, something important I need to do, and I need Hall. I roll, leaning over the railing to peer down at his form on the bottom bunk. His eyes are closed, long lashes fanning shadows over his freckles; he fell asleep with one hand cradled to his cheek as if to hold my kiss in place. "Hey," I whisper.

Eyes still closed, he mumbles, "I should have tried the corn bread."

"Huh?"

He blinks groggily, snatching his hand away, burying it under the covers. "What?"

I wait a few seconds for him to fully wake up, then climb down the ladder and perch on the edge of his mattress. "Want to go to the movies?"

He runs a hand through his hair, sticking it up in the back. "It's one in the morning."

"I want to go to the movie theater with you. It's on your bucket list, remember?"

This snaps him the rest of the way awake. "Is Moonlit Cinema open this late?"

"No." I smile. "But you can bring the movie theater to us, can't you?"

He grins back. Drinks in the sight of me slowly. I can tell he's pleased that I'm taking initiative, inviting him on an unexpected adventure when he's usually the one filling that role. "Yes. I think I could do that."

Hall gives me a twirl. When I come to a stop, my outfit has transformed into a tea-length black dress embroidered with tiny gold beads, the hem of which he catches between two fingers as it flares. We both look at his hand, and he quickly lets the fabric go.

I admire his black suit, with a gold waistcoat and silver holly cuff links. "*Nice,*" I say with an appreciative whistle.

He bows at the waist. "I've got flair."

The bedroom expands, ceiling pushing up, shape-shifting into a cavernous theater. He keeps on holding my hand as the room moves around us, every part of it in motion, window stretching until it's swelled into a giant white screen between two deep red velvet curtains. A carpeted slope leads the way down aisles between chairs. Each light is the size of my fist, and upon a closer look, they're each small white-blue moons. He miniaturized the moon, then copy-pasted it.

I scan the faraway ceiling, the film-projector window. A second Hall stands ready to operate it, waving down at us.

"Popcorn?" the Hall beside me asks, proffering an old-fashioned red-and-white striped bag.

"Please and thank you."

We have the entire theater, of course, but after we treat ourselves to the seats in the center of the room, shadows begin to appear around us. Figures, setting the scene. When I watch them for too long, I notice that they ripple or glitch, features on some too murky to make out, while others are dim, grainy projections. Gregory Peck is seated next to Rita Hayworth. I hear Lucille Ball's laugh. They're suddenly everywhere, each one popping into being, milling about, settling in with coats and handbags. These are the same faces that hang on walls throughout the house with their names autographed in black slashes: Sidney Poitier, Frank Sinatra, Grace Kelly, Paul Newman, Rock Hudson, Sophia Loren. Grandma's personal idols, silver-screen legends of old, larger than life, inspiring my awe since I was small.

The screen's still blank. "What's playing?" I whisper.

Hall leans in, our shoulders brushing. He hands me a ticket stub, and I tap two knuckles against my grin as I read it.

Of course.

He pops open our vintage bottles of Coke, moon-lights winking out as the screen roars to life. The projector *click, click, click*s, spots and streaks blipping by in a succession of frames until the title card goes up. *His Girl Friday*. I have to tip my head all the way back to take it in.

Rosalind Russell as Hildy, eternal icon and *my* personal hero, appears. "I love her style," I gush in whispers, as though the shadow-profiles of James Dean and Dorothy Dandridge might overhear. "And her voice. I could listen to Rosalind Russell and Cary Grant ping-ping off each other all day. All that fast-talking, and how everything they say has two layers to it." I fold my hands over my heart.

I heard you the first time, Hildy's saying. *I like it, that's why I asked you to say it again.*

"Love how she eviscerates all these men," Hall adds. "What she does here with her hand. Everything I know about acting is that hand gesture." We both mouth Cary Grant's *A home with Mother. In Albany, too.*

"How many times have you watched this?" he wants to know.

"Couldn't tell you. I love screwball comedies. Did you hear that? He ad-libbed that." I nudge him. "Look at how Walter looks at Bruce when he asks if there were no twins."

Hall missed it, so he gestures to the other Hall up in the projection room. We rewind seven seconds, both grinning at Cary Grant, master banterer. A fizzy sensation powers up in my bloodstream to hear the soft surrounding laughter, Hall's arm touching mine on the shared armrest, the planes of his face aglow with my favorite movie. I bite my lip hard. If I let that smile out, there'll be no putting it away again.

"I wish I could pull off hats like that," I whisper, then soon grow aware of a slight weight on top of my head. Hall's given me Hildy's hat, which I adjust until it's the perfect angle.

"Watch him dab his eyes like he's crying."

"I know. His talent was unrivaled, really. Did you catch that?" I tap the back of my hand against his shoulder. "She said 'classified ads' but it's a play on 'ass.'"

He shakes his head at me, but he knows I'm right.

We take turns muttering the dialogue, and though he doesn't have it memorized as well as I do, he's an enthusiastic thespian.

My head lolls along the back of the chair, left to right. "You wanna know something?"

He waits, watching me.

I wave a hand toward the screen. "I miss wearing retro outfits. My polka dots. I hate to admit it, but I loved those swing dresses."

I wonder how it's possible for his eyes to shine like that. "Why do you hate to admit it?"

"Because I didn't want to be Little Bettie. I wanted to be my own Bettie."

Maybe I've gotten into my own head a little bit, about being perceived and judged and disliked by literally all of planet Earth. Maybe he's right and I'm the one who's been judging and disliking myself, projecting those insecurities onto the expressions of every passerby. And if anyone actually does dislike me?

I'm starting to wonder why it matters.

I swallow, settling back in my seat. "You know, that one GIF of Cary saying 'Get out!' comes from this movie." Hall's hand has slipped over to my side of the armrest, finding its way beneath my fingers. "Ohh, *look* at how he looks at her."

My gaze swivels from the screen to his face, and his expression knocks the wind from my chest. In my mind, my feet come out from under me—*whoosh!*—and I land, hard, in unfamiliar territory. Dazed, I tell him, "Cary Grant was in a movie called *Holiday*."

His head dips, a barely discernible tic. His eyes go dark and time itself seems to deepen. "I know," he breathes.

My eyes lock on his mouth. "I can't have him because he's dead, and nobody else will do." My eyebrows draw together.

He's looking at me like . . .

Like *that*.

And then swiftly away. His mouth purses, a serious expression overtaking his features as if he's just changed his mind about something.

"What?" I whisper.

He shakes his head, innocently replying, "Nothing."

My eyes narrow. "Hm."

He stretches his legs, shifting subtly away from me. "Pay attention to the movie."

Oh my, he's *blushing*. And secretive! Since when is Hall secretive? He used to process every single one of his thoughts and emotions verbally, and now he's dodging me with this "*Nothing*" business, just like a self-conscious human. And right when we were having a gazing-adoringly-at-each-other moment. Which probably doesn't bode well for the romantic notions I've been entertaining (they involve a horse-pulled carriage ride through Central Park and a broken axle, leaving us stranded with only each other's body heat for warmth).

On further, and disturbing, reflection, gazing-adoringly-at-each-other moments are a frequent occurrence for Hall. He gazes adoringly at my mother when she compliments his pies, and gazes adoringly at Hallmark Christmas movies, and icicles when the sunlight hits them just right, and . . . truly, I can't think of anyone he *doesn't* gaze at as though they're the most important, special being in the universe.

Hall leans in again, although he doesn't look at me. He keeps his face angled toward the screen. "I was just thinking," he whispers, "about one of your evil schemes."

"Which one is that?"

"To make an enemy's pillowcases scratchy for the rest of their life."

I don't believe for a moment that this is really what's been on his mind, but I indulge with a "Have you come to the dark side, then?"

"For one scheme only. I don't like that Ted Cruz guy."

I giggle. Someone two rows in front of us, four spaces down on the right, twists around, holding a finger to their lips. It's Greta Garbo. I'm being shushed by Greta Garbo.

Hall lowers in his chair, sliding all the way down out of sight. We both laugh. More people shush us.

"This is fun," I murmur in his ear when he braves coming back up. "We should come here more often."

"If you think this is fun, you should see what I can do with the tub in the purple guest bath. Hint: I can expand it into a lake and re-create a Viking ship inside it."

"Really?"

Up on the big screen, Cary Grant and Rosalind Russell stop what they're doing to turn in our direction, giving us reproving frowns. *"Shhh!"*

It's the best thing that's ever happened to me, even if it isn't all the way real.

CHAPTER FOURTEEN

Countdown to Christmas: 4 Days

IN THE MORNING, it takes me a minute to figure out where I am.

I sit up on my elbows, hair a wild tangle about my face, and squint at the bedroom. "What happened in here?" The red pickup truck and *fresh-cut Christmas trees* décor have been swapped for a nautical theme. A ship steering wheel takes up one wall. The curtains are white with a lobster print. Instead of Christmas trees, we've got signs that say GONE FISHIN' and JOE'S CRAB SHACK. Even the design on my phone case is different, seashells instead of elves.

"Felt like we could use a change," Hall announces, rolling off the bottom bunk. His sweater displays Santa Claus in board shorts, surfing the waves. "It was getting stale in here."

"Very beachy."

"I thought about bringing in real sand to cover the floor with."

"Grandma would murder you."

He glances nervously at the door. "I might've already put some in the den."

"In the *den*?"

"A beach theme needs sand!" He magicks together an outfit for me, laying it out on the bed: a seafoam maxi dress, floppy hat, and oversized sunglasses. It wouldn't be at all out of place in Hawaii or Los Angeles, but we're in Colorado, days away from Christmas. You'd think he'd be trying to stuff me into every outfit from *A Christmas Prince*, forcing a wardrobe change once an hour.

"What would you like to do today?" he asks, a blurry hurricane zooming from here to there, making adjustments to his beachy knickknacks. There's so much driftwood. And starfish.

Ordinarily, I'd say I want to go back to bed. Followed by grazing on snacks in bed while playing on my phone, until at least three in the afternoon. But this is Hall's first holiday with a family, and I've been shamefully half-assing it.

After I dress and return from the bathroom, Hall takes one look at me and stands up straight, eyes widening. He takes a step forward, then back, resting a forearm against the wall. *"Wow."*

"I take it you like the dress you picked out." By his reaction, you'd think I was wearing something unbelievably hot, but it's only a simple dress, albeit more form-fitting than what I'd usually wear.

He slips his hands into his pockets, laser-focused. "Do a little spin for me?"

I oblige.

He gives a low whistle, eyes dark and glittering with appreciation. "I was right, you look like a dream. Like a sea nymph. Like . . ." He circles me, then stops in the doorway and leans against the frame. "A goddess from Atlantis."

I blush. "Oh, stop."

"Never."

I do another spin, because I am incorrigible and I love how slack-jawed it makes him. "Today, we're going to make salt dough ornaments together."

He stares at me like I've asked him if he wants to get married. His attention darts to the ceiling above my head, and I watch the minutiae of anxiety play across his features, a blush on his throat.

"We can shape them like candy canes." When he still doesn't respond, looking oddly deer-in-the-headlights, I prompt, "Hall?"

"Uh. Hang on a second. Close your eyes."

"Why?"

"It's a surprise."

I do as requested, frowning when I sense movement overhead, stirring my hair ever so slightly. "What in the world are you doing?"

"Nothing. I think I heard someone calling my name. Gotta go, bye." Then he runs out the door, down the hall. I hear footsteps thump on the stairs.

The spot where Hall had been swirls with crushed peppermint dust and an uncharacteristic ocean tang.

Okay, then.

The rest of the house has received a drastic makeover. The red, green, and gold ornaments are now aqua, coral, and tan. We've got oars on doors, fishing nets, an octopus coat hook, sand collar drink coasters, LIFE'S A BEACH wall decals. A saltwater aquarium that takes up half the sitting room and which I am unsurprised to find comes with every fish featured in *Finding Nemo*.

"He told me he's thinking about becoming an interior designer. Asked if he could practice on the house," Grandma is mentioning to Mom from behind a tiki bar with a MARGARITAVILLE banner. "He must have rented a truck for all this shit." She sips her mimosa. "You know, I kind of like it, though."

I finally track down Hall as he's emerging from Grandpa's study, a stack of thick texts balanced in the crook of his arm.

"What are you up to?"

He doesn't slow, moving swiftly toward the living room. "I've got so much to read. There's a list called One Hundred Books to Read before You Die, and I've only read two of them. How am I supposed to learn about the Dow Jones at this rate?"

"Why do you need to learn about the Dow Jones?"

"I've been thinking." His brows slant down as he revolves, adding a book to his pile. "Do you want to go to Orlando? I've got unfinished business in Orlando."

"Are you all right? You're acting a little off today."

His jaw locks, and I watch a thought crystallize in his brain. But before he can open his mouth to explain it, there's a knock at the door.

"Ah, that's for me," sings Marilou, sweeping down the stairs. We all turn, puzzled, as she opens the door and a strange man enters. He's tall, handsome, dark-haired, a dead ringer for Henry Golding.

Felix stands. "Who's this?"

"This is Jake." Marilou smiles prettily. "You're going to duel him. If you win, you get to keep me as your wife."

∗

The staggering silence lasts five seconds.

"Excuse me, *what*?" I blurt.

"What? Who's Jake?" Felix's head swings from his wife to the man, whose name he cannot grasp. "What?"

"*Jake.*" Marilou peers at him with an impatient, meaningful look. "Jake Lim! You know?"

"Your scuba instructor from forever ago?"

"Hey." Jake Lim waves.

Marilou's irritation clears, her brilliant smile back in place. "That's right."

"Who's this?" Grandpa asks, strolling into the room. He's carrying one of his wooden mallard ducks under his arm, which I see has been glued to a small surfboard. Hall leaves no mallard unturned.

"This is Jake Lim," I tell him brightly. "He was Marilou's scuba instructor, we are learning."

"When I met Marilou," Felix says to us, staring numbly at Jake, "she was dating both of us. Jake and I both wanted to be exclusive. We presented reports, ten pages, double-spaced, discussing what each of us could bring to a relationship." I believe it. Marilou's very pragmatic, with a love of laminated pro/con lists; she tutors fifth-graders and regularly tasks them with writing letters to their representatives, reminding them of promises they've yet to follow through on.

"And I picked you." Marilou's lip curls. "How lucky. Did you even type that yourself, or did you have somebody else do it?"

"How could you even *ask* me that?"

Felix's gasp is a dead giveaway. Marilou seizes him by the wrist, then drags him out into the front yard. Jake is holding a sword. Two swords. Two long, slender swords with crimson cross handles. Marilou snatches one, tossing it to my brother, who high-steps to the side to avoid getting nicked.

"What are you *doing?*"

"Who is this?" It's Grandma, joining us in the yard, gesturing to Jake.

"It's Jake Lim, from scuba-ing," Sean pipes up, eyeing the swords doubtfully. "He's going to duel Felix, and if Felix loses, Marilou's leaving him."

Jake waves politely again. "Hey, what's up."

"Now we're cooking." Grandma rubs her hands together. "A duel! I haven't seen one of these in years."

Felix doesn't budge, gaping at his wife. "Are you kidding me?"

"I am not." She's telling the truth. I've never seen her like this—her smile is pleasant as always, but a cold fire flares in her eyes. Hall notices, too. He kicks one of the swords farther away from my sister-in-law.

Felix tries for an I'm Too Adult For This pose, fists on hips. "I'm not dueling anybody. There are *children* present."

"Fight!" Domino and Minnesota Moon yell, bloodthirsty. "Fight! Fight!"

"There's no need for that." Hall raises his arms, a figure of peace. "Let's go inside and talk about the common habits of contemporary American adults. I, for one, keep opening up the LinkedIn app on my phone, even though there's never anything good on there. But right after I close it out, *whomp-whomp!* Next thing I know, I'm right back on one of my four favorite apps." He lets his arms fall. "Just a relatable little anecdote about me."

I pat his shoulder. "I think you're using 'whomp-whomp' wrong."

"You mean 'whoomp,'" Grandpa shouts helpfully.

Marilou looks at Felix and shrugs. "Duel for my hand. Or forfeit, and I divorce you. These are my terms."

"Hey, Felix." Kaia cups her hands around her mouth, stage-whispering from fifteen feet away. "I think Marilou saw Callista's Instagram."

"Shut up, Kaia!" he snaps, because he really wants to yell at somebody, and if he yells at Marilou, he's going to have to give her the house in Corona del Mar. He'll be left a pauper with homes only in Pacific Palisades, New Orleans, and his favorite: the Miami Beach condo with mirrors on every ceiling and a six-foot neon flamingo.

"Nice day for a duel," Dad notes, appraising the lovely blue sky. He's right. I knew something was different, but until now, I couldn't pinpoint what. All the snow's melted, not an icicle or snow fortress in sight, just greenish-brown grass.

"Did you stop making it snow?" I whisper to Hall, who pulls out his phone and begins to tap on the screen. The phone has no logo, so it must be magic-made.

"I've got the most *horrendous* data plan," he declares loudly. "Oh, look!" He chuckles, waving the phone about. "Right back on LinkedIn! Typical. The stocks are at it again."

Jake swings his sword.

"Aghh!" we all scream.

"No! You leave him alone! You leave my baby be!" Mom tries to throw herself at Jake, but Dad and Grandma hold her back.

Grandma needs the excitement. Athena used her tea for home-made facials, and she's been in a rotten mood ever since. "Let's just see how this plays out."

"The tips are capped with rubber, don't worry," Dad reassures everybody as Felix whines, "I'm not a baby." He grudgingly picks up his sword, poking its tip to ensure that it is indeed rubber.

"So, what?" Felix yells at Jake, at Marilou, at a cat walking by. Definitely at the small clump of grass that trips him up. He kicks it in retribution. "If Jake wins, are you leaving me for him?"

"No."

"But you flew him here specifically to fight me?"

"That's right." Her voice darkens as Jake takes another swing, and Felix's eyes bug out. "Look alive, Felix."

It is dawning on my brother that this is happening.

"No crotch shots!" he entreats. "And no face stuff. My face is expensive."

"Mine's insured for thirty grand," Athena tells us all.

Jake is agreeable. "Yeah, it'd be cool if you left my calves alone, too. My wife is super into my calves."

"You're married?" Felix sputters. "For fuck's—then why are you—? Bunny! I don't understand why you're going about this like *this*."

"Don't you *Bunny* me," Marilou spits. "Your right to call me nicknames is on hold. What are you, drunk? Lift your arm higher! Fight, you idiot!"

"I'm not drunk, I'm hungover," he grumbles, dodging Jake. Jake moves with easy grace, bright-eyed, cheerful. As if dueling an ex-girlfriend's husband is a regular activity for him. He whistles as he passes the sword back and forth from hand to hand, ambidextrous. Grandma claps. Dad is visibly wondering where he went wrong in parenting.

Felix plays defense only. He has no strategy for offense, bleary-eyed, hair a mess, bags under his eyes. That midnight eggnog is catching up.

"You're supposed to be the normal one!" I exclaim to Marilou.

So all the time that she's been here, she's known what he did? And she's just been saving her fury for when Jake arrived? I have to admire her restraint.

Her eyes narrow on my brother, watching him swerve and duck. "He promised to stop responding to Callista's attempts to contact him, and I thought he could use a wake-up call."

Kaia is staring at Marilou in wonder.

"Are you going to intervene?" I ask Hall.

"Can't. Duels are protected from magical interference. It's all in the legislation."

"I would like to see this legislation."

"There is legislation that prevents you from seeing the legislation. Your eyes are too mortal."

Naturally.

"What are you doing?" I peer over his shoulder to see what he's so preoccupied with over there on his phone. There are thirty-six tabs open on his Chrome browser.

> Plastic surgeons hate her! Phoenix woman's secret to smooth, ageless skin.

> *Love Island* star flaunts sculpted butt on the beach. NSFW!

> Are your brunch tastes more Gen Z or Millennial? Take this quiz.

"Oh, *Hall*," I say in hushed tones.

He furiously tries to X out of his pages, but the screen freezes up. I don't think Hall is ready for the Internet.

The first jab from Jake certainly wakes Felix up and reclaims my attention. He's too slow to react, absorbing Jake's parry in the left pectoral muscle.

"My pec!" He gazes imploringly at Marilou. "He got my pec. You *love* that pec."

"That pec is dead to me until you've won this duel."

"Marilou, please. I *love* you."

"That's fine." She is unfazed.

"Think of Adrian. He needs his parents to stay together. Do you want him growing up sad and miserable in a broken home?"

Two of Felix's children from previous marriages throw pine cones at him. Meanwhile, Jake's sauntering fluidly about, smirking as he feints, knocking Felix off-kilter.

"Mr. Jake, what is your job?" Avenue pipes up.

"I've had many jobs. I've been a diving instructor, a lifeguard, a karaoke host at Knott's Berry Farm, and a guest experience associate at Hollywood Wax Museum. But now, I'm a fireman."

"Oooh!" they chorus. Mom and Marilou raise their eyebrows appreciatively.

"Do you have any pets?" Octavian asks.

"I have seven." He stabs Felix in the thigh, then dances backward. "A rabbit, three fish, a dog, a cat." He winks at Minnesota Moon. "And a pony. She's a sweet old girl named Savannah."

"I wish *Jake* were my uncle," laments Honeysuckle Lou. "Why did we have to get stuck with Uncle Felix? He doesn't even have any ponies."

"I heard he's employed by *nepotism*, whatever that means," Ichabod adds.

"I saw a picture of him from 1998 and his hair had frosted tips," says Domino. The kids snicker.

Felix scowls. Lunges for Jake.

I can't help but root for him. He's so hapless and uncoordinated, but slowly, determination is mounting. He can't let this guy with amazing calves destroy him in his grandparents' perilously steep front yard while his wife and kids watch. "Come on, Felix!" I yell. "You can do it!"

He doesn't glance my way, but there's a trace of surprise on his face. He blinks. Gets a good hit in on Jake, who exclaims loudly.

"Touché!"

"Thanks." Felix rolls his shoulders, jumping from side to side like a boxer in the ring. Grandma shouts corrections about his form, which was inescapable because she did a boxing movie twenty years ago and still fancies herself an authority. "You're not gonna steal my girl."

"No interest! Happily married, man."

"How'd you convince him to come here and fight Felix?" I ask Marilou.

She smiles wanly. "I offered him money, actually, but he turned it down. Said he'd do it for the story."

Right. The chance to fight Felix Hughes must be tempting. He's landed on a lot of Most Punchable Celebrities lists.

Jake has better technique, but Felix has desperation. He's unpredictable, steps jagged, and after sneaking one successful jab he builds up his confidence to land another. Another. Another. A small smile plays at his lips. Jake stumbles, falls; he shakes his hair from his face as he stands, breaths deepening. They circle each other like wolves, dragging their swords against the earth. Rich people settle their disputes in really unhealthy ways.

Hall takes me aside, looking agitated. "I'm experiencing ugly-colored feelings about Jake's dexterity with a sword. I've seen jealousy exhibited in others, but I've never felt it from my own point of view. I'm astonished by the physical aspects of this emotion. My stomach is sick! I'm trying to seem happy so that nobody notices, because I don't want to vocalize these unacceptable feelings, but smiling when my stomach feels like mildewed oatmeal is unnatural."

Jealous Hall! He doesn't know how ridiculously cute he looks, frowning like that. "We've all been there. Ashlee Simpson threw a White Russian smoothie out of her car window at me once when I was out jogging, because she was jealous of my custom Nikes."

"I won't throw a White Russian smoothie at Jake from my car."

"That's good. Keep a handle on those urges."

He looks away. "Maybe a Mello Yello from a bicycle."

Meanwhile, the fight is still going on. "Is he actually *winning*?" Kaia says, marveling.

A clump of snow in an overhanging tree bough slips sideways, falling with a *splat* on Felix's head.

Felix jumps, sword slanting midstrike, and I notice, too late—

"The cap! The rubber cap fell off!"

Jake's staring up into the tree where the snow fell from, and Felix pounces on his distraction to go in for the kill.

"For . . . my . . . marriage!" he bellows, bringing down the sword. It slices Jake's left arm off.

"Aghhhhh!" we all scream again. Blood spurts where Jake's arm used to be, spraying Felix's traumatized face. Jake stares down at his own exposed bone and his eyes roll back into his head.

"Jake!" Marilou shrieks.

Felix drops to his knees. "I didn't mean to!"

Marilou picks up Jake's arm and smushes it against the wound as if she can reattach it. "I thought those couldn't cut!"

"Of course they can, they're longswords," Frangipane yells out, scathingly. "*Rapiers* are dueling swords." He and Octavian roll their eyes at each other.

Hall and I look at each other in panic. I raise my eyebrows in silent question, and he nods. He seizes my wrist, and we're turning, turning, sucked through black space, spitting back out on the front lawn as it appeared a couple of minutes before. Jake's arm is whole once more, all of his blood safely inside his body, where it's supposed to be. Nobody notices our reemergence, all eyes on Jake and Felix as they circle each other. The déjà vu makes me queasy. Kaia says once again, "Is he actually winning?"

"Wait! Pause!" I wave wildly. "Felix, the rubber thing on the end of your sword fell off."

He lifts it, twisting the blade in the sunlight. Makes a face. "So it has. Nice catch."

"That could've been bad," Dad mutters as the sword is recapped.

"Doubt it," Jake says. "I'm too quick." Snow falls from the tree and splats him on the head this time.

Felix backs him up against a tree ("Oh, yes," Marilou murmurs), sword to his throat. "Surrender."

Jake drops his weapon. "Okay, you win."

Mom, Grandpa, and I cheer. I think the others were more excited in the other timeline.

"I win!" Felix whoops. He grabs his wife. "I'm so sorry. I'll get a restraining order, I promise, and we should probably check the cameras when we get home to make sure she hasn't planted more poison ivy in our flower bed. I know I'm messy, but I love you so goddamn much and I want to be with you forever. Life means nothing without you in it." He's breathing heavily. "This means you'll stay with me, right?"

"That's what I said."

"*Whomp-whomp*," Ichabod crows. To Hall, he adds, "That's how you use 'whomp-whomp.'"

Felix throws Marilou over his shoulder, marching straight into the house. Jake wipes the sweat from his brow with one sleeve, grinning. "I let him win."

Chapter Fifteen

JAKE STAYS FOR lunch, then gets caught up in a marathon of *What We Do in the Shadows* with Grandma. "I'll give you five thousand dollars to come back and do that every Christmas," she offers him when he leaves.

"Bye, Uncle Jake!" the kids yell, waving.

Before Jake can say anything else, Hall shuts the front door on him. "He's not bad with a sword, but if you want to see something *really* impressive, watch this." He brings out a collapsible top hat, taps the brim with his plastic magic wand, and then a real rabbit jumps from inside it. "Here, you can keep this," he tells Octavian, who is instantly told by three adults *You're not keeping that*.

"Where'd you get that rabbit?" Athena demands.

Hall flourishes the magic wand, doing jazz hands. "With my very real magic wand."

I poke him in the stomach. "You told me you can't magic things to life. Where'd you get that rabbit?"

"A magician never tells." He shoos me away.

Hall behaves erratically all afternoon. I overhear him asking Mom what her favorite brand of lemonade powder is and happily complaining to Athena about traffic. (Just traffic as a concept.) He asks my nieces and nephews if they've "heard any hot goss lately." I discover two orange road cones in the truck bed, which I'm fairly certain he stole.

I don't know what to make of it.

Hall slips off while I'm wrestling the swords away from two excited nephews. I check the bedroom, the purple guest bath, the tower. I duck behind palm trees and the stack of presents that's begun to accumulate in the living room. "Has anyone seen—"

My attention lands on the yellow bench that's usually flush against the basement door, and which is now pushed outward. Ahh.

He's gone to visit Little Teller City.

When I was around ten, Grandpa went through a phase in which he obsessively built a child-size village in his basement, working on it night and day for the better part of a year. Every time we visited, he was down in that basement, door locked, drilling and painting and injuring himself a good bit. "You don't have the knees for cobblestones, you old goat!" Grandma would yell down.

The grand reveal was thrilling. We made a special trip out for it, the first visitors to Little Teller City. He'd recycled a few props from movie sets, as he used to be a set designer and still had a few connections. The winding street, paved with real cobblestones, is named Bettie Boulevard. ("That's not after you, it's after Grandma," Athena told me, in case I got any ideas.) There's Rocky Road Ice Cream Parlor with fake ice cream scoops and a cash register that dings, Mountain Express Post Office where you can dress up with mail bags. A milk bottle delivery service. Old-fashioned bicycles with baskets on the front. Gold Rush Bookshop.

Teller City Market with its miniature shopping carts and The Little Red Schoolhouse, with four desks for the grandkids.

Grandpa followed us from one area to another, pointing out any cool details we might have missed. It was delightful, a tiny town all to ourselves. My siblings and I bossed each other, fighting over who got to deliver mail, who got to be the teacher, who had to work at Gold Rush Bookshop (it was the smallest building packed mostly with books from the '80s that made you sneeze when you turned their pages). Teller City Market was the clear favorite. It was the only building that could comfortably fit all four of us at once, and the fake food was so high quality we agreed we could probably trick our parents into thinking it was real. Little Teller City ends in a painted mountainscape, a rather slapdash mural of flowers and sky—by that point in creating the town, Grandpa was burned out and wanted it to be done.

I step carefully down the steep cement stairs, cool air wafting up to greet me. Above, the dryer hums, vibrating the exposed beams. Grandpa had meant to install a realistic sky on the ceiling, but building this place took ten years off his life and he couldn't bring himself to lift a paint roller one more time. Hiring somebody else to do it was out of the question. Lawrence Watson would rather raze this basement to ash than let another man lay his incompetent mitts on it.

Our interest wore off after a couple of years, largely because there are no televisions in the Mayberry-esque time capsule. I haven't been down here in a good while, so I expected cobwebs (the great-grandkids aren't allowed in the basement because they "don't appreciate it enough") and dust. Maybe I'd crawl into the market and reflect on ye olden days, in which I was small enough to fit properly, and how Dad was a good enough sport to play along, pretending to be fooled by our plastic cheeseburgers. How the bite marks he left in them made us fall over with laughter.

But I see that the market, extraordinarily, has grown right along with me into adulthood.

Every building on Bettie Boulevard has sized up to accommodate a grown-up or two, ceiling pushed skyward a few extra feet. Teller City Market bears a wreath on the door. A model train whistles as it chugs around its tracks within the display window of Frontier Hardware. The bicycles are now red pickup trucks with chopped trees sticking out the backs, boughs still thick with snow. There are soft Christmas lights strung from every surface, arching rooftop to rooftop over the cobblestone street, which has acquired a dusting of white fluff.

Near the end of the lane, a familiar shape is busy etching frost onto the glass door of the Blue Moose Café, perfecting each frozen snowflake by hand. His back is turned to me as he hums, lost in his work.

"It's beginning to look a lot like Christmas down here," I observe, sliding my hands into my pockets.

Hall jumps. Whirls. "Ahh! Bettie!" It's like I've caught him with an adult magazine. He fidgets, the apples of his cheeks glowing.

"So. This is where all the stuff from upstairs went, hm?"

"You weren't supposed to see it."

"Why, is it a surprise?"

His jaw tightens, an unspoken *no*. Interesting. I step forward, ignoring his obvious distress at my presence. "Grandpa's going to have a cow."

"He won't know. It doesn't look like this when I'm not here . . . I change it all back whenever I go upstairs."

"When did you start sneaking down here to change the village?"

"Three thirty this morning. I've been up and down all day."

I watch him shrewdly. "Why?"

He lifts a shoulder, then lets it drop.

"You can tell me."

"I'd rather not."

Very interesting.

"Oh, no," he moans, dread-filled gaze locking on a spot above my head.

"What?" I begin to look up, but he grabs my hand, tugging me toward him.

"Look at that!" he shouts, pointing at the flower shop. There are poinsettias painted where tulips once were, waving ever so slightly in a breeze. I hear dim voices of pretend customers deep in the shop, which is still flat, painted on the wall.

"Wow, you added an audio feature? Nice touch."

I turn back to Hall, who's gone red in the face.

"What's going on with you?" I squint up above my head, but nothing's there. "Are you okay?"

He sits down on the curb and lets his face fall into his hands. *"Urnngghhhh."* Keeping one hand over his face, he jerkily waves the other in the direction of the schoolhouse, silencing the Christmas music from it.

"I am melancholy," he confesses, conjuring a thesaurus. He leafs through its pages. "And simultaneously famished, which I am learning makes any emotion worse in conjunction."

I sit down on the curb beside him, smoothing my dress over my knees.

"And then there's this." He whips out a graph from nowhere, so large that I have to lean back to view it in full. It looks like a stock chart, a jagged mountain landscape in red marker. Beneath the peaks and valleys are names.

Jimin from BTS. Janelle Monáe. David Bowie. And three separate times, *Little Women*: (*1994: Professor Bhaer; 2019: Jo; Book version: Laurie*). *Bettie Hughes.*

"What am I looking at?"

"These are the people I find myself the most strongly attracted to."

I stare at the graph. My name sits at the highest peak, twenty points above Jimin. Clear, irrefutable confirmation that Hall likes me.

It feels like my heart has turned into bubbles.

His brow furrows like a frenzied scientist boggled by his own creation. "Crushing has hit me with a vengeance, barreling out from around a corner to punch me right in the brain. But it seems that out of all possible personalities, my favorite type is you."

Me.

Out of all of his favorites, I'm the *very* favorite. He's been telling me all week that he thinks I'm spectacular. Giving me hugs, compliments, a kiss. The way he gazes at me as if I invented hot chocolate. I had to take his ardent attentions with a grain of salt, because he celebrates *everyone* like this. Which is a quality I adore about Hall, but it's good to know that I'm special to him in a different way.

I feel my face break into a smile, but the balloon of big, happy feelings pops when I see that Hall doesn't look pleased about this development at all. He isn't smiling. Which . . . okay, I sort of get it if his attraction is reluctant. My life was a mess when he showed up. But it's been steadily improving and, in my opinion, can only get better from here. He and I are good together. Our spark feels magical, distinctly Bettie-and-Hall; I don't think either of us could replicate it with anyone else as a partner. We enccurage each other to dream big, shoot for the moon, reaching out a hand when the other gets stuck, bringing the other down to earth whenever one of us gets too carried away—a perfect balance. Being with Hall is so fun, so easy, so *just right*. I never knew a dynamic could be like this. I always thought romantic relationships had to be dramatic battles dominated by tears and stress.

The graph disappears. "And that's not all," he goes on. "There's so much I want to try. I'm thinking about everything I still haven't done, and it's got me in a panic. Look at this." He summons a mug of coffee from thin air. Or not coffee, knowing him. "Red velvet creamer."

I knew it.

"I love red velvet creamer. I love it with all of my heart. And peppermint mocha, sugar cookie, and gingerbread latte creamer. Not eggnog latte, though, it tastes too much like teleportation. But what about caramel *apple*? What about pumpkin *spice*?" His eyes are tormented. "They're not on shelves anymore."

"Can't you magic some up?"

He shakes his head miserably. "It's not the same. I want to try autumn flavors in *autumn*. Are there summer flavors? Spring? What is Coffee mate keeping from me?"

"You have to be patient. Seasons come and go at their own pace. I imagine this is annoying for you, when you've got magic that lets you take shortcuts to get whatever you like."

"That's just the thing. I love the changing of the seasons. I want to endure every torturous in-between; how it's cold in the mornings in springtime, then hot by afternoon. I want to watch the leaves turn color slowly at the end of the year, the contrast of red maple against a white sky when a cold snap rushes in."

I press my lips together. "I'm . . . not following. Do you want me to check the pantry for . . . what was it? Caramel apple? I bet they have some. Grandma and Grandpa don't check their expired products frequently enough."

"*No*," he groans, forcefully. "It's no good if the weather isn't that perfect autumn crisp that makes me wish I ran an inn in Vermont." He laughs in a hopeless sort of way, pressing the heels of his hands to his eyes. "I sound ridiculous, I know, but I want to carve pumpkins in October. I want to pick apples with you in September."

He could have said *I want to pick apples*, but he said *I want to pick apples with you*. My heart softens like butter in a pan. "We can do that."

The gentleness of my tone only serves to prod him closer to the edge. He springs to his feet, hands behind his back. Oh, no. It's never a good sign when Hall paces.

"The longer I'm in this form, the more human I'm becoming. The more I want and need, like a human. I want to stay here and do all the human-type things I always dreamed of, which requires time. Years and years of it. But my role is magic, which isn't compatible with humanity or the teaspoon-sized amount of time that fits into the human experience. I didn't expect to *feel* this much. And the momentum is so quick: at first, I felt only a little bit human, with the smallest human needs. But then they grew bigger and bigger, so fast, new ones cropping up that I've never had before, and I don't know how to deal with it, how to juggle it all. There are needs that didn't exist for me a week ago that I can't stop thinking about now. The more of this world I interact with, the greedier I get for more. Do you see the bind I'm in?"

He's talking rapidly and mostly to himself, hair mussed, shirt wrinkled. He stops short in front of me, gaze yearning and just a little bit lost. I see him again in the theater, eyes roving my face, barely blinking. I see him in the kitchen, slowing time to protract our kiss as Grandma's *long may they reign* rings in the air. I hear his voice again and again, on loop: *Do you need me to kiss you in front of them?*

I let go of a few of the words at the end, the unnecessary ones. *Do you need me to kiss you?*

I think that my answer to that has turned into a yes. I stand up and he moves toward me, closing his eyes as I lay a hand against his cheek; but right as my mouth begins to brush his, he pulls back. Settles a hand on my shoulder.

"Bettie," he says delicately.

My pulse stabs at the hinge of my jaw, and the room blurs as my vision adjusts, pupils expanding. This is the problem with letting my heart go soft. Now it's so much easier to prick.

"But you said you . . ." My throat is coated with sandpaper. I gesture to the graph, the proof that he likes me, but it's gone.

The light in his eyes shutters. "All of these new feelings are for nothing. They're all futile."

"They're not," I whisper.

"I'm sorry." His tone is like a kiss on the forehead. "If only I lived here permanently, it would be different. I would act on the feelings. But since I don't—I'm watching your happiness climb day by day, and it's wonderful, but that means we're near the end . . . I can't change what I am. I've tried. And I've tried delaying the inevitable, but it *is* inevitable."

We look at each other with the most miserable understanding. He's right. We've developed feelings for each other, which should be wonderful, but to discuss it out loud will just make it worse when he goes, as he must.

"Never mind all this." He gestures at nothing in particular. "Never mind me. I'm not here to blather on about myself, am I? I'm here to give you holiday cheer. I'm here for *you*, to help you be merry and bright."

"If you're not feeling merry and bright, how can I? Not everything's about me. You can be about you, too."

"I can't." He sighs. "That's not my role. I'm being selfish, and I'm sorry."

"You've never been selfish for a whole second of your existence."

"I stole a menu from Cracker Barrel. And some traffic cones. I don't know what possessed me to take them. I've never felt like this. I'm losing my grasp on myself—I get an impulse and I want to follow it no matter what. Is that what it's like to be human?"

"You'll learn impulse control." Except he won't, if he'll be leaving soon. Who will he be when he returns to his old post? Will the feelings ebb away, or will he be forever dissatisfied up there, wanting this world when his purpose is to remain apart from it?

He shakes his head a few times.

"I can't change the seasons," I manage to tell him, blinking back a hot prickling in the corners of my eyes. "But if you want to go somewhere else in the world where it's summer, we can pick apples. We can go on a trip."

"That's not what I'm supposed to be doing. But thank you." He grasps my hand, squeezing lightly.

"Something else, then?" I paper over my hurt and disappointment with a too-bright smile, a sunny tone that feels heavy in my chest. There will be time to miss Hall later, after he's gone. I don't want to waste however many precious weeks we may have left being miserable. "How about a winter-approved activity?" The perfect idea strikes. "I know exactly what'll cheer us up."

I take his hand, leading him toward the stairs. Behind us, Little Teller City shakes off its skin of magic, shrinking back to usual size. "Come, Holiday! Let us bake some delicious secular cookies, partake of glasses of milk, and revel in the ensuing warm and fuzzies."

He returns my grin on a slight delay. Cookie baking! This should make him happy, which has spawned an unfortunate cycle of making *me* happy, which means his time will be up even sooner. When we trudge up the stairs and into the kitchen, a cold wind of despair follows after us, threaded with all the words we'll never say out loud.

Chapter Sixteen

....

Countdown to Christmas: 3 Days

W HAT DID YOU put in these cookies?" I'm on my sixth and I can't stop.

Hall is aloof. "The ingredients. You were there last night, you saw."

"You had to have added something extra. These taste too good to be normal cookies."

"I added love." He clears his throat. "In the general sense, of course. Love is in the air. Love is all around us." He looks like he wants to shoot straight up through the ceiling with a jet pack.

"It certainly is," adds Mom as she passes by, grabbing a cookie. She pats Hall on the head. "Thank you, son-in-law."

His gaze moves sharply to mine, but I have to look away. She's going to be so disappointed when a wedding never happens.

Hall bustles over to the dishwasher to unload it, but Athena beats him there. This is no coincidence. When Hall cleared the dishes from the table after dinner, Grandpa was so exuberant in his gratitude that my siblings were bothered. If somebody receives positive attention, that is attention the others are not receiving. Listening to Hall praise everybody has Felix peer-pressure-complimenting Marilou more often. Dad mentioned privately to my sisters and me that Hall is "growing on him," so Athena is now talking up her husband's alleged positive attributes. This flattery, in turn, has prompted him to behave extra generously. Sean has asked me twice if I need assistance opening my drinks.

The drive behind these behavioral changes isn't altruistic, but when somebody is kind to you, you tend to be kind back, so we're in the midst of an odd paying-it-forward train that is just as alien as it is surprisingly pleasant. Kaia has even been putting her phone and iPad down to join in family conversations.

"Hurry up, Betts!" Dad barks from the living room. "We're about to press play!"

I wander into the living room with my seventh cookie as Mom pops a tape into the VHS player. "What's that?" Ichabod asks.

"A videocassette tape," Dad tells him. "It's like a DVD."

Avenue folds up a used Band-Aid and flicks it at Ichabod's ear. "What's a DVD?"

"It's Netflix for old people," Domino replies, as I feel my ancient, brittle bones dissolve.

"When your parents were little," Mom explains gently to her grandchildren, "we would record them on the camcorder." Thankfully, there are no tapes here memorializing me as an awkward teenager, as Grandma only has the old videocassettes.

On the screen, a much younger Hughes family is at a campground, but my working memory of this trip is obsolete. Mom's voice is overly loud, which my off-camera father remarks on. "Oh, shush," Present-Day Mom says in unison with her younger self. "I have to talk loud, or the sound won't pick up!"

"Listen to Dad!" Kaia laughs. "Your accent was so much stronger!"

Dad glowers. "I sound the same."

The camcorder pivots, capturing Dad in his full thirtysomething glory: spiky brown hair, a blue sweater with artistic holes around the collar, svelte.

"Who's that?" Minnesota Moon asks, and Dad hollers.

"What do you mean, who's *that*? That's me."

She looks him up and down. "Doesn't look like you."

He points at her. "Watch your mouth."

"You know, sometimes I forget how he landed you," Grandma remarks to her daughter. "I remember now. Although I still say you got married too young."

"You married young, too."

"We can't all be the exception to marriage statistics, darling."

We all scream when we're blessed with Great-Grandma (rest her soul) in culottes and a fanny pack. She shields her face from the camera, pushing Mom away, who films a chubby-cheeked Kaia waddling around in a diaper. Little Athena is unrecognizable with her brown ponytail. In the distance, Grandpa is fishing at the edge of a lake. Felix stands next to him, shirtless and deeply suntanned, his scraggly mullet sun-brightened nearly to blond. His kids immediately yowl in reaction to his hair.

"It was the style," he and Mom both insist.

"Where's little Bettie?" Grandpa (present-day) asks, five seconds before (younger) Dad asks the same question.

"She's in time-out," we all hear Mom respond. She turns and zooms in on a scowling little creature in a blue bucket hat and pink jellies, wispy black hair in pigtails. Little Bettie is bouncing on a metal and plastic lawn chair, kicking up rocks. The screen goes black for a few seconds; when the video flickers back on, we're no longer at the campground.

"Ooooh, look at this!" Young Mom exclaims, very loudly, shaking a rattle in Kaia's face. "Look at this!" She shoves a baby doll in Kaia's face. Kaia presses her small hand into the cake that is presented to her and watches it ooze between her fingers in fascination.

"Grandma, are you *smoking*?" Honeysuckle Lou exclaims.

"That's a candy cigarette."

"There's smoke coming out of it."

"Look! You're smoking right in front of him!" Octavian gestures to a small Felix, head buzzed, front teeth overlarge, who's helpfully trying to persuade Kaia to play with her toys as a stream of smoke wafts directly into his eyes. Young Mom thanks him and calls him a big helper while Young Dad, who's doing the recording this time, tells him to back off and let Kaia play with whatever she wants. Felix is standing on the back of a chair, hopping up and down excitedly. Young Dad tells him to cut it out, which he does. Present-Day Dad grimaces.

"This is why I have asthma now," Felix informs Honeysuckle Lou. "Grandma, I can't believe you blew smoke right into my face."

"It was a different time."

"Mom, you look hot," Athena says. It's true. Mom's got short, flippy blond hair in this video, very sleek, with a black turtleneck and deep red lipstick.

"That's weird," one of her kids replies. "You can't call your mom hot."

"Why not? I'm *your* mom, and I'm hot."

Mom sighs. "I *was* hot, wasn't I."

Dad tugs her to him. "You've always been hot and always will be." I notice he's exaggerating his accent. Mom smiles, snuggling against his side.

A small voice in the video pipes up. "Can I come out of time-out now?" And the camera swerves to land, predictably, on a little girl with black hair and a pink Popsicle stain around her mouth, perfectly dry but wearing a bathing suit. She's sitting on the bottom step of the staircase, hands under her bottom, heels thumping the floor.

"Are you going to be good?" Young Dad asks.

"No."

"Then you can't come out of time-out."

"See, she's always been a gremlin," Athena reminds us.

"It's why we love her," Kaia rejoins, reaching across Hall to grasp my hand for a few seconds. She pulls away, smiling.

Young Felix walks over and hugs little Bettie, gives her the baby doll Kaia doesn't want anything to do with, and calls her his little buddy. We all go, "Awwww!"

The video goes black again and refocuses on a new scene. It's my birthday.

"Do you remember that clock?" Mom asks Dad now, pointing at a clock on the wall in the background. "We lost that in the move to Fresno, didn't we?"

"I thought we gave it away."

"I wouldn't have given that away. I miss that clock."

"Look at that wallpaper. That is the *ugliest* wallpaper. I always hated it."

"I loved that wallpaper!" Mom gapes at him as though he's insulting one of their children. They continue to notice old stuff in the background that nobody else cares about, wondering where it's all disappeared to. All the while, little Bettie is tearing into her presents with the help of Felix, who hands her each one and offers to get them out of their packaging. Young Dad tells him, a little snappishly, to back off and let little Bettie open her presents by herself. Present-Day Dad grimaces again.

"I'm sorry, Felix."

"I'll let you help open my presents on Christmas, if you want," I offer.

"*Thank* you," he replies, with a haughty expression for our father. "It's about time I'm appreciated."

I'm watching my miniature self, how easy it is for her and her siblings to hug each other, to be in each other's space. Tangling up together like a rat king, play-fighting and real-fighting and forgiving so quickly, arms around shoulders, holding hands. Someone always hugging somebody else. I find myself tearing up over it, but when Sean rudely points this out, I scowl and say I'm only misty-eyed because I miss what it was like to not know him.

Mom's misty-eyed, too, because she and Dad were separated at the time this particular video was recorded, coming together only for our birthdays and holidays. Watching herself struggle, even though it's impossible for the rest of us to tell she was struggling, is dredging up some bad memories. Grandma's misty-eyed because she doesn't know what happened to the ruby earrings she sees her younger self wearing and accuses her dead mother of stealing them. Most of the kids have left the room by now, even though they were promised this would be a captivating stroll down memory lane, and they call us narcissists for watching ourselves with so much enthusiasm. Peach Tree cries because she's not in the videos with us. *"I'm left out of everything! It's not fair!"*

Even Hall is teary. "Aww," I whisper, smiling. "You big softie."

He wipes his eyes, backing away. "Excuse me for a moment."

The tape ends. Mom sifts through a stack of videos with labels like *'03 Christmas Play, Sweetheart Pageant,* and *Kaia Talent Show.* Everyone is clamoring for videos in which they are the star. Mom has veto power, eliminating any video in which she doesn't like her hairstyle. We're all exclaiming that we'd forgotten about Diana, our cocker spaniel who passed away the day I graduated high school, when I realize Hall is still gone.

I find him in our room, perched on the edge of his bed, shoulders rounded to fit beneath the top bunk, staring at the floor while his hands idly play with a snow globe. His eyes are red-rimmed and bright, and my heart drops, a cold stone, down into the pit of my stomach.

I thought he was being sentimental, like the rest of us. This isn't sentimental-sad. This is *sad* sad.

"Hey," I say softly.

"Hi." The snow globe contains two miniature figures ice skating, holding hands, their scarves flying behind them.

I close the door behind me. "How are you doing?" As soon as the door's shut, I'm pulled into the magic he's cast over the room, and I see that he isn't sitting on the bottom bunk after all. He's sitting on a red bench at the edge of the ice rink, watching a memory of the two of us skating together. Whenever it ends, he hits replay, and we go round and round again.

"I have something to confess," he says, still riveted on the snow globe. Inside it, there are two miniature people sitting on a bunk bed side by side.

I join him on the bench.

"I put an extra tablespoon of brown sugar into the cookie dough. I—I just really, really wanted you to like the cookies we made together. I've been talking up cookie baking so much and the pressure got to me. I cracked."

"Is that all?" I huff a relieved laugh. "Hall, you had me worried. I don't care if you added an extra teaspoon of brown sugar."

"Tablespoon. I'm diabolical."

"I think we can get through it." I offer a rueful smile that he doesn't immediately reciprocate.

"I want to thank you for coming on this family trip with me." I bump his knee playfully with mine, trying to raise his spirits. "It hasn't been too bad, with you here. My family loves you—even Dad and Grandma have come around, and they're the hardest to convince. Usually, this week is a disaster, but this year I'm enjoying myself."

"I can see you're a lot happier these days."

"And it's all your fault. Well done, you." I say this last bit in my dad's embellished accent.

He nods broodingly. His expression is so far away, making my heart pinch. "Watching you become happier, laughing with your family, is a spectacular thing, which I am proud to watch. Even if it does mean my time here is tapering off." He cocks his head. "Humans are the most fascinating creatures. You're all so intelligent and yet you often use that intelligence to accomplish the most baffling of goals. I've enjoyed being one of you, having the freedom to put my energy toward nonsense, more than you can know. Not having a sole, single purpose. Down here, you can have loads of varying purposes all at once. You're not a . . ." He holds up his fist, thumb and forefinger pinched together. "Not, like, a—a *function*, you know? What you are, is more than I am."

I take his hand between both of mine. "You are *everything*, Hall."

"Now that I know what I've been missing, I feel like I'm only

halfway filled up with experiences. I'll return to my old life knowing that I'm only half of what I could've been. I've got to live with
that, not knowing what the rest of me should look like." He pats
my knee clumsily. "Sorry. My default used to be pure, unadulter-
ated joyfulness, but now it's shot through with dozens of other
emotions. What a mess." He tries for a smile. "Know any good
jokes to lift my spirits, by chance?"

"Actually, I did make some jokes for you. Of a sort."

I reach, and even though I can't see the old rolltop desk, my
hand finds it, along with a thin stack of folded construction paper.
It appears when I pull it back.

"I made you a few more cards, since you liked the last one so
much."

He takes the first from me, the cover inexplicably illustrated
with a camping scene. Inside, it reads: *Surprise! Lacey Chabert is behind you.*

A reluctant *hmph* emits from his nose. "I'm not going to look
behind me. I refuse." (Then he does, surreptitiously.) He reads the
blue card, which I've drawn a pastoral scene for, with flowers and
tiny cottages. *Wishing you all the zest with your orange scones.*

"Have I ever made orange scones?" he wonders.

"I tried to come up with universal sentiments, but everything
came out very niche. If you ever meet someone who bakes orange
scones, this one will really hit."

He opens the yellow card, its front featuring all of the nutri-
tional information on a box of Kraft macaroni and cheese for no
reason whatsoever. The gem inside is: *I might be your best option.* The
most crucial detail of designing my cards is that the artwork must
be unrelated to the message, for maximum chaos.

"And one more, because I was on a roll." I open this one up for him myself, giggling at my own joke. *It's time to move on, Chris.*

"I love it!" he exclaims. "Who's Chris?"

"We don't know!"

Hall's eyes gleam. His knuckle grazes my cheekbone. "You're right. Very niche. Thank you, I love these."

"I try."

His expression changes, eyes darkening. He holds my stare for a long, loaded moment, and then something above me snags his attention. His jaw hardens.

"What?" I look up, but all I see is a puff of smoke. It smells like mint, like magic. "Why do you keep doing that? What's up there?"

"Nothing." His face is flushed. Definitely not *nothing*, then. Maybe I'm being haunted.

Snowflakes from the memory land on his shoulders, instantly melting. They last longer on my clothes than his, star-frost sparkling against my coat. Hall presses the pad of his finger to a snowflake that's landed on my sleeve and crystallizes it with his magic, marveling over it for a moment before he tucks it into his pocket.

"I am feeling terribly human today," he says at length, settling the cards on his knee. "I used to find those characters on CW shows unrelatable, but now I'm all *moody* and I just want to put on a black cloak and wail mournfully in . . . in a park full of fog. I want my cloak to billow behind me as I storm down an alley at midnight, the shadows scattering fearfully." His hand tightens into a fist. "I want to wander through a cemetery in the rain and curse my feelings."

"I understand. We've all been there."

He nods again.

"Would it help if I said I've thought of the perfect white elephant gift?"

"Maybe." He's skeptical.

"I have two ideas, actually. The first is a papier-mâché Lacey Chabert from *Family for Christmas* and a papier-mâché Lacey Chabert from *A Christmas Melody* meeting and realizing they're twins who were separated at birth."

His spine snaps straight. *"Nice."*

"The other is a puzzle. We'll need to use magic for this one, though, because whoever gets the puzzle, the picture on it will be whatever their favorite Christmas memory is."

He smiles one of those slow, happy, skin-crinkling-around-the-eyes smiles that tells me I've got a winner. "I like that."

"Wonderful."

"Spectacular."

"Fantastic."

"And if you were the one to get it?" he asks. "What would your favorite Christmas memory be?"

I cock my head. "I'd forgotten how much I used to love this time of year, when my siblings and I were kids. One year, we went sledding on the hill behind the movie theater, and then when we got back, Grandpa made us hot chocolate and put on *Home Alone*. We'd discussed how we could easily overpower any burglars, then made all the adults really mad when they found our traps. Syrup on the stairs, nails sticking out of walls, that sort of thing."

He holds in a laugh, shoulders shaking.

"But I think that my best Christmas memory," I go on, "is this one time when I woke up in the middle of the night. I was probably about eight years old. I was hoping to catch Santa filling up stockings, so I tiptoed downstairs, but there were no presents under the tree, nothing in the stockings. Then I looked out the living room window, and . . ." My gaze strays as I replay the scene in my mind's eye. "The world was blue magic, the yard filled up with moonlight so bright I could see every tree, the shapes of cars parked all the way down on the streets in town. The glowing cinema sign, snow sparkling on the gazebo in the town square. There wasn't a single sound in the whole house, because I was the only one awake." I pause. "I think that might be the most peaceful I have ever felt, but I haven't thought about that moment for a long time."

He's watching me with a half smile, and I feel wretchedly perceived, like I told him something I didn't mean to.

I deflect. "What's yours?"

He hands me the snow globe, and I give it a little shake. The memory playing out before us goes loose and dissolves, blossoming into Hall and me in the movie theater. We watch ourselves watching *His Girl Friday* for a minute, and then it becomes us watching Hall watching *me* watching *His Girl Friday*.

"Our greatest hits?" I ask, giving the snow globe another shake. Now we're looking at ourselves baking cookies.

He takes the snow globe from me, contemplating diminutive Bettie and Hall for a moment, before sliding it away into another dimension for safekeeping. "Like my own VHS player."

We stand up, in the bedroom once more, memories gone. For a moment, all we do is stare at each other. "Would it help if we went back in time?" I ask quietly.

He gives an almost imperceptible shake of the head. "We'd just carry it with us."

The seconds tick on, each one a terrible throb. His expression shows that he wants to say something else but can't bring himself to.

"All right." I try to inject cheer into it when I add, "Puzzle time, then."

"Definitely. And you know, we should go ahead and do the papier-mâché thing, too. If I post a picture of it online, maybe I'll get her attention. I would very much like her attention."

"I am going to get you Lacey Chabert for Christmas, Hall. I swear."

He laughs hoarsely. "Meet you in the den in a few minutes?"

"Mm-hmm."

I leave the room, closing the door behind me so that he can have privacy. And then I go straight to the living room, which thankfully only has my dozing grandfather in it, and begin removing lightbulbs from the Christmas tree.

CHAPTER SEVENTEEN

Countdown to Christmas: 2 Days

N O MATTER HOW many candy canes I throw away, it keeps getting worse.

The beach furnishings are gone, and Hall has redoubled his Christmas cheer efforts with laser-focused intention. Grandma and Grandpa's house is once more a swarm of red and green, silver and gold, hazy with mint (although no one can detect the source of it), towering Christmas trees in every room, bedecked in so much garland and ornaments that you can't tell the lights no longer work. I've been snatching up decorations and stuffing them behind cereal boxes in the lazy Susan, hiding them in closets and storage tubs out in the garage, but it's not enough. There's too much to keep up with, and we're surrounded. Hall can no longer hold himself back from doing what he was designed to do, showering us with every trimming you'd want for a perfect Christmas Eve: fluffy snowfall, instrumental music drifting from corners, a cozy fire, and an almost drowsy sort of happiness, one where you feel you could curl up in an armchair and be content forever.

Hall's gone all out with the food, too: bibingka, traditional Christmas pudding, peppermint bark cheesecake, leche flan, pumpkin spice and cranberry babka, a Yule log cake that will take weeks to devour, gingerbread truffles, and a truckload of meticulously decorated sugar cookies.

It's devastating.

Grandma's relaxing on the sofa with her feet up on an ottoman, wearing a lazy, feline smile as she rereads letters she claims a prince ("I won't say which one") once wrote for her. Mom and Athena are watching *Feud: Bette and Joan*, Dad growing annoyed by the number of times Mom has mentioned how handsome Stanley Tucci is. The kids are in the den teaching Grandpa how to play Minecraft while Sean feigns interest, enjoying his cheesecake. Kaia's curled up in the window seat with her guitar, gamely taking all our song requests, plucking away tranquilly and stopping every now and then to write down music.

If I'm going to keep Hall on earth longer, that means I've got to build a giant wall between myself and any modicum of cheerfulness and embrace Emo Bettie. But Hall has noted that I'm not as merry as the others, and he won't rest until that's fixed. He keeps experimenting with sounds and scents, learning what triggers my nostalgia, torturing me with Mariah Carey and the smell of maple syrup and butter. I try to hide from him after lunch, Kaia's saddest ballads blasting in my earbuds, reminding myself about all the despicable people and despicable things that make me upset. I've drawn up a list: *Kelly Frederick. Lucas Dormer. Chip and Joanna Gaines. LuLaRoe. Capital One. Piers Morgan. David Letterman.*

"Please don't," I beg when he floats over to me with my coat and boots in hand, having rounded up all the others for a snowball fight. I'm on the top bunk, halfway through a "When You Want To Cry" Spotify playlist. "Let me lie here and be depressed."

"I can't do that." He smiles sadly. "Come on, Betts. Let's make the most of today."

"No." I turn over onto my side. "Today can get bent."

"If you insist on lying in bed, I'll have no choice but to bring the fun to you. I can transform this bedroom into an episode of *The Adventures of Paddington*, 'Paddington's First Snow.' Don't make me turn you into a cartoon."

"Fine." I shove to my feet. "I'll go throw snow at people! But I refuse to feel cheerful about it."

"I'm truly sorry." He clasps my hand, helping me down. "I can't resist anymore. You have to understand—it's all pent up inside me."

It isn't an easy task, being a Holiday Spirit who physically *must* spread good feelings. Hall's need to bring joy will win out over any desire of his. That's just who he is.

I don my mittens and hat, which naturally he's knitted for me, with crotchety grumbling. *Daytona Beach*, I think determinedly. *Lorne Michaels. Carl's Jr.* Andromeda Magazine. *The Duke of Cambridge*. If Hall can't resist bringing me joy, then it's up to me to resist feeling it. Today I am going to dwell on the melting ice caps and stranded penguins.

We troop to the front door. When Hall turns the knob and opens it, a snowball flies directly at my chest. Snowballs are whizzing everywhere. "Hey!" I yell. "I'm not ready yet!"

"The safe zone is Mrs. Bannerman's tombstone," Hall says, pointing to a foam prop. "We're split up into two—"

Oh, this sweet, naïve angel. This family doesn't do *teams*. I watch Grandma take out Kaia with a snowball aimed at her left leg. When I see Felix and remember him telling me I'm not an actress, I bean him in the head, but he dives toward the tombstone too fast. It's a souvenir from a role Grandma played in the early 2000s. She was promised by the director that she'd have just as many lines as the lead actor, but the script was rewritten and her character was killed off in the first ten minutes of the movie as the catalyst for the husband's high-octane revenge tour. Her character didn't even get a first name. Every few years, some writer or other comes to visit Grandma for an interview, and the publications always include a photo spread of these tombstones stippling the yard—MRS. BANNERMAN, HIS WIFE—and Grandma feels vindicated.

Felix's children and nephews wait in the trees for him to leave the safe zone, then fire the cannons. Years' worth of rage over watching Felix flirt with their teachers and their friends' moms is coming out.

Marilou takes pity on him, a knight in puffy pink armor. As Felix hovers behind her, agog at his wife's accuracy, I think back on the little boy who tried to help me open my presents, who brought me a toy when I was in time-out. How big and open his heart was before chasing fame messed it up.

He's an idiot sixty percent of the time. He messes up constantly, like I do, like we all do, but I study his happy, animated face and you know, I think I might have a soft spot for that idiot under all the annoyance.

The soft spot firms up with a quickness, though, when Felix tricks me into thinking he hurt his knee, limping, only to knock me down with a snowball the size of my head. He pulls the same stunt on Mom, who rushes over to help him only to receive a cold white splat to her hip. When he comes for Athena, however, my older sister has no compassion and blasts him right in the gut. Then she makes sure no one can retaliate by shouting that she might be pregnant. Sean locks himself inside his car for half an hour, forehead against the steering wheel, sobbing. He doesn't get out until she admits she lied.

Minnesota Moon pelts Grandma, who isn't as spry as she used to be. She's a tall woman wearing all black, a stark contrast against the snow, which puts her at a disadvantage in this game. "I've got you covered, Grandma!" I cry, running up behind Minnesota Moon. I grab her, hefting her over my shoulder. I zigzag through the yard, tackling children, delighting in their shrieks. Hall grins from the sidelines. I'm struck by a long-ago memory of Grandma playing with us when we were little, too. I only remember one time in the winter—she dragged us in a long wooden sled from the back of the house over toward the woodpile. Athena tipped over the side when Grandma went too fast, knocking out a loose baby tooth. The tooth fairy brought her a guilt-ridden eighty dollars that night, which she spent at Rocky Road Ice Cream Parlor. She bought Felix, Kaia, and me ice cream cones every day for the rest of the visit.

Hall strolls over to me, wearing the smile he dons whenever he's feeling particularly pleased with himself, and I automatically smile back at him.

"What?"

He observes the air around me. "Your happiness meter has been climbing higher by the day. When I walked over to you just now, it went up another notch."

"It did not."

"It did so, and that is because you're happy to be around me, which you shouldn't be embarrassed about. You can't see my happiness meter, but if you did, you'd see it's bursting through the roof." He wriggles his fingers, miming an explosion. "Wires and sprockets everywhere."

My lips twist. "You've been hiding from the carnage you provoked."

His mouth flattens as he cuts the house a long, world-weary frown. "I got sidetracked talking to Kaia about her custom of ending relationships out of fear, even when she still loves the person."

I stare at him wonderingly. "What on earth possessed you to do that?"

"Have you listened to her singing lately? Somber love songs. The closer we get to Christmas, the more somber she gets. Sometimes, people don't know how to healthily communicate, so the requests end up coming out backwards or sideways or invisible. Sometimes, people could use a hug, but they ask for it by half-heartedly flinging a snowball at your face."

"If you say so." I am somewhat disturbed by his assessment of Kaia. Maybe I should be giving her more hugs myself.

"I just told her that I saw her happiness was low and said that if she opens up to her family instead of dealing with her struggles alone, she might feel better." He levels me with a *look*, so that I know exactly who he's segued into talking about.

"Opening up is not a Watson-Hughes family forte," I reply thinly.

"I think people can work out anything, as long as they put in the effort. Even though you've argued with your family a few times this visit, you haven't left. You're still here."

"That's because you're here. You make it better."

The light in his eyes dims somewhat, smile fading. But he

hooks his arm in mine and briskly changes the subject. "Time for dinner. I fixed a turkey, with all of the traditional sides, so that I can pretend it's Thanksgiving. Kind of a two-in-one! We're eating a bit early because I have a surprise in store for later."

"Oh? Do tell."

*

"Oh, not *that*!"

"Yes, that! Come on." Hall grabs my arm, steering me toward the spiked black gate bordering my grandparents' property, opening it up to the sheer, plunging driveway. He's always been a whirlwind, but his velocity is especially powerful this evening. He rushed us through dinner so that we could get to this part, but by dinner's end, when he was trying to convince us all to accept third helpings, I could tell he was regretting not taking his time. Now we're overstuffed and the last thing we want to do is go on a walk, but the bracing air does feel nice.

"Caroling!" Mom cries, clutching a song booklet to her chest. We've all got a copy, but I don't think any of my family members have examined the covers closely enough to realize that the vintage artwork of the group of people singing is *us*. "I adore caroling!"

Kaia belts out a few lines with such easy and enviable talent that Athena pouts. "It isn't fair to make me sing alongside a professional."

"You sang in that J.G. Wentworth commercial," Sean reminds her, but is silenced with a glare.

"This is going to be fun!" Hall says. "I promise." It comes out sounding like *or else*.

He leads the way down to Old Homestead Road, the conductor

of our caroling train. The children keep zigging and zagging, shouted back into place by Grandma, whose favorite part of the holidays is getting the chance to boss the youths. Felix is showing off his baritone, asking Mom who's the better singer, him or Kaia. I make up the caboose, because I'm still trying not to have fun. It's a lot more challenging than I'd expect considering it's quality time with my family. I'm on the dangerous precipice of smiling for no reason.

Peaches and cream oatmeal, I think to myself, focusing on the ills of this world. *Tucker Carlson. The cancellation of* Pushing Daisies. *The dog from the Bush's Baked Beans commercials.* Family Guy. (They've made fun of me before.) *The way Play-Doh smells like it should be edible.* Hall's got the Watson-Hughes clan singing "Here We Come A-Caroling" and he hasn't had to threaten anyone's lives to do it. Sean and a few of the kids had laughed off the suggestion, but here they are, louder than all the rest, showing off their pipes. Mom, Grandma, and Grandpa harmonize effortlessly. Dad hums, which is his limit. I hum under my breath, too, lip-syncing whenever Hall glances over his shoulder.

I refuse to be joyful. I haven't been the most stubborn human on earth for twentysomething years in a row just to break that streak now.

"Psst."

Hall has smoothly materialized at my side, syncing his steps with mine.

Ahead of us, Grandma is radiant, making up for all the emotions I'm attempting to strangle. Kaia has a little more pep in her step. And up front with Felix, Marilou sings off-key on purpose to make him laugh, wearing baby Adrian in a sling.

"Psst," Hall whispers again.

I ignore him. I know what he's up to—he's only trying to put me in a good mood, and I won't have it.

He leans in. Murmurs in my ear, "I've got a hamster in my pocket."

My head swings. "You what?"

He slides a thumb into his pocket, stretching the fabric enough for a small, furry head to poke out, as well as two tiny paws.

There is a hamster. In his pocket.

I stare at him in exasperation. He grins, eyes lit up, and *oh*, what a nasty trick—I grin back, shaking my head.

"You're something else."

"I know. Her name is Hildy. You'll take good care of her, won't you?"

"Don't you dare saddle me with a hamster."

"Look! She loves you." He raises her up to give my cheek a kiss, then stows her away again in his pocket. Damn, now I'm in a good mood against my will, and this is very unkind of him, and so very unfair. But it's too late now, our arms brushing as we walk past Cheers Chocolatiers and its vintage mural of an apple-cheeked young woman in a bonnet and yellow summer dress, tasting a chocolate. Silver Mine Dining is aglow, plates and forks jangling in the kitchen as the back door opens and closes behind one of its workers, who walks briskly into the alley to throw out garbage. The roads are lined with lamps tied up with big red bows, old-fashioned clocks on posts, wreaths and multicolored lights. The sky's silver-white with snow, bright without any sun, the shadows of houses falling across us in stripes long before we pass them.

Teller City is a strange little place for the great Bettie Watson to end up in. Small, charming, and utterly normal, just like Grandpa's personality, with a long-closed Coca-Cola plant and a dance studio whose sign reads NOW DANCE AWAY, DANCE AWAY, DANCE AWAY, ALL! Surrounding mountains like enormous chunks of rough white howlite, jagged edges scraping the sky. Neighbors are delighted to be serenaded, opening their doors as we pass by in our discordant parade. Some wave and shout our names. Some get out their cameras. A man who is probably college age proclaims his love for my grandmother, who laughs when Grandpa jokingly rolls up his sleeves to square up. Mary from Mary Had a Little Boutique waves at me, and an image strikes me out of nowhere, unbidden: my strange little cards on her store's shelves, next to homemade soap and mittens. A description tag scrawled with *Artisanal greeting cards by local artist Bettie Hughes.*

I can see the image so clearly in my mind that I pause for a moment, committing it to memory. Hall glances at me and follows my gaze, not seeing what I'm seeing, but something in my expression makes him smile. I fold up the thought and tuck it into my pocket for later.

On we go, past the market, the bookshop, the post office, singing "The Holly and the Ivy." Hall, without my knowledge, has slipped elsewhere into our group, leaving me shoulder to shoulder between my sisters. Kaia throws an arm around me as she sings, pushing me over to Athena, who nudges me back toward Kaia, in a game we used to play when we were kids, walking together. I'd forgotten how it feels to be on the inside of that club again.

I study Kaia, realizing I've been looking out at her from a distance for a long time, seeing her as less real than she is. Then

Athena's self-conscious mumbling gives way to a top-of-her-lungs spectacle, which makes me smile, genuinely, and I'm overcome with a strange, earnest tug to do the same. This persona we've all adopted, that we don't care, that we're untouchable, is a protective second skin that we maybe don't take off often enough. Maybe if I let my persona rest around family now and again, they'll feel safe enough to do so, as well.

"Have we ever gone caroling before?" Mom asks. "I feel like we have."

"I did in a movie," Grandma replies. *A Very Warren Christmas.*

"We've never gone caroling," Felix says.

"Well, I think we should do this every Christmas," adds Mom, who doesn't like the spotlight but is happy to be part of a pack.

"But you'll have to go caroling *here*," Grandpa tells her with an authoritative nod. "Where there's snow."

Dad shocks everyone by suggesting, "Next year we'll all fly out to visit my parents and surprise them with caroling. Have you ever been to England, Hall?"

"Yes." But not in person.

"It's the loveliest country," Mom declares. Dad throws her an amused look, as Mom has never visited England without complaining about the weather. "You two could even get married there!"

Neither Hall nor I say anything.

We pour past the Blue Moose Café, past my gingerbread town house, which is starting to grow on me, Teller City Trading Company, clanging our bells, shouting to the heavens, singing the *Hall* part of "Deck the Halls" extra loud. Then we sing "Santa Claus Is Coming to Town," and Hall changes *you'd better watch out, you'd better not cry* to *you'd Bettie watch out, you'd Bettie not cry.*

I slip my hand in his. "Your hands are probably cold. Thought I should keep one of them warm." I clear my throat. "I'm very chivalrous like that."

"You're a saint." He laces our fingers together. "Hmm. Is your cheek cold?"

"It's all right."

"Because if so, I was thinking that I should probably kiss it," he ventures. "For warmth."

"Oh." Delighted surprise swells. "Yes, I'm *freezing*. Can't feel a thing. Might be dying."

He kisses my cheek, and it warms me from the top of my head to the tips of my toes.

"Feel that?" he asks under his breath.

I can certainly feel that I'm a smitten, dreamy-eyed puddle. My breath catches at every little part of Hall that gives away what he's thinking about: the glint in his eyes, how intent they are, how fierce, absorbing every detail of me in turn. His reactionary swallow when my stare runs long. The way his hair curls, specks of snow bringing out the russet tints as they melt and darken, and my body goes absolutely haywire over it. Tingling extremities. Fairies in my stomach, diving and fluttering. My pulse is like if someone took my heart and skipped it across the surface of a lake. My gaze drops to his lips, full and dark in the wintry air. "I think my mouth might be frostbitten," I say.

"Oh, I have a cure for that."

He chucks a finger under my chin and leans in, expression turning serious. Just before his lips can brush mine, a snowball splats all over our fronts. I scream, not just because it's cold but also the timing was very rude.

"Get a room!" Ichabod crows.

"Devil child," I snarl. "I'm stuffing snow down the back of your shirt. Come here."

He cackles and speeds ahead. The other adults turn to see what's going on, Marilou pays Ichabod back with a snowball of her own, and a small war breaks out until Grandma gets hit in the butt and swears she'll lock us all out of the house. Hall gives me a somewhat shy sidelong look and I bite my lip, glancing away; then I look at him and *he* looks away, and we both laugh. My heart swoops with panic even as my smile grows, and I think he knows, because his grip is tight, like he wants to never let go.

Valley Visitor's Center & Sleigh Ride Depot passes out Oreo-flavored candy canes to us all, which makes Hall's *month*. A clerk from Loggerheads Law Offices spots us coming from afar, dashing out with Hershey's Kisses for the kids. By the time we reach the flickering Lone Wolf Motel on North Platte and unanimously decide to turn back, the streetlamps have all sprung to life.

"Can we race?" the kids ask their parents.

"No, you'll get hit by a car."

"We'll stay on the sidewalk!"

Sean picks up his youngest daughter, settles her on his shoulders, and bolts. She squeals. The others take off with or without permission. The adults hurry a bit faster so that they can keep an eye on them, except for Grandma and Grandpa, who accept a ride from one of their friends passing by.

"See you at home!" Grandma cackles from the backseat, wiggling her fingers. "Walking uphill is for suckers." Mom flips her off, and then she and Dad cross to the other side of the road to be alone, arms entwined.

Hall and I slow our pace until the others have outstripped us, falling quiet.

The Grand Canyon, I think, heartbeat faltering. *Chalk. Herbie the car. Every math teacher I've ever had.*

"Oh, this'll never do." He groans. "I'm supposed to be cheering you up! I'm the shame of holiday-spiriting."

"You're *not*. You're the best, only I wish you weren't. I wish you were rotten at your job."

"I once got employee of the month for one hundred and eighty-two consecutive months," he tells me. "Toppled from my throne in 1996 by a Holiday Spirit who helped Adam Sandler come up with 'The Chanukah Song.' Brought him the chorus in a dream, and after that, yours truly was old news."

"I don't believe you."

His lips curve, eyes scanning the horizon. The rest of my family have wandered out of sight. The sky has gone to sleep, fading to black when we're not looking. Snow hangs suspended in streetlamps' beams, fluttering without appearing to be falling. Hall magicks a red umbrella for me, a green one for himself; we twirl them, listening to sleet pitting off the nylon. When I let my umbrella list to the side while spinning it, a cyclone of snow goes curling off the top, a bright spray in the dark.

The wind ruffles his hair. "Do you see what I see?"

In the air, like a soft wind, a faint chorus of "Do You Hear What I Hear" accompanies, and I feel my cheeks lift.

"What do you see?"

He twists a lock of my hair around his finger, wistful. "A beautiful girl who makes me laugh. Who, the longer I'm with her, the more unbearable it feels that I must ever stop."

My smile falls.

He clears his throat, looking away. "And, I see a world I have so much affection for. A tiny little town of silver and gold." He toes a rock aside with his shoe, brow lowered. I think he's trying to fight back the thoughts that are troubling him, but willpower can only get you so far. He's learning that being human means dealing with your feelings as they strike, and not simply choosing more pleasant ones with the click of an internal button. "Do you like it here?"

I haven't always. But now? I'm not so sure.

He follows my attention, sweeping in a wide western arc across the indigo sky, up to the west, down again like a looping roller coaster. This town was supposed to be a temporary stopover, an irritation to overcome and then forget. But, unclouded by those feelings, all I see is alpine beauty, triangles of mountain that flush red, purple, blue in the sunset, like paper cutouts. The big, round clock of Town Hall glowing like a full moon, tower shrouded in fog, its cobblestone courtyard strung with twinkly lights. Streetlamps twined with garland and red velvet bows mark each corner, the one-way gravel tributaries that wind off into the trees, into the mountains, disappearing into nowhere.

"It has its qualities."

Hall's eyes find me, playful yet solemn. "Do you hear what I hear?"

A lonely train whistle, boxcars rumbling across a stone viaduct. I catch snatches of curling white print on the train: *Wish Come True Express.*

I wish he'd stop making the world feel as magical as he sees it, but I'm resigned.

"I bet it's pretty here in the spring," Hall observes, lifting a hand toward the bare trees. I like what the shadows do to his face when he tips his head back; they close in on either side like dark fingers of a glove, and I visualize him in a twilit bedroom, palms pressed to a windowsill as he gazes down upon a lively street. Then, without even shifting his gaze, he'd be seared with awareness of me, knowing intrinsically that I moved into the room. Somehow I already know *exactly* how his muscles will tense: with equal parts restraint and longing, because he draws out every moment that gives him pleasure and will make himself wait until he can't any longer. Those gorgeous eyes would look like moonless nights, hands reaching for me, bringing me flush against him. I can see the rise and fall of his chest, the anticipation. I can hear his steady breathing in that quiet, faraway room, even from where I stand in the road inside a timeline that won't ever let us have that moment.

It's painful, how badly I want it.

Some trees fill with pink blossoms before our eyes, others pale green. Birdsong begins to chirrup from somewhere hidden, and I can smell it—earth and rain and that uniquely spring scent, like wet sticks, a doused fire.

I watch the pink blossoms blow away as green leaves unfurl and grow, a warm breeze shuddering through. Even though it's dark out, sunlight warms my face, rebounding off the umbrella. As quickly as summer arrives, it gives way to autumn. The world is crimson, copper, gold, with pumpkins on doorsteps and scarecrows hanging from shadowed doors. Hall watches the progression with contemplative eyes that are, I notice, more brown than they are green.

When his hand falls, the trees are snow-laden, skeletal once more.

"You could see it," I tell him. "If we're careful, you can stay long enough to watch the seasons change. You could stay forever."

"I need you to be more responsible with your money," he replies, out of left field. "Okay?"

"Hall."

"I'm serious. Please listen—I'm going to be upset if I see you struggling, and there's nothing I can do. My magic works differently up there." He lifts his chin. "I can only wrap you in feelings, not things."

"I don't like this. Don't talk about going away."

"I am going, though. There's nothing we can do to stop it."

"There has to be."

He steps close, that golden, comforting warmth encircling, making me briefly close my eyes. "It's every time you catch me looking at you," he says so quietly I barely hear it. His breath hitches. A slow blink, eyes darkening. "It's every time I laugh."

"What is?" I whisper back.

His hands cradle my face. He's so close that I make out new freckles, too faint to be detected from even a foot away—on his brow bone, three beneath his left eyebrow. Secret freckles. There's still so much I don't know about Hall, that perhaps I'll never know.

"You get a little bit happier," he responds with a smile that doesn't reach his eyes. Those strange eyes, more human now than ever, but still not completely of this world. There's an inner light in their depths—if I turn my profile at just the right angle, I can see it flickering. "It's a good thing that my purpose is close to being fulfilled. I tell myself it's a good thing."

"I don't want to be happy." I swallow a rising lump in my throat. "I don't want to be happy anymore if it means you'll go, okay? Make my wish come true."

Instead of making my wish come true, he holds me close. My

thoughts stumble into the future, to a Bettie who won't have this luxury anymore, who won't be able to hold him whenever she wants. I love the way I feel when we're together, bubbly and light and safe, whether alone or in a crowded room. The way he casts a glow over the atmosphere like *anything* can happen, mysteries around every corner, old concepts taken for granted shining in a new light. Even the bad days, with Hall, are adventures. Just thinking about how I'm going to lose his caring touch, and the opportunity to admire him while he . . . While he *everything*. Bakes with my mother, side by side, sending me flirty winks and secret smiles because he can feel my close attention on him. How could I want to look anywhere else?

He helps my grandparents by wheeling their garbage cans down the road for pickup, which is terribly attractive. If he walks through the kitchen and notices the oven timer has less than ten minutes left on it, he sticks around just to make sure someone's there to get the food out before it burns. He answers the landline when everybody else ignores it, striking up friendly conversations with telemarketers. He tinkered with a grandfather clock on the third floor, making it chime the tune of one of Kaia's songs. He performs magic tricks for the kids, involving all of them in unique and personal ways, making them feel special. They like how they get to pretend there is real magic in this world, but more than that, they like how he listens to them. He doesn't act as though he's above them talking down. I'm not all that maternal, although I think I could be someday in regard to my own children, and no power weakens my knees like the sight of Hall rocking baby Adrian to sleep while wearing a paper crown Honeysuckle Lou gifted him eight hours beforehand.

How can I give him up and not fall apart? To not be able to roll over at night and see him reading on his Kindle as he often does when it's late; and then when he catches me looking, immediately begins reading aloud, giving each character a distinctive voice. My throat closes up. That feeling I wish I could stamp out only grows.

"I'm scared of feelings," I admit. "This is the punishment I get for them."

"I know." He gently squeezes. I feel like I'm up on a mountaintop, losing air. What happened to all the oxygen? I can't breathe properly.

"It isn't fair." My complaint is muffled by his shoulder. "Can't you choose to stay?"

"No."

So definite. A swift kill. *No*.

"Can't you lie?"

"If you like." He withdraws enough to see my face. "I get to stay forever."

I frown.

"Didn't help?" he guesses, the laugh lines around his mouth deepening.

"I'm trying to figure out a way to trick you into staying. A loophole. If you go, I won't be this happy anymore, which means you'll have to come back. Every time you go away, I'll be unhappy again, so you'll have to keep coming back to me over and over."

His sad smile is enough to dash my hopes. "I'd be happy to let you trick me, if it worked that way," he says, tapping my nose. "I wish there was a loophole. I'm so sorry there isn't."

"But if you go . . . what will I do?" It's not about the things. I don't care about the things anymore, which I think he knows. What use do I have for thousand-dollar purses and yachts when the person who gave them to me is gone?

He wipes a wayward tear from my cheek. "We'll have to muddle through somehow," he says lightly. Then he pulls away, like he can't take being this close to me.

We walk and walk, my toes numb in my boots, ears stung by the frozen air. The snowflakes up in the streetlights tremble in their orange slant, and slowly, Christmas music expands into the atmosphere, ringing clear as bells. Dancers spring out of the snow in colorful costumes—a girl and a Nutcracker Prince, a court of snowflakes in starlight skirts, a Sugar Plum Fairy. They're on the edge of transparent, almost ghostly.

"I love a good musical," he confides. His holiday cheer momentum is a train without brakes, barreling downhill. There is no stopping it. All I can do is brace myself for the crash.

One of the dancers leaps so close that I can taste the mint in my mouth. "Amazing."

To the orchestra rising from the opposite side of the street, he calls, "Play us out!"

Trumpets, horns, and violins swell.

We walk home in the night, our pair of umbrellas spinning off snow like sparklers, as he covers me in the merry and the bright.

And something else—

Another feeling, one that burns long and low rather than the flashes he was designed for, and which he never planned, that has awakened with such a power that there can be no possibility of it being rewound.

※

Chapter Eighteen

⸺⸺⸺⸺

T'S TRADITION FOR us to watch *It's a Wonderful Life* before bed on Christmas Eve night, so that's what we're doing, piled together in the living room. Hall and I are on the floor, sharing a turkey sandwich. I look at Grandpa, as it's tradition for him to shed a tear when the movie ends. But he's serious and sharp-eyed, watching Hall and me.

"Can I sleep in the living room?" Avenue asks.

"No, Santa Claus won't come if you're out of your bed."

"But I'm not in a bed. I'm in a sleeping bag."

"I can't go to bed unless I'm wearing purple socks," says Ichabod, opening the floodgates.

"I can't go to bed unless Ichabod's wearing red socks," says Octavian.

"Why can't I watch *Euphoria*?"

"Can I have some cereal?"

"I just saw a hamster! It ran into the laundry room."

"Is it true there's a miniature town in the basement and

Grandma will make us live down there forever if we leave our dirty shoes in the hallway?"

Honeysuckle Lou attaches herself to Athena's leg and screams that she's never going to bed, ever. She wakes up Adrian, who wails, and Marilou kills several children with her eyes. Grandma threatens to shoot Santa Claus off the roof with her crossbow if they don't all pipe down, which only makes them cry more.

"Actually, I have a present for everyone," I announce before the chaos gets its feet off the ground. "An early one."

I haven't had time to wrap them, so they're still in the plastic they arrived in today thanks to next-day shipping. Only Mom knows about this present, as I needed her help figuring out everyone's sizes. Moms have a knack for knowing everything, especially last-minute.

Hall turns to me in surprise.

It's kind of a dumb present. I don't know why I got them, really. Everyone's going to think this is dumb. They're going to think it's corny—

"Aww, that's so cute!" Kaia cries, unfolding her pajamas and holding them against herself.

"I love them." Hall hugs his, eyes soft. The material is an icy blue, featuring the Coca-Cola polar bears.

Mom elects herself distributor. "I've got a size twelve over here. Who needs a twelve? Here you go. I'm looking for an eight. Jim, here you are. I've got a child's ten. Minnesota, ask your dad if you're 5T."

Athena wriggles her fingers high in the air. "Anybody see a ladies' four?"

"Little tight on my biceps," grunts Felix, who peeled off his shirt to try on the new one, flexing his arms. Grandpa snorts.

Even Dad tries on his, which Mom praises him endlessly for doing, as the positive reinforcement might persuade him to try couples' Halloween costumes next year. "Everybody in front of the tree! I want to take a picture. Peach Tree, where are your new pajamas? Well, go get them out of the bathtub! Frangipane, get over here, there are no hamsters in this house." She and Grandpa herd everybody. Athena clotheslines a nephew in her haste to get the best spot, practicing which smile she wants to use.

"Wait!" Athena dashes upstairs. "Don't take it yet!"

When she hurries back down, her lips are tinted, hair smoothed. She settles down on one knee and holds a tube of bareMinerals liquid foundation in her palm for the camera.

"Oh my *God*." Felix rolls his eyes.

"Shut up," she seethes. "It's Christmas."

Mom sets a timer, then throws herself into the crowd. "Three, two, one—smile, everybody!"

We gather around her phone to check out the picture. Only three of us were prepared for the camera to go off. Dad tries to weasel out of participating by insisting he be the one to take a redo, but Kaia saves the day, figuring out how to set the timer for fifteen seconds.

"Everybody scoot in!" Mom yells like our lives depend on it. "Bettie, scoot in! More!"

I'm practically in Hall's lap. He eases an arm around me, and I can't help it. I do a very fiancée-type thing, and lay my cheek against his shoulder. Hall tilts his head slightly to rest on mine, which pleases me more than it should. *Please don't let my meter go up*, I think. The camera flashes and I glance askance, half expecting Hall to be gone. But he's still here.

I sigh in relief.

"Did we get it?" Mom asks, running back to the camera. "Oooh, that's a good shot." She lifts it and unexpectedly snaps another of just Hall and me. "Lovely! You could use that to announce your engagement, Betts. Do you want me to take some of you two out in the snow? Making snow angels! Now *that* would be cute. We could write your wedding date in the snow, if you have a date. First thing in the morning, that's what we should do."

I don't answer, kissing her cheek good night. Then I turn, catching Hall as he changes the channel from *Frosty the Snowman* to the local news. I raise my eyebrows.

"It's a sad movie," he says by way of explanation.

"It's a Christmas cartoon. I'm shocked you don't love it."

"Frosty melts." He places the remote very carefully on the TV stand so that he won't have to look at me. "When the winter fun is over, he has to go away."

My heart squeezes. "Oh." *Right.*

We all do the good-night rounds. I'm the best aunt ever because I can reach the cookie basket that Sean hid on top of the fridge, handing out cookies in secret because c'mon, it's Christmas Eve.

"Night, Grandma." I air-kiss my grandmother, who has paired her pajamas with a matching blue wig. "Merry Christmas Eve, everybody." I hug Grandpa, who keeps me for a second longer. I assume he's going to press some pocket money into my hand, but instead he surprises me.

"Don't let that one go," he murmurs at my ear.

"Huh?"

He nods at Hall, who's hugging Dad tightly, eyes closed, smiling beatifically (Dad is trying to be annoyed but failing). "The way he looks at you. I've been paying close attention, to make sure he's good enough for you . . . He's just *enamored.*"

My mouth is dry. My gaze irresistibly flits to Hall, who feels me watching, and our eyes lock. He flashes that devastating grin, and it's automatic, how quick I go boneless.

A gleam strikes Grandpa's clever eye, and I realize: he knows we've been pretending. Grandfathers are very good at knowing secrets, especially the heavy-of-heart ones. Maybe it's my lack of wedding talk, or the way Hall and I are with each other. He doesn't ask what my motives are, likely guessing that I did it (as I do most things) for attention.

"You see?" he whispers. "He's carrying the whole moon over there. It shines out of his eyes when he looks at you."

This is the last thing I need to hear. "I suppose," I mumble uncomfortably.

"You *suppose*? I hope you see what's in front of you, and that you appreciate who you have." Grandpa is rarely stern with me and can't keep it up for long. "I worry about you."

"I know I'm lucky. I appreciate Hall very much." I'm going to cry if I don't get out of here. "Night, Grandpa."

"Merry almost-Christmas, sweetheart." He pats my back fondly, letting me go. I walk on wobbly legs upstairs, dodging children hiding from their parents. I close my bedroom door behind myself, gulp down a sharp and shaky breath, and have to sit down. Except the bunk bed is gone.

Hall enters with two steaming cups of hot chocolate, expression turning sheepish when his gaze travels from me to the bed. Bed, singular. "Sorry about this. My magic is, ah, blinking out a bit. Happens sometimes."

"Your magic spontaneously turned the bunk bed into . . . what is this, a queen?"

He nods slowly, eyebrows high. "I'm as surprised as you are.

I'll do a maintenance check on my magic in the morning, but I'm so exhausted right now from a very long day of Christmas Eve magic-making that I can't possibly set it right tonight." He looks convincing, but I eye one of the romance novels he bought at Gold Rush with suspicion, lying on his nightstand with half its pages dog-eared to mark favorite passages.

"All right." I slide into bed on the left side; he climbs in on the right and then passes me a hot chocolate. I'm incredibly full; if I consume one sip or bite of anything more, I might explode, and also I just brushed my teeth. But I accept it, of course.

"Nice bedspread." I tug the covers up to my middle. It features a giant red pickup truck with pine trees sticking out of the bed. HALL'S CHRISTMAS TREE HAUL.

"Thank— Oh? I hadn't noticed. Would you look at that! Yes, so it is. I'm glad my subconscious magic picked it."

"Your subconscious magic has good taste." I glance at him, then away, then back at him. He's in an old-fashioned stocking cap, the end of it drooping onto his shoulder, with a fuzzy white pom-pom. "Never mind."

"What, this?" He reaches up to touch it. "It's traditional Christmas Eve garb. You want one?"

"No."

"Your loss." Under the bedspread, he crosses his ankles. Sighs dreamily. "My first Christmas Eve night in a human body."

"Did it live up to the hype?"

"It *did*, Bettie. It lived up to it so much that all my past dreams have shattered into a billion pieces. Ka-boom. I'll remember it always." He turns to me. "Will you?"

"I can't imagine forgetting a Christmas Eve that involves dancing Sugar Plum Fairies and a hamster in your pocket."

"Hildy. Don't forget to take care of her."

"Hall."

"I've added some savings to your bank account, but not so much cushion that by the time it thins out beneath you, you'll have reverted back to your old habits."

"Hall."

"I wonder if I've got one more trip to Cracker Barrel left in me. I'm haunted by the chicken tenders I could've had."

"Hall, you're making it snow."

He stops chattering. Stares around. "Oh. Sorry." He rubs his palms together and the flurry ceases, then disappears. "We've got a big day tomorrow."

"You must be excited."

"You can't possibly imagine. I've been waiting to be on the inside of a happy, cozy home for Christmas morning—well, for always. Do you think I should get a Christmas piñata? Is that a thing?"

"We could make it a thing."

"Good idea. I can't wait to have the whole family sit down together, hold hands, and recite what we're grateful for." He sighs again. "I hope your grandmother says she's grateful for the life-size wax mannequin I made of her, in character as Priscilla Presley from the 1993 movie *My Life with Elvis*, for which she won Best Supporting Actress. If I were here in summer, I would take her to the opera, and we'd wear bedazzled denim jackets. That's the dream. Along with being a meteorologist."

He's being serious about the meteorologist part (every morning he watches the weatherman's report with naked envy), but I think he's laying the rest on thick, trying to turn my blue thoughts toward sunlight with good-natured rambling. He goes quiet, perhaps thinking about what he would really do if he were here in the summertime. I bet he would love picnics. I bet he'd want to go to every small-town street fair in the Midwest and sample deep-fried novelties. Visit every amusement park. Join a local Wiffle ball league. I've never done anything like that and wish we could go on all those adventures together. Hall's immortal, yet he's had such a short life.

I switch off my bedside lamp, he flicks off his, and together we stare at the arctic moonlight spattered over the wall, broken up by shadows of snowflake decals he's affixed to the window.

"Best holiday ever," he declares.

"Yes, you are." I turn my face to catch his grin.

He closes his eyes, lips still curved into a smile, propped up on the pillows as if wanting to stay awake. As though he can't stomach the idea of missing a single moment. "What does tonight feel like for you?" I want to know. "As the Holiday Spirit, I mean."

He ponders the question. "Like a precipice, and like a pit, depending on whose mood I'm picking up. I feel all the wishes, all over the world, of other people. I feel their loneliness, their anticipation. It doesn't brush as close now—my focus has only been you lately—but it tends to be either a wonderful night or a painful one. If I could go to those suffering, I'd wrap my arms around their whole house like shielding someone from a bomb about to go off. I'd give them all of my peace."

Of course he would. I wonder if he's ever done that for me, on one of my cold and lonely nights. There have been many.

"And when you're out cheering everybody else up," I say, "who cheers *you* up?"

"I've always been content enough with my lot." He drifts off, hesitating, an unspoken *but* loud in the silence.

We let it hang there.

He touches my hand instead, covering mine with his. I think about what might happen right now if he were an ordinary human man, and not a feeling made personified, a greater purpose I have to share. I think about how I would shift onto my side to face him, tugging on his hand to bring him closer. I would strive to articulate how special I think he is, and how I can't help but want more and more of something so good that it almost hurts. But then again, if he were an ordinary human man, I wouldn't have let him get this close—it's been a gift, this chance to trust someone implicitly. To be myself in the open, grudges and impulses and mistakes and all.

"Are you asleep?" he whispers some time later.

I shake my head. "Can't."

"Would you like some help with that?"

With his magic that he claims is down for maintenance. I smile into the pillow. "Okay."

He tousles my hair in gentle strokes. "I didn't understand, before I met you," he tells me. "The whole time that I was up there, without a body, I wasn't really *creating* joy. I was only setting the scene for it. Then when I came here, I couldn't *make* you feel holiday cheer, not with trees and ornaments and lights. None of that worked. Then, suddenly, you started participating."

Because I wanted Hall to enjoy Christmas.

"I think, although this comes dangerously close to sounding cheesy," I reply, "that the holiday spirit might not actually be about those things?"

"I think you're right."

"I think it might be about sharing good feelings with others." There are better ways to phrase this, but I intentionally dance around them all. "Being with special someones, maybe. Spending time together."

His pitch drops. "I think you're right about that, too."

A beat passes. My throat closes up.

"When will you go, exactly?"

"I don't know. Soon." His breath hitches. "You're up to a nine point two on the scale now."

What absolutely awful news.

I can almost hear that ticking clock in his head as the silence carries on for a while longer, with the sleigh-bells-and-crackling-ember-atmosphere that is distinctly Hall. Then he begins to hum. There's no spellwork laced into the sound, no holiday fog that will send me off to dreamland. This is a human gesture.

And it's what I needed. I drift off with his low reverberations against my shoulder, one song blending into another, into another . . .

✳

I sit up with a start, as though a lost voice has found its way into my ear, quiet as a breath but noticeable enough to snap my eyes open.

The bedroom's still full dark, blue tint sliding to a different wall with the adjusted angle of the moon. The bed is empty, comforter tucked in tight on the other side to seal in my body heat with what's left over of Hall's. But the body that's supposed to be stretched next to mine is gone.

"Hall?" I call quietly. Maybe he's sitting on the floor working on a scrapbook.

No response.

I slide out of bed, tiptoeing down the hallway, hugging my

arms against a chill that catches me now that I've left my blanket behind. "Hall?" I ask again, tentatively.

Has he . . . ?

He can't have.

The den, sitting room, and kitchen are empty. When I find him in the living room, my knees go loose and watery with relief and I clutch the arm of a chair. He's standing in the golden star-burst of light surrounding the Christmas tree, watching the snowy world beyond the glass patio doors with a tilted head, absently toying with a Popsicle stick ornament. When he spots my reflection drifting up behind him, he turns.

"Hey." My voice is shaky. "What are you doing down here? Don't tell me you're snooping through presents."

His expression transforms with that crackling-fire smile, twin flames in the depths of his eyes. "And if I was?"

I poke him in the chest. "That's cheating." But I'm a hypocrite, so I start snooping, too.

"I'm still working on your gift." He waves a hand, within which a shiny, book-shaped package appears. "Not finished yet, but I hope you'll like it."

The grandfather clock gongs midnight, and I bite my lip. "I *suppose* I can let you take a peek at what I got for you, now that it's officially Christmas."

He hits me with that solar flare of a smile. "Yeah?"

My hand slides up his wrist, tracing his forearm. "Yeah. I think you should have the honor of opening the first present. You've done so much for all of us."

My gift to Hall lacks presentation. I went overboard with the tape, and it's lumpy, but you'd never guess I did a bad job by his reaction. "Oh my." Hand over his heart. *"Bettie."*

"What do you think?"

I already know the answer. He's so easy to please. He smooths the new sweater against his chest and tucks his chin down to appreciate it. The sweater says HALL I WANT FOR CHRISTMAS IS YOU (Bettie Hughes, in collaboration with Madeline Watson-Hughes, $29.99 plus supplies).

"Something else, too," I add, a little shy. I go fetch his other present from the laundry room, where I'd stashed it earlier, fiddling nervously with my hair when he accepts it without a word: a bouquet of mixed flowers in crinkly wrapping. It comes with a note: *From your secret admirer.*

"You mentioned that you've always wanted one," I rush to explain. "The flowers and the, uh, secret admirer. I know it's not the same as a proper Valentine's Day secret admirer, but—"

"It's the best present in the world," he replies, voice rough. He clears his throat, blinking rapidly, distraught and pleased in equal measure. "You shouldn't have."

"I couldn't help myself."

He turns the bouquet in his hand, memorizing every blossom: carnations and Gerbera daisies, tiger lilies and sunflowers. The friendliest, happiest flowers I could rush-order. In a faint breath, he adds, "I wish you had."

He places the bouquet carefully on the sofa, then twists toward me. "These are generous gifts, and I adore them. But there's something else I really want." His gaze drops to my mouth. When he finds his voice again, it's low and jagged. "It's *all* I want. I can't stop thinking about it."

My heart somersaults with a heavy, clumsy *thump*, then accelerates so fast that I get light-headed. "Yeah?"

A slow nod as he steps forward, attention lifting to the space above me. I look up, too, watching as a small plant blooms in mid-air: a cluster of green teardrop-shaped leaves, tied together with a red bow.

Mistletoe.

"It keeps appearing above your head," he confesses. "Whenever I think about how much I want to kiss you, mistletoe manifests, and I have to hurry up and get rid of it before you notice. Sometimes I get rid of it and it immediately grows right back, even bigger than before."

I smile. "That explains a few things."

"You're a powerful woman, Bettie Hughes." His lips twist. "When you kissed me, I legitimately think it rewrote my DNA. And ever since, I've been dying to kiss you again."

I tip my head up slightly. "Me, too."

We look at each other for a long moment, letting that settle.

Then his hands spear the ends of my hair, admiring how the strands slip between his like silk, dark gaze lingering on me in question. We both exhale, no need to hide emotions anymore, to suppress. This is it.

He skims his thumb along my lower lip, and I kiss it.

I've got to make this good. I've got to make it so good that he never forgets, that when he's looking back on the memory of me one thousand years from now, it still stands out crystal-clear.

Our first brush of lips is just holding. Familiarizing ourselves with the zing of each other's skin when it makes impact, the nerves-going-haywire charge that tingles all over. It's like being zapped by static electricity, then coming back for shock after shock. I expected a reverent touch, but he can't bear to be soft because he doesn't have the time, and he requests *more* with a rumble at the base of his throat. Cradles the back of my head and peppers me with little kisses that make my vision swim.

He tastes like peppermint bark, like snowcaps and starry nights. He feels like sunlight poured into the shape of a man, liquid and hot and golden. He can't get close enough, hands all over, clinching me to him.

My head empties. I cage his jawline in my hands and kiss him fiercely, not holding back. A quick flash of his face shows me his eyes are shut, forehead furrowed like he knows this isn't enough, that the more he takes, the faster he'll have to go, but he can't stop now. This is the precipice, and I know what comes next, so we'd better make the most of our fall.

It's snowing in the living room, dusting our hair, the Christmas tree. Music fades in and out from nowhere, lamps flaring to life— reaching excruciatingly bright crescendos just before the bulbs turn black and die. Hall either doesn't know or doesn't care as he goes on kissing me like he's breaking down from the inside out and every touch could be the last. He doesn't take any of it for granted, doesn't beg or bargain. He simply takes and savors. He makes me wish we could rewind to the moment he was conjured and spend our whole time together just like this, even though that would be impossible. When we met, we were different. We had to grow into new versions of ourselves before we could grow into this version of us.

We part for air, unsteady on our feet. My vision is dark and vibrating at the edges, all except for Hall, who glows like a star.

I can't stop staring.

"Look at you now," he says tenderly, mouth hitching into a smile that can't help itself. "Oh, that's the most beautiful happiness I've ever seen."

"You don't look as happy," I tell him, my chin quivering. "I took it all from you. Take it back."

"I wouldn't dream of it."

"Please, Hall." I hear my desperation, edged with mania.

"You deserve only the best, do you understand me?" He holds me close. "I need you to internalize that. I want you to treat yourself as I would, with kindness and respect. Promise me."

My eyes well with tears, then overflow. I need to keep him here, but I can't make this harder for him than it already is, so I say, "I promise."

"I wanted so much more." His words are raw, almost shaking, palm curling against my cheek. Hot tears splash his fingers. His expression is so anguished that I have to close my eyes. Only for a second.

They're still closed when the hands slip away from my skin. His heartbeat no longer beats against my sternum; no curling tips of his hair tickle my forehead. The dependable solidity I've been leaning against gives way so abruptly that I stagger to catch my balance, arms wrapping only around myself. But his last words still press to my throat like a kiss.

"I'm so sorry," I say, even though it's too late for him to hear it.

When Hall disappears, there is no dramatic puff of smoke. There is no remarkable sound or scent or special effects to mark the loss; there is only nothing in the space where he was. An absence of that extraordinary feeling he embodies and radiates outward, especially toward me . . . which I can say honestly, only now that he's gone . . .

Is love.

Chapter Nineteen

....

Christmas Day

W HAT DID I tell you about sleeping on the couch? I won't
be responsible for any pregnancies, Bettie Gardenia."

"What?" I mumble, opening my eyes. Why are my eyes so
sore? My chest is aching, too.

Ah. I catch sight of the bouquet of flowers Hall left behind and
remember why I feel like I've been bulldozed.

I slowly drag myself upright on the living room couch, meeting
my grandmother's hawkish, annoyed stare. "Sorry."

"Where's your fiancé? I came downstairs and there wasn't a
hot breakfast waiting for me. What the hell is up with that? I refuse to get used to it."

"He had to leave."

She reels back. "On Christmas morning?"

"It's not his fault. He didn't want to go." I stand up, all the
blood in my body running down my legs. I've had a long, emotional night, and my circuitry doesn't know what to do with itself.

I slept with Hall's sweater as a pillow, the sight of it making my heart squeeze. My gaze drifts over the hill of presents gathered around the tree, the shape of a gold-plated guitar I bought for Kaia with Hall's money. Jennifer Lopez's stolen Versace dress rests next to it, tied up in a bow for Athena.

These gifts, which I'd congratulated myself for picking out so perfectly, rub me the wrong way in the stark morning light. Staring at them now, I wrinkle my nose. They're gaudy displays of wealth I don't actually have. I envision Kaia holding the guitar in her lap, and how the big, impressive reveal will actually look to her and everyone else: like I've got a chip on my shoulder and something to prove. They'll smile and thank me and say the presents are amazing, but they'll know the intention behind them. If they found that obnoxious, I couldn't blame them.

I don't want to watch any of that happen.

Quickly, I grab all my presents and rush them back up to my room. Without Hall's magic, and on such short notice, I don't have anything to offer anybody. So I decide to take a route I haven't visited since I was a kid and go for homemade.

While the rest of my family works together to cook breakfast, I round up construction paper, washi tape, and glitter, going to town making Christmas cards. Each of them bears a Christmassy cover: trees, wreaths, candy canes, with a goofy sentiment or joke inside. When I'm finished, I have four cards per person, which I slip into boxes folded from cardstock I found in Hall's scrapbooking supplies. Then I use his stamp kit to emboss each with *Hughes & Co. Cards: Holiday Chocolate Box Edition.*

Because inside, you never know what you're gonna get.

I return to the living room as children are beginning to accumulate, faces sticky with cinnamon roll icing, impatient to learn what Santa brought. They all start ripping into their presents as my mom trails behind, cleaning up shredded paper and bows (and a million wrappers from Band-Aids, which are this year's stocking stuffers of choice). She's always the one cleaning up messes, never the one who gets to relax on the sofa and enjoy. I take the trash bag from her, forcing her into a chair. She keeps trying to get back up, helping Domino remove tags from her shirt, recovering Ichabod's glasses before Frangipane steps on them, fetching Avenue a muffin. "Sit *down*, Mom," I order, bringing her a cup of strong black coffee. I press a button on the side of her armchair to make it recline, draping a blanket across her legs. "Relax."

Astonished, she tries to project relaxation, sipping her coffee with a timid air, like she's gotten away with a crime spree.

Dad smiles.

"Josh Groban's tied up in the bathtub," Peach Tree reports placidly, bricking together a new Mario and Yoshi Lego set. "He says a weird man stole him yesterday and told him that if he ever wants to see his family again he has to serenade Aunt Bettie all day long."

"It's not nice to lie on Christmas," Athena scolds her. "That's how you get coal."

"Look! I got a five-pound jar of peanut butter!" Minnesota Moon screams, holding it up over her small head. "That's just what I wanted!"

Soon, the children are applying Band-Aids to each other and then taking turns to mercilessly rip them off, filling the house with howls and shrieking.

The presents in silver foil—Hall's signature paper—are big favorites: Russell Stover chocolates for Dad, which remind him of his first date with Mom so long ago—*"Wonder how Hall would guess that?*"—and a weaving loom for Mom. A picture of a new surfboard for Marilou (the real thing shipped to Marilou and Felix's house, so that they wouldn't have to lug it to the airport). A child-size, twenty-five-pound wooden mallard duck for Grandpa that the kids waste no time climbing on (and which has been only modestly bedazzled). Celine Dion collector's edition Barbies for Athena. For Kaia, a blacksmithing book called *Edge of the Anvil*, along with a propane forge for metalworking. "I'm gonna make so many swords," she says with a wicked glint in her eyes, thumbing through its pages.

Felix shakes a Magic 8 Ball that produces a new kernel of wisdom each time you turn it over—Hall's gift to him is a bottomless well of advice for how to make good decisions. From me, my brother gets the confession that *My Eyre Ladies* isn't real. "I knew it!" he cries, pointing his finger at me, at the ceiling, at Grandma, who hasn't done anything bad (for once). Then he weeps, collapsing against a wall. "Oh, I'm so glad. I can't stomach competition."

"I've been meaning to tell you." Felix and I aren't big huggers, but I suck it up and give him one, anyway. "*Thornfield* really does sound like an interesting movie. I'm sorry I wasn't more supportive when you told me about it."

"Nah, it's not a big deal . . ." he replies halfheartedly.

"I was an ass."

He grins. "Yeah, okay, you were an ass. But I get it. I give you shit all the time."

I hug him again. "Love you, Felix."

He bumps the toe of his slipper against mine. "Hall's really rubbing off on you, huh?"

"Nonsense. I've always been an angel."

When I'm finished sweeping up ten pounds of gift wrap, I return to my seat, where a pile of presents waits with my name on them, next to a pile of presents for Hall from my family, which I don't touch. I go through the motions of opening mine and fixing on a smile, saying thank you. But I don't absorb any of it. I can't concentrate on gifts when all I want is for Hall to be here with us, with family, which he's so badly wanted all his life and so badly deserves. I'm having a delirious, out-of-body experience, putting on a front while internally crashing. How can my family smile? How can they enjoy themselves, when the holiday spirit is gone?

Watching them laugh and hug each other, trading candy from their stockings, I wonder if their ability to carry on being merry is because Hall gave them so much of himself. They've already soaked up all the holiday cheer they need.

There's one more gift on my lap, rectangular, weighing about as much as a book. *To Bettie. Always your Hall.*

My hands hesitate before my brain tunes out all the noise and I'm tearing it open without thinking, opening not a book but a journal, the first two pages filled with his elegant, tidy script.

I snap the book shut, heart racing.

Then open it back up again to the first page.

ONE OF A KIND

One's edges need not be rounded
for them to be a good shape
Behold, the paper snowflake—
It is perfect!
And has so many points to make

I reread it, not comprehending what exactly it is that I'm seeing right away. Poetry? I've never heard him express an interest in poetry. There are only two finished poems in here, all the rest blank or occupied by rhyming word banks. He'd gotten a few other poems under way, then abandoned them, lines crossed out, frustrated inkblots leaking between pages.

"Bettie, did you make these?" Kaia's voice grabs my attention. She's holding up a colorful fan of papers. *We should do something about all those cans of paint in the basement,* one reads. Then another: *Divorce is very sad. It might help you to know that we never liked him.*

"Yeah . . ." I'm tense for a moment, but then she grins.

"I love them."

Mom is beside herself with enthusiasm in a way that only a mother whose child presents them with colorful doodles on craft paper could be. "Oh my gosh!" she cries. "You used to draw these when you were little! Remember, Jim?" She pokes on a pair of reading glasses to examine hers. *"You let my birds pair off into cliques while I was in Atlantic City and I won't forget it."* She frowns. "I don't remember you ever having birds. Bettie, when did you ask me to watch your birds?"

Athena laughs, the sparkly ink on hers flashing in the early light. Her illustration is of two pineapples riding a skateboard past a toxic waste plant. *Please don't make me choose what we eat for dinner.* "Look, Sean. It's our relationship in a nutshell."

Felix shows his to Marilou: *I didn't understand* The Goldfinch.

"Neither did I, to be honest," Marilou muses. Baby Acrian sticks a red ribbon to her cheek, and she blows raspberries into his palm. He giggles wildly.

There are no duplicates, so my family starts passing their cards around, reading the ones they didn't get.

Mom's wide blue eyes are confused. *"It's hard to find episodes of* The Mentalist *anywhere.* What? I don't get it."

"The randomness is the joke," Kaia informs her. I cover my face with my hands and smother a laugh. "It's supposed to be weird."

Mom reexamines the card. "Oh. Hah." Then a minute later: "Have you looked on Hulu for *The Mentalist*? Sometimes when I can't find something, it's on Hulu."

Watching everyone, I don't think they would have enjoyed the extravagant gifts nearly as much as they're enjoying (well, with the exception of Mom, whose humor doesn't quite match mine, but you can't please everyone) these extremely stupid homemade cards.

Grandma reads hers aloud, mouth tilted. *"You're my abettor half! See you at the trial.* Imagine getting something like this in the mail. Watch your back, Hallmark."

I smile at her, but *Hallmark* makes me think of *Hall* and how much he'd love this tableau. My eyes burn with tears. How dare he not be here for this.

It's so utterly unfair.

One by one, members of my family notice his absence, and question me about it. I expect to be berated—*What'd you do to screw it up?*—so it knocks me off my balance when they're supportive instead. Marilou brings me a waffle, even though my appetite has shriveled up. Dad asks if I'd like to help him with a puzzle. Grandma forces me to wear her lucky wig (a platinum bob with green glitter), and Grandpa whips up a bucket's worth of hot chocolate and passes me a handkerchief for my damp eyes.

Their unexpected affection prompts me to blubber, which I do privately in the kitchen pantry with my waffle (I'm not hungry, but maybe eating something sweet will help, I tell myself).

While I'm sagging against a box of Ritz crackers in the dark closet, soaking the scarf around my neck with tears, it hits me:

Maybe I can bring him back somehow. Maybe if my behavior is really, really good, the mystical cosmos will reward me with Hall, but this time he'll be here for keeps, and then I can properly tell him how I've grown to feel about him. We'll have more than just two kisses.

"Everything all right?" Mom asks when I cut back through the living room on my way upstairs.

"It will be," I reply firmly, thundering up the staircase with purpose. I don't have to be sad. This can all be temporary.

I whisk into my bedroom, which is exactly as it was when we arrived: cramped, dim, with an odor of disuse. It contains a single twin bed and one flat pillow. It's as if Hall was never here at all.

I haven't accessed the Internet in days, haven't Googled myself. This is the longest social media hiatus I've ever taken, and my fingers itch to log into those portals to hell when I open my phone. Like an addiction. But those spaces haven't been healthy for me, which is more evident than ever now that I've gotten some distance from them and feel better about myself. Hall's wall-to-wall schedule of activities for this week has incited a cleanse—now that I've gotten a taste of what it feels like to not care so much about what others are saying about me, I want to keep that streak going.

I've been so angry for so long, but I've been telling myself I don't care. But I have cared far too much, for far too long, about what everyone else thinks of me.

What is the best way to earn good behavior points? It can likely be determined by behaving polar to my impulses. If there's any way to get magic on my side, it's got to be holiday do-gooding.

I type *how to start an online auction* into my browser's search bar and giddily run through all the possibilities. At first, I'm conservative with what I decide to donate. What if I want to learn how to play the guitar someday and wish I hadn't sold the one originally meant for Kaia? What if I end up *needing* all the costumes from the 2013 film *The Great Gatsby*? But as I add items, I find myself liking the way this feels, feeding the high by giving more and more. I'm going to sell all this shit, which, it turns out, I maybe don't actually need as much as I thought I did, which will make the world a better place. No exaggeration! I am actively contributing to society—*me*, Bettie Hughes. What a thrill!

The yacht, which Hall conjured for me during my Wish For Everything In The Song "Santa Baby" Extravaganza is presently stuck in the mountains, and is going to find new significance raising money for children in need. I am calling the organization Yachts for Tots. Having started off with a bang, I keep up the momentum by brainstorming as many sellable items as I can bear to part with: all the custom jewelry Hall designed for me, ball gowns, my collection of Valentino Rockstud bags that I craved to fill the void of having to sell all my bags when I went bankrupt. My La Californienne Large Cartier Tank Wrap Strap Watch joins the auction, and I just know that it's going to end up on an ungrateful TikTok star. But this watch is four thousand dollars! Why do I need to impress strangers with brand names, anyway? Watches are useless. Time is a construct, so I do not recognize its authority. Time is math, which is another construct that I do not recognize.

The next order of business will be figuring out how to return all the stuff I can't, in all good conscience, sell: Amal Clooney's engagement ring. Elizabeth Taylor's engagement ring. JLo's green dress. Louis Armstrong's trumpet. I'll have to hire my nieces and nephews to shoot these items out of T-shirt cannons, over security gates, to land on the doorsteps of their rightful owners. And then run away very fast.

My notes app fills up with more stuff I asked Hall to procure for me: rare shoes, first-edition copies of old books I wanted purely for bragging rights, photographs of galaxies beyond the reach of our technology, a marble bust of Rihanna. And one big-ticket item I've been holding on to for years, despite the bankruptcy, which I bought with my first big paycheck: the oil painting above my bed in which I'm wearing a feather boa and nothing else, oiled-up legs dangling over the arm of a zebra chair. The way the light hits my cans is breathtaking, and I want to see if my tastefully decorated rack fetches fifteen grand—which, according to a GoFundMe, is how much a small town in Virginia needs to build a new playground. Maybe they'll even name it after me. My attention flits toward the ceiling, imagining a mist somewhere above the roof of this house. Not that it matters. I'm not doing this for clout. You hear me, mystical cosmos? My motives are completely pure.

I only hope Hall's feelings haven't changed, now that he isn't human (or at least he'd gotten close to being so) anymore. I hope that my good deeds will be enough that I'll earn him back.

Later today, when I return to the town house (Christmas is over, and we'll all be branching off to our own respective homes, cities, and states over the next few days), I'll take pictures of everything and bring the auction online. "We're going to get him back," I promise Hildy, who's currently sleeping in my bra. I tug the front of my shirt down to stroke the tiny animal down her soft back, and love bursts inside me against my will. Hildy is surprisingly docile, and cute, I suppose. She's used to Hall, who gave her lots of lovin's, so I'm trying not to disappoint her too much by being . . . not Hall. He sets a high standard.

A knock at the door commands my attention, followed by my

parents and grandfather poking their heads in. "All right?" Mom asks. "We don't want to bother you, just want to see if you're okay."

I set my phone down. Suck in a deep breath.

"Actually. Could you come here for a minute?"

They trickle inside curiously, Dad leaning on the wall with his arms crossed while Mom climbs into bed beside me and Grandpa perches at the foot.

"I haven't been entirely honest with you."

I'm emotionally wrecked and I know their support will make me feel better, but in order to get that support I have to endure the hard part and come clean. I don't tell them Hall is the Holiday Spirit, of course, because they'd worry about my mental state, but I confess that I never recovered from all my financial problems like I claimed to have. The string of mistakes I made: how when I teamed up with brands to start my own labels, I didn't know what I was doing and took bad advice. I didn't save any of my windfall. I tell them I've been living in Teller City for months, in a dead woman's house. Mom goes rather pale with worry, and I can tell Dad is trying hard to suppress judgment. He swallows all of his *you should have done x or y*, surprising me by gathering me into a hug instead.

"We would have helped," he says softly.

"I'm sorry."

"Bettie, you can *always* come to us when you need help," Mom tells me. "No matter how old you get."

"I didn't want you and Dad to argue over it. And . . . it was embarrassing. Athena, Kaia, and Felix—"

"Have needed help, too," she interrupts. "I can't tell you all the times Felix has needed a guest room to stay in because a relationship didn't work out. Kaia loaned your dad and me her car when we were having car trouble. I go with Athena every time she visits the doctor. Felix mows our lawn and collects our mail when we're away. I still bake Kaia's favorite zucchini bread and mail it to her, wherever she is in the world. And did you know that Athena is one of the producers for Felix's *Thornfield* movie?"

I shake my head, dumbfounded.

"Helping him out, like he helped her out when she needed capital for a makeup line."

"I didn't know Athena had her own makeup line."

"It fell through. She didn't come to us when that happened, either, and when I found out, we had a long talk. She thought I'd insist on giving her money, which she didn't want from me. But all I wanted was to be there for her, give her support."

"And advice," Dad interjects huffily. "We're not half bad at it, you know. We didn't come by all this wisdom for nothing. Let us pass it along to you."

Mom smiles. "Athena's going to be trying again, with different products, when she's ready."

"Yes, we *do* want you to be independent adults," Dad adds as I digest this new information, "but we also want you to let us know when you're in trouble, in times when you can't be independent. Shit happens. We're here for you when it does. And if you want, you're welcome to move back in with us temporarily until you're back on your feet." He says it so confidently, as though he has no doubt I'll prevail.

"Thanks, I appreciate that. But I'm going to keep living here for a while, I think. I got a new place downtown." All I need now is a job.

Mom and Dad, mouths open, are the picture of shock. "You want to stay in Teller City?"

"Yeah. I mean, I know I go on about how much I love the beach, but . . ." I think of Hall and me together in the red truck, driving above the valley, its glowing grid, beams shooting up into the clouds like searchlights. I see us caroling in the streets, all the smiling, friendly faces in doorways. The dollhouse that flowered between two buildings, which I'm going to call home, and that tight-knit sense of belonging that I've come to associate with Teller City. Wouldn't it be lovely to preserve a shred of the way Christmas makes me feel now that I've known Hall, to hold that feeling close all the time? "I like it here," I finish. "The town's grown on me. Besides, you can't beat the free grocery deliveries, and the complimentary tire-changing services."

"Complimentary tire-changing?" Dad's eyes zip to Grandpa, who shakes out his newspaper and disappears behind it, like Hall does whenever he wants to memorize new weather forecast phrases. "Is that a thing?"

"Who knows?" Grandpa replies airily. "I'm all the way up here on this hill. Don't know about anything that goes on down there."

Dad just stares at him, then at me. I wonder how long my grandparents have known I've been lurking on their turf, or why they let me get away with my production of Look How Great Bettie Is Doing. Then again, Grandma's an exceedingly proud woman to whom image is everything, and I get more than just my name from her. Perhaps she understood.

"Thanks for the groceries, Grandpa," I say quietly.

He flicks the newspaper to another page. "Don't have any idea what you're talking about."

When they leave the room, I expect despair to swallow me whole again, but it strangely doesn't. It's as if their love parted the curtains of that darkness, shining a light in. And even though they've gone downstairs, even though the half-finished mug of hot cocoa on Hall's bedside table makes my eyes sting, I think that light will remain.

✳

CHAPTER TWENTY

··

I WAKE UP ON December twenty-sixth back in my town house, afternoon streaming through gold gossamer curtains, breathing deeply for any trace of peppermint.

Nothing.

I fly downstairs, hoping against hope that Hall will be bustling about the kitchen, which he's made adjustments to in our absence—it's more practical now, with powder-blue polka dot dishware and tropical houseplants that are mercifully fake. He's transformed what was his bedroom into an office space. Instead of a sleigh bed, it holds a craft table laden with calligraphy sets, a Cricut Joy Machine, a printer, and containers of sequins, glue, and stickers.

While the gift makes me smile, his absence feels like a big red *REJECTED* stamp over all my efforts. Christmas is over. Hall is gone, which I can't undo, no matter how strong my willpower might be. "It's not fair," I mumble. "I discovered the true meaning of Christmas! Isn't that enough?" Honestly, what's it going to take?

I was up in the wee hours of the morning methodically planning how many new leaves I'm going to turn, estimating how much better I'll have to become as a person before I'm rewarded for it.

Something else that isn't fair: Teller City is gorgeous today. We've got crisp white heavens and six inches of snow, when in a world where there was any justice it'd be slushy right now, sky a gloomy gray blob. I hear laughter wafting from outside, where children are inconsiderately enjoying themselves, and my first instinct is to go ruin it. I'll shoot ornaments off the giant Christmas tree in the town square with a BB gun, then start slinging snowballs at children who dare to come admire my pretty gingerbread house.

Dressed in Hall's sweater, which now he'll never be able to wear himself, I thump outside and puncture a hole in a blow-up Nutcracker soldier with an icicle. I'm going to be a typhoon of misery! I'm going to spread it everywhere! If I can't be happy, then—

There's a small parade flowing down the street.

A parade of Watson-Hugheses.

Mom and Marilou are carrying pies; Sean, Grandpa, and Felix are holding boxes of dishware; Grandma's got a painting under her arm that looks like a genuine Edgar Degas; Athena's got a cutting board; Kaia has a hand-painted *Home is where a Hughes is* key hook. The children are busy swinging around baskets, soap dispensers, and embroidered hand towels. Ichabod chucks a vase like a football at Frangipane but misses, and it shatters on the sidewalk. Kaia gives him a gentle noogie.

"Happy housewarming," Dad tells me, planting a kiss on my cheek.

"Look, it's shaped like Colorado!" Athena says brightly, handing me the square cutting board.

It's all too much. My mouth wobbles.

"Oh, sweetie." Mom's smile falls. "What's wrong?" She already knows the answer, not giving me room to reply before continuing, "Where did he go? Why'd he have to leave?"

"It's complicated. I don't want to talk about it. I . . ." I glance around at all their gifts, my rib cage suddenly too tight. "Thank you, everybody. This is incredibly thoughtful of you."

"We can't stay long, but we wanted to give you a proper housewarming," Marilou tells me. "Felix and I are taking off in an hour, and your parents' flight is at six."

"We also wanted to snoop." Felix invites himself into the house to deposit all my stuff in the kitchen while everybody else pokes at the lawn ornaments. "Grandpa told us this is where you live."

Mom tips her head back to contemplate the house. "Well, isn't this the *cutest* little place. How long's it been here?" She takes in the location of my neighbors, the café and gift shop. "Where'd the milk truck go? Am I imagining that there used to be an old milk truck here?"

"Bettie!" It's Grandpa. "What do you say about going to the movies today?"

Going to the movies reminds me of *His Girl Friday* and sweet, handsome Hall in the seat next to mine, our hands touching in the popcorn bag. My face crumples. I'll never meet anyone that wonderful again. This planet is wall-to-wall with men who only want one thing, and that one thing isn't copying the décor of the Cheesecake Factory for a magical treehouse, the blueprints of which I found stashed under Hall's pillow after he left.

"Or not!" he hastens to add. "We could go to . . . the Bahamas?"

Dad shoots him an incredulous look. He throws his hands up. "What? Who doesn't love the Bahamas? I'm helping!"

"Sister of mine," Felix interrupts, and I notice that the scarf Hall knit for him is draped around his neck. "If you're not making *My Eyre Ladies*, do you mind if I do? I've been rethinking my script, and you know, there's some room for improvement. I'll give you credit, of course . . . not that you'd want it, probably."

"Bettie, I love your hair today," Athena tells me with a straight face, holding her arms out to offer a hug. Baby Fang twists in his BabyBjörn, chubby hand up. It is the final straw.

I'm sobbing on the sidewalk in broad daylight.

"There, there." Athena motors over, petting my hair robotically. "We're here for you, Betts."

To the kids, Grandma snaps, "Be supportive of your aunt Bettie! Her incredible fiancé has left her all alone, possibly forever, we haven't gotten to the bottom of it yet, and, to make things worse, she doesn't use retinol anti-aging serum. With all this crying, she's going to have regrets."

The children chorus a distracted, unconvincing "Love you, Aunt Bettie!" peppered with "Love you, aging serum," by the youngest ones.

Felix pats my head, hand heavy. Grandma doesn't offer any hugs, but she *does* offer me a drink from her thermos, which is a dash of coffee added to Baileys.

"So, the movie thing," Felix cuts in. He's got his Notes app out, *Blake Lively and Ana de Armas as the nannies* splashed across the top. "D'you think you could sign off on that, give me permission so I can get this thing going, or . . . ?"

"Not now," Kaia growls. "She's having a hard time, you half-wit. Bettie, I'm sorry we didn't get the chance to say goodbye to Hall. I don't know what's going on between you two, but I know you can make it work. You looked so much in love."

I sob louder, tears dripping into the thermos. Grandma observes it with a grim set to her mouth. I'm diluting the alcohol with my salt, which is wasteful.

"Don't say *Hall*," Felix loud-whispers out of the corner of his mouth. I notice he's got lipstick on his jaw that matches the shade Marilou's wearing. Nearly everybody has somebody, except for me. Why did I have to fall in love with an immortal mist!!

I shake Kaia's shoulders, trying to rattle some sense into her. "And *you*."

"Me? What'd I do?"

"Why did you let Courtney go? You loved her but you let her slip through your fingers because you're scared."

My bewildered sister can't form a reply.

"Go get her back!" I exclaim. "Do you know how much I wish I could—" I stop. I can't fully explain, so they'll never understand. But even though they don't understand, they close in, anyway.

"I'm okay." I try to wave everyone off, but it's like one of those Chinese finger traps—the harder I resist, the tighter they swell around me, until my eyes are bulging and my throat is constricted with the amount of attention they're cramming down it. I'm snarling like a feral alley cat, but nobody is scared of me, and it's insulting. I'm shooting off *leave me alone* signals that they're misinterpreting as emergency *please help me* smoke flares. Hall has destroyed my family culture by imbuing these people with a caring spirit. I'll never forgive him.

A sunburst of emotion fizzles bright inside my chest. My mind rewinds to when Hall and I first arrived at the Watsons' house, when we were in the sitting room while everyone else congregated in the kitchen. I felt isolated, ignored, because they didn't come to me. But I didn't go to them, either. I hung back, lingering. What might have happened if I'd walked into the kitchen? If I'd hugged someone hello?

"I love you, Mom," I force myself to say to her now, the words thick.

Surprise and pleasure unfurl on her face in a brilliant smile. "Oh, honey. I love you, too."

"I'm sorry I didn't come to Thanksgiving."

"Baby, it's—"

"I'm sorry I don't call enough. I'm going to start calling you all the time, and save up money so that I can visit. I'm sorry about . . ." My apology generator is rusty. I reflect on using her emergency credit card to buy a three-hundred-dollar vintage Ouija board so that I could talk to Rue McClanahan when I was seventeen. "A lot of things."

My mother holds me tight, rocking me back and forth. "I will always love you, no matter what. I will always support you, even if it doesn't look like it. Sometimes support looks like disagreeing with you or telling you that you're on the wrong path. But your heart is in my heart, always, and all I want for you is a good, healthy life."

Kaia begins to establish plans for us to all get together in mid-January, and I believe her when she elbows me, saying I'd better show up. I don't fight Athena when she volunteers to pay for my airfare, because I can see now that she isn't doing it to look superior. My family *wants* me around. It's taken my whole life to realize that not being the center of attention isn't the same thing as being ignored.

Is this growth? I don't care for it. It's like wearing the wrong size clothing. I analyze their faces—well-meaning, frequently annoying, but unconditionally at my back. A support network. No matter what, they love me; no matter what, I truly love them. This circus is mine.

It's something to hold on to.

The youngest children try wandering off, which sends the adults chasing after them with loud apologies tossed, that they still have packing to do. As I shout my goodbyes, Grandpa loiters behind, his gaze snagging on my kitchen table, where the record player rests. "Oh, good! You must like the birthday present I picked out for you, then."

"*You* picked out the record player?" Usually Grandma is in charge of gift-buying for birthdays and holidays, and Grandpa simply signs the cards.

His whiskers twitch. "You're shocked."

It's true. "Am not."

He passes me a chocolate from his coat pocket, then unwraps one for himself, nodding. "I bought that at an auction, as a matter of fact, at the Magic Towne House in New York City from a man by the name of Walter B. Gibson, many years ago. I rediscovered it sitting in my closet a few months before your birthday and had to work hard to convince your grandmother that a beat-up old Kinollghy could be spruced up enough to be a fine present for our Bettie. Enabled me to do plenty of tinkering, so it was a present for myself, too. I got to lug it back and forth to an electronics shop in Greenbriar, since the one here in town said the task was beyond them, but they got invested emotionally, came along to Greenbriar to watch. You should have seen it—a room full of old tinkers putting their heads together, making it good as new, while I threw out suggestions in the background about the color of wood stain as if I were helping. But you like it, then?"

"I love it."

He's pleased. "I can't wait to rub it in that I was right. Your grandma's vote was for a dartboard that screams when you hit it."

"Oh, definitely get that for me next time. But thank you, the record player is perfect. You did a terrific job with those updates— I thought it was brand new."

"On second thought, forget what I said." He waves an arm to get rid of the secret. "Brand new. We'll pretend it cost me a fortune, shall we?"

"I like it even better with a history."

"Which is why I'm your favorite in the family, I assume? Since I'm ancient." He winks, then begins walking down the sidewalk toward the others. "Come visit more often, all right?" He points up the mountain. "Right there. Can't miss it."

"How does lunch every Sunday sound?"

"Fabulous. Now, I will see you later, and you *be good*. I'm off to go tell your grandmother she was wrong."

"I'll pray for your survival."

He pauses. "You know, maybe I won't. She might still have those darts."

✳

SHE GLOWS

Snow!
Falls upon your nose
which crinkles, and
away it goes—
Blow!
It drifts up to your hair,

and I
hold my
own breath to spare
the crown of stars that's gathered there.
Glow!
How I wish that time would slow,
leave me here to age and grow.
I've got your hand,
which holds my heart,
your smile sparkling up the dark.
Oh!
Aren't you just the starriest thing
Round and round and round I think
how wonderfully lovely it would be,
if magic didn't make us fall apart,
to be with you here in the spring.

I take a walk that evening, a pair of skates held tight in one hand, Hall's unfinished book of poems in the other. The sky is already darkening, church bells reverberating with five gongs. There is no difference between today and Christmas, aesthetically—the fountain in the town square still spits up diamond-bright water, illumined by the Victorian lampposts. The gazebo still glimmers with white string lights, benches empty. The ice rink remains an impossible miracle on the corner of Pools and Old Homestead, where an empty car lot ought to be. I'm so deeply glad that all of Hall's tangible fingerprints on the town didn't disappear along with him, like Cinderella's coach turning back into a pumpkin. If I couldn't cast around and find traces of Hall in everything, everywhere, that would make my heartache all the more unbearable.

Directly across the street from the skating rink, holiday music still curls from Gold Rush Bookshop's speakers. *Do you see what I see?* Each ghostly syllable hits with a sharp pang.

Flurries tumble down, pressing me in the direction of the ice. It's snowing because of weather, because it's winter, because it's cold and there's precipitation. There's no magic here anymore.

And yet.

It doesn't feel like there *isn't* magic here, either. I dither at the edge, surveying the glinting blue-white surface. I don't have anyone to hold me up this time, to help me along. I set my book of poems on the bench, lacing up my skates.

This day has not unspooled like I thought it would.

Instead of wallowing, I began job hunting. I need to get better at taking care of myself. I want to prove to myself that I can hold down a job, that I can build my savings, that I'm going to be okay without relying on wishes. I went door to door in town, asking businesses if they had jobs available, and the experience wasn't anything like how it used to be, when I lived in big cities where people recognized me from tabloids. Here, they recognize me as the granddaughter of the formidable woman who leers down at them from her nightmare gargoyle house, and they are all *very* nice to that woman's granddaughter.

The Blue Moose Café needs a dishwasher, a job I'm confident I could perform. North Park Realty said they'll hire me if I obtain a real estate license. Last Dollar Lanes has a job opening, but I'd be the only staff on third shift and I'd have to deal with the rowdy Late Night League—I don't know what the Late Night League is aside from it being for old people, but the teenager who explained the job to me sounded scared. I've gotten a couple other offers, too. I'm not sure what I want to do yet; I'm giving myself another day to mull it over.

I position one skate in front of the other, wobbly at first. I hear music, laughter, as doors open and close, businesses locking up, flipping their signs from GOOD TO SEE YOU to MEET AGAIN SOON.

I skate through the darkness, on and on, surroundings shrinking down to the circumference of this rink, the blazing lanterns. My legs grow accustomed to the exercise, calves and thighs burning as I push myself to go faster. I am successfully skating without any help. I can *do* this, which is a pleasant shock. I can do this on my own.

The wind in my hair, biting cold or not, gets the endorphins pumping, and it's as if the ice isn't here at all, as if I'm soaring through sky. My reflection in the silver mirror below ripples as if I'm burning, smoke trailing off my fingers and hair. I gain confidence, trying out a twirl. I sway, but before I can fall, I feel a pressure, a presence. A force without weight. It coils around me, easing me back up.

I don't fall.

Phantom hands lightly stroke my jaw, as if there is something alive in the wind that has taken a shine to me, that wants me to know I am precious. I gaze up at the place where Hall's face should be, his secret freckles and lopsided smile, springy locks of brown hair that gleam mahogany when he turns just so, and a hot tear slides down my cheek, freezing into a star.

An invisible thumb wipes it away.

All I can think is *please, please*, but it's stuck down low inside my

ribs. I am stock-still, the blood racing to my heart, pulse so clamor-
ous in my ears it's like a relentless fist pounding on a door. As each
snowflake drifts onto my collar, it melts instantaneously, as though
flickering out from the warmth of another person's breath.

I can't pinpoint the moment those hands leave me. It happens
so slowly, so fuzzily, that I wonder if time has been manipulated.
If he pressed pause on it for a few minutes. Or, I think, as doubt
begins to seep in along with how perfectly ordinary my surroundings seem, maybe I imagined the whole experience.

"Come back," I whisper hoarsely, pleading with the stars winking over the mountains. "Please. Make my wish come true."

He doesn't come back.

My breaths escape me in shuddering plumes. My limbs are
shaking, teeth chattering against each other. It was him. He was
here. I *know* it.

I scour the sky for any hint of him, but all is as it was. Nothing
else is out there.

He was here, he was here.

But where did he *go*?

I swallow, throat burning, and walk on trembling legs back to
the bench. I wrench off my skates, noticing that a breeze has flut-
tered the poetry book open as I yank on my boots.

Tucking windblown hair behind my ear, I flip the book right
side up. The fifth page, which had been obstinately stuck to the
back of the fourth one, contains a poem I haven't yet read. It
smells of spilled peppermint hot chocolate, the paper crinkled and
warped, rough at its rises and soft in the valleys. My eyes dance
from left to right, at this new fragment of Hall that's taken form
right when I thought I'd gotten the very last of him.

What I See

Some of your mischief is disguise
All the granite is for show
I've seen the way it leaves you
when
we're standing all alone
The fire that flickers in your eyes
makes me burn up in the cold
You'll laugh and say, "Oh *Hall*,"
but you
are softer than you know

My gaze lifts to the stars again, no longer wondering where Hall went.

He went, quite clearly, back into everything.

To where he's always been. Standing by, giving cheer, twinkling in the streetlights, the snow, turning the mundane into the magical. Most of the sadness in my heart is for him, who can't participate, who can only give and never take. Or he takes from what he gives, I suppose: deriving pleasure from pleasing.

I press a hand to my mouth, scanning for shadows, for wherever Hall might be, because I want him to see that I'm going to be all right, that I won't fall apart. What if it breaks his heart to see me heartbroken? I couldn't bear that.

He's everywhere, though. When I trudge home and close the front door behind me, the noise sounds like his voice, urgent, quiet: *Bettie*. When I twist the tap of the bathroom sink to wet my toothbrush, the falling water sounds like *Even ten minutes*. Which I am certainly imagining, because *even ten minutes* doesn't make any sense.

Ten minutes until what? But the water gurgles out that exact same sound again, just as I shut it off: It goes down the drain in a mystifying *even ten minutes.*

Even ten minutes.

When I lie down for the night, the sighs of the pillow feel like the kiss of heat you get from kneeling before a blazing hearth. I think I feel snowflakes landing softly in my hair, but when I reach up to touch the strands, I come away with nothing.

And when I fall asleep, I dream of places I've never been before, people I've never met, visions I've never fathomed—I see houses hundreds of miles from mine, the smiles of strangers from an aerial view. I feel a flame that will never go out in my tight, aching chest as I look down at *myself* from someone else's point of view, someone who loves me, as I sleep curled up in bed.

*

Chapter Twenty-One

··

T'S DECEMBER THIRTY-FIRST, and I'm on my lunch break.

In the immediate aftermath of Hall's departure, I tried to bring him back a hundred times. My record player can't hold its liquor too well, so I've ruined my vinyl of Mariah Carey's *Merry Christmas* by repeatedly playing it backward, doused with wine in an attempt to re-create that holiday miracle. In between attempts, however, I managed to get a few other things done.

First, I deleted all of my social media accounts except for Instagram, which I'm making private for now. External validation isn't a viable substitute for self-esteem, according to my surprisingly wise parents. I don't want to waste more of my life trying to look like someone I'm not. I'm hoping that if I keep my social media presence small, I'll learn how to manage it more authentically, and have a healthier relationship with it. As Mom has reminded me and then reminded me again, taking care of myself isn't weakness.

Second, I went back to the Watsons' house to dig Felix's *Leon of*

Naples screenplay back out of the tower, because I couldn't stop thinking about whales and railings. As soon as I finished reading it, I called Felix and begged him to let me email any and all of my old Hollywood contacts because—*My God*. It's the most ridiculous plot ever created. If I can't watch Neoprene Bontpont in all of his anachronistic glory on the big screen at Moonlit Cinema, it will be a life half lived. He let me run with it, and we're both excited about some positive reception we've already received from a heavy-hitting actor with comedic tastes that appreciate the weird and the over-the-top. Not to name names, but I might have once stolen his wife's engagement ring.

Third:

"How's the job going?" Kaia asks, waiting on the sidewalk for me to shuffle out of the store with my purse over my shoulder, ready for lunch.

"On the downside, I broke a scanner today, then cried when I couldn't figure out coupons," I report. "On the upside, I get a discount on merchandise."

She flashes a smile, then tamps it down. "Have I ever told you that you have the prettiest smile?" I say. She shakes her head, ducking self-consciously, but I can tell she's pleased. Mom, Dad, Athena, Felix, and their families have all gone home, but Kaia's holding out, staying on an extended holiday at Grandma and Grandpa's. She says the house has inspired her songwriting. I think she might also be gathering her bearings, working up to an act of bravery.

She flicks my nametag. "I'm proud of you."

"Me, too. Did you know that evening gowns hand-sewn by Teller City's own designer Samantha Tan are affordable and one of a kind? She never uses a design twice. Local legend has it that her pieces are enchanted to make the wearer's romantic wishes come true. A Cupid, if you will."

She gives me a playful shove to the side. "Did *you* start that local legend?"

I grin. "And you don't wanna miss Jackson County Ironworks's spring collection. So many cool pieces to choose from! Your sculptures will be the talk of the town."

"Stop or I'm going to make a citizen's arrest. I'm serious."

"Personally," I go on, doing a twirl, "I never leave the house without my trusty Through the Snow at Twilight candle, unless I'm feeling fun and flirty, in which case I use their environmentally conscious vanilla bean wax melts."

I've decided that being environmentally conscious is going to be My Thing now, as it's one of the ways I can affordably better the world. I'm all out of yachts to auction off for charity, but I can still contribute. I've been drinking water from a stainless steel thermos rather than my beloved plastic Evian bottles, and so far today I've yelled at two different people to pick up their litter. You're welcome, Mother Nature.

We cross the street, a breeze gusting Kaia's short brown-blond hair to make it curl around the edges of her ball cap. On this stretch of Cottonwood Lane, snow never melts off the cars parked on the street because they're chilled by the shadow of the Watson house rising far above. Grandma's such a menace. I want to be more like her someday, but not the acting and accolades part, or the fake gravestones in my yard. I want to be an intimidating matriarch with loads of great-grandchildren underfoot to bring me the remote when I bark for it.

"I *get* it," she laughs. "You're shilling for Mary Had a Little Boutique now."

"A shopping hot spot in the Colorado heartland," I reply airily. "Don't miss out on all their best steals and deals! For a limited time only you can get half off any purchase online if you use the coupon code *BETTIE* at checkout." Mary's on Etsy, as well, where she sells quilts and headbands for babies. Half of my job is double-checking shipping labels and making trips to the post office.

"I think it's cool that the shop is going to let you sell your cards there, too. I'm happy for you."

"Mary's a gem. I won't forget her when I'm being interviewed by *Forbes* someday."

When she offered me a job, Mary explained that I'd be frequently communicating with local creators, who are the backbone of the store. I mentioned my Hughes & Co. cards, she invited me to bring in a variety box, and ended up ordering twenty boxes of fifteen cards each, with a special request for extra copies of one with an owl yelling I HEARD WHAT YOU SAID ABOUT ME. The adrenaline rush from my first sale was unlike anything I've ever experienced in a work environment. Looking back, passion was the missing component from all my other business endeavors. With my lipstick line, my Bettie Gardenia fragrance, the jewelry collaborations, I'd simply been throwing products at a wall to see which might stick. I didn't get any creative fulfillment from them. These cards, however, are *mine*. I draw and package each one myself. I care as much about making them and having fun doing so as I do about selling them.

My goal is to become a worldwide sensation, naturally, but for now I'll start local, working my way up from Mary Had a Little Boutique salesgirl to president of Hughes & Co., home of niche cards that nobody asked for but everyone definitely needs. You should see me at it—I'm like a puma with the customers. I could sell a shark to a clownfish, and I'm going to put Magnolia Hope Chest out of business.

I am granting myself this one tiny grudge to keep me warm at night. Chip and Joanna Gaines's folksy shop is direct competition for Mary Had a Little Boutique, and for that unforgivable reason, they must go.

"*Bettie.*"

"Huh?" I whip around.

Kaia returns my stare emptily. "I said I'm happy for you."

"No, it was . . . it sounded like someone else just said my name."

We both survey the crop of buildings: Cheers Chocolatiers, Rocky Road Ice Cream Parlor, Moonlit Cinema, sidled up against each other like cozy old friends.

Nobody I recognize is afoot, but I dart along the crosswalk anyway, peering into the chocolaterie, at a husband-and-wife team in tall white hats who sculpt chocolate while patrons look on. Then I hear it again:

"Bettie."

The voice keeps slipping in from changing directions: now it's coming from behind me. In the big glass display window at a Verizon Wireless, there are about thirty cell phones lit up with a familiar face, thirty identical Halls waving.

I stop dead.

Before I can move again, the image wipes, screen blank before readjusting to read *Verizon Wireless*.

"What?" Kaia asks, following my gaze. I press my fingertips to the glass, staring, waiting for Hall to come back. "Do you need a new phone?"

"No," I croak. "Hold on, I'll be back in a sec."

Her attention falls upon Silver Mine Dining, where we're currently supposed to be enjoying grilled cheese sandwiches. "How long is your lunch break?"

"I'll be quick."

I duck into the store and check out the phones, thinking maybe he left evidence of himself somehow. But there's nothing. When I return, Kaia squints. "What was that about?"

"I thought I saw Hall on the phone screens."

She glances. "Was he?"

"I don't know."

We start walking again, but my muscles are rubbery. I keep craning to glance back at the store. "I know what you mean," she says conversationally. "I keep thinking I hear Courtney's voice. Or I'll see a purple jacket or a purple sign, and it's like my heart tries to jump out of my body because for a millisecond, I think it's her." At my inquisitive expression, she adds, "Courtney has purple hair."

"Maybe your heart is telling you that it wants to see Courtney."

She sighs. "My heart needs to shut up."

"Feel your feelings, Kaia."

"I refuse."

We head into the diner, grabbing two counter seats. But just as we're about to order, someone walks through the door and in the brief space of time before the door swings shut behind them, I hear Hall's voice again. "Hold on," I blurt, then run back outside, my poor sister disoriented behind me.

There are four people on this side of the street: a mother and her two young children, and an old man. I whirl around, watching my own puzzled reflection in the window of Teller City Market. There are no display phones with Hall waving from them, but

I do notice something else: speakers fixed to the other side of the store are blaring a Christmas song, and I am fairly certain the correct lyrics aren't supposed to be *It's beginning to look a lot like Bett-iiie.*

"Bettie?"

Kaia joins me outside, handing me my purse. "You okay?"

"Listen!"

"What?" Her eyes zip up and down me as though I might be hurt. "Listen to what? What *is* it?"

"That!" I point at the speakers. This is proof that he's here in some capacity, watching. Trying to be with me from up in that everywhere.

"*It's beginning to look a lot like Christmas,*" Perry Como croons.

My hand falls. "It was . . . it wasn't that, though, it was Hall. I heard him singing. Right there! He was coming out of that, right there. But instead of Christmas, he was saying . . ." I drift off, hearing the words falling out of my mouth. ". . . Bettie."

I cover my face with my hands.

"Oh, honey."

"Nooo, not the *oh, honey.*"

"Yes, babe. C'mere." She drops our purses onto the pavement and scoops me into a hug. "It's gonna be okay, okay? I've got you. I know I'm not a hot guy in a sweater, but I give good hugs."

"You really do," I reply, words muffled by her shoulder. "Your perfume is amazing." I deeply inhale the raspberry and vanilla fragrance, which has a calming effect.

"Can I make a confession?"

I pull back slightly. "Yeah?"

"This is the perfume Courtney wears. I bought it so that I could smell her all the time."

Now it's my turn to smush her into a hug. "Oh, honey."

"I *know*."

"You need to go to her. You need to grovel."

She looks anguished. "I don't know how."

"I bet you've written songs about her."

She groans, betraying the truth.

"Exactly." I'm triumphant. "Serenade her with one of your songs. Toss long-stemmed red roses at her window. Who could resist?" I squeeze her hands in mine. "If you want her, you have to tell her, all right? Don't be stupid."

"I hate feelings-talk."

And then we both have to laugh, because *hoo, boy*, is that a genetic trait, and also because a couple of teenage girls are staring at us from about four feet away, bug-eyed. I sling an arm around Kaia's waist. We're about to go back into the diner when one of the girls nervously steps forward, fidgeting with her hands. "Um."

We pause. "Hi?" Kaia prompts.

"It's just." She bites her lip, forcing herself to meet my gaze. "Would you sign something for me?"

"Uh, sure." I was betting that she'd ask for Kaia's autograph. I start digging in my purse for a scrap piece of paper to sign.

"Actually." She blushes to the roots of her hair, then begins to unzip her jacket with unsteady fingers.

"Whoa, whoa," Kaia begins, but the jacket's already unzipped, and when we get a good eyeful of the girl's shirt, my jaw hits the floor. It's four Raisin Creme Pies, in neon colors, overlapping like an Andy Warhol painting. The caption initially curdles the coffee in my stomach, but then I read it again. And again. #RespectFor-BettieIsOverdueParty

Surprise plonks me on top of the head, but it's a delighted surprise.

"I got a Sharpie," Kaia announces, riffling through her bag. "Hold up, let me find it. Where'd you get that shirt? Is that custom-made?"

The girl tells her where she ordered it from, and by the time she's finished with her sentence, Kaia's already ordered the shirt for everyone she knows. "Team Bettie, always," she says.

With my signature emblazoned over the hot-pink Raisin Creme Pie, the girl rushes back to her friend, squealing. They jump up and down. Before Kaia and I are out of earshot, the girl's friend shouts after me, "You're her hero, you know!"

Kaia nudges me, grinning. "Can you sign my shirt, too?"

"Only if you sign mine." I think about how my little sister pulled me back from the grips Lucas Dormer had me in. How, even though we weren't particularly close, and I didn't want to listen, she knew enough to know I needed help.

Backlash has finally arrived for the previously untouchable Lucas Dormer. It seems that his stint on *Dancing with the Stars* soured his image, so now it's acceptable for Lucas's girlfriends who came before and after me to tiptoe through, brave enough to speak out now that they feel they might be listened to. I've been trying to curtail the attention I pay to this news, but it's not looking good for him. Even his ex-bandmates have put out a statement saying they *are shocked and appalled to learn of this behavior*, as if they didn't try to silence me when I told my story. But at least the tide is turning now, so more women will have warning. Even though no one wanted to believe me back when my voice was the only one, I'm proud that I spoke up. And as for my closure, I keep a rubber snake on top of my microwave at home—I smile every time I pass it.

"Can I just say? And I'm not even kidding—you're my hero, Kaia. I'm so lucky to have you as a sister."

She makes a "pfhhhshhhaw" sound, turning away so that I don't catch her wiping a misty eye. Then she tackles me with a noogie, because that is how she expresses her affection aside from creating music. Gratitude for my family, even when we drive each other up the wall with our collective obnoxiousness, brings an irresistible lilt to my heart. And so, by the time I'm back behind the counter at Mary Had a Little Boutique, dreaming of new cards I'm going to create, that light shining through the curtains of my heartbreak is a mile wide and forever long—a searchlight that will never stop looking out for me.

*

This is how I spend my New Year's Eve: curled up on the sofa with a platter featuring every type of cheese the market deli offers, glittery extensions pinned to my hair because maybe looking cute will solve all my problems, watching *His Girl Friday* with mascara tracking down my face. Perhaps I am a masochist. Perhaps I'm hoping to re-create a feeling.

Hildy the hamster is passed out next to me, her small stomach bloated with blueberry yogurt treats. She's living her best life. "Good for you, Hildy," I tell her, then swing my gaze to the television. The movie's barely started. *What did you just say?* the other Hildy's asking.

Her fiancé, who won't be her fiancé by the movie's end because she belongs with Walter, of course, replies, *What?*

Go on. She smiles encouragingly, and I mouth her next line: *Well, go ahead.*

Well, I just said, "Even ten minutes is a long time to be away from you."

I glance down at the Kinollghy record player, which has turned itself on and lit up green. I halt the movie to go shut it off. As soon as I sit back down, though, it lights up again.

My focus sharpens on that dial as I slowly get up off the couch and float over. I shut it off. It turns itself back on, quicker this time.

I lift the lid, peering suspiciously at the red *Merry Christmas* record still housed inside even though it stopped working thirty attempts ago. Now all it gives me are scratchy squeaks.

I remove the album, gingerly mopping up sticky wine stains with a wet washcloth, then forage for the record sleeve. I locate it behind the player, tipped against the wall; and just behind that one is the second album I'd forgotten Marilou gave me as well: *Merry Christmas II You*, Mariah Carey's second collection of holiday hits.

"Next year," I promise Mariah, since I've listened to enough Christmas music during the past month to last me for eternity. But then my gaze falls to track 12: "All I Want for Christmas Is You." The same magic song from *Merry Christmas*, but on a new, unspoiled record. I slide it out of its sleeve and decide to give this one a try, because what do I have to lose?

I mess with the arm, skipping around the track, reversing it once we've reached the end. I sweep the room for signs of what happened last time, but the lights don't dim or intensify, and a man doesn't appear from thin air. The only sound in my house is Mariah, singing forward and backward and performing magnificently either way. The version on this album is more upbeat, a little faster. It should make me feel bubbly and positive, but the lyrics only serve to highlight that awful feeling I've been struggling to keep at bay. Because all I wanted for Christmas was Hall, and now he's gone.

"I'm sorry," I murmur to no one. "I'm trying to keep my spirits

up. I really am." I begin to twist the volume knob counterclock-
wise to shut the record player off.

The television remote, which I left hanging precariously on the
edge of the couch cushion, somersaults to the floor, smashing the
play button.

Startled, I go, "Agh!" and look at the hamster, as if she's the
one who turned it back on. She's passed out cold in my fuzzy slipper, which I've made into a bed.

I heard you the first time, Hildy says in the background. *I like it.
That's why I asked you to say it again.*

I repause the movie, glowing numbers on the cable box below
my television flashing from 11:59 to 12:00, one year to the next,
and over on the Kinollghy, the song number rolls over right along
with it. Goose bumps race along my arms.

Should auld acquaintance be forgot Mariah sings. The machine
rattles, dial colors flushing from standard blue to vivid green to
yellow-gold. A voice that is definitely *not* Mariah Carey's crackles
from the speakers, cutting her off. "Operator. You have unlocked
your New Year's Resolution."

My legs almost buckle. "What? Hello?" I turn the volume up,
which saturates the room with static. "Can you hear me?"

"I can hear you," the female voice replies, sounding *bored,* as if
it's totally normal to converse with somebody through a radio. I
stare at the round band of warm yellow light. There's a subtle
shimmer in it, like tiny glitter specks that turn sideways as they
tumble through midair, flashing briefly, illuminating my hands,
which are clutching the mahogany box in a death grip.

"Who is this?" I ask.

"You played 'Auld Lang Syne' on New Year's Eve at precisely

the stroke of midnight using a magical musical mechanism, did you not?" she inquires, a few degrees above exasperated.

"Yes to the first part. To the second, I don't think so? My record player is just a regular old record player."

"It's never exhibited any supernatural behaviors?" The radio dial waffles back and forth like a compass needle, tipping from AM to FM.

"Well." I bite my lip. "It once summoned the Holiday Spirit."

"In that case, I'll repeat: you have unlocked your New Year's Resolution. You may cast it now or at your next convenience."

"New . . . Year's . . . Resolution," I repeat slowly, trying to untangle her meaning. "Can you clarify?"

She inhales sharply through her nose, and the yellow light flickers. "Is this a prank call? Those punk interns from Arbor Day? I've had enough of you hooligans. The holiday switchboard is busy enough at this time of year without you giving me extra work."

"No, no, this isn't a prank!" I exclaim, panicking. If she hangs up on me, I don't know if I'll be able to get her back. "I'm a human. Uh, from earth. Down here. I get to do a resolution? What is that, exactly?"

"A resolution is a decision or determination. With magical influence behind it, the determination then acts as a wish. Some rules and restrictions may apply."

I lie down on the floor, head spinning. "A wish."

I have so many wishes, I could springboard into a pool of them and not sink anywhere near the bottom. I want to rewind time. I want to repeat the last two weeks of December on a loop. I want to go back to Christmas at midnight and live inside that moment, building castles and kingdoms in it, and to never have Hall taken away. I want to not feel like I've got a beehive inside me, a restless swarm, whenever I'm not in the spotlight or whenever I'm in the spotlight but it isn't for good reasons. I want to live a hundred different lifetimes and see who I might have been in each of them, and I want Hall to be able to taste every flavor of coffee creamer, and I want all of my siblings' dreams to come true. I want for everyone I know and love to be marvelously content, always. But I've already cast my wishes; I've cast hundreds of them

All I can think about is the whirlwind force that is Hall and how much he's changed my life. How much I admire him, how much I want to be like him. If I'm going to be like Hall, then there's only one way to respond to a once-in-a-lifetime chance like this. "Can I grant somebody else's greatest wish?"

I jump back at the sound that emits from the speakers, a click followed by an ethereal and exceptionally loud *Ahhhhhh.* "*Rare achievement unlocked,*" a clear new voice resounds in monotone. "*Paying it forward.*"

"That's new," the operator remarks, sounding almost interested. "I've never had someone donate their wish before."

I'm feeling weak by this point. "Yeah, well. I figure I've already had my turn."

"Noble." She's back on her sass. "To whom am I paying your wish forward, then?"

"Hall. I want for Hall's greatest wish to be granted. He deserves it." I swallow. "He's just, this absolutely amazing person, with the most dazzling smile conceivable and adorable sweaters he knits himself, and he deserves the best, anything he wants." If he wants to roam among the dinosaurs, he should get to. If he wants to be flattened and digitalized as a *Peanuts* character to live inside the world of *A Charlie Brown Christmas,* then so be it. Even if I never see him again, it lights me up with the best feeling in the universe to know that for *once*, I'm going to turn the tables and be the one to make *his* dreams come true.

The operator has no patience for my sentimentality. "A wish that's been paid forward operates at a higher frequency, with fewer regulations. The last time this happened, the quokka was invented."

"Wait. How loose with the regulations are we talking here? Last I checked, there were tons of restrictions on what a holiday spirit could and could not do."

"*Do*, yes. But we're talking about *receiving*, by another subset of magic with its own power and rules. The New Year's Resolution laws and licensing are a different beast entirely, which most fail to appreciate. I can't tell you how many holiday spirits only bother to learn about the laws of their own preferred holidays. It's all in the legislation! I don't know why everyone who calls in here is so unfamiliar with the legislation: it's only eighty thousand pages, and you're human, so it's not like you have anything better to do. What, do you *need* to watch another episode of *Storage Wars*?"

I have approximately one billion follow-up questions. "So then—"

"Nope!" she interrupts in a faux chirpy voice. "I'm suuuper busy, so let's not. What is Hall's location?"

Where *is* his location? My mind blanks. "He's a holiday spirit? So maybe—"

"Hold, please. Connecting."

The lights hiss and dim, digital numbers on the cable box blinking as they rearrange. I think it's supposed to read *BOOT*, but the *T* is missing.

"Somebody call for me?" a voice over my left shoulder booms. I turn, and there is a man in my living room. But this might be even more bewildering than the last time it happened, because instead of a cheerful, grinning Hall in an ugly Christmas sweater, there's a tall strange man with shoulder-length black hair that is halfway between Rod Stewart and The Rachel, in white face paint and heavy black eyeliner. He spreads out his arms to show off the costume bat wings attached to a bright silver jumpsuit, the lights in my ceiling fixture flashing orange and purple. Dry ice fog curlicues out of the carpet, swathing his lower half, which includes thigh-high platform boots with sparkly spiders sewn on. "BOO!" he thunders. Lightning flashes.

"Who the hell are you?"

He spits fake vampire teeth into his hand. "I'm Hall," he says jovially, giving me a wave that brings his fright factor down a few pegs. His Party City bat wings flap "Who're you?"

I rear back, aghast. "You're not Hall."

"Am so. Hall O'ween. I'm the Holiday Spirit!" He peers around. "This is a large bathroom."

"It isn't a bathroom. This is my living room."

"Did you not summon me? Go into a bathroom, lock the door, switch off the lights, spin around three times in front of a mirror while chanting 'Bloody Mary'?"

I smack my forehead. "She sent the wrong one."

"It's the lemon poppy seed muffin part that most folks forget," he goes on. "That's your sacrificial offering! Never forget the muffin. Now my pal Bruce is totally different, he only accepts cranberry, but you don't want to summon Bruce. He has six heads and his skin is transparent, so you can see all the blood lava."

The information that someone can beckon this particular Holiday Spirit merely by presenting a muffin to a mirror while chanting "Bloody Mary" opens an endless stream of doors in my head.

The way I've been accessing holiday magic has been through the record player, but it's staggering to contemplate how many other methods might be out there. What if someone in Tallahassee is watching a VHS tape of *Weird Science* that they stole from a Blockbuster in 2002, then pause it at 4:44 a.m. exactly, and due to the rules of National Science Fiction Day, I am teleported to that person's bedroom so they can obtain the perfect woman? There are hundreds of holidays, each probably with their own weird trip wires and access points. It's only down to sheer coincidence (and Mariah Carey) that I met *my* Hall.

"There's been a misunderstanding."

But Hall O'ween isn't listening. He's helping himself to my charcuterie board, dipping grapes in goat cheese. "So, what can I do you for? Ex-boyfriend need a dose of what he's got coming, maybe? I passed a 7-Eleven on my way here; we can hit it up for toilet paper and go festoon some trees." He rubs his hands together. "Where's your nearest cemetery?"

"Not that I wouldn't love to toilet-paper trees with you, but I'm searching for a more Christmassy holiday spirit who also goes by Hall," I explain. "Can you help me find him?"

"Oh, honey, you're gonna have to be more specific than that." He touches one of my throw pillows, turning it black, with a glittery purple skull and crossbones design. The air is pungent with the scent of candy corn. "There are literally thousands of Christmassy holiday spirits." He fills an ornamental bowl with rubber spiders, then flicks his black-painted fingernails at a lamp. It transforms into a gnarled wizard's staff with a round, cracked glass globe at the top, and a live crow on top of that. "Kind of a basic lot, if you ask me."

"Here, I've got a picture!" I run to grab one (of forty-three)

scrapbooks Hall left behind, brandishing it under his nose. A Polaroid of a very smug Hall and a disconcerted mall Santa gleams
on the page. Hall was giving him tips on how to look convincing.

"Oh, *that* guy. He's been super bumming everybody out lately.
His magic stopped working, so now he just kind of drifts around,
all gloomy-like." He makes an exaggerated sad face.

I lower the scrapbook. "His magic stopped working?"

Hall O'ween shrugs. "Happens sometimes, if you're having
personal issues. I'll go fetch him for you. Don't forget to leave a
jack-o'-lantern on your doorstep on Halloween night to ward off
bad luck! Or not! I don't know what you're into!"

He throws a bat-winged arm across the lower half of his face,
spins, and vanishes in a puff of acrid smoke and a "MUAH HA
HA!" A plastic cauldron filled with Reese's Pumpkins rattles in
his place.

Hello? another voice echoes three seconds later, and my chest
tightens in response.

"Hall!"

But he isn't here.

I analyze the golden pool of light slanting from the record
player onto the carpet, the dials waffling back and forth of their
own accord.

I twist the volume knob as loud as it'll go.

A low voice crackles through the speakers. *"Hear me?"*

"Hall?" All the fine hairs on the back of my neck stand on end.
"I can hear you!" I grab the record player on both sides, tunneling
gaze fixed on the silver Kinollghy logo.

"Can hear you, too," the static replies.

My heart is a hummingbird, beating so quick that it hurts.
"Where are you? Are you down here or up there? Can you see me?"

"I'm somewhere in between."

The line cuts briefly, blipping between *somewhere* and *between*, but it's Hall's voice pouring out, when I didn't think I'd ever hear it again. My hands tremble.

"Are you all right?"

A few beats, and then: *"No. I learned how to have a will of my own down on earth, but I don't know how to make it stop."*

"Listen, maybe I can help. I want you to think of your greatest wish, right now, whatever that may be. Something you want with all of your feeling." Nobody feels more than Hall, so whatever it is, it's going to be powerful. A sonic boom.

I'm thinking about it, he replies. I can picture his eyes shut tight in concentration, a pinch between his brows. Loose curls on his forehead. This isn't about me—for once, it's about him, and only him—but a small white flame still blooms in my rib cage, hoping.

"The magic words?" I prompt, for old times' sake.

There's a lull, airwaves hissing and popping. I hear him draw a breath. Time clicks to a standstill, sound and oxygen and all movement, everywhere, thickening into a strange solid matter as, far, far above, a glittering substance *breathes.* It feels like comfort and companionship, waiting, watching, listening. Marveling: *what would the person whose role is to think only of others want for himself?*

I hear the smile in his voice, scattering throughout that mist, breaking apart all over the planet and lighting it up bright and shining for one moment that is happier than any other moment has ever been. Everything that is alive must feel it; every head must turn in wonder.

"Make my wish come true," he says.

*

IT TOOK A while for Hall to come back to me completely. He started off in a mirror.

"You're one-dimensional!" I cried. "How do I get you out of there?"

It looked like he was standing right beside me, but whenever I turned my head, all I could see was empty space. "If you haven't already guessed," he announced (his visual and audio components were not yet attached to each other, so his voice emitted from the animatronic Billy Bass fish mounted to the wall), "I am the spirit of the Holiday Spirit. As in, I *used* to be the Holiday Spirit, but now I am a Real Boy, like *Frosty the Snowman* if it had the correct ending. I've been withdrawn from one plane of existence and re-submitted into another, as this plane is more fitting for my entity's ability to thrive. My greatest wish was to thrive, as a human." He cocked his head. "With you."

Then I started to cry, so Hall tried to reach through the mirror to hold me but he couldn't, which made *him* upset, and it was frustrating to not be able to touch each other. But at least he was *there*.

"You really want to be with me?" I blubbered, wiping my eyes.

"More than I've ever wanted anything," he replied seriously. "I've done nothing at all since I returned but plot how to come back to you, trying to bend all the laws, hunting for loopholes. I didn't care anymore about what I'm ostensibly meant to do, or who the universe thinks I'm supposed to be. What I am is a man in love, and you're mine, Bettie. Nothing and no one is going to keep me from you. Not time, not legislation, not magic."

Naturally, I began crying harder. "Get out of that mirror. I love you, too, and I want to kiss you."

"I have a feeling we'll have to wait a week or two while I reconstruct myself. Which is very irritating," he replied, teeth clenched. "I'm used to instant gratification."

I lifted the mirror off the wall and rested it on the couch. "We'll pass the time by building suspense."

And then he noticed the decorations left behind by Hall O'ween, so I had to explain that, along with everything else he missed (he asked me to turn on the Weather Channel and rotate his mirror). He told me what it's been like to be outside his body, determined to return. We did a lot of staring at each other and calling each other's faces perfect, sniffling, beaming, and finally laughing, because it was us against the universe and we won. We got to keep each other.

"Also."

Then he revealed a folded slip of paper from his mirror-pocket. The words in the birth certificate were flipped backward in the glass, but I know him so well that I could have guessed, anyway.

"Hall Monica Bettie."

"I thought I'd need some documentation. A forged birth certificate and ID, so that Cracker Barrel will hire me. They're putting one of those in Springhedge, did you hear? A few well-placed whisperings in the ears of sleeping entrepreneurs has worked out nicely for me."

"You gave yourself Bettie as a last name."

"Of course!" That warmth I'd been missing began to radiate again, but this time it was radiating from *me*. I felt myself glowing from within, and I knew from the glimmer in his eyes that were almost all the way brown with only the thinnest band of green in his left, that my light had reached him. "It's the best name I could think of. *Bettie* has all my favorite things in it."

The following day, he left the mirror and appeared as a low-lying mist that hovered in my living room. Which was alarming for me but absolutely terrifying for the FedEx delivery man, who saw it all happen through the window and who now leaves my packages on the farthest step from the house.

Slowly, as the days of the new year passed, Hall absorbed more and more of the physical world and his form began to take shape. It was an arduous process that took all of his concentration, so I sat by quietly for moral support whenever I was at home and, to avoid distracting him, spent a lot of time at work or at Grandma and Grandpa's house. He built up his matter out of his surroundings: he took the color of the coffee table for his irises, crafting his hands from the smoke of a candle. Piece by piece, Hall was reaccumulated, nearly identical to the old Hall but painstakingly constructed into a specimen that could not be easily wiped away by a magic clock ticking down to goodbye. He is no longer a feeling, a larger purpose. What he likes to say, whenever I ask him "*What are you?*", is:

"*Well, I am yours, of course.*"

By the end of the weeklong transformation, Hall had disentangled himself from the magic, pushing it back out into the atmosphere where it belongs. At the time, I was walking home from work late in the evening and from a block away, I noticed the lights in my house were all on. I ran down the street, threw open the front door, and there he was, standing next to the fireplace waiting for me. I dropped my purse to the floor, tears filling up my eyes as I stared. I heard myself whisper, "Hey, there."

He was Hall, but different. I didn't realize until he'd become human all the ways in which he was once supernatural: How his clothes never wrinkled before, and his shoelaces never came untied. How, when he doesn't have his grooming choices set on autocorrect, he develops a five o'clock shadow.

He bit his lip, lopsided smile stunning as always, holding a bough of faux mistletoe over his head in invitation.

He said to me, his voice all the more honeyed and attractive without its notes of sleigh bells and crackling embers, "Want to start where we left off?"

I leapt at him and wouldn't let go. He didn't mind at all when the cookies, which he'd put in the oven to celebrate his "birthday," burned to charcoal briquettes.

Afterward, he opened his Christmas presents, which I'd kept under the tree in my living room, and didn't have the heart to put away. ("Scrapbooks! A camera! I love all of this!") Then I marshaled my relatives onto FaceTime so that he could say hello, assure them he loved me, that he wasn't going anywhere ever again and had been tied up with an unavoidable work thing, and that he'd quit his job over it.

Now, Hall is simply a man: unmagical, and yet the most magical person there ever was.

＊

It's been nearly a year since he returned. Today is Christmas, and we are at the Watsons' house.

"My vote's for the wedding to take place in Lapland," Grandma is saying, for the fifth time in an hour. There's no reason for her to still be bringing this up, as if Hall, her biggest fan, has a prayer of going against her wishes. "I want to be the matron of honor."

"Mom's the matron of honor, Grandma."

Mom pivots so that no one will tease her for crying. She keeps bursting into happy tears whenever she's reminded that I asked her to be my matron of honor.

"Then I want to be the best man. With a black lace tux."

"Yes. Done," Hall responds at once. I shake my head at him, bemused. He's going to pass out when he traipses down the aisle to discover Lacey Chabert standing there as officiant, which is a surprise I'm working hard to pull off. By that, I mean that Athena has dirt on the Hallmark Channel and has called in a favor.

We've set a date for the wedding, next year on December twenty-first—it's a long engagement, the reason being that Hall hasn't finished proposing yet. He's intent on bringing to life all of his ideas that were left on the cutting-room floor when he first proposed (spontaneously, forgetting the fireworks). It'll be months before Hall's proposed to me in enough ways for him to be satisfied. It took an eternity to narrow down which season we wanted the wedding to take place in, because he loves the idea of summertime nuptials just as much as he wants to get married under a maple tree in the fall. Don't even get me started on his scrapbook of possible themes, thirty percent of which involve a reindeer-pulled carriage and excessive burlap. Mark my words, we're going to end up renewing our vows every few years so that he can carry out his many (many, many) ideas.

A lot is different about this year compared to last. For starters, there was no nifty teleportation to carry us here—we had to make do with a regular old airplane (as we were coming back from a trip to Santa Monica), which made Hall bright-eyed with nostalgia. *I was somewhere up here when you granted my wish*, he said. *In the clouds, watching the world's lights blink on and off and feeling like mine would never turn back on again.*

Also, he lost the ability to shape-shift our twin bed into two bunks. Neither of us is upset by that at all.

And lastly, it turns out that Hall cannot ice skate for his life. Without magic, his legs splay like a newborn goat's. But he won't give up trying—Hall's been out on the rink every morning at dawn, practicing. With his determination, he'll go pro. Between bussing at Cracker Barrel and working for Channel 10 News (he's the most charismatic weatherman the station has ever known, and his good looks and enthusiasm have attracted a national audience), he's quite busy. He's only made it one one-hundredth of the way through his latest list of hopes and dreams. My list is much shorter, and I feel like I've achieved so many wins that it would be pushing it to ask for more. Last week I sold my one thousandth box of cards, and I've successfully kept a houseplant alive since August. Hall brings me breakfast in bed every Sunday morning.

Life is good.

Hall doesn't mind going about his life "manually," having to pack the snow into snowmen by hand. He doesn't mind measuring out exact ingredients for his pies, waiting for the clouds to decide they want to gift us with snow rather than spurring it on with a click of his fingers. The only magic he can accomplish now is the David Copperfield variety, which is his favorite, anyway, as he so loves to say with a mysterious and enigmatic air: "And for my next trick . . ." right before he sweeps me off my feet with a kiss.

He adores watching the seasons change at their leisure, too, and has admitted in the dead of night, in a hushed whisper, that he thinks he might like autumn the best. But I am not to tell a soul. He's the Holly King, after all.

"Take it from me," says Felix. "A spring wedding is the way to go."

Felix finally gave Marilou the big wedding of her dreams in April, and their relationship is still going strong, so he believes his curse has broken and he is now an expert on all things wedding and marriage. "Felix," I groan. "Stop giving Hall ideas. I've already settled on wearing a velvet cape over my wedding dress, and a giant crown that looks like it's made of icicles. I'm going to be a vision for the ages. Icicle crowns and velvet capes don't fit with spring!"

He talks over me. "And of course, I'm going to be in charge of the bachelor party."

"No," I reply in tandem with at least five other voices.

Felix is undeterred. "You'll have to lock down my services soon, because my calendar's filling up. Shooting starts in June."

"You'll be finished long before December," Mom reminds him.

"I know. But we've gone thirty minutes without talking about my movie, which gives me indigestion." *Leon of Naples* will be filming in Toronto. My sisters and I will be there to lend our enthusiastic support.

"Felix." Hall pivots. He's wearing the HALL I WANT FOR

CHRISTMAS IS YOU sweater, which has a few runs in the fibers from excessive wear. "Tell me every little molecular detail about your movie."

"It's a good movie." Dad clears his throat, sitting forward earnestly. "Very fun, very strange. I'm proud of you, Felix. And all of your creative endeavors." He drums his fingers on his knees.

Felix glows. "Thank you, Dad and favored brother-in-law. Well, it starts with an old-timey man called Neapolitan—" We all groan.

Sean tosses a blueberry muffin at my brother's head.

Grandma cranks up the volume of the TV, drowning him out. Felix throws her a peeved look. But soon, even Hall and his award-winning attentiveness can't resist the allure of Freeform's 25 Days of Christmas programming. "Is this . . . ?" His face colors.

It is the 1966 classic *How the Grinch Stole Christmas*.

"I will not," he declares, beginning to rise to his feet, but I shove him back down.

"Yes, you will. You're going to finish this movie."

Hall's eyes darken. He crosses his arms defensively over his chest. "Fine," he grumbles. "I will finish this movie. But I will not enjoy it."

The movie is twenty-six minutes long. By the end, he is in tears.

"I just!" He lifts his arms. "That's so!"

"I know." I rub comforting circles on his back.

"They got all their presents! They got their roast beast! I never knew."

"The Whos and their goodness made him want to be a better Grinch. Reminds me of someone else I know."

He blows his nose on a mitten he's knitting. He's not exceptionally skilled with nonmagical knitting, so it looks more like one of those mitts you fit over a baby's hand so they don't scratch themselves. "I enjoyed that very much."

"Anyone want to go caroling?" Mom asks, to which a few of the kids chime, "Me! Me!" But none of them louder than Hall, who flings himself at the door so fast, he forgets it's a closet.

Marilou, Courtney, and Kaia scramble out of his way. This man takes his caroling seriously.

"There's something off about that one," Sean mutters.

"Don't say that again." Grandma gently touches his hand. "Or I'll put a hex on you. I have my ways."

Grandpa slips me five dollars. "For the Band-Aid collection."

I hug him. "Hall filled your bedroom with inflatable ducks. I'm so sorry. *Woman's Day* won't stop sending us magazines, and he finds the most unbelievable coupons."

He pulls back, glaring at Sean. "Why don't you ever bring me inflatable ducks?"

Sean sputters.

When I bound outside, I have to bring Hall his coat because he was so excited that he forgot it. He's singing, "*Have yourself a merry little Bettie,*" when I walk up on him. "*Let your heart be mine.*"

I launch into his arms. He laughs as he catches me, a shimmering peppermint cloud of a laugh ringing in the air. He doesn't feel like himself without the holiday spirit fragrance, so he's been wearing candy cane cologne.

"I wish . . ." I go *hmm*, thinking hard. "That you would give me a Hershey's Kiss. You've always got some in your pocket."

"Granted." He hands one over. "I wish . . . that you would give me a kiss, too."

"Granted." I capture his mouth with mine, and I'll never get used to this—how he puts his entire body into a kiss, making each and every one an ardent *I love you* in which I can taste each letter of my name, fulfilling promises he'd made to himself back when he didn't know if we'd be together again, vowing that if he ever got the chance, he'd better kiss me like every time was the last. As a perfectionist, he is a *very* good kisser. Spectacularly unrivaled. When he finally withdraws, he's gone rosy and there's a dark haze in his eyes, gaze so intent on my face that I blush. Personally, I have forgotten where I am and what we were doing, which he must be able to tell, because his dimpled smile turns a touch smug. He's deliciously all-over human these days, but he still grants the *best* wishes.

Ah, yes. Now I remember. We're going to go caroling until our feet ache and our throats are sore, and then we're going to come back to the house and drink hot cocoa that Hall is consistently flabbergasted does not auto-refill. *Then*, we are going to spend the rest of our lives endeavoring to make each other merry and bright.

"You forgot your hat," he points out.

"I'll be fine."

"It's cold outside. You need a hat. Here." He taps that cheap plastic magic wand of his against a gloved palm, and my lumpy knitted hat shoots out of the white-capped end.

I seize the wand, inspecting it closely. "How'd you do that?"

"Magic." He raises his eyebrows, chin tilted up with airs of superiority.

"No, *really*. Did you have my hat up your sleeve? Or inside your coat?"

"I've been telling you all along that this is a magic wand, Bettie. The real trick is getting you to believe it."

"Oh, fine, then, don't tell me," I huff, and he laughs.

As we walk side by side down the road into peaceful blue

twilight a little ways behind the rest of our family, our amusement melts into small, contented smiles and hands clasped like they cannot bear to let go, and nothing—*nothing* else has ever mattered as much as this man's off-key singing that makes the world a more joyful place to live in, and his frequent, grateful, so-happy-to-be-here kisses pressed to the back of my hand, and his love in my heart, where the magic lives on.

"And for my next trick."

Hall flicks his wand once again toward the North Star, and, in a truly remarkable coincidence, snowflakes begin to flutter down from the sky.

The End
And Happy Holidays

Acknowledgments

THE IDEA FOR this story popped into my head one morning when I was half-asleep. I opened Twitter and began to type up the idea as a joke, because of course it was a joke, but then I tilted my head and thought . . . well, what if I actually wrote it? I saved the Tweet to my drafts and did just that. Bettie and Hall's story is a level of bonkers that I found personally very fun to play around in, but I wasn't sure if anyone would actually want to read something like this. I mean, the source of magic in this world could very well canonically be the chicken parm sandwich from Domino's, depending on whether Hall was serious about that (and he might have been). I am endlessly shocked and grateful to have such a brilliant agent, Taylor Haggerty, who was supportive from the jump.

Thank you to my editor, Kate Dresser, for your invaluable guidance, to Tarini Sipahimalani, Jasmine Brown at Root Literary, Emily Mileham, Maija Balcauf, Linda Rosenberg, Hannah

Dragone, Marie Finamore, Tiffany Estreicher, Katy Riegel, Erica Cuculic, Lyris Bach, Heather Lewis, Christopher Lin, Sally Kim, and to everyone else at Putnam who has had a hand in bringing *Just Like Magic* to life. Thank you so much for publishing me.

I have tremendous appreciation for my author friends whose texts and emails have kept me from turning off the Internet and escaping into the mountains forever. There are many of you, but I have to mention Martha Waters, Sarah Grunder Ruiz (shout out for helping me brainstorm the *Dancing with the Stars* scene), Chloe Liese, and Mazey Eddings in particular. Thank you so much to the authors who kindly agreed to read early copies of this book, and who have said lovely things about it, or even kindly offered blurbs. You're all my heroes!

A special thank-you to Samantha and Shahad, who contributed to the Romancelandia for Afghan Women auction, bidding on a copy of this book and the book's dedication. Your generosity is so very appreciated.

And then, of course, my family—you're my favorite people in the world. Simply the coolest crew ever. Without a doubt, I could not do this whole writing thing without the support of my husband, Marcus, who protects my writing time and who good-naturedly lets me steal some of his qualities to put in my romance heroes. I haven't stolen from my children yet but look forward to the opportunity.

Thank you, readers, for continuing to make me cry when you tell me you've just discovered one of my books and loved it. My first book debuted at the very beginning of the pandemic and I honestly thought it might be curtains for me before my career really even began. I can't tell you how grateful I am that you're still finding Naomi, Nicholas, Maybell, and Wesley. (And now Bettie and Hall, too!)

But of course, the biggest thank-you of all goes out to the real star of *Just Like Magic*; a literal queen, a legend, an icon: the one and only Mariah Carey. You're Christmas magic.

Just Like Magic

SARAH HOGLE

———

Discussion Guide

———

Excerpt from You Deserve Each Other

———

BOOK
ENDS

PUTNAM
— EST. 1838 —

Discussion Guide

1. Bettie feels pressured to live up to her family name, but also to the Bettie name, which she inherited from her grandma. To what extent does she attribute her successes and/or failures to her lineage? How do you think family history can impact a holiday celebration?

2. Why do you think Bettie puts so much pressure on gift-giving? How does this compare to the way she uses social media? Discuss the role that location plays in both these rituals in this book.

3. If your very own Hall appeared in your life, what would your first wish be? Which wish would immediately make Hall disappear from your life?

4. When Bettie first arrives at the Watson-Hughes Christmas dinner, she doesn't feel that she has succeeded in making the grand entry she wanted, because no family member gives her much notice. Why do you think this was? What do you think Bettie wanted from her relatives?

5. Bettie pretends she's starring in *My Eyre Ladies* to steal Felix's spotlight, and Felix gets angry. How does sibling rivalry play a part in *Just Like Magic*? How are the siblings able to make progress in their adult relationships by the end?

6. Bettie and Hall go on their holiday shopping road trip when Bettie grants Hall some of his greatest wishes by showing him mundane human experiences. Later, when Hall returns at the end, Bettie describes him as "simply a man: unmagical, and yet the most magical person there ever was." Discuss the implications of the word *magic* in this story.

7. Mariah Carey's "All I Want for Christmas Is You," in all its magic-fueled renditions, perfectly encapsulates Bettie and Hall's bond. Play the song with your book club and discuss how the song plays into the themes of the novel.

8. Hall has the magical ability to statistically know how happy Bettie is. How does Bettie's involuntary vulnerability propel their relationship? How are happiness and love entwined and in what ways do they differ?

9. What does it mean for Hall's purpose to be to instill happiness in others? How does author Sarah Hogle demonstrate Bettie's happiness apart from Hall? How do you think their happiness will evolve after the events of the novel?

10. In writing *Just Like Magic*, Hogle pays homage to the gleeful spirit of the holidays. What makes holidays feel so special? Discuss with your book club your favorite holiday, and how your respective Halls would appear to you all.

Keep reading for an exciting excerpt from
You Deserve Each Other by Sarah Hogle.

PROLOGUE

....

I THINK HE'S GOING to kiss me tonight.

If he doesn't, I just might die. It's our second date, and we're parked at a drive-in theater pretending to watch a movie while sneaking looks at each other. This movie is two hours and five minutes long. We have spent one hour and fifty-five minutes not kissing. I don't want to sound desperate, but I didn't contour a third of my body with this much highlighter to not get any of it on his shirt. If all goes according to plan, he's going to be limping home tonight with ravaged hair and enough shimmer powder on his clothes to make him reflective to passing cars. He's going to smell like my pheromones for a week no matter how hard he scrubs.

I haven't been shy with the hint-dropping, drawing attention to my lips by licking, nibbling, and idly touching them—advice I got from *Cosmopolitan*. My shiny lip gloss was developed in a lab to magnetize the mouths of men, effective as fanning peacock feathers. Nicholas's primitive instincts won't be able to resist. It's also a magnet for my hair and I keep getting the eye-watering taste of extra-hold hair spray in my mouth, but sometimes beauty requires sacrifice. On top of all this, my left hand drapes across my seat palm-up for maximum accessibility in case he'd like to pick it up and take it home with him.

My hopes begin to wither when he looks at me and then quickly away. Maybe he's the kind of person who goes to the drive-in to actually watch the movie. As much as I'd hate to consider it, maybe he's simply not feeling this. It wouldn't be the first time a smooth-talking charmer dropped me off with a good-night kiss and ghosted right when I thought things were getting good.

And then I see it: a signal that eating my hair all night has not been in vain. It arrives in the form of an empty mint wrapper sitting in the cup holder. I subtly sniff the air and heck yes, that is definitely wintergreen I smell. I check the cup holder again and it's even better than I'd thought. Two empty wrappers! He's doubling up! A man doesn't double up on mints unless he's preparing for a little move-making.

My god, this man is so handsome I'm half convinced I somehow tricked him into this. I like every single little thing about Nicholas. He didn't wait three days to call after the first date. All of his texts are grammatically correct. I have yet to receive an unsolicited dick pic. Already, I want to reserve a ballroom for our wedding reception.

"Naomi?" he says, and I blink.

"Huh?"

He smiles. It's so adorable that I smile, too. "Did you hear me?"

The answer to that is no, because I'm over here admiring his profile and being way too infatuated for it being so early in our . . .

I can't even call this a relationship. We've only been on two dates. *Get it together, Naomi.*

"Zone out a lot?" he guesses.

I feel myself flush. "Yeah. Sorry. Sometimes people talk to me and I don't even register it."

His smile widens. "You're cute."

He thinks I'm cute? My heart flutters and glows. I give an inner thank-you speech to my false eyelashes and this low-cut (but still classy) blouse.

He cocks his head, studying me. "I was saying that the movie's over."

I whip my head to face the screen. He's right. I have no idea how the movie ended and couldn't tell you what the major plot points were. I think it was a romance, but who cares? I'm much more interested in the romance happening here in this car. The lot is now deserted, granting us enough privacy to make my imagination go wild. Anything could happen. It's just me, Nicholas, and—

The pink cardigan folded neatly on his back seat, which obviously belongs to a woman, and that woman isn't me.

My stomach drops, and Nicholas follows my gaze. "That's for my mother," he says quickly. I'm not quite convinced until he shows me a HAPPY BIRTHDAY card beneath it, which he's signed and added a personal message to. *Love you, Mom!* I inwardly swoon.

"That's so nice," I tell him, acutely aware of how isolated and intimate it feels in his car. I'm a mess of nervous butterflies, and the discarded mint wrappers keep snagging my eye. The movie's over, so what's he waiting for? "Thanks for taking me here. Not many drive-ins left these days. Probably only a couple in the whole

Midwest." It's even rarer to find one that operates year-round. Luckily, we were provided with a complimentary electric heater to offset the insanity of doing something like this in January. We've got a few blankets spread over us, and for an out-of-the-box winter date it's been surprisingly cozy.

"There are eight left in the state, actually," he says. The fact that he knows this piece of trivia right off the top of his head is impressive. "Are you hungry? There's a frozen yogurt stand near here that has the best frozen yogurt you've ever had in your life."

I'm not a fan of frozen yogurt (especially when it's cold out), but no way am I being anything but agreeable. We don't know each other that well yet, and if I want to score a third date I need to come off as low-maintenance. I'm easygoing Naomi, fun to hang out with and *definitely* fun to make out with. Maybe after the frozen yogurt he'll kiss me. And possibly unbutton his shirt. "That sounds great!"

Instead of fastening his seat belt and driving away, he hesitates. Fiddles with the radio dials until static fuzz tunes in to an upbeat indie song called "You Say It Too." It hits me that he's fallen so quiet because he's nervous, not disinterested, which surprises me because up until now he's exhibited nothing but confidence. There's a charge in the air and my pulse accelerates with intuition of what's to come. The rhythm of my blood is a chant. *Yes! Yes! Yes!*

"You're beautiful," he says earnestly, turning to face me in full. His eyes are hesitant as he bites his cheek and I'm stunned that *he's* the nervous one here. My heart skips as he leans toward me an inch. Then another. His lips part, gaze dropping to my mouth, and just like that I can no longer remember any other men I've ever dated, he's eclipsed them all so utterly. He's intelligent and charming and perfect, absolutely perfect for me.

My heart is now lodged firmly in my throat. His fingers stroke through my hair, tilting my head up to meet his. Nicholas leans in that final inch and lights up my world like a shooting star, anticipation and wonder and a feeling of tremendous rightness barreling through my veins. He kisses me and I'm a goner, just like I knew would happen.

What a magical, extraordinary night.

MARCUS HOGLE

SARAH HOGLE is a mom of three who enjoys trashy TV and provoking her husband for attention. Her dream is to live in a falling-apart castle in a forest that is probably cursed. She is also the author of *You Deserve Each Other* and *Twice Shy*.